The Stones Corner Series

Volume One

Turmoil

Jane Buckley

Oakleaf Press

Cover Photograph: A British Army (BA) helicopter on patrol over St Peter's School in the Creggan area of Derry/Londonderry. This aircraft was the 'Scout' helicopter, used for observation. The BA had access to a range of helicopters for carrying out different jobs, such as moving equipment or large numbers of soldiers. Photographer: Eamon Melaugh, August 1972, Circular Road, Creggan, Derry.

Sincere thanks to Dr Martin Melaugh, CAIN Director, CAIN Archive - Conflict and Politics in Northern Ireland, Ulster University, for permission to use this image.

WARNING: This book contains scenes of violence, strong language, and sexual references. It also includes the kind of language used during the 1970s, which some readers may find offensive. While this is a work of fiction, parts of the story are based on real events.

To understand and move on from the Troubles in Northern Ireland, we first need to understand how and why it all happened. We need to recognise the pain and hardship that people lived through, and take time to reflect on what we've learned. The Stones Corner series was written with that in mind.

Every effort has been made to get permission for any lyrics, quotes, or copyright material used. If anything has been missed, I apologise and will gladly include proper acknowledgements in future editions.

Jacket design: TSL.ie. and Jane Buckley
Copyright Jane Buckley 2025

Thank you, Lynn Curtis and Anne Macdonald
I couldn't have done it without you. JB x

In memory of Daddy, Charles, Brian and Frank, sorely missed and
much loved
and to all the victims of the Troubles.

*'The answer to difference is to respect it. Therein lies a most
fundamental principle of peace: respect for diversity.'*
— **John Hume**, Nobel Peace Prize Lecture, Oslo, 10 December 1998

Volume 1: Turmoil (First Published 2021) ISBN 978-1-9123-2871-0
Revised edition 2025 ISBN 978-1-0687599-0-1
Volume 2: Darkness (First Published 2021) ISBN 978-1-9142-2559-8
Revised edition 2025 ISBN 978-1-0687599-8-7
Volume 3: Light (First Published 2022) ISBN 978-1-9155-0216-2
Volume 4: Hope (First Published 2023) ISBN 978-1-3999-7265-9

About the Author

*J**ane Buckley* grew up in Derry/Londonderry during the Troubles, and her writing pulls no punches. Her *Stones Corner* series - *Turmoil*, *Darkness*, *Light*, and *Hope* – cuts straight to the heart of one of Northern Ireland's darkest chapters. These are character-driven stories with bite. Brutally honest. Deeply human. The kind of books that stay with you long after the last page.

She doesn't soften the blow or romanticise the past. There's no gloss, no filter, just truth, told with grit, empathy, and a sharp eye for the everyday details that shaped people's lives. Her stories are rooted in actual events, voiced in plain language, and built around ordinary men and women trying to survive the extraordinary.

Nor does Jane write to shock. She writes to make sense of it all. To honour those who lived through it. To make sure it's not forgotten.

Having completed the fourth book in the *Stones Corner* series, *Hope*, Jane's next work, written for the US-based Project Children, steps back to the powerful true story behind the initiative featured in the series. Between the seventies and nineties, 23,000 children from both sides of the divide were flown to the United States, welcomed into homes, and given a taste of peace.

It's a story of hope, healing, and the quiet power of kindness. One child. One family. One summer at a time.

USA Indie Award Winner 5* Review

'Hard-hitting, informative, richly detailed, and filled with food for thought, TURMOIL is an historical novel fit to sink one's teeth into. Set in Northern Ireland during the 1970s, Turmoil paints a vivid picture of life amidst armed struggles. It's a story of people trying to get on with their lives against a backdrop of discrimination, bigotry, revolutionary conflict, state collusion and suppression. And it's the little things of bravery and kindness that make this book such a joy. Knowing she can't afford them, the uncle buys his niece a pair of tights for her new job. A woman berates the masked gunmen by telling them she'll complain to their mothers. The wealthy boss who visits his injured secretary is naïve about his flashy car's impact on her impoverished and dangerous part of town.

There is universality at work here. We could be in any country where there is conflict – where bosses are trying to save their factories, where young men are seduced into a cause, where psychopaths use conflict as cover for their dark work, and where people – despite everything – are flirting, laughing, and falling in love. The author has created a set of characters here that the reader can quickly identify with and, in some cases, genuinely care about. The various sides of the conflict are represented with an even-handedness, which aids our understanding of the complexities of Northern Ireland's conflict.'

Prologue

Over the years, stories have circulated in numerous British Army barracks about the first deployment to Derry/Londonderry in 1969: Operation Banner.

When 300 troops from the 1st Battalion, Prince of Wales's Own Regiment of Yorkshire, arrived, the Catholic community welcomed and cheered them.

The regiment was brought in to relieve the exhausted Royal Ulster Constabulary (RUC), who had just endured a fierce three-day battle in the Bogside area.

This conflict had started after a march by Protestant Apprentice Boys and turned violent. Despite the use of CS gas, water cannon, and eventually firearms, the RUC was unable to quell the rioting.

The Catholic residents of the Bogside were jubilant, believing they had broken the morale of the much-despised police and their auxiliary force, the B Specials, often referred to as the 'Protestant Army.'

Within an hour of the regiment's arrival, the predominantly Protestant RUC withdrew from the chaotic scene, and the British Army, somewhat naïvely, took their place.

Catholics largely thought the 'Brits' had arrived to safeguard them, viewing them as unbiased peacekeepers. In those initial peaceful weeks, local women even offered tea and biscuits to the young soldiers as they patrolled the streets.

The British Army's view was that Operation Banner was a restricted intervention, and the soldiers were initially inexperienced and poorly equipped. They appeared almost comical in riot gear from Aden, still bearing Arabic writings on their shields. Many senior officers who had served in Aden and Cyprus viewed Northern Ireland as just another British colony.

But, they quickly realised this conflict was unlike others. Here, it was impossible to identify the enemy by appearance; here everyone looked the same.

Soon, the air became thick with tension and peril. Fear gripped the community. Catholic Republicans, Protestant Loyalists, the RUC, and the British Army engaged in shootings and bombings as retaliation for the numerous atrocities committed by each side. The escalating desire for revenge became insatiable, with each group as angry and determined as the other to achieve victory.

The British Army being there angered several key Unionists and Loyalists. They criticised the government for interfering in 'their' province, feeling the army was too lenient on the Nationalists and Republicans, allowing them to establish no-go areas with little resistance. However, their views soon changed when the military began to escort and protect Loyalist Orangemen marches and protests. The honeymoon period was over.

The first British Army death of the 'Troubles' occurred in February 1971, a young gunner. During the first of many raids, over 300 suspected Republicans were arrested. The army's intelligence was so outdated that some of the listed Republicans were dead. Only a year later, the first Loyalist was detained.

Internment proved to be a catalyst for a wave of violence and protests by outraged Republicans.

STONES CORNER, TURMOIL, VOLUME ONE

In January 1972, during a civil rights march in Derry that became known as 'Bloody Sunday,' the British Army shot dead thirteen
unarmed Catholic civilians and wounded another fourteen, one of
whom later died.

Consequently, the province saw a surge in unrest, which then
prompted Operation Motorman, the British Army's effort to end
Republican control after eleven months. Westminster suspended the
Northern Ireland Parliament and imposed direct rule.

In 1972, 500 people died, including just over half who were civilians. This year marked one of the most significant losses of life in the
entire conflict, and at the time, no one could have imagined that the
bloodshed would spiral out of control and continue for decades.

In the heart of Creggan, by the Army base,
Barbed wire, sangars - soldiers in place.
Stones bounced off Saracens, flames hit the sky,
Kids legged it laughing as tear gas rolled by.
But the factory stayed open, no time to wait,
Women linked arms, heads down to the gate.
Mothers stitched, fathers on the dole,
No work for the men, just rage in their soul.
Windows shook as the riots swelled,
Bricks through glass, balaclavas held.
Smoke in the air, glass under feet,
Another night burning, another defeat.
Love kept quiet behind locked doors,
A name unspoken, a fate that was sworn.
Fingers brushed briefly, eyes turned away,
A world too dangerous for hearts to stay.
But Derry still stood, scarred but strong,
Fighting for more than the same old song.
A day would come when the guns fell still,
When hope outran the urge to kill.
Still the needle ran, the thread pulled tight,
Keeping the wages, holding the light.
Rocola stood while others fell,
Its heartbeat steady, determined as hell.

JB
2025

Chapter One

Derry/Londonderry, 1972

They were hyper – almost manic – fuelled by a hateful rage. All day, they'd sat through briefing after briefing, their frustration building until unbearable.

Finally, it was time. They'd had enough. A few sneaky vodka shots only intensified their fury as they prepared to leave the barracks, faces smeared with camouflage paint, expressions hard and unyielding.

Some men climbed into Saracens or Centurions, while others set off on foot, gripping their berets against the fierce wind created by three lit-up, stationary RAF Wessex helicopters. The ear-splitting roar of the whirling blades matched the men's eagerness for action – an eagerness underpinned by simmering revenge. The promise of air cover was a small comfort, but what they craved was payback. Tonight was bound to get messy, and they welcomed it.

After Operation Carcan, the biggest British military push since Suez, and the chaos of Bloody Sunday, they'd taken shit from every direction. Now they wanted blood. And were they ready? Fuck, they were beyond ready. For Queen and country!

Warning shouts filled the air as the illuminated giants, resembling monstrous dragonflies, launched one after another, slicing through the relentless rain squalls west towards the city. The remaining men and vehicles followed in haste.

Within minutes, the flying predators reached their destination and hovered menacingly, descending lower and lower over the rows of semi-terraced houses. The downdraft from the whirling blades rattled doors and windows as the few working streetlights fought to remain intact against the battering. Steel rubbish bins clattered and scraped across the tarmac as their contents blew over the pathways. Almost immediately, the street's inhabitants woke in panic, scrambling out of bed to switch on the lights.

Nineteen-year-old Caitlin McLaughlin was luckier than most, not snatched from sleep but already lying awake, restless in her single bed. Against the bitter chill of the barely heated house, she curled into herself, knees tucked to her chest, arms wrapped tight, shivering beneath a doubled-over blanket. She couldn't sleep, not with her brother Martin on her mind. She kept thinking about where he was and, more importantly, if he was safe. The RUC had taken him days ago. Not a word since.

At first, she didn't know what was causing the racket, but it didn't take long to figure it out. A helicopter was right above the house, close enough to rattle the roof tiles and windows. Caitlin clamped her hands over her ears, trying to block out the relentless thudding. Dizzy and shaken, she pulled back the thin floral curtain and stared out at the madness unfolding on the street below.

Before she knew it, a searchlight tore through the window, sweeping across the room, up and down the walls, over the bed, and landing right on her. She pulled her cardigan tighter over her nightdress and stared back, unblinking. The light lingered on her, as if expecting more, then slipped away, almost disappointed in its find.

Outside, the scene was like something out of a nightmare. Her heart pounded as she heard the screams of women and children from the houses backing onto their street, the sickening squeal of tyres, and the shouts of men.

Saracens and jeeps, lit up with powerful spotlights, sped along the narrow road, stopping randomly to park halfway across the pavements. Armed men scrambled out of the vehicles – some running to take cover and observe, while others marched towards the pebble-dashed houses. RUC officers struggled to restrain their snarling German shepherds, the dogs barking and salivating at the end of their leashes. Urgent hand signals passed between the raiders as they assessed their surroundings. Soldiers and policemen strode up garden paths in pairs, heading for the front doors. Local street dogs barked and snapped at the heels of the darkly dressed figures, who kicked them away, swearing. Fists hammered against locked doors, soon followed by the splintering of wood and the smashing of glass. Loud, confident English voices, hated by the whole street, called out names from lists held in gloved hands.

Mothers tried to bundle small children under the stairs, terrified they'd be trampled or shoved aside by the invaders. The soldiers searched living rooms, kitchens, and bedrooms for the listed men, leaving destruction in their wake. They overturned furniture, emptied drawers, and ransacked cupboards with a sweep of an arm or the kick of a boot.

In the hallways, the women stood trembling, clad in nightclothes and bare feet, watching the brutal violation of their homes. Some tried to soothe crying, half-asleep children or clutched their babies as the gun-wielding troops continued their onslaught.

In house after house along the street, lights blazed as front doors were rammed open, dazed men and women hauled from their beds. Cruel batons pushed aside the screaming wives who tried to take their men back from the aggressors.

By now, Caitlin was shaking. This was the worst she'd ever seen. She jumped as her younger sister Tina bounced into the room, her fiery red hair bristling and freckled face tight with anger.

'Jesus, Caitlin, you've got to come!' Tina's words were muffled as she struggled to remove the braces she wore on her teeth. 'It's the Brits again. Another raid, there's gonna be murder.' She yanked her braces free in frustration and bundled them in the pocket of an old school blazer she'd pulled on over her pyjamas.

'The bastards are lifting loads. I've only seen them grab a fella by the hair. Hammered him and threw him in the back of a Pig. Mammy's off on one, and Daddy's shoutin' his head off!' she cried.

'Ah shit, Tina, not again,' Caitlin replied, recalling the night of Martin's arrest. It'd been bad, but not this bad.

She rubbed her eyes, still dazzled, and searched the room for something warmer to wear against the bitter cold. She spotted her father's heavy Aran on the floor, and having worn it earlier that evening, flung aside her cardigan and pulled the thick woollen jumper over her head. Without pausing to find shoes, she pushed Tina out of the door ahead of her.

On the landing, they saw their wide-eyed mother, standing at the top of the staircase, supporting herself against the wall with one hand and the handrail with the other. Caitlin sighed. It was clear Majella McLaughlin had been drinking again as she let go of the railing to fumble with the silver crucifix around her neck. She swayed a little but stayed on her feet.

The three of them jumped at a heavy knock below, followed by the crack of the front door being kicked in. Two soldiers burst into view at the bottom of the stairs, kitted out for war, their faces half-covered in black paint and scarves. They started up the steps as Majella launched into a stream of abuse.

Somewhere behind them, Caitlin heard her father's voice, raised in panic, demanding to know what was happening.

The lead soldier climbed on. Halfway up he yanked his scarf down, a twisted grin cutting across his face. His boots thudded on the carpeted stairs, dull but deliberate, every step a threat. His combat jacket sleeves were rolled high, and Caitlin caught a flash of red ink on his forearm — a tattoo. The wooden stock of his rifle pressed tight to his chest, the white issue number scrawled by hand. Just below, a baton swung from his green-webbed belt, ready.

Unlike his tall, skinny partner behind, he was short and compact, with a thick neck bulging with muscle beneath a thin mesh scarf. She noticed his eyes were brimming with excitement and sensed danger.

Her mother stopped her tirade and leaned close as the intruder approached. With her face only inches from his, she hissed, 'Ye English bastards, Martin's not here. Youse have him already.' She lashed out with her ringed hand and struck him hard across the cheek.

'Leave us be, and fuck away back to whatever rock ye crawled from!' she cried.

The soldier didn't say a word. Instead, with one brutal swing of his arm, he knocked Majella clean off balance. She smashed her face against the wall, and then fell to the floor. Caitlin flinched as the sound of skull hitting plaster echoed through the landing. Blood spurted from a deep gash above Majella's eyebrow, trickling fast down her cheek. Caitlin dropped to her knees, her heart racing, and checked her over. Majella's skin had turned ghostly pale, her eyelids fluttering, lips slack. She looked dazed, like her brain was struggling to catch up, and for a moment Caitlin feared she was going to pass out.

The Brit touched his face to assess the damage. Majella's rings had only nicked his cheek, but it was bleeding. He stared down at the horrified woman and a cruel smirk crept across his face. Still silent, he simply shook his head in mock disapproval. Caitlin knew with absolute certainty that this night was far from over. It was only going to get worse. Much worse.

Her father continued to shout as the soldiers nodded to each other and took out their batons. The bleeding soldier searched the bedrooms while the other stood watching the women.

'Clear,' came a call from Caitlin's room.

They could hear other soldiers joking and laughing downstairs. The noise was unbearable as they tore through the McLaughlins' home, wrecking the place.

Caitlin gripped her mother's hand, watching as the first soldier stepped towards a closed door. He opened it and found the walk-in linen cupboard. With his back to them, and to get under their skin, he started rummaging through the shelves, tossing out the methodically folded linen onto the floor. All of which Caitlin had spent her entire Sunday ironing.

Worse still, he stamped across the lot, grinding the pristine laundry under his wet, muddy boots. He sucked in air through his teeth, glaring at Majella, and growled, 'By the way, you mad bitch, we're not here for Martin. We're here for that husband of yours, Patrick.'

Caitlin froze, her eyes as wide as saucers. He wasn't English; he was Irish! That threw her. She must've stared because he noticed, gave a smug little nod like he was proud of the fact, then strutted straight into Martin's open bedroom. His gaze swept the walls, taking in the IRA posters, a Tricolour, the 1916 Rising memorabilia, like he was sizing it all up for later.

Sneering, he added, 'Nice décor,' before tearing the posters from the walls, spitting on them, snatching the Tricolour, tossing it aside and leaving the room.

He soon reached her parents' room, where Patrick McLaughlin lay. He'd been bedridden since his son's arrest and could hardly get up without help. According to the family doctor, his heart was weak, and his son's detention had only worsened his condition.

The pair of soldiers exchanged a look and entered the room. Caitlin glanced anxiously at her mother, who'd pulled herself up from the floor but was slumped against the landing wall. Barefoot and wearing a short, well-worn nightdress that had ridden up around her hips, she was oblivious to her lack of underwear as she rubbed her throbbing head and saw the blood on her hand in surprise.

Caitlin took her arm as she peered through the open bedroom door, 'It's okay, Mammy. It'll be all right.' The older woman bowed her head and wept, her frail body rocking back and forth. For the sake of modesty, Caitlin readjusted Majella's nightie.

From the bedroom, Caitlin heard loud cries and bangs, by now her heart pounding even faster. *What in God's name are they doing in there?!* In desperation, she turned to Tina and cried.

'Tina. Help me quick. Get Mammy into our room, out of the way.'

No chance. Tina stood there in shock. Useless. Her eyes wide and brimming, she shuddered as she clung to the doorframe of Martin's room, as if holding on to it for dear life.

Another round of thuds and shouting from the bedroom made Majella lose it. Her breathing quickened as she clutched Caitlin's wrist.

'Do somethin', Caitlin, please. They can't hurt him, love. Please go in and see!'

Caitlin ran. What she saw stopped her in her tracks.

Her daddy stood naked and spreadeagled against the far wall, his arms raised, fingers separated and spread out in surrender. His fragile body trembled from strain and humiliation. Under normal circumstances, she'd have died to see him like this, but not now. What she saw was not shameful; it was cruel, degrading and deeply wrong. She made to run for him, her hand outstretched, but before she knew it, the Irish soldier lashed out again, knocking her sideways.

His face twisted with rage as he bellowed, 'Stand back, you stupid cunt. Don't touch him!'

With his scowling face in hers, he yelled at her again, eyes bloodshot and filled with something rotten: 'Or we'll lift you too.'

From behind, her father wailed, 'Jesus Christ, get her outta here, will ye? Get her out. I don't want her to see me like this!'

She saw the tears glistening on her daddy's face, raw with shame. Then, unexpectedly, the soldier struck Patrick's lower back with his baton, causing a horrifying crunch that made her sick to the heart. He went again, this time landing a blow across the backs of his legs, each strike more brutal than the last.

Patrick howled and collapsed to his knees. Caitlin crawled to him, trying to help, but a massive hand caught a fistful of her hair, and yanked her back. She cried out in agony as her scalp burned and the roots tore at her skin. When the hand let go, she crumpled beside her father, who reached out to comfort her.

A voice cut through the madness, 'Fuck that, Morris. That's enough!' shouted the gangly soldier, stepping in to pull his partner away.

'Leave it be. We've got what we need.' He scanned the room for anything Patrick could wear and spotted a pair of underpants on the floor. With a word, he flung them over, and Patrick, now on his feet, fumbled to pull them on.

The Irishman crouched beside Caitlin again, his baton at the ready. 'So tell me, you Fenian bitch, before I give you something to *really* cry about, would ye happen to be hidin' anyone else here in the house?'

Caitlin stared him in silence, fury and hatred churning behind her tears. He raised his baton again, but before he could strike, the other soldier was faster and grabbed his arm mid-swing.

'That's enough, I said, Morris. We're outta here.'

Private Billy Morris grunted and lowered his baton. 'Okay, right. I hear ye.'

Although disgruntled, he rose to his feet, snarling at Caitlin, 'I'll see you again, sweetheart. Ye can count on it.'

With that, he slipped his bloodied fingers into his mouth, sucking them with a twisted pleasure that sent a wave of revulsion through her. She shrank back but never took her eyes off him as he pulled something from a pouch and opened it: a black sack-like hood that he tried to place over her father's head.

His partner protested again and grabbed his arm. 'You're going way overboard, pal. I don't like this!'

'Not a chance. Outta my way. It stays.' Morris snapped. He grabbed Patrick, who was still half-naked, yanked the hood down over his head and pushed Caitlin out of the way. With a sickening thud, Patrick's face hit the doorframe after he tripped, staggering, blind and off balance.

Caitlin cried out in horror, her hands flying to her mouth. 'Jesus Christ, he can't see where he's going! Take that thing off him and let him get dressed. He's sick, for God's sake. He can't go out like that!'

She darted forward, desperate to help, but a sudden crack of pain exploded in her skull. Her legs buckled, the floor rushed up to meet her, and everything went black.

Chapter Two

Craigavon Bridge

Private Robert (Rob) Sallis of the 2nd Battalion, Royal Regiment of Fusiliers, jumped up to his bunk and laid his head on a thin, hard pillow before stretching out his long body. He took a deep breath and released it, thinking back over the events of his day.

Eee heck, it never stopped raining here. So far, their six-week stint in Londonderry offered a few sunny days. Cold and miserable, today had been especially rough. He'd spent hours manning the checkpoint on Craigavon Bridge. Not only was he soaked to the bone and freezing, but he'd become more and more depressed as he'd stopped traffic, facing open hostility from almost every driver. It was getting to him, to all of them.

He'd soon become fixated on the news, reading the papers to grasp the essence of the Troubles. The British media appeared government-aligned, sometimes distorting events in this God-forsaken, forgotten region. They hadn't even scratched the surface of the despair and bigotry he was seeing firsthand. Reading or watching it on TV was nothing like experiencing it up close.

Like so many back home, he'd paid little attention to Northern Ireland. He hadn't cared. Now, his homeland resembled a war zone, a reality Rob and his friends were unprepared for. They couldn't make sense of the relentless hatred they faced. Weren't they still in the UK, for Christ's sake? And weren't they only doing their jobs? Their pre-deployment briefing had been short and vague: 'The situation is an internal security matter between the Roman Catholics and Protestants.' That was it.

Rob's initial confusion regarding the city's two names soon vanished. The Catholics called it Derry (Doire in Irish, meaning 'oak grove'), while the Protestants called it Londonderry (named after the Protestant London merchants who helped pay for and build the walled city). This little detail was a big deal when they questioned suspects. If someone told them they were from 'Londonderry,' they were dealing with a Loyalist or Unionist, but you still had to keep your wits about you. If they used 'Derry,' you had to be extra careful – they were a Nationalist or, worse, a Republican. Maybe even a member of the Provisional Irish Republican Army, aka a 'Provo.'

Day after day, the routine was the same. The soldiers were forever stopping, questioning, and searching people in cars or on foot. Their orders were to gather as much intel as possible about the suspect: name, address, age, occupation, where they were headed, where they'd been, even to note their clothes and how they acted. Everyone could be a Provo, especially the teenagers.

Back home in Byker near Newcastle, the Sallis family was worried sick about him. Rob could sense their fear and concern from their frequent letters. He tried to sound cheerful when he wrote, telling them not to worry – it was a doddle. But deep down, he had to admit he was scared shitless. He hated the open hostility, especially from the Catholic Republicans. The irony didn't escape him – Rob had grown up Catholic himself.

Tracey, his fiancée, was as anxious as his mam and dad. Hoping she would include his mam in their wedding plans for the coming summer, he encouraged her to stay in contact with them. It gave them all something to look forward to. Rob was an only child, and his mam had taken to Tracey the moment they'd met – he was relieved; the same woman could be a funny one when it suited. Anticipating the big day, and particularly their Spanish honeymoon, he could almost feel the sun, a world apart from Londonderry's cold and damp.

With under three months until his next leave and twenty-first birthday, making it even more special, he hoped he wouldn't have to do another tour here, but it seemed likely. As luck would have it, most of the lads were relieved beyond words at being stationed in Londonderry and not in the brutal South Armagh region – nicknamed Bandit Country. South Armagh was a Provo rural stronghold, bordered on one side by the Irish Republic. Gun battles, ambushes, and sectarian murders were a daily occurrence on its never-ending maze of country roads. Over time, it became so dangerous that the troops had to travel by helicopter. No one wanted to end up there.

Rob's body started to warm up, and with a hidden smile, he silently thanked his mam for the thermals she sent. When he'd first opened the parcel, he cringed with embarrassment – they were ridiculous, and the lads had taken the piss something rotten. Now, he couldn't care less; they were a godsend. The cold in their damp, draughty barracks was brutal.

'What a bliddy awful day,' someone groaned from the lower bunk.

Rob smiled and leaned over the edge to look down. Val Holmes, his best marra. They'd been inseparable at school in Byker. When neither could land a Swan Hunter apprenticeship, they'd joined up together.

Rob shivered and replied, 'Yeah right. Thought me balls were gonna fall off with the cold. At least on patrol, you can keep moving. It's rotten here, Byker's tropical to this!'

'Pussy', Val shot back, laughing.

Val's laugh could've raised a smile out of a corpse. It started low, rough as a dog's growl, then shot up into a squeal that sounded like a hyena on speed. Rob, like everyone, thought it was bizarre and it drove him crazy, but he laughed about it.

'Howay, man,' he continued. 'Patrol's no joke. Hundreds of eyes on your back the minute ye step out. Waitin' all the time for that fucken pop and *whoosh*.' He mimed a gun firing at the side of his head.

'Even little kiddies shoutin' all sorts of cursin' words I don't get and tossin' bricks and bottles. I'm tellin' ye. I could've sworn I saw a bairn in nappies chuckin' stuff at me. No joke.'

Rob leaned back and pictured the scene. Humour was crucial in the job, and being close to Val was a howl. His marra was famous throughout the regiment for his stash of jokes and entertaining stories. Salt of the earth he was; kept them all sane.

The bunk rattled as Private Billy Morris slammed a hardback book against its metal frame. With a clipped English accent, he sneered, 'So, gentlemen, how was your day? Bet it wasn't as good as mine.'

Neither Rob nor Val reacted. They couldn't stand Morris. He was a Protestant from Portstewart, a staunch Unionist town in County Londonderry, a stones throwaway from the city. His hatred for Catholics, Republicans, Fenians, Taigs, left-footers, whatever term he felt like spitting out, was intolerable. It wasn't a matter of politics; it was the man. Something mean and rotten simmered under the surface. Everyone knew it. One day he'd cross the line, and nobody wanted to be dragged down with him. Most of the squaddies gave him a wide berth. Always alone, circling for trouble, like a stray dog in a butcher's shop.

An ugly fella, he was built like a brick shithouse, with beady eyes perched above a hook nose and a thin-lipped mouth – none of which did him any favours in the looks department. His square head was shaved to the bone, and he wore baggy black tracksuit bottoms and a short-sleeved white T-shirt that showed off a massive, overworked torso.

On his lower forearm, visible to everyone, was a large tattoo of the Red Hand of Ulster with 'No Surrender' written above it. Besides all that, Rob noticed a fresh red cut slashed across his cheek and wondered who'd done it, probably some poor bastard trying to fight him off. The question wasn't how Morris had made it into the army; the question was how he'd ended up back here, among his own people. The lad was poison, always stirring it, always sniffing out Republicans.

Their silence clearly riled him as he smacked the bed frame again, and in his harsh Ulster accent, he shouted louder this time, 'Did youse not hear us?'

'Piss off, Morris,' Rob replied sourly.

From the lower bunk, Val cried, 'Divvent give him the satisfaction, Robbie lad. Ignore the knobhead.'

Morris paced at the foot of the bunk, fists clenched and unclenching, a vein in his temple bulging like it might pop. He stared them down, desperate to cause trouble.

'Youse is a pair of lazy twats, ye know that?' he spat, this time booting the bedframe hard.

'Don't ye wanna know how I gave some Fenian slag aright smack the day? Knocked her out cold.' The pair of Geordies didn't even look at him.

Morris tutted, puckered his lips and muttered, 'Fuck youse,' before strutting off, belting out some mangled version of a song about feeling good and the like. The second he was out of earshot, Rob looked down at Val, screwed up his face and shook his head.

Val raised an eyebrow. 'What is your man all about? The state of him.'

Rob chuckled. 'A right gack, ain't he?'

'More like a complete bellend,' Val replied.

They burst out laughing and together yelled, 'Bellend!' for all to hear.

The day sucked, but at least hassling Morris made things more bearable.

Chapter Three

Honey

He'd been tasked with finding someone like her for some time, and his first sighting was weeks before, when she was hanging around the Guildhall Square, talking with a small group of friends.

He wasn't attracted to her, but he saw promise. From a distance, he watched her until he finally went up to her. She didn't expect it. The poor girl looked scared stiff, like she was about to shit herself. He bowed, took her hand, kissed it, and then, in a deep, velvety voice, gave his best performance.

'Mornin', I'm Kieran. Kieran Kelly.'

After letting out a nervous laugh, she replied, 'Hello.'

Although she initially dismissed it as her imagination, she had, in fact, noticed him hanging about. The idea alone made her tummy flutter. This boyo was something else and well out of her league. The guy was about eighteen, and he had that look – like one of those flirty Spanish foreigners on the telly – with his thick fringe, long, jet-black curly hair, and tan skin that seemed to make his chocolate-brown eyes pop out. Those lashes!

There was something wild and feral about him. Tall and slim, he was dressed in spotless flared jeans, an expensive corduroy jacket, and a crisp, open-collared white shirt. But what stood out was his habit of constantly pushing his heavy fringe out of his face while speaking. He was undeniably gorgeous, as anyone could see.

'How about us grabbin' a cuppa tea?' he asked, to her bewilderment.

'*Seriously*? Ye wanna go for a cuppa tea with me?!' she blurted, her heart banging like mad, barely able to believe that a fella like him, was asking her out!

Kieran grinned cheesily, enjoying the effect he was having on her.

'All right then. When?' she asked impatiently.

After chatting with her for a while, he realised the girl was ideal. Needed a bit of work, but ideal.

Up close, the way she barely met his eyes and how she spoke like she wasn't quite sure of herself confirmed what he'd suspected. She was vulnerable, completely unguarded, and it wouldn't take much to get her tucked tight under his wing. Already, he pictured the ease of grooming her, making her feel seen, desired, and significant. Once she trusted him, he could manipulate her into doing anything he wanted, making her believe it was love. That was the plan and, judging by her expression, it'd be a piece of piss.

'Okie dokie. The Rainbow then, five the 'marra!' He yelled, glancing over his shoulder as he crossed the busy street. She wasn't sure if he'd caught her reply, but his friends made plenty of noise, jeering and whistling as they clapped him on the back, howling at his flirting.

'See you then,' she'd called after him. He must've heard because he threw her another funny bow before swaggering off towards the city centre.

Before she knew it, she was spending all her free time with him. He was dead sound – clever, funny too – though always banging on about Ireland, his hatred for the Brits, and all the horrors their so-called empire had left behind: famine, internment, massacres, the lot.

At first, she only half-listened, nodding along to keep him happy. But bit by bit, she started paying proper attention. What shocked her most was how interested she became. The more she listened, the more questions popped into her head, and every time she asked one, he lit up. Said he could see a bit of fire in her now, like she was finally waking up.

He started calling her '*Honey*' and, laughing, told her, 'You're suckin' up everything I'm tellin' ye, like a wee bee to honey.'

She loved being around him, even if half the time she hadn't the foggiest what he was on about with all his big, fancy words. *Screw it.* Her feelings were so strong that she would have done absolutely anything for him. Convinced he was the cleverest and bravest man she'd ever met, she listened intently to his every word. He was more than her friend now; he was her hero.

By the end of round one, the poor girl didn't stand a chance. She was soft as butter in Kieran Kelly's hands, and he knew it.

Chapter Four

Aftermath

Caitlin woke up feeling as if she was going to die. Her head was spinning, she was nauseous, and she could taste blood at the back of her throat.

Disoriented, she tried to sit up and say something, but a gentle pair of hands pushed her back onto the pillow, and a soft, familiar voice murmured, 'Shush, love, shush, take a minute.'

Her mother sat on the bed. Patrick's black dressing gown pulled tightly over her blood-splattered nightie. One side of her face and neck was crusted with brown stains, already drying in patches. At the foot of the bed stood Tina, still pale-faced and sad.

As it all came rushing back, Caitlin tried to throw back her bed covers, panic rising in her throat. 'Where's Daddy, Mammy?!'

Majella held her down again, gently but firmly and silenced her once more. Dread was already creeping in, and Caitlin braced herself for the answer she knew was coming.

'They took him, love. The Brits. He's gone.'

'Ah, Mammy, no... I think I'm going to puke.' Caitlin's hand went to her throat.

She stumbled into the bathroom and dropped to her knees on the freezing tiles, barely scooping her tangled hair back from her face in time. The overpowering stench of bleach stung her nostrils, mixing with the bile rising in her throat as she retched into the toilet bowl. Each convulsion wracked her body with sharp, twisting pain, her stomach heaving in relentless spasms that left her gasping. Her head pounded, her limbs trembled beneath her, and for a moment she simply knelt there, slumped over the bowl, trying to steady her breathing and make sense of what had happened.

In time, she allowed her hair to fall forward again and shield her drawn face. She sighed, dragged herself up, one hand on her aching belly, and only then noticed the blood on her daddy's Aran. He'd kill her; it was his favourite jumper, and no one else could wear it. Except her. *Bugger.*

After flushing the toilet, she opened the door to find her mother and Tina waiting outside. Caitlin could see they'd already tidied up the strewn contents of the linen cupboard.

Tina stood barefoot, still in her favourite pink broderie anglaise pyjamas. With her braces back in, she looked much younger than her seventeen years, more vulnerable, and nervously chewed what remained of her fingernails.

'Better, love?' Majella asked, looking Caitlin over. 'Believe it or not, that'll help.'

Caitlin wiped her mouth with some tissue. She wasn't sure but replied anyway, 'Hope so. My throat's raw, and me head's about to explode. More importantly, are *you* all right?'

Majella placed a hand on her forehead. 'Aye, I'm fine. Doesn't help having a friggin' hangover. Guess it's me own fault... Tina's been next door already, rang Tommy. He'll be here in a sec. He'll sort things out.'

Tommy was Caitlin's uncle. The man was like a magician in a crisis: calm, quick and always knew what to do. A go-to guy for fixing just about anything. She turned to Tina.

'What time is it?' she asked.

'Half-five.' Tina replied.

Despite her pounding headache, Caitlin managed a smile while keeping her voice light.

'Tina, you've got college. Get some kip. Okay? I'll stay with Mammy and sort this place out. Don't worry; we'll get Daddy back.'

But Tina wasn't having it. She shook her head, tears rolling down her cheeks.

'I don't wanna go to bed; I wanna stay with you. I'll not sleep after this.' Her arms flailed in frustration.

Caitlin stared at her. Her sister's curly red hair was wild, tumbling loose but proud around her shoulders. Ever since they'd hit their teens, their bodies had gone in opposite directions. Caitlin had shot up tall, a willowy beanpole, shy of six feet, with barely a curve to her name. Tina, nothing like it.

Caitlin's beauty bugged Tina, who, at a disappointing five foot four, was apple-shaped with full breasts. A bit of a tomboy, she didn't fuss about clothes, make-up or boys, while Caitlin was all about keeping up with the latest fads, spending her spare time flicking through magazines like *Jackie* and *Seventeen* that the girls shared around the factory where she worked.

At times, Tina's skin would flare up with painful eczema rashes, and despite trying every remedy under the sun, nothing worked. Puberty had dealt her a rough hand. Luckily for Caitlin, she had flawless porcelain skin, striking blue eyes, and a lush mane of long black hair that tumbled halfway down her back. Most girls would've killed for it, though it hadn't done her many favours, merely left her with only one close friend and a great big dollop of jealousy.

'Trust me, Tina. Go, please. Hit the sack,' she said.

Tina caught Caitlin's no-nonsense tone and gave a small nod of defeat, finally giving into the tiredness written all over her face. They usually shared a room, but she'd been bunking in Martin's since he was lifted.

'All right. G'night,' she mumbled, not exactly happy about leaving them but ready to crawl into bed.

'Night, love,' they both replied.

The door clicked shut, and Caitlin turned to her mother. She shivered again, rubbing at the bloodstained jumper.

'I need to get this off before it soaks in. Go you on down and stick the kettle on for Tommy. I'll only be a sec.'

Majella nodded and tightened her husband's oversized dressing gown around her, the sleeves trailing down past her hands.

Caitlin watched as she made her way down the stairs, sluggish and unsteady, gripping the banister with both hands. She must have some thumper of a headache too, Caitlin reckoned. Probably for the hundredth time, swearing she'd never drink again, and gasping for a cure.

As far as Caitlin knew, there wasn't a single drop left in the house, and the thought of phoning the doctor again for more tablets made her squirm. It hadn't even been that long since the last lot was picked up, and at this rate, they'd be the talk of the surgery. Her mother must've been scoffing them like sweets, the way kids do when no one's looking.

Once Majella disappeared down the hall, Caitlin turned back into her own room and began rummaging through the wardrobe, dragging out a black ribbed jumper and a half-decent pair of blue jeans. She got changed in quick, painful movements, then made her way into her parents' room.

The bed was a mess; the covers tangled and tossed, and for a moment she stood there, shaking her head at the state of it all. At the window, she parted the curtains and peered out at the street below. It was a pit, with rubbish, scattered dustbins, and lids everywhere. She saw a few people moving in and out of houses, trying to figure out who was taken. Even inside, the reek of petrol and burning rubber from a hijacked car set ablaze up the street was everywhere.

Sitting on the little stool at her mother's dressing table, Caitlin picked up a tarnished silver hairbrush and slowly dragged it through her tangled hair. After tying it into a ponytail, knowing she'd need to wash it later for work, she gazed at her reflection: a swollen face and the beginnings of a black eye. *Just lovely.*

With a sigh, she stood up and went downstairs to face the raid's aftermath. She started in the living room first, trying to sweep up the broken glass from the picture frames, clearing away the rubbish of torn books and scattered newspapers. Not that they'd much to wreck in the first place, she knew it could've been worse.

From the kitchen, Majella shouted. 'Your tea's here, love.'

Pausing by the kitchen door, Caitlin watched her mother anxiously wipe down the smeared worktops with a damp cloth. Once upon a time, the place was spotless, but of late, she'd let it go to pot.

A round wooden table sat in the middle of the kitchen, surrounded by six mis-matched chairs. Over the years, the family had shared secrets, slagged each other off and laughed till they cried around that cheap pine table. Everyone had their own chair, with Tommy usually claiming the sixth, since he spent more time here than his own place. This kitchen was the heart of the McLaughlin home, and on the wall hung a crooked portrait of Pope Paul VI, with a set of broken rosary beads draped over it, barely hanging on by a thread.

Majella handed her a chipped teacup, and Caitlin asked quietly, 'Where do we go from here, Mammy?'

Before replying, the older woman grabbed a cigarette from a pack on the windowsill. As she realised it was her last, she shook the empty box and tossed it onto the table. She lit the fag, took a long deep drag, and let the smoke roll from her lips, watching the curls swirl around the room like they might answer for her.

'I honestly don't know, love,' she sighed. 'Martin's been gone ages, and not a word. Nothing. And now this. Your daddy's not gonna cope. Not with his heart, and now I'm down to me last fag... for feck sake.' She took another long, steady drag.

'I ran after them with his pills, ye know, but that turncoat had a go at me again. If it weren't for that other one, hate to think what he woulda' done.' She jabbed at Patrick's dressing gown, her voice cutting.

'Wouldn't even let your poor Daddy put this on.'

Caitlin nodded, remembering the hulk-like figure, and blurted, 'Yeah, what was he about, eh? Him Irish, too.'

'Irish, me arse. Didn't you see his tattoo? Red Hand of Ulster it was. A bloody Orangeman.' Majella snapped.

Caitlin groaned. That explained it. *Unbe-fucking-lievable.*

Sipping her tea, Majella relished her last few drags. 'Anyways, what goes around comes around. He'll get his comeuppance one day. Ye mark my words.' Caitlin reached across the table and gave her hand a gentle squeeze and said.

'Forget him now, Mammy. As for Daddy, they'll let him see a doctor, I'm sure. He'll be grand.' Majella gave a half-hearted nod, her eyes already drifting to the empty fag packet on the table.

'I wonder...' she murmured, barely audible. Then, letting out a dramatic sigh that was far too familiar, she whispered, 'Sweet Mother of Christ, but I'm dyin' here,' as if to confirm Caitlin's prediction on the staircase.

In solemn silence, they waited at the table until the back door was flung open, and a slab of a man stormed into the kitchen, bringing a blast of icy wind and rain with him.

Uncle Tommy. Not the tallest by any stretch, but built like a brick wall, with a barrel chest and a thick, freckled neck rising from broad, square shoulders. He wore his usual dark green and khaki fur-lined parka over jeans, both soaked through. His flushed face was streaked with rain, the water running down from his drenched red hair and thick moustache. Caitlin spotted the spidery veins around his battered nose and high cheekbones, signs of too many jars and too many late nights.

The moment he stepped into the warmth of the kitchen, his thick black-framed glasses steamed up, hiding his stormy blue eyes. He whipped them off, blinking hard, and searched his pockets for something to clean them with. He gave up and used his jumper. Then, nodding towards the seated women, he said, 'Someone grab us a cloth, will ye?'

Caitlin stood up to fetch one as Tommy hugged her mother. 'There, now. Tell us what's happened.'

Tears ran steadily down Majella's face as she fought for words, each one catching in her throat and broken by the struggle to breathe. As the unfortunate story unfolded, Tommy's eyes narrowed, and he muttered a curse upon seeing the cut on the side of her head.

Waiting for her mother to slow down, Caitlin rammed a dry dish-cloth into Tommy's hand and raised her voice above Majella's weeping.

'Jesus, Tommy, they dragged Daddy out with some sorta hood on, wouldn't even let him get dressed. Kept battering him with a baton, he could barely stand, never mind see where he was going. It was awful.'

It was her turn to take a breath before she went on. 'Mammy was saying they wouldn't take his dressing gown or his tablets. *And* they've friggin' smashed the front door in. What's going on?'

Before saying a word, Tommy wiped his face and head to stop more water from dripping onto the floor. His voice was muffled and angry under the cloth, and the women strained to hear.

'It's a right fuck up, is what it is. They've torn Blamfield Street apart, rounded up about forty men, your da included. Nobody's saying a fuckin' word. Fuckin' nothing. God forgive me for cursin'.' He crossed himself and muttered the start of an Act of Contrition, but didn't get very far.

Tommy was a Sinn Féin 'community worker,' well-liked and re-spected by the Catholic community. He was charismatic, clever, and trustworthy, known locally for his patience and letter-writing skills. For those who couldn't read or write, Tommy would run letter-writ-ing campaigns to sort out all sorts of unfair prejudices, especially around housing. His success rate was high, and his knack for commu-nication had earned him respect even among the Unionists.

After smoothing his moustache, he picked up the Liverpool FC mug of tea Caitlin had set out. She was unnerved to see her uncle, normally calm, so upset.

'Things are gonna get worse,' he sighed. 'It's bad this time. They're liftin' everyone left, right, and centre. Do ye know there wasn't one Prod lifted? Not one. There's Catholics lying dead in Belfast 'cos of this.'

He gulped his tea and, shivering, looked at his sister's pack of fags on the table. 'Christ, I'm freezin' me arse off here. Any of those left, Majella? I need a smoke. Bad.'

'Nah, Tommy, sorry. That was me last one. Maybe you'll find some butts lying around in there,' she replied, offering him a week-old, half-filled ashtray, then suggested he stand by the gas ring to warm himself. He grimaced and waved her off.

'You're grand, thanks. I'll grab some later. There's talk of beatings at that camp the Brits opened in Magilligan. Looks like they've put the hardliners in there. Eight or ten huts for prisoners right in the middle of all those Brits, an army camp – how about that? Sayin' they're setting the dogs on them and starvin' the poor bastards. What's worse, they won't let them sleep. It's like the feckin' Gestapo.'

Caitlin was horrified. 'There's gotta be something we can do, Tommy!'

Tommy replied, his voice low, 'Nah, I don't know, love. I'm at a loss for once. Mind you, there is some good news – well, sorta good news. Found out about Martin. He's in the Kesh. He'll be in rough shape, I'd say. I'll get Brendan Doherty to come up with me, check him out.' Brendan was the family's trusted solicitor.

'If he's in the Kesh, there'll be nothin' left of him,' Majella cried. She'd heard about the terrible conditions at the prison and wanted to join Tommy on his visit.

'Ye can't love; they're not lettin' women in – not yet, anyway, Jella,' he replied, using his pet name for his sister.

'But listen to me, don't be thinkin' about that for now. I'm gonna find Patrick first, then I'll see Martin, hopefully the 'marra. Brendan'll drive, he's goin' anyway.'

To this day, no one understood why Tommy had never learned to drive. He drained the rest of his tea, stood up, and clicked his fingers as he thought of something.

'Come to think of it, Jella, ye'd better pack a few bits for Martin. Clean clothes, throw in a bit a' food – if you can.'

He patted down his trouser pockets. 'God, I need a ciggie. Sure you've none about, Jella?'

'Sorry, love. I'd better go sort out Martin's things,' she replied, looking a tad guilty for not being able to offer her brother a decent smoke.

Once she was out of sight, Tommy started rooting for Patrick's half-empty toolbox in the under-stairs cupboard. Muttering to himself, he said, 'I'll see what I can do with that front door of yours.'

Caitlin thanked him and kept tidying up while Majella rummaged about upstairs. After a while, Tommy let out a grunt and stood back to assess his handiwork – it'd have to do.

Back in the kitchen, Caitlin gestured for Tommy to sit. 'I'm dead worried about me Mammy,' she said.

'I don't think she can take much more. She's up to her eyes in those pills, Tommy, and drinking like a fish. She's dying the day and keeps saying Daddy won't survive being locked up. What's it gonna do to her if something happens to him? What's it gonna do to all of us?' The thought of it alone was enough to push the lot of them over the brink.

Tommy ran a hand over his face. 'You've no idea, love, I'm up to me eyeballs with people askin' for help. All sorts a'people. No one knows what's gonna happen next. The world's gone ape shit.' He paused for a moment.

'But today's not the day to think about all that. First things first.' Careful not to drip any more water, he reached for his sodden parka and turned to her.

'I know your ma's fallin' apart. Half the town's fallin' apart. One step at a time, okay? Let's sort your da' out the day, first? And do us a favour, keep an eye on Jella for me, will ye?' He'd always had a soft spot for his sister.

As if on cue, Majella stepped into the kitchen with a crumpled white Spar bag in hand. She'd packed a change of clothes and the bare essentials for Martin, then moved quietly to the cupboards. There wasn't much to give, but she still managed to pull a few bits of food together. Times were hard.

She told Tommy the rioting hadn't helped. Patrick's Giro was late again because of the post. Most postmen wouldn't come anywhere near the estate. No-one could blame them, not really. It was a risky job these days, with the Provos out hijacking most of the Royal Mail postbags and vans.

Patrick hadn't worked in years. Not for lack of trying, but there was nothing going for men like him. Unemployment among Catholic men was through the roof, especially at his age. Most company ads didn't even bother hiding their prejudice, but came right out and said it: 'Protestants only need apply.' And with that sort of carry-on, whole generations of youngsters had no choice but to pack up and leave for England and beyond, all promising to send money back home.

Tommy thanked Caitlin for the tea, pulled on his parka, and eased the back door open against the wind.

'I'll phone as soon as I hear anythin',' he said. 'Promise.' He cursed the weather as he stepped out, wind and rain lashing at him before he'd even made it to the gate.

Inside, Majella groaned and carried the empty cups to the sink. 'That man is sooo good.' She turned to Caitlin, 'I'm sorry, love, but I have to put me head down.'

Caitlin nodded. 'Course you do. I'll finish up here. See you after.'

'You're as good too. I don't know what I'd do without you.' Majella breathed.

With a kiss, she disappeared, and Caitlin got on with what she needed to do. By the time she was done, her body ached and her head was still thumping. She grabbed the only aspirin she could find and watched them dissolve, all the while trying to make sense of the last few hours. Sick with worry and feeling lost, she had that feeling again, the kind she could never quite explain but couldn't shake either, the kind that filled her with dread about what tomorrow might bring.

Whenever one of her feelings came about, it was seldom wrong, and always meant the same thing.

Turmoil.

Chapter Five

Rocola

After a couple of hours of restless sleep, the new day rolled in. At breakfast, Caitlin struggled to swallow the toast that Majella had placed in front of her and barely sipped her tea. Tina sat next to her, looking worn out but, for once, not moaning about her breakfast cereal mixed with their usual Marvel. She hated the dried milk, but Marvel was all they could afford; full-fat milk was a treat.

For college, locally known as 'the Tech,' Tina could wear whatever she liked, and she was pleased as punch to ditch her much hated school uniform to the back of the wardrobe. Today, she wore a mishmash of colours: a torn, short black skirt with grey tights, a pink blouse, and a purple-braided cardigan. Her wild hair hung loose, framing her tired face, still swollen from crying.

Majella hovered at the sink, bleary-eyed and foul-tempered, a damp cloth in hand. She couldn't keep still. But kept wiping the same spot over and over like it might settle her nerves, muttering under her breath every so often, though none of it made much sense.

'Don't get upset, Mammy,' Caitlin said, attempting to offer some comfort. Tommy's got Daddy covered. You know what he's like, he'll call as soon as he hears anything. And remember, he's going to see Martin tomorrow. That's good news, at least.'

Tina's face lit up at the mere mention of her brother. She adored him. In her eyes, Martin McLaughlin could do no wrong.

'Martin? What's that about Martin?' she asked excitedly.

'Ah, sorry, love, we should've told you. He's in the Kesh.' Caitlin replied. Tina's face dropped.

'The Kesh? Why the hell is he in the Kesh? Martin wouldn't hurt a fly!'

It was common knowledge Martin was tight in with the Provos and wasn't the innocent his little sister thought he was, but Caitlin knew now wasn't the time to break it to her.

'I know. But they're cracking down everywhere. The Brits are paranoid. They think every Catholic on the planet's involved. Tommy says not a single Prod's been lifted. Not one. You shou—, '

Out of nowhere, Majella snapped. Her glare could've cracked glass as she rounded on Tina.

'Jesus Christ, give it a rest, will ye? Me belly's churnin', me head's poundin', and I've had it up to here with your bletherin'. Will ye shut it, the pair of ye. I need peace, not a bloody debate!'

The sisters exchanged a look and rolled their eyes to the heavens as Majella went on.

'Tina, finish that cereal and get your bag. You'll be late. Keep your head down, and if there's the least sign of trouble, straight home, d'ye hear? And stick close to Emmett. He'll keep an eye on ye.'

Caitlin knew fine well Tina neither needed nor wanted anyone to be 'keep an eye' on her. She watched as her sister flung her spoon into her half-empty bowl and strode off to her room. Her mother's outburst said it all.

These days, Majella was a basket case, and it was starting to get to Tina too. Life was shite, and getting worse by the day, for all of them. And now poor Tina had to spend her morning hanging about with *Moronic Emmett*, as she called him.

Emmett was one of the McFaddens who lived next door. Two years younger than Tina, the pair had grown up side by side. They were an odd match – her with her fiery moods and quick temper, him all laid-back and love-struck, forever hanging around like some obsessed puppy who didn't know when to give up.

Speak of the devil, there was a knock at the back door. Majella opened it and said, 'That'll be himself now.'

And there he was, standing loyal as ever on the back step in his St Peter's school uniform. His black blazer was stained with food and the crest on the top pocket half torn off. A baggy V-neck jumper, crumpled white shirt, and flared hand-me-down trousers hung off him, the hems nearly swallowing his shoes. A school tie dangled from a battered brown leather bag slung over one bony shoulder, and a thin plastic belt held the lot up.

Tina came back into the kitchen, looking anything but pleased. She hated being seen with Emmett; he was just a wain, but her mammy insisted they walk to the bus stop together every morning.

'How's it going, Emmett?' Majella smiled.

'Not great, Mrs McLaughlin. Me mammy's goin' off her rocker. It's our Joe, he's back in trouble. She's thinking of sending me to me Aunt Trish in Greencastle over the border. I've told her I can't miss school. We're hardly back and I've got me exams soon.' He wasn't for stopping, with lots more to say.

'Did you hear the Brits are parking their Pigs in our school car park? It's a laugh, but they keep talkin' to us, all nice and friendly. It's bad though, cos we can't talk to them, can we? They're even askin' us to play footie,' he blabbered.

Majella planted her hands on her hips. 'Heard that. Don't go gettin' mixed up with the likes. Keep your head down and outta it. Wee dote.'

She gave the top of his head a quick rub. 'Bless ye, thinkin' about your exams too. Good on ye.'

Emmett nodded, eager and brimming with hope. He'd told everyone on the street what he wanted to do when he left school. He'd get out of Derry, go to university, land a crackin' job, and make it big. One day he'd be loaded, rolling in it, with more money than he'd know what to do with. He'd once told Caitlin he was angry, watching his ma slog her guts out while his useless da sat about smoking and watching the horses. Determined to carve a better life, he swore he'd live in Australia when he grew up. Sun, beaches, blue skies that never ended. Even Tina might come with him. And his ma too, if she'd ever leave that big clout of a father.

Majella patted his back and nudged him towards the door. 'Off you go now with laugh a minute there. Stick together and straight home after.'

Still in a huff, Tina elbowed Emmett through the door first, and before they knew it, they were away.

'Bye then. You have a good day too!' Caitlin called after the slamming door.

She thought about Tina. When it suited her, the girl could be a proper pain in the arse. Still, she was the lucky one who got to stay on at school – a chance Caitlin never had.

At sixteen, Caitlin had no choice but to leave school. She started out as a runner in Rocola, the local shirt factory, and now worked as an administrator. Mrs Mugan, her favourite teacher, had urged her to get some qualifications before she left, so she took a secretarial course and passed with flying colours.

University was never on the cards. Just wasn't. Most girls her age left school and went straight into the factories, starting out as hemmers, cuffers, or button hole makers. The work was dull and repetitive, but payday made up for it. The idea of getting dolled up and heading to a dance or disco kept their spirits up. When the horn went on a Friday evening, the streets filled with the women's chatter, laughter in the air as everyone was itching to get out and hit the dance floor.

Caitlin shot upstairs and gave her hair a quick rinse under the luke-warm tap. With the heating barely on, there was little chance of getting clothes dried properly, so she wriggled into a clean but damp pair of Lee jeans, grabbed her bits and pieces, and headed back down to the kitchen.

'Gotta run, Mammy. I'll be straight home after,' she cried.

Majella sat at the kitchen table, her sad eyes staring at the empty chairs, remembering the good days. She rubbed her temples, barely holding it together.

Her eyes flicked over Caitlin until she said, 'Right love. Your sand-wich's there too, it's only bread and sugar, sorry. Cupboard's empty after Martin. I'm headin' to the sortin' office to see if your daddy's Giro's in yet. Might give it to me early. If not, I'll have to go see me mother.'

Caitlin gaped at her. 'Seriously? We're not that desperate and I'm paid soon. Forget that, Mammy! You know what that woman's like. Honestly, we'll be grand. Go on up and lie down. I'll see you later.' Majella stood and kissed her daughter on the cheek.

'Aye, suppose when ye think of it, I'll leave her be. Bye, love. Hope work's all right with your poor face and everything.'

Caitlin wasn't best pleased at the idea of them going anywhere near her granny. Mary O'Reilly had never taken to her daddy, always saying he wasn't good enough for her only daughter. She'd wanted Majella to bag herself a *professional*. The old bat was a total snob.

When Patrick and Majella did get together, Patrick was working the docks, but the work dried up when the shipping companies switched to sea containers. After that, plenty of dockers had no choice but to sign on. Many turned to the old drink and what started as a lifeline ended up like a bloody great noose round their necks. Numerous city billboards screaming, 'The Dole Destroys the Soul' only twisted the knife in. It was awful seeing so many hardworking men left with nothing to do. Depression was rife.

An explosion had blown Caitlin's granda to smithereens in the Second World War, so Mary O'Reilly made it her life's mission to find a rich husband for her daughter, but she failed. Love won out, and Majella soon married Patrick McLaughlin, a poor but hard working docker. To make matters worse, the woman was cold as ice to her grandchildren. Never once did she show an ounce of care for any of them.

Mary preferred to keep to herself, but what she didn't realise was that Majella and Tommy weren't the least bit bothered by her lack of love. They had each other.

As for the grandchildren, they all thought she was a spiteful old hag and they, too, weren't bothered. Caitlin hoped Majella wouldn't end up grovelling to the crabbit cow, she'd never let them hear the end of it. Tommy was spot on when he warned them, 'The old bat never forgives, never forgets.'

Thankfully, they rarely saw her, and when they did, it was only out of duty. Christmas, Easter, that sort of thing.

Chapter Six

The Factory Girls

C aitlin stood on the front step, staring out at their half-fenced garden. It was a disgrace. Crumpled cans, chip bags, and scraps of newspaper were scattered across the muck-soaked grass, which was patchy at best. The gate hung off-centre, and with her daddy so sick, no one had fixed it. She was mortified, especially knowing the McFaddens next door always kept theirs neat and tidy. Maggie would be out sweeping the steps while her boys trimmed the hedges. It only made number 30's effort look worse.

She wrestled with her ancient umbrella, trying to force it open. Doors slammed up and down Blamfield Street as tired women and girls stepped out, heading off to what was left of Derry's few remaining shirt factories.

The glory days of the shirt industry were long gone. As a child, Caitlin remembered the sight of crowds of women linking arms, laughing and chatting on their way to the dozens of factories scattered across the city.

Back in the 1920s, Derry had boasted forty four factories and over 8,000 women employed from a population of around 45,000. She'd heard they could stitch a shirt from scratch in sixteen minutes flat. But then came the downturn. Factory owners started outsourcing work to the Far East, where women were paid buttons, a lousy £2.50 a week, far less than the Derry girls. Most of the factories had shut down, one after the other, but Rocola, where Caitlin worked, had somehow hung on. Just about. It was still the biggest in the city.

She drew her coat tight, shut the front door behind her and set off. As she turned the corner, her best friend Anne sprang on her from behind.

'Mornin missus,' she cried, giving Caitlin a big hug and linking arms. Their umbrellas bumped, and they giggled like mad, until Anne inspected Caitlin's face and gasped, 'Mary Mother of God, what happened to that face?' Caitlin touched her cheek gingerly.

'Weren't we raided this morning, and a bleedin' Brit smacked me one. Well, not exactly a Brit, an Orangeman dressed as a Brit. They took me Daddy, him only in his underpants. No more. We don't know where he's gone, nothin... Long story. My head's still killing me, well sore.'

As they walked, Anne wanted more detail, so Caitlin filled her in.

'Ye sure you wanna go to work?' Anne asked.

'Have to, Anne. Need the pennies. If I don't, Parkes'll deduct it – you know what she's like.' Mrs Parkes was Rocola's notoriously stingy office manager.

'Think she'll notice?' Caitlin asked, carefully touching her eye again.

'Forget Mrs Parkes. That woman wouldn't notice if a great big dick was stuck down her Proddy gob!' Anne burst out laughing at the thought and shuddered.

'I swear to God, Anne, you're awful. Don't make me laugh, it hurts!' Caitlin screeched. 'I don't believe you sometimes. That is so a sin! If Father McGuire heard that, you'd—'

Anne squealed. Caitlin's naivety never ceased to amaze her. 'Ah, for feck's sake! You're a wile prude, wee girl. Will ye grow up for once, I was only jokin'!'

Caitlin threw Anne a loving glance, realising she was the only bright spot in her otherwise dark world. After the raid, she'd thought she'd never laugh again, but there was Anne Heaney, within minutes, making her feel a million times better.

Anne suddenly had an idea. 'Didn't you catch that Orangeman's number so ye can report him?' She stepped closer for a better look. 'Ouch, that's gonna be a beaut.'

With a shake of the head, Caitlin replied, 'Get real, Anne. Report a Brit? Waste of bloody time. It'd be his word against mine. Compared to the other stuff that's going on, I'm all right. Tommy says there's been brutal beatings and loads of houses wrecked. Men lifted everywhere.'

'And you don't know where your da is?'

'Not a clue. Tommy's on it though.'

'Good old Tommy.' Anne replied. She liked Tommy – everyone liked Tommy O'Reilly.

Caitlin couldn't help touching her swollen face again as the morning's events played through her head. She didn't want to say much more, especially about her mammy's drinking, but Anne's eyes said she could imagine it.

'It'll be grand. Try not to stress,' she said gently, though they both knew full well it probably wouldn't.

The way things were going, Anne wasn't sure about anything anymore. The Brits had even lifted a few teenage girls from the bottom of their street. Everyone knew they weren't involved. Not the type. Ordinary Derry girls who worked hard as cleaners at the local hospital.

As they chatted, the rain eased off, and the two of them barely noticed the angry slogans sprayed across the walls of Creggan. 'Don't ball lick the British, fight them IRA/P, 'and 'They can kill a revolutionary, but not a revolution' – a few of the latest.

Arm in arm, they soon made their way down the steep slope of Blighs Lane towards Rocola, stepping over broken paving stones and the ruin left behind from the rioting. Petrol bombs had scorched the road near Stones Corner, where a couple of kids were already out picking through the debris for spent rubber bullets, hoping to show them off later. Glass, wood, and burnt-out car parts lay everywhere.

Housing was a sore point in the city. For Catholics, getting a council house was near impossible. When it came to allocations, the Unionist council always favoured Protestants.

Creggan, built in 1947, now held around 15,000 Catholics. It had been deliberately designed to pack Nationalists into one area, thereby keeping the Unionist government in control of the voting boundaries. Classic gerrymandering.

'Tell you what, let's change the subject,' Anne chirped. 'Have you heard from hunky Seamus lately?'

Seamus was Caitlin's ex. They'd been on and off for ages, and he'd proposed the year before. Caitlin didn't love him the way he would have liked, and it all got too much. She was determined to hold out for Mr Right. For true love. Seamus was a nice fella, but when she turned him down, he'd gone to America in a huff. Majella had been furious with her for weeks. She'd adored him. Thankfully, her daddy had stood by her.

Caitlin gave Anne a cheeky smile. 'He's not my *hunky* Seamus. And no, haven't heard a dicky bird. Don't expect to either.'

Suddenly, the heavens opened again and they ran like the wind until they reached the factory gates and melted into the crowd.

After clocking in, Anne headed for the stock and dispatch room, yelling over the roar of the machines, 'See you tonight, missus. Don't worry. And try to get somethin' for that eye.'

Caitlin waved her off, wiggling her fingers in a mock nag: 'Nag, nag, nag...'

As she made her way to the admin block, she felt the loss of Anne's company already. A sudden wave of exhaustion hit her as she clocked the sign taped to the lift door.

'Out of Order.'

Just my luck, she thought, dragging her sore self up the stairs to the fifth floor. She couldn't stop thinking about her daddy, convincing herself he'd be back home and in one piece by the end of the day. Everything would go back to normal, or as near to normal under the circumstances.

At the top, she walked along the narrow corridor lined with office doors, each etched with the names of the managers: Mr Henderson, General Manager; Mr McScott, Accountant; and so on. She reached the last door, where Mrs Parkes, her two junior assistants, and Caitlin worked.

First to arrive, she stepped into the cold room and hung up her coat and scarf. After a few failed tries, she managed to get the old gas heater going and left it on the lowest setting. Mrs Parkes was well known for her frugality, never allowing it on high, and as a result the girls were often laid up with colds or the flu through the winter. When she, who must be obeyed, finally appeared, Caitlin noticed the familiar dour face.

Petite, barely five foot, with a long thin face, wired rimmed glasses and a black pudding bowl haircut, Mrs Parkes was slim as a rake and reminded Caitlin of the *Wicked Witch of the West*. Rumour had it she'd married a Derry man she couldn't stand and now longed to go back to Bangor, her home town and a Loyalist suburb of Belfast.

'Morning, Caitlin,' she said in her broad East Ulster accent, shaking out her umbrella and waiting for a reply.

When Caitlin didn't answer, Mrs Parkes eyed her face, but said nothing. No doubt, Caitlin reckoned, grumpy drawers thought she'd been given a crack by her stotious father. Or worse. Shows what she knew. Patrick never touched a drop, unlike Majella, nor had he ever laid a hand on any of them.

'Morning,' Caitlin finally replied.

Mrs Parkes gave a sniff, grunted, and hung up her coat before shuffling off to make her usual cuppa. She never offered the girls a hot drink, either. Not that they'd ask. You'd get a look that'd turn you to stone if you did.

Not long after, her workmates, Sinead and Mary, arrived – full of chatter and giggles – until they spotted their boss. They stopped dead, muttered a polite 'Good morning,' and got the usual grunt in return.

After peeling off their wet coats and dumping their brollies, they sat down and tried not to laugh. Sinead had swiped one of her brother's dirty magazines from under his mattress, and the pair of them were still sniggering about it. Nevertheless, it didn't take long for them to notice Caitlin's face. Their looks turned slightly to concern, but Caitlin's eyes told them quickly enough to leave it and not ask.

After lunch, an unexpected knock on the office door broke their routine. A distinguished-looking man in a classic black three-piece suit strolled in, white shirt, red tie, the works. It was Roger Henderson, Rocola's big cheese. The owner himself. Normally looking very much the part, with his neatly trimmed steel grey hair and tailored suits, today he appeared pale and tired looking, with dark, heavy bags under his eyes.

Caitlin didn't see much of him, but when she did, he was always polite and seemed decent enough. Behind him came a younger man none of them recognised. Roger nodded to Mrs Parkes and offered a smile to the girls.

'Mrs Parkes. Ladies.'

The office manager leapt to her feet like a cat on a hot tin roof, smoothing her thick serge skirt as she stumbled forward.

'Wh...wh... why, Mr Henderson, good afternoon. What a surprise!' She hated surprises. Hated them with a passion.

Roger smiled and spoke in a soft Derry accent. But posh. Caitlin caught it straight away, that trace of a privileged upbringing.

'A quick visit is all, Mrs Parkes. Wanted to introduce another Henderson — James. My nephew. He's recently moved from Scotland and will be joining us here at Rocola.' He gave James a brief nod and smile.

Caitlin's eyes flicked to the newcomer as he shook Mrs Parkes's hand, then glanced around the office. When he stepped fully into view, she had to admit he was the last thing she expected to see around these parts. He was without question the most beautiful man she'd ever laid eyes on. *Beautiful* – a word she'd never use to describe a fella, but it was the only one that came to mind. As silly as it sounded, he was *beautiful*.

Tall and well over six foot, he made Mrs Parkes look like a midget. With thick auburn hair and sea-green eyes that could kill, he was dressed as if for a wedding. Whatever aftershave he wore drifted through the office, rich and musky, the kind that made you want to get closer and take a long, greedy sniff.

'Mornin', ladies.' His husky Scottish accent rolled out.

'Mornin', sir,' Sinead and Mary sang back. Elbows nudged, smothered giggles broke out, the girls' insides flipping as they tried and failed to keep quiet. They couldn't get over him. *Jesus, but wasn't your man something else?!*

Roger Henderson, aware of the swooning women, rubbed his hands and gave a sly grin.

'Best keep moving James, before I lose half my workforce!' He turned to the office manager.

'I'll catch up with you later, Mrs Parkes, as James here will need a secretary.'

Sinead let out a snort and elbowed Mary again, who burst into a giggle loud enough for the whole office to hear. One look from Mrs Parkes was all it took – their faces snapped into perfect little masks of fake innocence.

As Roger made to leave, James stepped aside to let him pass, but not before scanning the room again. His gaze stayed on Caitlin. Instinctively, she quickly raised a hand to hide her bruised face, but caught the flicker in his eyes as he dipped his head and said, 'Thank you, ladies. See you again.'

He threw in a cheeky wink for Sinead and Mary before pulling the door shut behind him. The second it clicked closed, Sinead's jaw dropped.

'I'd be his secretary any day. For that, I'd type with me feet, starkers!'

Mary clutched her sides. 'Wait 'til we tell the girls downstairs. Wasn't he outta this world?'

'Out of this solar system more like!' Sinead joked.

As usual, the ever-grumpy Mrs Parkes growled, 'Enough of that now, ladies. Back to work!'

The day dragged on for Caitlin until the horn blew at five o'clock.

Feeling rotten and unable to eat, her sad little sandwich sat untouched on her desk.

Mrs Parkes had been training the others elsewhere in the building all afternoon, leaving Caitlin more than happy to have some time alone. She gathered her papers and locked them back in the drawer, then stretched out her arms and let out a deep, much-needed groan. Once everything was in its place, she grabbed her coat, umbrella, and scarf, ready to get home as fast as her legs would allow.

Outside it was still lashing down, and, as usual, Anne waited by the entrance, leaning against the wall under her umbrella, puffing on a fag like a chimney. She was one of those naturally beautiful women, a proper Irish colleen who, beneath all her bravado, never quite realised the effect she had on men. Her pale strawberry-red curls framed her face perfectly and, like Tina, no matter how many times she tried to tame them, they always bounced back.

Caitlin had to admit Anne's face was a sight to behold, even with a half-soaked ciggy stuck to her perfect rosebud lips. She'd tried often enough to get Majella and Anne to quit, but it was no use.

'Ugh, will you chuck that smoke away?' She nagged, flicking a finger at the packet. 'You know I can't stand them. They'll kill you one day, and you'll reek.'

Anne jumped up, gave Caitlin a playful pout, and flicked out the half-finished butt before tucking it back in the pack for later. Without a word, she passed Caitlin her umbrella and, taking her sweet time, swapped her dull flat pumps for a pair of bright red stilettos. She tossed the pumps into her bag and flashed her friend a wide, know-it-all grin.

'That's better now, isn't it?' She gave a wink and added, 'Sure, the world's easier to face in these beauties.'

Caitlin shook her head as Anne took back her umbrella, and the two girls linked arms.

Anne was mad about her three-inch stilettos and loved anything 1950s rock and roll. Much to her sister's annoyance, their bedroom was plastered with posters of glamorous movie stars and singers from that era, crammed with wide-petticoated skirts, pencil skirts, and tight tops. She swore by her stilettos, convinced they were man-catchers, adding a bit of height to her petite five-foot-two frame. Her dream was to own a pair in every colour of the rainbow. Caitlin couldn't figure out how she walked in them, even in the rain, but she rocked it like a model, flashing her perfect shaped legs and winking at any fella caught staring.

When they met at primary school when they were five, Caitlin thought Anne was pure magic, a scream. She couldn't imagine life without her and would do anything for her.

They walked on home, going on about their day, with Caitlin telling Anne about the newbie, James Henderson. Anne wasn't that interested; she'd a date that night and mentally kept changing her mind about what to wear.

After saying their goodbyes, Anne wandered off to her family's run-down terraced house, where she lived with her many siblings and her eternally exhausted mother. For as long as Caitlin could remember, Anne's mother was either pregnant or had just given birth. Her family was dirt poor.

As to Anne's father, he was barely seen, but when he was, it was obvious he was popping in for a quick 'you know what' before disappearing again. An old IRA man on the run, he spent most of his time in the Irish Republic. Everyone knew he had another woman set up down there, but no one dared mention it to his wife. It was never talked about. Her older brothers had already flown the nest, her sisters worked at Rocola too, and the younger ones were still in school, so the family relied on the working women to stay afloat.

For years Caitlin had listened to Anne talk about meeting a rich, tanned Yank who'd sweep her off her feet, marry her, and carry her away to America, like their great-aunt Rose, and other Derry girls had done during and after the war. Anne wasn't joking. One way or the other, she'd her heart set on living her dream in the good old US of A.

Chapter Seven

A Telephone Call

Drenched and cold, Caitlin arrived home, cursing as she searched for the door key in her oversized handbag while trying to hold on to her umbrella.

As soon as she found it, she quickly opened the partially repaired door, shook the umbrella out on the doorstep, and placed it in the corner of the hallway.

She called out, but silence greeted her. The house was bitterly cold as she hastily removed her wet coat and hung it under the stairs.

She tried again, 'Mammmmyyyyy. Tina anyone in?' Nope. No one in.

Practically crawling up the stairs and across the landing to the bathroom, she perched on the edge of the white enamel tub and turned on the hot tap. Still feeling rough, she pleaded with all the saints that the water would be hot. With her hand under the tap, she waited, fingers crossed, as it flowed. It was nearly dark outside. The wind howled, and the rain slapped against the small, frosted bathroom window.

Sensing the water heat, Caitlin thanked God and sighed with relief as she placed the stopper in the plughole and let the hot water flow over her hand. Goosebumps crept up her arms as steam formed in the cold air of the bathroom, but as if detecting her absolute need for heat, the water cruelly receded, only to be replaced by a freezing flow.

'Shit, shit and shit!' she cried. No chance of a bath. Next, without warning, the bathroom light went out, leaving her sitting in the dark. Wound up and anxious, she tried the switch, on and off, on and off. The electric meter must've run out.

She muttered a series of quiet curses and did everything but cry. Her mother obviously hadn't got the Giro, so Caitlin wondered if there was any money lying elsewhere in the house.

With the help of the street lights, she rifled through the bedrooms, digging deep into jacket and trouser pockets, cupboards, and drawers. It was like scouring for gold and coming up empty-handed. As a last resort, she asked herself if Tina had cashed in all the lemonade bottles she and Emmett collected from the nearby building sites all summer. The workmen always left empty Maine bottles for the kids to find and return to the local shop for a few pence.

In the darkness, Caitlin knelt and lifted Tina's bedcovers, peering underneath as she searched. At first, she couldn't find anything but stretched her arms as far as she could until she felt something. She pulled out whatever it was and thanked God to see a few empty bottles inside a Wellworths bag. Only a few, but it was a start.

As she hauled the bag out, she gasped when she smacked her elbow on the bed. After holding it in and swallowing the pain, she waited a moment, then she heard the front door open, followed by her mother's voice from downstairs, 'Caitlin! You there?'

There is a God, Caitlin decided before running down the stairs with her prized bottles. 'I'm here. Any luck with the Giro?'

She watched Majella remove her wet mac and place it next to Caitlin's under the stairs, and talking to her from inside the small cupboard, she replied, 'Should be here tomorrow, love; decided I couldn't face your granny, not today.'

As Majella walked into the hallway, she gazed up at the ceiling. 'Why's it so dark in here?'

'Meter's run out. Do we have *any* money?' Caitlin asked, exasperated.

Majella scowled, picked up a shopping bag, and held it up like she was stocking up for a Sunday roast.

'Got the dinner,' she said, then walked into the kitchen, where she checked her purse. 'Only forty pee. That's it. For Jesus sake. I was hopin' it'd last 'til the mornin'.'

Caitlin trailed her into the dark kitchen, feeling depressed. 'Doesn't look like it. Where's Tina?'

Majella placed the bag on the table and attempted to examine Caitlin's cheek. Distracted, she reached out and stroked it.

'Tina? Oh, next door helping Maggie with somethin'. She'll be here in a minute. God love ye. That eye looks sore, even in this light. Gonna be a beaut.'

Caitlin half-laughed, recalling Anne's using the same words. 'You're not the first to say.'

Her mother appeared unsteady. Had she been drinking? Caitlin wondered.

Majella noted the plastic bag in Caitlin's hand. 'What's that for?'

'A couple of empties I found under Tina's bed. She'll have to take them to the shop. Hopefully, there's enough with your forty pee and these to feed the meter. Mind you, I think she's been saving them.'

'Don't worry about Tina; leave her to me. There's some old candles 'round here somewhere. Put those cooker rings on full and get some heat goin'. It's like an icebox in here.' Majella replied, along with a sigh of relief; hopefully it'd last the night, get the pipes going and a bit of heat in the house. Before she knew it, all four gas burners were lit, and Caitlin took her chair. She watched as Majella rummaged through a cupboard for the candles. *Thank you, God!'* With a warm smile, she held them up.

'There now. We'll be sorted in no time.' She took out her lighter, lit the candles, and set them on saucers from the draining board, then placed them on the windowsill. The room filled with a warm, almost magical glow, and funny enough Caitlin thought, peaceful in a way.

'Any word on Daddy?' she asked.

'Fraid not, love. Still waiting to hear,' Majella moaned. She opened the shopping bags and removed a half stone bag of potatoes, an extra large onion, and two packets of Irish special mince for a stew. Next, she placed a Mother's Pride loaf and, as a treat, a pint of Old City Dairy milk on the table, talking as she put the food away.

'I've been here all day, prayin'. No calls next door, so I ran out to get this stuff.'

Their neighbours, the McFaddens, had a pay phone in their garden shed that locals could use to receive and make calls. They kept it locked, and you had to ask for the key to use it. It was a community initiative, allowing those who couldn't afford a phone at home to talk to their families in far-off countries. Vandals had damaged most, if not all, of the pillar box-red public phone boxes in the area.

The front door soon opened, and Tina walked into the kitchen a moment later. Her face and hair were soaked. It didn't take a brain surgeon to see she'd made no effort to protect herself from the downpour as water dripped onto the floor from her nylon quilted coat. After shaking it all over the place, she asked, 'Any news?'

'Nothin', I was just sayin' to Caitlin, still waitin' to hear,' Majella replied, facing the sink, then turning around. It was only then that she noticed how drenched her youngest was.

'Jesus, wee girl, hurry up, will ye? Get that coat off before you catch your death. The electric's gone. Dry yourself off, take a sec, then grab my mac and nip 'round to the shop. We need to top up the electric with those bottles and this. And don't forget a fifty-pence piece!'

Tina flung her soaking coat aside – *she'd only walked through the bloody door!*

She snatched the coins from Majella's outstretched hand, eyes blazing, lips pressed into a tight line. Caitlin could see the rage brewing on her sister's face, furious that she'd found her hidden stash of bottles.

'I'll go then, shall I?' Tina fumed, muttering under her breath and biting her lip. In a foul mood, she grabbed the bag and stalked out, stubbornly ignoring Majella's offer of her mac.

Half expecting it, Caitlin heard the battered front door slam. She felt bad for Tina. Her sister was a funny onion, always off in her own world, hiding away for hours and keeping herself to herself. Sometimes, she wished they were close, like Anne was with her sisters. But she'd wised up over the years – when Tina got into one of her moods - best to leave her be. Sad, perhaps, but that was how it was in the McLaughlin's house these days.

An hour or so later, dinner was cooked, and the house had warmed up a little as the three women sat in the kitchen. Majella had kept the lights off and let the candles burn, allowing them to enjoy the soft, soothing atmosphere.

Now that Tina was back and had got off her high horse, Caitlin asked how things had gone at the Tech and whether there'd been any bother between the students. It was one of the few places where Catholics and Protestants mixed.

'No, no trouble, not today anyway,' Tina muttered sulkily at first, then back to herself as she told them Maggie, next door, had heard nothing about her eldest son Joe, who, like their Martin, had been lifted ages ago and was worried sick. She added that the Brits had kicked the Mullans' poor dog so hard when it went for them that the loyal old mutt had conked it. And the eejits had only gone and lifted a thirteen-year-old boy, believing him to be someone else. Only under pressure from a blazing Father McGuire, who'd stormed into the Strand Road barracks like a man possessed, did they let the fella go.

Majella couldn't believe it and said Maggie was right to think about sending Emmett over the border. As for Father McGuire, weren't they were blessed to have a parish priest like him. A saint.

Out of nowhere, the house quaked in response to an almighty boom – a bomb. There'd been nearly fifty so far that year, and everyone had grown used to the regular blasts. This one wasn't that close, but near enough to make them worry.

Moments later, a loud knocking at the front door echoed through the house. Caitlin ran to open it and found Maggie McFadden, the street matriarch and neighbour, standing on the doorstep, desperately shielding her bleached blonde hair, coiled in numerous coloured rollers, from the wind and rain. Coatless, she wore a floral apron tied securely across her ample bosom, accentuating its size. She jumped into the hallway as soon as the door opened.

Caitlin thought the world of Maggie. Everyone did. She was a kind woman who adored her roles as wife and mother. Like many Derry women, she worshipped her sons and kept her home immaculate, despite working full time as a catering supervisor at one of the large city hotels. She was highly regarded throughout the estate, and as a bonus, she earned extra money by hosting several Tupperware parties at home. In her rasping smoker's voice, she delivered a message.

'Hi ya, love. Tommy's on the phone looking for your mammy. I think he's been tryin' to ring before; sorry, I didn't hear him. Was upstairs with the hoover on. He sounds frantic. You'd better get her. Quick!' She spun around and ran as fast as she could back towards her own house.

'Tell her to hurry!' she shouted.

'Will do. Thanks, Maggie!'

Caitlin rushed to the kitchen, crying, 'Mammy, quick, Tommy's on the phone.'

At this, Majella took off full pelt next door. Caitlin squirmed at the thud of the front door slamming, the force knocking a piece of panel loose, sending it clattering onto the tiled floor. She couldn't understand how the same door was still hanging.

The sisters glanced at each other. Because she wanted to keep them busy and avoid overthinking, Caitlin suggested they set the table. They laid out the plates, knives and forks alongside tumblers of water and cheap paper napkins. Majella always insisted on napkins at every meal, including breakfast – even if it was just a piece of kitchen roll.

Caitlin set down the last glass and said to Tina. 'I know you threw a hissy fit about me finding your empties, Tina, but I'll make it up to you on payday.'

Tina shook her head. 'It's all right. It's only we've been saving them, that's all, and half the money's Emmett's. There again, he's driving me bonkers – keeps asking me to go to see *The Godfather*. I've seen it and wish he'd leave me alone. Give me head peace.'

Caitlin chuckled. 'Poor Emmett. He's got it bad.'

Tina smiled. 'Don't talk.'

Afterwards, Caitlin checked the front door and knew they'd have to get it fixed properly, by someone who knew what they were doing. The girls sat in awkward silence, waiting for Majella to reappear.

Tina stared at her sister and felt the same old pang of sadness. She'd always found Caitlin hard to talk to. They were so different. Caitlin was all chit chat and open, and Tina... well, Tina was Tina. Although she knew Caitlin tried to get close to her, she never quite knew how to meet her halfway. It was Martin who got her, but he was gone now. She missed him like hell.

Sometimes, it felt like something wasn't right with her. Inside. Like God had forgot to complete her. For as long as she could remember, she'd never had a sense of belonging, or of having a place or a voice in this house. It was almost as if she were standing on the outside, looking in. Her head played tricks on her all the time.

Finding the silence uncomfortable and getting anxious, she said, 'Taking her time, isn't she? Something must've happened.'

Chapter Eight

Dante's Inferno

Almost as if summoned, a frantic knocking came from the front door. The girls jumped up and ran to open it, bumping into each other down the narrow hallway.

Tina opened the door first to find a flustered and out of breath Maggie standing beside a visibly shaken Majella. A couple of rollers had come loose from her hair, and she hurried inside, gripping her neighbour and best friend by the arm.

Majella's eyes were red-rimmed and empty, her face pale with raw pain as she gazed at Caitlin. Heartache etched itself onto every line of her face; in the space of fifteen minutes, she appeared to have aged years.

'What is it?' Caitlin gasped, rushing over to support the distraught woman. 'What's happened?!' Majella couldn't get a word out, and Caitlin searched Maggie's face for an answer.

Maggie shook her head, her own face pale with distress, and said, 'Christ, Caitlin, your da's had a heart attack. They're takin' him to the hospital. Emmett's gone to get our Charlie to drive you over. It's not good.'

She turned to Majella and added, 'Your mammy was on the floor when I went to check on her. Poor Tommy was still hanging on the phone, screamin' down the line like a madman. He's in some state, but says he'll meet you at A and E.'

'Jesus Christ!' Caitlin replied. The small group of women were unsure what to do next, a creeping sense of dread hanging over them until with a calm voice, Caitlin placed her hand on her sister's wrist.

'Help me get Mammy into the living room.'

Together they eased Majella out of the hallway and placed her down onto their scrappy brown corduroy sofa. Her body was trembling, and she was mumbling nonsense to herself. Caitlin couldn't even offer her a drink to settle her nerves – as far as she knew, there wasn't a drop in the house. She cursed their poverty. There were pills upstairs, she was sure of that, but she hadn't a clue what they were for. No idea what to give, what was safe, what might knock Majella out more, or, God forbid, make things worse. The idea of screwing up completely stopped her.

Tea. They'd make some tea. In Derry, during any crisis, tea was the glue that held everything and everyone together. Once, she might have laughed. But not today. There was nothing funny about today. Not a single thing.

Tina was asked to make the tea. She didn't need to be told twice, grateful to be doing something, anything, rather than sitting in there watching her poor mother break down. Maggie and Caitlin sat either side of Majella, offering what little comfort they could.

Once the tea was made, no one moved, no one said a word. Only Majella reached for a cup, her hands trembling so badly as she drank, the rim tapped against her teeth.

The minutes dragged by as they waited for Charlie. The only sound was the ticking of their old-fashioned mantel clock, steady and relentless, each second growing louder, more annoying than the last. They could do nothing but wait, hope and pray Charlie would get there soon, all the while wondering if Patrick was still alive.

In the end, Maggie sprang to her feet. She couldn't sit still any longer. Caitlin watched as she yanked back the net curtain, like looking out might somehow drag Charlie up the path quicker.

Apart from Majella, she was fretting over her Joe. Her only comfort, if you could even call it that, was that he wasn't soft like Emmett. Her eldest was a tough nut, always had been. He'd been in and out of trouble more times than she could count, but that never stopped her worrying about him, not then, not now. Day in, day out, she carried it, but tonight, it was worse. The fear, the waiting, all of it seemed to settle into her very bones like lead.

A loud thump on the front door sent Tina running. She opened it to find 'Big' Charlie McFadden standing in the rain, looking well cross. He brushed past her and shouted out for his wife.

'In here,' Maggie called.

He followed her voice and stepped into the living room, looking suspiciously at Maggie first, then Majella's pale, stunned face.

'What the hell's goin' on, love? Our Emmett's near givin' me feckin' heart failure, grabbin' me outta Mailey's like that. The stupid git's been talkin' gibberish the whole way. What's up?'

'It's Patrick, Charlie. He's had a heart attack in custody. Have you had much to drink? Think you can drive them over to the hospital?' Maggie jerked her head towards Caitlin and Majella.

'Awe shit. Poor Patrick. Aye, no bother. I'll go get me keys. I'm grand, only had a pint. It'll be some journey, mind you. Didn't ye hear it? Bomb's gone off in some café near Fort George.'

Without waiting for a reply, Charlie turned and went next door.

Caitlin knew the drive over wouldn't be easy. After any bombing or whatever, there was always a mad scramble to find whoever was behind it. The whole place would be crawling with army and police, every check point backed up, every road watched. Since the device had gone off on the city's west bank, all the ambulances would need to cross Craigavon, the city's only bridge. The general hospital was quite a distance away on the east bank, the Waterside. A permanent checkpoint on the bridge caused mayhem with local traffic on a normal day, but after today, the journey time was anyone's guess.

Caitlin, after snatching their coats, offered to help Majella with hers. The sugared tea had settled her a little, enough to stand, enough to move, but she still looked like one wrong word might knock her over. She nudged Caitlin away.

'I'm okay, love. I'll do it.' Her eyes went to her youngest, she couldn't miss the fear written all over her face.

'Tina, shush now. Stay here and watch the house. We'll phone as soon as we know what's happenin'.'

Tina glanced at Maggie, who bobbed her head in agreement and gave her an encouraging smile.

Charlie reappeared and jingled his keys with a scowl. 'Let's go before they start riotin'.'

Tina stepped in and kissed her mother, then moved to Caitlin, 'Promise you'll phone when ye can,' she begged.

'I will,' Caitlin whispered, pulling her into a tight hug. Unusually, Tina clung to her, then let go.

The three of them headed out, hurrying down the path to the waiting car. Caitlin looked back to see Maggie and Tina still on the doorstep, watching.

Charlie's red Ford Zephyr was his pride and joy. His 'baby' the one he'd spend hours polishing, making sure its immaculate bodywork gleamed like it was ready for a garage forecourt.

Tonight Caitlin was glad of it and once inside and cosy in its fleece-covered seats, they left. She scanned the houses as the Ford inched through the battle-worn streets. Given it was teatime and drizzling, the rioters wouldn't be out until they'd eaten and the weather had eased.

Small groups of older men gathered on street corners and warmed their hands by the flames burning in cut-down oil drums. Teenagers attempted to play football with discarded Coca-Cola cans. They acknowledged the Zephyr as it drove by and descended Abercorn Road, which led to the bridge's upper deck. Predictably, there was a long traffic queue, and the vehicle soon stopped at an army checkpoint. As if straining against the need to crawl, the Zephyr's engine roared mightily, filling the air with its impatient growl.

Caitlin moaned. 'It's going to take forever to get through this. What if we tell them we're trying to get to the hospital, do you think they'll let us through quicker?' She was struggling, on the brink of tears, and could feel a lump forming in her throat.

Charlie exhaled and leaned back against his headrest. He was so big he almost touched the roof of the car. He tutted.

'Won't make any difference, love. They'll likely keep us longer for badness. We'll have to wait. Don't worry; we'll get there soon enough.'

By now, it was pitch dark, and the rain began to pour harder, drumming against the roof and sides of the car. Since they left Blamfield Street, Majella, who sat in the front passenger seat, hadn't spoken a word.

Caitlin thought back to the last year or so, how things had changed. Her mammy, once the strong one, now popping antidepressants and drinking like there was no tomorrow. With Martin in deep with the Provos and her husband sick, she'd cracked. Until then, she'd always kept it together, but now, even with a handful of tablets and drink to calm her, she was twitchy and, most of the time, three sheets to the wind.

The car edged past the red-and-white signs warning oncoming drivers to dim their lights. As they queued for inspection, ambulances sped past, carrying their human cargo.

The Ford inched forward for twenty long minutes until they were finally next in line. Charlie rolled down the window and held out his driver's licence.

Caitlin tucked herself into the rear seat, staring straight ahead to avoid looking at the Brit, who'd stopped them and was now deep in conversation with Charlie.

'Where you off to, mate?' he asked.

'Altnagelvin. The woman's husband's had a heart attack.' Charlie gestured to Majella.

The soldier bent down and shone his torch into the back of the car. He spotted Caitlin first, before moving the narrow beam towards Majella. The light remained as he attempted to get a better look. Since he saw she was upset, he looked across at Caitlin, who was staring ahead. He straightened, scanned Charlie's license with the torchlight, then handed it back with a brief nod.

'Move on, but be quick. There's been a major incident, and the hospital's expecting casualties. Good luck.'

Charlie rolled up the window and muttered, 'Bloody miracle. Bastards are human, after all.'

The rest of the drive, barely three-miles, took way longer than usual, an eternity. The Zephyr's wipers howled in protest as they battled the downpour. Charlie stuck to the main roads, keeping clear of the Loyalist enclaves of the Waterside, where the kerbs were painted red, white, and blue – accompanied by limp Union Jacks that drooped from the same red, white, and blue painted streetlights.

The Waterside was where most of Londonderry's Protestants had settled. Over the years, they'd drifted east across the river, leaving the west bank behind. Here, there was a sense of prosperity, unlike the slum terraces and jobless Catholics on the other side. Here, men worked as firemen, policemen or in the Civil Service. Some even ran their own businesses, and most of the homes were privately owned. Only a handful of public sector jobs were open to Catholics, and even then, very few applied. Most Republicans found it difficult to swear allegiance to the Crown.

Swathes of Loyalists had moved out of the *Fountain*, a shrinking district near the city walls, when redevelopment propelled them out. Few came back. Now a minority, those who stayed felt uneasy, living so close to the Republican Bogside, where threats were constant. Frustration ran high, and many of the Apprentice Boys from the Orange Order began acting like vigilantes, defending their homes from attack a stone's throw from the infamous walled city.

The traffic remained heavy as they approached yet another army checkpoint at the entrance to the hospital. Four or five cars queued ahead. Charlie slammed his hand hard on the dash board, and Caitlin felt her mother startle in response.

She placed her hand on her shoulder in reassurance as Charlie, in a deep blue rage, growled, 'So many feckin' checkpoints.' Caitlin didn't reply but knew that if the soldiers saw Charlie angry, they'd only make it more difficult or, worse, arrest him. She told him to relax.

'We're here now, Charlie; take it easy. Whatever you do, don't let them see you're rattled. They'll wind you up worse.'

The girl was right, but they'd been winding him up something awful lately, and he was raging. There was only so much a man could take. It was the same every time: stop, search, go; stop, search, go, and Charlie, like the rest of them, was fed up to the teeth. He couldn't understand how it had come to this. No matter where you went, there were soldiers everywhere. Pigs and Saracens sitting everywhere, watching everyone. None of them ever imagined that one day, 22,000 soldiers would be living on their shores and, after *Bloody Sunday*, they'd be here a long time. Like most of his buddies, he was filled with dread and anger.

Next in line, he rolled down the window again and got his licence ready. The Brit who approached was soaked through, wrapped in a heavy camouflage cape, his face half hidden beneath the hood. He snatched Charlie's license without a word, gave it a quick run over, then finally spoke, his voice clipped and cold.

'Where've you come from, sir?'

'Creggan,' Charlie replied, rolling his eyes and resisting the urge to snarl.

'Why you here, sir?'

'The woman's husband's been brought in with a heart attack.' Again, Charlie gestured to Majella.

'When, sir?'

'When what?'

'When was he brought in... *sir*?'

'I don't know, do I? Last we heard, he was in an ambulance.' Charlie blinked. *What was this twat up to?*

'Step out of the vehicle and open the boot, sir,' the soldier ordered. Charlie slapped the steering wheel. He was livid.

'You've gotta be jokin' me, we've got to get to A and E. For all we know, the man could be dead!' Majella gasped beside him, her hand covering her mouth.

Harsher this time, the soldier repeated his request, ignoring Charlie's outburst. He was as fed up as Charlie, having stood in this pouring rain at this godforsaken checkpoint for hours.

'Sir. Don't make me repeat myself: climb out of the vehicle and open the boot. *Now.*'

Charlie turned off the engine, let out a deep, pissed-off groan and climbed out. Rain poured down on him with a vengeance. Grumbling, he fished out the car keys, popped the boot, and lifted it open.

The Brit leaned in, dead casual. He waved his torch around and had a good rummage, lifting things and tossing them back in, blatantly to anger the driver. He nodded, making a point he was finished, and Charlie slammed the boot shut.

Then, taking his time, he ran the torch slowly over the Zephyr's bodywork, crouched low to have a nosy underneath, and carried on round to the front. He wore a sly grin the whole way, clearly enjoying how jumpy the big Irishman had become.

As he reached the bonnet, he threw in a smile for good measure and said, 'Pop it,' like it was an afterthought.

Caitlin watched on as Charlie stood still, so close to blowing his top. *Please, Charlie, don't,* she prayed. Reluctantly, with no choice, Charlie lifted the bonnet, and the soldier flashed his torch inside – nothing worth noting. With another curt nod to move on, Charlie, drenched through, stiff with anger and fuming, slammed the bonnet shut.

Seriously taking the piss, the soldier dragged it out, starting with a long look at Charlie's licence before handing it back, then shining the torch straight in his face like he hadn't a care in the world.

'Move on quickly, sir, can't you see. You're holding up the queue. We haven't got all day,' he muttered, smirking like he was doing Charlie some great favour. And before he knew it, without another glance, the Brit turned on his heel and wandered off to the next car, as if Charlie McFadden had never been there.

It took Charlie a minute to find his voice once he was back in the Ford. He shook his head, shut his eyes, and swore something inaudible under his breath before turning the key.

As the car rolled into the hospital car park, he mimicked the soldier's words with a bitter, hateful resentment: '"Why ye here, sir? Where've you come from?" What the hell does he think we're doing 'ere – out shoppin'? It's a feckin' hospital!' His knuckles were white as he drove into the car park, ranting like a kettle on the boil. Majella and Caitlin stayed silent, letting him simmer down.

In time, they slipped into a car parking space, far enough to get soaked as they made their way to the hospital entrance.

They'd expected mayhem, sure, but this was something else. The second they stepped into A and E, the shrieks, the stench of blood, and a burning smell hit them like a wall.

It was carnage, raw and unfiltered, as if they'd stumbled straight into Dante's Inferno, with no way out.

Hell.

Chapter Nine

Melrose

Not far away, in a fine residence in Prehen, James Henderson finished a delightful dinner of partridge, served at the long, linen-draped table in his uncle's opulent, candle-lit dining room.

James adored this room. His uncle had taken great pride in preserving its original design, including the restoration of the Adam fireplace, where flames danced, casting a warm red glow over the hand-painted Chinese wallpaper.

He observed the men dressed in evening wear around the table. His father, James Snr, sat proudly at one end, while Roger faced him from the other. Father and son stared at each other as James considered how alike the two brothers were. Both were tall and well-built, with steel-coloured hair, but their temperaments couldn't have been more different. Chalk and Cheese.

His moustached father was ex-army, a former British Army captain who had served in World War II, and various other campaigns until retiring a few years ago. He was a severe man, a devout Presbyterian, and James found him difficult and argumentative. He suspected he was jealous of his older sibling's success, while his elder showed James Snr, nothing but support and generosity in return. Along with James, several of Ulster's most prominent business men, entrepreneurs, politicians, security personnel, and senior Rocola staff sat to his left and right.

James was bored stiff as, inevitably, the 'Troubles' reared its ugly head. The guests heatedly discussed their concerns about the shifting political climate as James's mind drifted back to his first day at the factory.

He'd been restless all afternoon, reflecting on Mrs Parkes and the office staff. Since spotting the girl, his thoughts had often wandered to the beauty with the bruised face. Surprisingly captivated, he'd taken only a brief look at her, yet sensed both fragility and a serene nature. A wave of protectiveness washed over him. Despite her injuries, she was breathtakingly beautiful. This train of thought confused and irritated him more than he cared to admit.

He sipped some fine red wine from a Londonderry crystal glass and tried his best to shake such thoughts off. It was beyond ridiculous. His career came first, always had. He had plans. Grand plans and with this opportunity, this golden ticket Roger had handed to him, he'd no time for women, breathtaking or not.

He'd always been upfront with the women he'd bedded: no strings, no fuss, a bit of fun and, with luck, great sex. If they didn't like it, they could walk. Most had. He didn't lose sleep over it. Some might call it cold, but he saw it as efficient. It suited him. Swift and clean, the way he liked things, swift and clean. He wanted a simple life, built around ambition, no flowery feelings or needy attachments, thank you very much. Oxford had been a buffet of liberal-minded women, and he'd taken full advantage, drifting from one night to the next with ease.

But this girl? This one was different. There was something about her that got under his skin straight away. The pull had been instant and unsettling. It took him somewhere unfamiliar, threw him off balance. A first for him, like someone had pulled the rug from under his feet. It wasn't only her looks, though she had them in spades. It was something else, something remote and harder to pin down. Innocence maybe. Such emotions he imagined, were trouble, they got in the way, and he certainly didn't want to be anyone's hero. Not with what he'd been tasked to do.

His attention returned to dinner as he glared across the table at an intoxicated, bloated, red-faced individual sitting opposite. James had been introduced to him earlier by his father, who appeared to know the drunk pretty well.

Charles Jones was a businessman from East Belfast, reputed to be wealthy, with substantial interests in the city's shipyards, amongst other things. A major backer and powerbroker in the newly formed Democratic Unionist Party (DUP), he had a reputation for being ruthless in both business and politics. But most of all, he was known for one thing – his flagrant hatred of Catholics. Not the odd grumble or prejudice you might hear in a bar, but full-blown loathing. His rants weren't political – they were personal. For Jones, the very existence of Catholics was a problem. Full stop.

Almost immediately, James had taken an intense dislike to the ugly, dictatorial effort of a man. He listened, expressionless, as Jones proclaimed to the assembled diners.

'We are a divided party. This talk of a "Sunningdale Agreement" — why, it's poppycock. Those Westminster bastards are betraying us. The very idea of Papists being near, let alone inside, Stormont... Over my dead body!'

'Calm now, Charles, please,' Roger replied. He gestured to his nephew for some form of help.

'James, kindly top up Charles's glass, will you?'

James reached across the table with obvious reluctance and topped up Jones's empty glass with the barest splash of claret. Deliberate. Petty even, but satisfying.

He could see his uncle was nervous at his guest's hectoring as he replied. 'There isn't anyone round this table who doesn't agree with some of what you say, Charles. However, I think we need to consider the future. You've seen the news, so many dead this year, and these Shankill murders are especially unsettling.'

Jones shook his head and slammed his fist on the mahogany table. The shining cutlery and glasses jumped under its impact as he screeched.

'The vermin deserve it. We *cannot* and *will not* lose control of our country. Our country, gentlemen. One that many of us fought for and died for, am I correct?'

He waited for someone to agree, but no one spoke, nor moved an inch. 'What about the Somme? Isn't Ulster ours? It's not for those Fenian fuckers in the South to tell us what to do with it!' His hateful words sprayed through a mouthful of the finest Médoc.

Roger shivered at this barrage of hatred, and James knew he had to step in somehow. He was incredibly fond of his uncle, and he wasn't about to let some pisshead upset him in his own house, at his own dinner table.

Roger was a fair-minded man, loyal to his monarch, and he, too, a World War II veteran. Like many, he never talked about his service to King and Country. He hosted these dinners not out of obligation but for his love of Rocola and the city, using them to forge alliances within Ulster's business community, and stay informed about political and economic changes. As one of the biggest employers in the area, he felt torn by the brutal events unfolding across the province. He loved Ireland, was proud to be Irish, but lately, laughter and good humour were in short supply, and he suffered for it.

James was about to interject, hoping to end Jones's rant, when a large, balding, distinguished-looking man nearby spoke up in a commanding voice.

'Charles, we must try to stop this violence. We need a middle ground, and comments such as yours certainly don't help.'

The speaker was Chief Constable George Shalham of the RUC, son of a retired Westminster Member of Parliament. A great friend of the family, he knew the city through and through and was known for his impartiality, except the Republicans who were outraged that the son of an English MP should head a police force of which ninety-three per cent was Protestant. Shalham was a modest and practical being who lacked airs and graces. Against strong advice, his telephone number and home address remained in the phone directory, exposing him and his family to potential assassination. But Shalham wasn't deterred. Like his friend Roger, he loved his hometown and Ireland.

Not happy about being interrupted and reprimanded, Jones grabbed the bottled wine near James and defiantly filled his glass to the brim, causing some of the liquid to spill onto the pristine white tablecloth. He hollered on, disregarding the overspill.

'Fuck the middle ground, George! Hang them all, and their bloody offspring. That Glenanne gang's doing us all a favour. It's what everyone wants, yet nobody has the balls to say so. Eliminating Papists and Rome!' A chorus of shocked gasps rippled around the table. Cutlery froze in mid-air. Food and wine forgotten. Roger had warned James that Jones, drunk or not, could cause trouble.

It was time to stop such talk, so James took charge and turned to a guest seated to his other side – Albert Brown, a local solicitor – and, in a voice loud enough for the whole table to hear, asked.

'So, Albert, do you think Mary Peters has done the right thing by ignoring the threats to her life by coming home?' Relieved by the change of subject, Albert replied.

'Credit to her, James. She's a tough cookie. Most women would have given up the ghost, then I suppose that's why she's an Olympian. We should be proud of her.' Albert was right: it shouldn't matter what the athlete's background was. James agreed, but their conversation was interrupted by an angry Jones.

Complaining, he said, 'I call it a fucking disgrace.' At such language, even the furniture seemed to groan in embarrassment.

'The woman is brilliant. I mean, to win a medal for her country, come back to Ulster and be warned she can't go home. A disgrace. She's made of steel, that one. A toast to her.' He swallowed the remains of his drink, still oblivious to the other guests, who sat in silent embarrassment, looking at each other with raised eyebrows.

'Enough now, gentlemen,' Roger exclaimed, his eyes pleading with James again for help.

Shit, James thought. *Will this night ever end?*

'Uncle, I walked around the factory floor this afternoon. I'd forgotten how enormous it was. I mean, it's amazing, and so streamlined. That time-and-motion study is something too. I'd like to talk to you about it.'

'Of course, we'll do it tomorrow,' Roger replied, his shoulders relaxing now James had shut Jones up. James raised his voice and joked as his eyes wandered around the table.

'I don't think I've ever seen so many women in one place. It's terrifying!' The guests chuckled in agreement as the atmosphere relaxed.

Roger gave his nephew a warm smile of gratitude and joked, 'Too true, James, too true. Been there and it is bloody terrifying.' He laughed. 'But competition is growing and costs increasing. The unions are putting us under pressure as well. There's talk of more strikes against internment. Eight thousand across the City walked out last month. We need to think about the future, and fast.' His own words seemed to sadden Roger as he drank.

'Then I've some ideas,' James told him. 'I'll tell you about those tomorrow too.'

'Wonderful,' Roger replied with a wink.

The conversation continued into the evening, long after the candles dimmed. By now, Jones was in a drunken stupor and bored by the small talk. He stumbled from the table and slumped into a chair by the fire. Without a care in the world, he drifted off to sleep after closing his eyes.

After brandy, James felt he'd done his best for his uncle and rose. He set down his napkin, took in the remaining guests, and joked, 'Gentlemen, you must excuse me. I've a long day tomorrow – it appears my new boss is looking for inspiration! I'll have to get my thinking cap on. Thank you and goodnight.'

With James gone, Alfie McScott, the factory's accountant and life-long bachelor, decided to leave too. A nervous individual, he was awkward and self-conscious, with huge glasses that always reminded his boss of a wise old owl. Roger trusted him. Alfie was a first-class accountant, fully dedicated to his job and Rocola's success. Always a bit clumsy, he somehow saved his glass of water from spilling as he stood up from his chair.

In his unassuming voice, he announced, 'Yes, yes, time I headed off as well. I hadn't realised it was so late.' He gave a half-bow to Roger, thanked him for a lovely evening, and bid goodnight to the other guests who were starting to leave too. The commotion stirred Charles Jones, who grunted an insincere thank you to his host and staggered out, ignoring the remaining diners.

As the candle-lit room emptied, only the two brothers remained, Roger and James Snr, sitting together by the fire.

Hypnotised by its flames and enjoying the heat, James Snr mumbled, 'I'm worried, Roger. These are serious times. I believe this province is in real danger of collapsing. The Republicans aren't going to give up easily, so Jones is right to be concerned. I've a feeling this is going to be a long and gory struggle. The Provos are exploiting *Bloody Sunday* to recruit volunteers – hundreds of youngsters, men *and* women.' He peered at his brother, waiting for a reply.

Roger considered his words, but was uneasy. 'I agree, James, but I'm not sure about the company you keep. Our Mr Jones. That man is lethal, brother. The narrative he uses frightens me to death. His words, the hatred he holds for Roman Catholics, it's like it's seeping out of his very pores.' James Snr decided not to comment, but listened as his brother went on.

'And this referendum in the spring will be a farce. Most Republicans won't even vote – they'll be told to abstain. It's a disaster, all of it, and on top of that, what about the issues I have at the factory?'

Again, James Snr kept quiet. Not because he had nothing to say, but because he was up to the teeth with Rocola. It was always Rocola this, Rocola that with Roger and now that his son was in the thick of it, he dreaded the thought of having to listen to the pair of them going on.

With no response from his brother, Roger paused, staring into the middle distance, trying to make sense of what he'd done. What a bloody fool he'd been, gambling with the factory like that, not just the money but everything tied to it. He'd dragged Rocola into a mess that couldn't be undone, not easily anyway. He couldn't believe he'd gone through with it. And now, facing the truth, there was only one thing he needed – another drink.

'You want another drink?' he offered. With his offer refused, Roger walked over to the table, refilled his glass, and sank back into his still-warm chair, feeling drained. Scared too.

Close to bedtime, James Snr quipped, 'Do you think it's safe for James to be here? He's surprisingly naïve. I don't think he understands the ins and outs of this place.'

Roger turned to him. 'You may be right, but remember, he's a bright lad. Needs to get a handle on things, that's all. And he will. You, of all people should know – he's your son. We know once that lad of yours make his mind up, there's no stopping him. Doesn't forgive easily either, and with that temper of his, anyone who crosses him is in for a rude awakening. There's no turning back.'

'You're right there,' James Snr laughed, 'I've had a taste of that myself over the years.'

Then, after snuffing out the candles, both men left the room, exchanged a quiet goodnight, and made their way up the wide wrought-iron staircase to the sanctuary of their bedrooms.

Chapter Ten

Bedlam

C aitlin led the way as they entered the reception area of the hospital's A and E department.

The screams of the injured tore through the building, mingling with the haunting wail of klaxons that reverberated off the walls, creating an atmosphere of pandemonium and doom. The stench of sickness, fetid air, and the oppressive heat of the hospital was overpowering.

All three removed their wet coats and tried to cover their noses to avoid the searing smell of burned clothing and flesh. The small group stopped and stared in confusion at the turmoil in the overcrowded space.

Bedlam.

With no waiting space left, patients and visitors overflowed down the narrow corridors, where doctors and nurses bustled from patient to patient. Orderlies rushed past with laden trolleys and demanded access to cubicles, most of them filled with distressed relatives and bloodied bodies.

The Great Hall, normally used for such emergencies, was out of action, awaiting the return of decorators the following day. Impatient staff fought to find space for the many casualties. In frustration, nurses yelled at anxious men and women, pulling back privacy screens in search of loved ones. Some even wandered into the X-ray room, oblivious to its many dangers. Armed soldiers with minor wounds stood huddled in corners as they watched the scenes of carnage unfold.

Stunned, white-faced men, women and children leaned against the two-toned green walls or, as a last resort, slumped on the grey vinyl floor. Patients with scorched bodies and torn clothes lay on stretchers, shrouded in a fine, grey-white powder. The blast had claimed some larger items of their clothing, and Caitlin couldn't help but stare as relatives and volunteers tried to cover their partially dressed bodies with green paper-like gowns. The nauseating stench of burning hair and skin grew stronger the further they moved through the hospital.

Two uninjured, middle-aged RUC officers attempted to question a teenage boy who could barely stand. His body shook, and the eyes he fixed on them appeared glazed. With zero empathy and frustrated by his lack of response, they barked their many questions, one after the other, at the astonished youngster.

'What's your name? Where were you when it happened? What did you see? Your name? Did you see anyone or anything suspicious?'

An attractive female doctor in a white coat turned up out of nowhere and attempted to push the taller policeman back. She was frantic as she placed her arm around her traumatised patient.

'Listen to me, you'll get nothing out of him. He probably can't hear you!' With a withering look, she added.

'Where's your sense of compassion, for Christ's sake? Look at him!' The smaller man pulled his colleague away and hissed something in his ear.

As they turned to leave, Caitlin heard him tell the doctor, 'Okay, but we'll be outside; we're not going anywhere. We know one of those bombers could be in here. Somewhere.' He pointed at the shocked boy.

'And it could be him.' After that, they walked straight past Caitlin and through the exit into the night. Charlie and Caitlin exchanged a look and then shook their heads. *Incredible.*

Caitlin scanned the room and spotted the admissions desk. Gripping her mother's arm tightly, they pushed through the sea of bodies towards it.

As they made their way over, Caitlin glanced at the unsmiling nurse staffing the desk. In her fifties, with greying hair, the woman's eyes were set remarkably close together with a nose that was long and pinched. Her whole expression screamed, *I-so-do-not-want-to-be-here.*

When they reached it, they found themselves at the end of a long queue. Caitlin sighed and sent Majella to wait off to the side, where it was less crowded and hopefully sit.

At the front of the line, a soot-blackened woman in her early forties was yelling at the dour-faced nurse. Tears streaked down her dust-covered skin, carving two pale lines across her grey-black face. The nurse hardly reacted when the woman kept shouting and leaned over the desk.

'She's five years old. I was holdin' her hand – right beside me, she was. Her hand! I had her hand, and then she was gone. Gone! Where is she? Is she here?!'

The nurse didn't look up as she told the woman she knew nothing about a missing child, but asked for her name again.

Caitlin stared in astonishment as the mother bent down, trying to make sense of the nurse's words. It was obvious she too couldn't hear properly.

'What? What?! I've told you a million times... Rosaleen McGuinness. She's only five!' she cried.

Charlie touched Caitlin's wrist and groaned, 'This is mad love. Let's go straight up to cardio.'

'Actually Charlie, I'll stay here with Mammy. You go up. At least that way, we're both on it. Mammy's no good to anyone.' Caitlin suggested. She jerked her head towards her mother, who looked like a lost child.

Charlie nodded. 'Right then, I'll be as quick as I can. I think Cardio's Ward Eight.' He strode towards the door leading to the lifts and excused himself as he pushed through the throng.

Caitlin looked around and was startled when a woman's voice called her name. Her eyes darted about, searching for the source.

'Caitlin McLaughlin, what the heck are you doing here?'

It was her cousin Kathy, Tommy's daughter. She'd recently finished her paramedic training and worked at the hospital. They hugged.

Caitlin could feel the pointy bones of Kathy's back jutting through her long black waterproof. She was amazed that her cousin could do such a job since she was a tiny wee thing, not a pick on her. However, Kathy's stubborn determination prevailed, and Tommy was proud when she joined the ambulance service. A necessity after *Bloody Sunday* and now with the Troubles, women, along with volunteers, played a crucial role in providing first aid and driving ambulances. Caitlin was never as glad to see her.

'Ah Kathy, it's good to see you. It's Daddy... We got a call to say he's had a heart attack, but we're getting nowhere here.' She motioned to the sullen nurse on the admissions desk. Kathy pulled back her hood and wiped her face with her hand.

'It's manic the night. They've probably taken him to Ward Eight. But, listen, I'm in the middle of all this and I can't stay. I've gotta head back. It's a mess, Caitlin, a friggin' mess, you wouldn't believe the things I've seen,' she moaned. 'Massive nail bomb. I can't help now, but I'll do what I can when I'm back.'

Caitlin nodded and encouraged her to go, but Kathy took a second look at her Aunt Majella, who appeared poorly and not quite there. She took hold of Majella's arm, coaxing her to move closer.

'Majella, let's get you sittin' down? You don't look the best.' She led her aunt towards a row of occupied seats and approached a young boy who sat swinging his legs back and forth. Fortunately, he was clean and tidy and showed no sign of injury. He lowered his head as he stared at the floor, bored out of his skull.

Kathy hunkered down to his level and whispered conspiratorially. 'You wouldn't do me a favour, wee man? Could you let this woman here sit down a minute? She's not feelin' the best.'

'Aye, no problem,' he replied, and with childish energy, jumped off the seat. Majella took his place with a tired smile and thanked him.

Kathy touched Caitlin's shoulder. 'At least your ma' can sit down a bit. I'll get back as soon as I can. And listen, your daddy'll be grand; he's in good hands up there.' She turned to leave, pulled her hood back up, and the crowd soon swallowed up her tiny, resolute outline.

Caitlin glanced towards the door leading to the lifts and caught sight of the same smoke-blackened woman from earlier, the one who'd been yelling at the desk. She was stumbling behind a trolley now, barely managing to hold on to a tiny, bloodied hand.

A nurse, wild-eyed and breathless, was pushing the trolley with a green-robed doctor at her side, both moving fast. They disappeared through the swing doors; the woman trailing behind. That had to be her child – Rosaleen. Caitlin crossed herself, silently, begging God to keep the little girl alive.

The queue shuffled forward until, at last, they were next. Caitlin called her mother over to join her. The cold fish of a nurse ignored them, more interested in the papers on her desk and not bothering to look up. Caitlin felt anger rise as she recalled this woman's callous attitude towards the distraught mother searching for Rosaleen – one who'd been here all along. *Sinful*. She knew the woman had power over her, so she kept her composure and refused to let the old hag intimidate her.

At last, the nurse turned her attention to them. 'Yes?' she spat.

'My father's been brought in with a heart attack. Do you know where he is?' Caitlin asked. She read the woman's hospital badge: Elizabeth Blood – had to be a Proddy with that name.

'What's his name?' the nurse enquired, her fingers continually sifting through the papers again, then placing them into a neat pile.

'Patrick McLaughlin.'

'Hmmm. Date of birth?'

'Twenty-fifth December, nineteen thirty.'

Elizabeth Blood flipped through a large red plastic index box, fuming that she should be working at all. It was supposed to have been a quiet night in, her, Tabby, and *Crossroads*. That was until the phone call ordering her to report for duty. Why did she have to deal with all this crap? She'd been nursing too long and wanted out. Her knees, they were killing her. But thanks to her deceased husband's cock-up with his pension, she was still here, working her arse off, day after day after day. Already resentful, she had to deal with this lot as well. Ah, for the love of God, she was tired.

She asked for the patient's address and waited for the tall girl to answer, all the while scanning the bruises on her face. Liz had seen the like before, a drunken row probably, and from the look of the older one with her, she was away with the fairies, or not far off. Stuck at this godforsaken desk, Liz could feel her patience wearing thin. It was shaping up to be another long, rotten night.

It didn't take long to find the patient's details and read them in a terse voice, 'Aye. He's here, Ward Eight. You can't go up. He's a Category A patient. No visitors. At all.'

'But he's my father; I have to see him,' Caitlin exclaimed, standing over the desk, her voice getting louder and louder. The nurse shot her a look of contempt, then stood and called over Caitlin's head to the next in line, crooking her finger for a woman to step forward and edge Caitlin aside.

'Come on ahead here. She's done. Hurry now!' Caitlin didn't know what to do. She looked at her mother, who was in a world of her own.

Sod that! Taking Majella by the arm again, they walked towards the double doors leading to the lifts.

But as Caitlin pushed through, Charlie met her on the other side. Still frustrated and angry, he updated her on developments upstairs while holding his nose against the stench. By now, Caitlin had near enough grown used to it.

Charlie rolled his eyes, pinched his nose, and told her in a thick voice, 'I was right. Ward Eight. The sister won't tell me anything. Me not being family. Only that he's not allowed visitors, not even you, love. And wait till you hear this one! An orderly I know says your da's in a private room with two feckin' RUC men guardin' him outside.'

Majella surprised them both when she reached for Charlie's arm and exclaimed, 'What's the RUC guardin' our Patrick for?!'

Caitlin stared at Charlie, and with a hint of false bravado, tried to appear in control.

'Charlie, do us a favour, take Mammy and see if you can get her a cuppa tea, will you? Anything to keep her going. I'm going up there myself.'

Guiding Majella towards Charlie, she added, 'Mammy, go with Charlie now and grab a cuppa. Leave Daddy to me.'

Charlie half smiled in agreement and led his neighbour back through A and E to the hospital shop/café.

With yet another deep sigh as they disappeared, Caitlin pressed the lift call button. She watched its slow descent, the numbered lights marking its journey to the ground floor.

She turned at the sound of a young female cleaner washing the bloodied floor with a crimson-headed mop. The girl didn't look up, just kept at it, dragging the mop back and forth like her body was on autopilot. Her mind seemed far from the carnage around her, lost somewhere else entirely.

Caitlin had no way of knowing the girl had only been released after being wrongly arrested and thrown in a cell for days. She'd been convinced she was on her way to Armagh Gaol, where the women were treated so badly, and the fear had near broken her. It was a wonder she'd managed to turn up for work at all.

When the lift doors slid open, two trolleys shot out, each carrying a broken, groaning body. One man's face was shredded and soaked in blood, the other was barely conscious, his leg bent at a sickening angle, bone sticking out through the flesh. The air stank of antiseptic, piss, and burned flesh. Caitlin couldn't move but held her lurching stomach. She couldn't help but stare, even as a nurse yelled at her to move. She backed away fast, her hand over her mouth. She'd never seen anything like it, and hoped to Christ she never would again.

She was worried sick, if Patrick was in a private room with policemen watching him, something wasn't right.

A second lift arrived, she squeezed herself in beside a crowd of silent, pale-faced strangers. The doors shut behind them with a clunk. The stench inside was overwhelming. A smoke-stained, wretched-looking man was propped up in the corner, gagging softly, barely able to hold himself. Caitlin tried not to gag as her eyes dropped to the floor, smeared with blood and bits of matter she couldn't name. The cleaner clearly hadn't got this far.

She tightened her arms across her chest and pressed her body back against the panel, desperate to breathe through her mouth and not think about what she was standing in. At least there were no trolleys this time, no mangled bodies or frantic nurses – only the quiet dread of people waiting, like her, to see what horror lay at the other end. The lift stopped at each level until Caitlin was alone with a tiny, black-clad old woman. They smiled at each other but said nothing.

When they reached the eighth floor, the woman got out, murmured, 'Night, love,' and disappeared down the corridor. Somehow, her presence stirred memories of old Irish grannies standing outside their cottages in grainy pictures. There had been something profoundly sad in her eyes, and Caitlin hoped all was well with her.

Could this day get any worse? She wondered, eyes darting left and right along the corridor, unsure where to go. Besides the fading footsteps of the old woman, the corridor was silent, in strict obedience to the 'Silence Please' signs stuck to the walls. She walked the opposite way until she spotted a sign for the sister's office, and before she knew it, she was standing outside the door.

Taking a breath, she knocked and waited until a petite, pleasant-faced nurse opened it, dressed in an immaculate stiff white cap, white-collared navy dress, and starched apron. Seeing Caitlin, she smiled warmly, and Caitlin smiled back. A name tag beside her fob watch read: *Staff Sister, Moira Gallagher.*

'May I help you?' She asked. She'd one of those kindly faces that put you straight at ease.

'Yes, please. My father's here. Patrick McLaughlin?'

'Ah, yes. Mr McLaughlin.' She stepped aside and waved for Caitlin to come into the small office.

It was modest: a small paper-strewn desk, two red plastic chairs, and a tall grey filing cabinet. Every inch of the wall was taken up with noticeboards, pinned with rosters, calendars, announcements, and thank you cards.

'You're his daughter, are you?'

'Yes.'

'What's your name, love?

'Caitlin.'

'Well, Caitlin, as I explained to the man before, I can't tell you much, only that the RUC have instructed us — no visitors for your daddy. Difficult as it is, I have to agree with them. He's a very sick man. I'm sorry.'

'Really? But Mammy's downstairs waiting. Have you any idea what happened?' Caitlin fell into one of the chairs lined up along the wall. She couldn't bear to imagine what her daddy had been through.

The nurse went on. 'Don't know for sure, but he's gotta crop of nasty bruises and cuts on his face. Marks on his back and the back of his legs as well. Between you and me, looks like he's had a real hidin'. Must've brought on his heart attack. It's all there in his notes.' She pointed at the desk where a hospital file lay open.

'I've already reported it.' She added. Hoping it would give the girl a bit of comfort.

Caitlin wrung her hands together and told the sister about the raid. 'The Brits beat the hell out of him, dragged him from his bed, even put a hood over his head. Him only in his underpants. It was awful.'

Moira placed a hand on Caitlin's arm. 'I'm so sorry. There's been terrible trouble 'cos of internment. Seen it with me own eyes.'

Silent tears fell, stinging Caitlin's sore and bruised face.

'What happened there?' Moira asked gently, eyeing Caitlin's injuries and hoping it was nothing more than an accident.

'Hit by a Brit. When I tried to help Daddy.'

The nurse shook her head. 'God love ye, ye poor thing,' she said.

After a brief thought, she gave Caitlin a firm nod. 'Tell ye what, love. Stay put a minute. I'll see what I can do. No promises, mind.'

And with that, she was out the door.

Chapter Eleven

Ward Eight

Caitlin waited in the sister's office until she returned, looking excited.

'Right, I've had a quick word with the doctor. He's a bit of a prick most times, but he's fair when he wants to be. You can see your daddy for a few minutes, but only you. No one else. And don't push it, hear me? This way.' Her smile told Caitlin she was half-teasing.

Caitlin turned left down the dimly lit corridor, following her guardian angel out of the office. Half-open doors allowed her to see into shadowed wards where rows of patients slept or caught her eye.

When they reached the last door, two burly RUC men stood outside, staring straight ahead. They ignored the women until the sister reached for the door handle. One of them, looking menacing, grabbed her tiny, freckled hand, and stopped her.

'No visitors,' he said in a forbidding tone.

Caitlin's ally smirked and, in a voice that could cut ice, gave him something to think about.

'Sir, I suggest you stick to your job, and I'll stick to mine,' she replied, matching his tone. 'Doctor Mahon has permitted this wee girl to visit her father. So kindly remove your hand and get outta my face.'

She paused, Then quieter, added. '*Please.*' The guard hesitated, then slowly stood aside.

Caitlin was impressed. The sister smiled at her, and once inside, closed the door behind them as Caitlin hurried to the bed.

Her father lay there, unmoving, wrapped in a coarse green blanket that had been pulled up to his waist. His face was puffed and purpled, almost unrecognisable, with deep bruises and angry red cuts slashed across his cheeks. His lips were split, dry and bloodied. Thick wires snaked from his chest and arms into a bank of machines nearby that blinked and gave off low, steady beeps. It wasn't much, but the sound gave her a sliver of hope. He was battered and broken, but he was breathing. Still here.

She spoke to him gently at first, her voice barely a whisper, but he didn't stir. The sight of him lying so still, hooked up to so many machines, was more than she could bear. Her panic rose as she leaned closer, her voice breaking.

'Daddy. Please. Open your eyes for me, please.' Tears streamed down her cheeks, blurring her vision. His chest lifted and lowered in a steady rhythm, but he gave no sign he'd heard her.

She tried again, more desperate now. 'Daddy, it's me, Daddy...' Nothing, but the soft, steady pinging from the monitors beside him.

The ward sister stepped forward, placed a hand on Caitlin's shoulder, and gently urged her back.

'Love. He needs rest now. I'll watch him through the night, I promise. It's late, and you're done in. Take your mammy home and ring the ward first thing. I'll be here.'

Caitlin looked down at her father one last time, brushing her fingers over the back of his hand, willing him to know she was there.

'But what if something happens tonight?' she asked. 'He'll be on his own. I can't leave him on his own. Please, Sister, let me stay.'

Caitlin fixed the nurse with a pleading look, and Moira Gallagher's heart almost broke at the pain she saw. She had no choice. Her orders were clear: a quick visit, no more. This was harder than she'd imagined. The poor girl was in such a state, so upset, but they couldn't stay much longer or those two hulks at the door would be in.

'You can't love. We have to go. You don't wanna get me into trouble now, do you? Sleep is the best thing for him. Please, we need to leave.'

Caitlin, broken with sadness, knew she'd no choice and the last thing she wanted to do was get the kind nurse into trouble.

Reluctantly, she let go of Patrick's hand, but tried one last time, 'Daddy, wake up. It's me. Caitlin.'

Not a peep. As she stood tall, she wiped her face with her coat sleeve, noticing her runny nose and a drip on her lips. She took a final look, bent down and kissed him on the forehead.

Moira decided it was time and guided Caitlin gently but firmly out of the room. The peelers didn't speak, but stepped aside to let them by, their expressions blank, but their eyes sharp as ever. Back in place, they stood like statues, saying nothing, giving nothing away.

Together, the two women walked slowly towards the lift, the corridor quiet but for the low hum of machines behind closed doors. Caitlin turned to Moira and murmured her thanks, her voice worn thin. The nurse offered what comfort she could, insisting Patrick was in good hands and would be watched closely through the night. They left with a quiet goodnight.

Moira walked away with her head down, heavy-hearted. She'd seen how much Mr McLaughlin was loved, how much his family clung to the hope that he'd be fine. But if she were honest with herself, if someone asked her to bet on it – would he make it through the night? Probably not. Not by a long shot.

Caitlin was in the lift forever, as it stopped at every floor before it finally reached the bottom. She stepped into A and E and noticed that the sullen-face nurse remained behind her desk, faced with an even longer queue of newly arrived and frightened visitors.

It was Charlie who spotted her first, and he and Majella made their way over.

'Any luck?' he asked, his forehead creased in worry.

Caitlin's voice let her down, and her eyes glistened with emotion.

'Say somethin', love. What's happenin',' the big man pleaded. Her answer was only to lose her breath until she could speak.

'The sister let me in, Charlie. His colour's awful; he's cut and bruised. His face, you have to see it. A disgrace. He's out cold. She reckons he's had some beating.'

With that, reality hit her as she fell into Charlie's wide-open arms, sobbing her heart out.

Because she saw her daughter so upset, Majella cried, 'What's wrong, Caitlin? Is he dead, love? Sweet Jesus, don't tell me he's dead!'

Caitlin quickly pulled herself away from Charlie and reached for Majella. 'No, Mammy! No, he's not dead, but he's bad. We have to phone back in the morning.'

Charlie swore and whispered to no one in particular, 'Bastards are panicking in case he doesn't make it, him bein' in custody an' all. There'll be murder if anythin' happens to him. C'mon, let's get youse home.'

In an instant, Caitlin remembered her promise to Tina and exclaimed, 'Bugger, I forgot Tina. I need to ring her. Does anyone have any change? She'll be worried sick. It'll take ages to get back with all this going on!' She waved her arms around in frustration. Charlie searched his pockets for some coins and handed over what little change he had.

With a grateful smile, Caitlin rushed to the payphone and rang the McFaddens'. To her surprise, Maggie picked up almost straight away.

Caitlin told her everything, and before hanging up, Maggie promised she'd head straight next door to tell Tina.

As they were about to leave, they met Tommy, who looked upset. He squeezed his nose against the dreadful smell and checked on his sister, who sighed with relief at seeing him.

'He isn't dead, is he?' he growled.

Majella took his arm. 'No love; he's alive, but in a sorry state. They won't let us in, but Caitlin saw him.' She looked at Caitlin. 'Tell him what the sister said, love.'

Tommy turned to Caitlin with a questioning look, and she met his tired blue eyes. 'It's not good Tommy. He's well out of it. I tried to wake him, but nothing. He's black and blue.'

She watched and heard him hiss as he put his head in his hands. 'I'm so sorry... but dear God if that man dies, I can't imagine what'll happen. There's riots in the Bogside already. It's gonna be a long, bloody night. And what the hell is that smell?!'

Caitlin looked around and explained, 'It's the bomb. Burnt skin and hair, I suppose. Christ Tommy, it's like something from a horror film in there. People with legs and arms missing, it's awful. I've never seen anything like it.'

Tommy was lost for words until Caitlin piped up. 'Any news on what happened to Daddy?'

Before he could answer, a chill ran down Tommy's spine, raising the hair on the back of his neck. Through the glass door, his eyes mapped the A and E filled with broken men, women and children weeping at the surrounding horror. *Dear God, why? Was it worth all this?*

He coughed to hide his crushed emotions. Then, in a whisper, told Caitlin what he'd been heard.

'I don't know all of it, but I had a word with Adrian Nixon, one of the youngsters lifted at the same time as your da. He's only seventeen,

a kid. Anyway, says after gettin' a good hidin' in the back of the Pig,
he and your da were taken to Strand Road barracks with two other
fellas. Told to put some kinda boiler suits on – bastards wanted their
clothes for forensics – then they'd have a medical. The other two boyos
refused. Next thing, the peelers grabbed the pair of them and took
them off somewhere. Didn't see 'em after that.'

Pausing, Tommy came up for air. 'Your da and Nixon got changed
and waited for the medical. Some medical. That so-called shit of a
doctor, Harris, walked in, all matter of fact, hardly looked at them –
even with blood tricklin' down Nixon's nose and handfuls of his hair
missin'. Tried to tell him your da wasn't well, Harris takes a quick look
at Patrick, signs some piece of paper, then turns 'round and says they're
both grand for questioning. Next thing he fucks off!'

Caitlin gasped as Tommy continued, 'Bastard didn't give a shite.
You should see the state of Nixon. Patrick's gotta be as bad.'

His niece nodded. 'Aye, he's had a good batterin' all right. His back
and legs. But it's his face, Tommy. It's worse – all cut and bruised.
They've put it in his notes and reported it.'

'A lot of good that'll do.' Tommy muttered and leaned back against
the wall.

Patrick's notes would be added to the growing pile of complaints.
Waste of bloody time. Tommy's head was swimming. He needed to sit,
but there wasn't a chair in sight.

'Nixon says they were questioned for a couple of hours until they
got back to the cell. He knew your da still wasn't good 'cos of his
colour. Kept keeling over and kinda' twitchin'. When Patrick started
to hold his chest, poor fella knew it was trouble and cried for help.
Ringin' the bell for ages. No one came 'til he practically kicked the
door down!'

He caught his breath again, his fury mounting. 'When the lazy fuckers finally show, they call Harris back and as soon as the wanker took stock of your da, he nearly shat himself. Rang for an ambulance. Mortal sin to call that man a doctor!' Tommy's anger knew no bounds as he spoke, still the women prompted him to go on.

'After that, well, Nixon reckons the reason they let him go was 'cos he saw the whole thing. Special Branch warned him to keep his gob shut, said if he breathed a word, they'd make a sample of him.'

'Bastards!' Majella squealed, her face like thunder. 'My Patrick! He's never been involved. Warned our Martin to keep outta it from the start, didn't he? From the very start. So many bloody times!'

Caitlin pulled her mother close and whispered, 'We know Mammy. But this... this has to be about Martin. Even with him locked up, they know he's well up in the Provos. So they go for the next best thing. Daddy. If I had my hands on Martin now. I swear to God, I'd... Her voice rose in anger. 'I'd kill him. Should be him lying up them stairs, not Daddy!'

No one had the energy to challenge her.

'We'd better go. I can't take this place any longer. That smells getting worse.' Caitlin sighed.

Majella shivered, and Caitlin turned to her uncle. 'You look sick as a dog Tommy. Best you go too. There's nothing to be done here now.'

The sorry group climbed back into Charlie's car once Tommy had promised he'd call at Blamfield Street first thing the following morning. The drive that followed was marked by a silence none of them felt able to break as they rolled towards the same checkpoints they had already faced earlier in the night.

The soldiers they met this time were in no better humour, their uniforms soaked through and their tempers shortened, every man looking like he was itching for a row. A handful of the checks were over quickly enough, but the rest dragged on, carried out with a deliberate menace by a line of wet, weary, homesick British lads who looked half-drowned, far from home, and spoiling for trouble.

Chapter Twelve

Mrs Parkes

J ames Henderson woke unusually early, a rare flicker of anticipation still simmering after a restless night. He'd spent hours scribbling notes, chasing every half-formed idea he thought might impress his uncle. Now his queen-size bed looked like a war zone of scattered papers, notebooks, and open books, the odd pen jammed between the pillows.

He stretched, arms above his head, then reached for his watch on the bedside table. Still early. He swung his legs over the side and padded across to the tall bay window. Drawing back the white shutters, he was met with a pale October morning. The sun hadn't climbed far yet, its light thin and washed-out, casting long streaks of greyish gold across the carpet. The air in the room felt cold. But it was clear out, and he took it as a rare bit of luck. As he began tidying the bed, he murmured, 'I'll go for a run.'

After rummaging through the tall dresser for his gear, he dressed quickly and moved towards the door, careful not to make a sound. He slipped out of his bedroom and began tiptoeing down the curved staircase, doing his best to avoid the creaky step near the middle, but halfway down, stopped dead, startled to see his uncle already up and standing at the bottom, dressed for work, a porcelain mug in one hand and a folded newspaper tucked beneath the other arm.

'Morning, James. Off for a run, eh? The forecast isn't great, best make it a quickie.'

'Righty-o. You good?'

'Not the best. Didn't sleep a wink. Massive bomb last night, surprised you didn't hear it. Major casualties. Honestly, it's heartbreaking. There'll be retaliation the day, lad, I'm sure of it, so be careful driving in.' James wasn't worried. He could handle himself.

'Och, Uncle, I'll be fine. I'm leaving all that political stuff to you and the rest. None of my business.' James smirked as he bounded down the stairs.

'See you after.' He never noticed the flash of surprise and hurt in his uncle's face as Roger's eyes followed him out.

Roger let out a groan and turned away, muttering under his breath. 'None of his business, eh? It'll be soon enough, my boy, sooner than ye think.'

Over breakfast, the three Henderson men sat reading the local papers. After a quick run, James had taken a long, hot shower and, as usual, was dressed to perfection.

Two papers were prominent on the table: the Catholic (Nationalist) *Derry Journal* and the Protestant (Unionist) *Belfast Newsletter*. Roger was summarising a story from the *Journal*.

'Says here, it was a bloodbath last night. A café. Who'd want to plant a bomb in a café? A Provo warning given, but they only got half the people out in time. Says there's a wee five-year-old girl dead.'

James Snr slammed his paper on the table and glared at his brother. 'Bastards,' he growled. 'Thugs – all of them. How could they? Needs sorting out.' He paused as an idea sparked in his mind.

'I know. Shoot the lotta them. And if not, lock 'em up for good and throw the key in the Foyle!'

Roger was taken aback by his brother's rage. He'd never heard him talk like that before and wondered if his growing ties with Charles Jones were having a bad influence. He'd talk to him later; it wasn't the right time with young James about.

'The poor mother and father must be heartbroken. Children shouldn't die before their parents. It's against the law of nature, isn't it?' Roger concluded.

The table fell quiet as his question hung in the air. James felt a change in the atmosphere and decided to leave.

He wasn't about to get caught in another debate, so he folded his newspaper, finished his coffee, and said, 'Right, I'm off. Want me to drive you in, Uncle?'

Roger shook his head and placed his newspaper back down. He'd read enough for one day.

'Not quite yet. Gotta few things to do here at the house. I'll catch you later.' Secretly, James was relieved. He loved Roger but enjoyed driving solo.

Rising, he said, 'That'll do. See you then.'

'Bye, James,' the two older men replied.

Roger, still fretful, called after him: 'Be careful.'

Too late, James had gone.

It was 8.30 AM when James slowly manoeuvred the sleek Jaguar down Melrose's long, tree-lined driveway. He loved this house, its award-winning rose garden, impressive white-rendered Victorian façade, and characteristic sash windows, a classic home of which he was proud.

His late Aunt Jocelyn, had spent hours tending its now mature garden. Sometimes, he could still feel her presence, especially amongst the roses. James had been extremely fond of her and spent most of his school holidays here with her and Roger, who were childless. He never had the nerve to ask why he had no cousins. Sad really; they would have made amazing parents.

James's mother had disappeared from his life when he was a child. He didn't remember her and only discovered years later that she had started a new life in South Africa. His childless aunt and uncle stepped in and took him under their wing, urging him to spend as much time as possible with them in Ireland. By then, his father had retired from the army, and James grew up knowing he could neither mention nor ask about his mother.

He came to believe his father resented the path he'd chosen, which might explain the drink and the gambling. Most days the man was in a foul mood and, without explanation, would vanish for days, sometimes weeks. James never let on that he knew the real reason they had lost their home in Ayrshire. They'd had no choice but to sell, to cover his father's debts. Gambling debts. James Snr was, like always, clinging to his brother, and taking whatever he could get. A lifesaver, Roger offered them a roof and did his best to keep his father's debtors at bay, though even he had his limitations.

Once James graduated from Oxford, he worked for a year or more at a large fabric manufacturer near Ardrossan, thirty miles from their old home. He'd enjoyed it at first, but soon grew bored and was thrilled when Roger offered him the chance to join the family firm in Northern Ireland. Yet another example of his uncle's generosity.

The drive into Rocola on the west bank of Londonderry, also known as the Maiden City – named as its walls were never breached despite three sieges over a few hundred years – was an arduous and frustrating journey.

James was stopped more often than usual at army checkpoints. Though he was new to the city, the security services recognised Rocola's black Jag and typically waved him through. Not today.

At the previous checkpoint, a soldier who looked like he'd just left nursery stopped and asked him a few dull questions, then quickly sent him on his way. James couldn't help but think how different their lives were – and how lucky he was living and working as he was.

Once at the factory, he eased the Jag into its allocated space, straightened his tie, and strode towards the office building, his briefcase swinging by his side. Annoyingly, his mind slipped back to the battered-looking girl, but he shook them off. No time for distractions, though he wondered if he'd see her about. This was his first day, and he wasn't here to chase women. He was here to pull Rocola back from the brink.

A short while later, there was a light knock on his office door. He didn't answer but sat back as Mrs Parkes promptly entered, carrying a china cup and saucer. God, what a wretched-looking woman, James thought, still in an attempt to be friendly, he forced a smile.

'Tea?' she offered rather grimly.

Not a great lover of tea in the morning, James wasn't going to start off on the wrong foot. Mrs Parkes was one of those iron-fisted, busy body, know-it-all types who could make your life pleasant or utterly hellish. Best to play it safe.

'Yes, thank you, Mrs Parkes. You're spoiling me. I can see now why my uncle speaks well of you.'

Mrs Parke's neck turned scarlet, and her face flushed despite herself. She looked unconvinced. *Was he toying with her?* Best to keep an eye on this one.

'Your uncle telephoned. Two o'clock to meet. Okay?' she said, back to business.

'Perfect. Thank you, Mrs Parkes.' She turned to go, but James called her back.

'Actually, Mrs Parkes,' he said politely in his most charming voice, 'there's one thing you *can* help me with.'

Mid-step, she turned back, combative but curious. 'Oh yes, what's that then?'

'Well, the meeting this afternoon is to discuss my new role, among other things. But, as my uncle was saying yesterday, I'll need a secretary and was hoping you could free up one of your girls. Uncle says, with your vast experience, you'll know what I'd need, but that it has to be someone trustworthy.' He flashed her his best smile, all teeth and innocence.

Resolved to ignore his flirty nonsense, Mrs Parkes was fuming when she felt the heat return to her cheeks. She pressed her hands to her face, trying to hide the blush creeping down her neck. She'd seen men like him before. Oh yes. Thought they were God's gift. Thinking they could get what they wanted with a cheesy smile and a wink. Well, not with her. And certainly not with any of her girls. She'd make sure of that.

'I don't think so, Mr Henderson. These local girls are naïve and quite inexperienced. *For someone like you.*' That'll tell him, she thought.

The barb wasn't lost on him, as she suggested. 'Best I do it meself. I'll speak to Mr Henderson when he gets in.'

Over my dead body, James thought, but aloud said, 'No. I wouldn't dream of it, Mrs Parkes. The hours will be long, and I wouldn't want to impose. I'm sure my uncle needs you more, but thank you all the same for your kind offer.'

'No, Mr Henderson, I insist. As I say, I'll talk to him.'

This one was used to getting her way, but James had no intention of backing down. He stood slowly and met her face on.

'I said no thank you, Mrs Parkes.' His tone was calm, but firmer now, with no room for debate.

'Let's not push this. I'd rather avoid a debate given it's my first day. Now, do you, or do you not, have someone you can spare?'

That did it. With a doubtful look, the office manager swayed from foot to foot. She wasn't used to being spoken to like that, not here. But she wasn't stupid either, he was the boss's kin. There'd be time to deal with him later.

'Ah. Well... In that case, I suppose there might be.' James smiled with quiet satisfaction and waited.

'Well... thinking about it. There's Caitlin. Caitlin McLaughlin. A serious girl. Keeps her head down but works hard. Not like the other two, talking rubbish or mooning after men.'

She shook her head. Between them, they hadn't the sense they were born with. A pair of chattering magpies, and not a brain cell between them. They wouldn't last five minutes with this boyo. No, Caitlin was his only option.

'Caitlin?' James tilted his head, feigning disinterest. 'Was she there yesterday?'

Mrs Parkes pursed her lips. 'Aye. The tall one, skinny. Too skinny, if you ask me. She's smart, no nonsense, doesn't give me too much grief.' James knew right off who she meant, and a rush of excitement coursed through him. Caitlin. The girl with the black eye.

Suddenly, Mrs Parkes's face darkened. Her mouth twitched, like she wasn't sure whether to spit out what she had to say. But said it anyway. 'Well... now... er...there is one thing, when I think of it. Best to warn ye.'

James raised an eyebrow, completely in the dark as to what she meant. 'Oh aye, what's that, then?'

She inhaled as if bracing herself. 'Well... the girl... Caitlin... She's a Papist. A Roman Catholic.' He looked at her, having to take what she said in and think of how to answer her. What she said was shocking.

'Sorry, you've lost me, Mrs Parkes. What exactly has that got to do with anything?!'

Regretting her words, Mrs Parkes fidgeted, yet she refused to take them back. 'She's Roman Catholic. The only one we've got up here. I thought... well... you know... some people prefer to know these things.'

His silence was glacial. Then he told her outright, 'Frankly, Mrs Parkes, I'm not *some people* and couldn't care less if she was the Holy Pope himself. Understand?'

Mrs Parkes bit her lip. His words hit hard. Her nostrils flared, and for a moment, she looked as though she might throw something at him, but thought better of it.

'Let me be clear, Mrs Parkes. I don't give a hoot what she is. I'll see her at noon. That suit?' James challenged.

Sorry she'd spoken at all, Mrs Parkes gave a quick nod, her lips squeezed so tight they turned near white. 'I'll bring her over meself.' Aware he'd made an enemy for life, James sat back down, angry but satisfied. Round one to him.

Barely holding back a laugh, he watched the woman give what looked like a twitchy wee curtsy at the door before marching out, stiff as a poker. *Boy, but she was a piece of work.*

He smiled as he removed his suit jacket and draped it over the back of his chair. So, the girl's name was Caitlin. Saying it out loud, he liked it: '*Kate-lin.*' A beautiful name.

Soft, but with a bit of steel to it – yeah he liked it. With no warning, a warmth stirred low in his gut. Bloody hell. Not now. No time for that sort of carry-on. What in God's name was going on with him?

Chapter Thirteen

Hook, Line and Sinker

At twelve on the dot, Mrs Parkes knocked and stepped into James's office, jerking her head for Caitlin to follow.

Despite the girl's plain dress, bruised face, and swelling black eye, once again, something about her knocked James off balance.

'Please. Come in, come in. Thank you, Mrs Parkes. Give us half an hour or so, and I'll get Caitlin right back to you,' he said, full of polite ease. The office manager wasn't too happy about leaving Caitlin alone in a closed office with him.

'I don't mind stayin',' she said. But James's expression told her she'd lost this battle too.

'Ah, right. If I must.'

She shot Caitlin a look and a tut, reminding her of their earlier talk. 'Only speak when you're spoken to. Listen, and don't rush your answers, or he won't catch a word of it. Probably won't understand ye half the time, anyway.'

Escorted by James, Mrs Parkes reluctantly left the office, and James promptly closed the door behind her.

Caitlin sat on one of the low visitors' chairs, feeling nervous and still not right in herself after yesterday. Her hands rested neatly on her lap, her head up and back straight, as her mother insisted.

The man across from her, smartly dressed and perched upright in his leather-backed chair, met her eyes with a measured calm that unsettled her more than it reassured. His aftershave, tangy, but expensive-smelling, filled the air between them, tingling her nose and making her blink. She didn't want to seem rude by wriggling or fidgeting, so she held herself as still as she could, trying her best not to let on how queasy and out of place she felt in such a posh office with someone like him.

He was handsome, that much was obvious. Powerfully built, with broad shoulders, those eyes, those striking green eyes were something else, and his skin. So clear and smooth it looked as if he'd never had a bad day in his life.

When she'd walked in, his smile had been warm, inviting even, which helped ease her nerves a little, though not entirely. The way he shifted in his seat, the tiny twitch at the corner of his mouth, made her think he might be as nervous as she was. The silence dragged, the awkward kind that made Caitlin want to cough to fill it. She stared at her hands, then back up again, and was about to speak when, *thank God*, he broke the ice.

'Thanks for coming Caitlin. I'm told you're trustworthy, which is vital for what I'm about to share with you.'

His voice dropped to almost a whisper. 'The fact is, Rocola's in trouble. Financially. And I've been tasked with finding investors. I need a secretary. A good one. Long hours, I'm afraid, but extra pay. Interested?' He looked straight at her when he spoke. She liked that. Good eye contact.

His Scottish accent was sexy, but more importantly, he'd offered her a job and, even better, more money. She'd do anything to escape Mrs Parkes and that cold, dismal office. God, yes. She'd take it; she'd take anything.

Fighting to control her excitement, despite Mrs Parkes's warnings, she blurted, 'Absolutely. I don't mind long hours. You've no idea. I'm thrilled. Thank you!'

James was pleased. 'That's wonderful.' His eyes crinkled with warmth.

They agreed she'd start the following week, and true to his word; he wrapped up the interview bang on thirty minutes. He even offered to walk her back to her office. She thanked him, politely refusing his offer with a touch of shyness, and left him standing in the doorway, watching her every step as she made her way down the corridor.

Back in his office, James let out a low groan and dropped into his chair. What the hell just happened? His head was scrambled, shot through with flashes and feelings he had no business wanting. He'd done everything right, hadn't he? Hired her fair and square, kept it polite, professional from start to finish. So why did it feel as if a charge had run through the room — and straight through him? Like a part of him had stirred awake, and now he wasn't sure he wanted to put it back to sleep.

She wasn't his type. Not by a long shot. Nothing like the women he'd gone for before, with their polished smiles and easy charm. The girl looked like she wore hand-me-downs; her scuffed shoes, the whole shebang thrown together. Poorly. There wasn't a hint of gloss about her. She belonged to a different world. Nevertheless, he couldn't help but stare at her. It wasn't only curiosity. It was the way she sat – shoulders back, hands clasped like she was steeling herself for bad news. No attempt to impress. Natural nerves and plain honesty. That alone hit harder than he liked to admit. He hated how he felt, but he couldn't deny it. She got under his skin.

He leaned forward, elbows pressed to the desk, rubbing at his temples as if he could scrub the thoughts away and be rid of the strange pull she had on him. It wasn't her face alone, though those pale, unguarded eyes seemed to take in more than they should. It was her composure, the quiet way she held herself even when nervous. No pretence. No games. Something decent. And in a world where most people acted or angled for something, she hadn't. Maybe that's what had got to him. She was genuine. Others weren't.

He wasn't some gawky wee eejit from school anymore, and he certainly wasn't in the business of letting his heart take over his head. That had never been him. Until now. Because Caitlin McLaughlin had somehow crawled inside his thoughts and settled there like she belonged. Worse still, common sense was shouting at him to walk away, to forget hiring her before it got confusing.

His instincts, shaped over closing deals and managing difficult people, were screaming danger. And yet here he was, slouched in his chair, grinning like a bloody sixteen-year-old, letting himself feel something dangerously close to elation. Christ, he couldn't tell you when, or if, he'd ever felt that before. Maybe never.

The admin office fell silent as Caitlin stepped back inside. Mrs Parkes's wordless disapproval speaking volumes. The thought of starting the job filled Caitlin with a kind of bubbling excitement she hadn't felt in forever. But it wasn't the new job that stirred her most. It was James Henderson.

'Is that it?' Mrs Parkes asked at last.

'Yes, thank you,' Caitlin replied.

'And?'

'And what?'

'When do you start?'

'Next week,' Caitlin said.

Mrs Parkes gave a grunt and turned back to her work.

At her desk, Caitlin found it hard to concentrate. Every word, every motion of the interview going over and over in her head. She couldn't put her finger on it. Aye, he was handsome, *beautiful*, but that wasn't the pull. This was different, the way he looked at her, the way he spoke, quiet but certain, as if the world couldn't touch him. So bloody confident, nothing like the men around here.

She wasn't naïve; she knew there were guys who looked the part but turned out to be shites or downright cruel. This was strange, a feeling so strong it left her caught, hook, line, and sinker. She should've been better prepared. But it was too late. Whatever it was, it had her, body and soul.

Friggin' heck, wait until she told Anne!

Chapter Fourteen

A Tar and Feathering

It was Rob's turn to go out on foot patrol in 'brick' formation alongside Val, two other squaddies and their lance corporal, or as they called him, their 'Lance Jack.' The smallest patrol unit the army allowed.

Their orders were to proceed cautiously alongside the multi-coloured terraced houses along the Lone Moor Road, a notorious Republican area in the Bogside. They'd just left the safety of their barracks, running out as fast as they could through a single corrugated gate at the back of the tall, iron-grilled barrack wall. Per usual, they'd zig-zagged across the open space, hoping to avoid snipers and find safe cover.

It was Rob's turn to carry the heavy riot gun. Most of the time, he preferred foot patrol, but for some reason, today he felt frightened, though he wasn't about to let on. He had a dreadful night's sleep, anticipating the difficult five-to six-hour patrol in the area they'd dubbed 'Provo-land.' The lads felt like fairground ducks exposed and waiting to be won as a prize by some gun-wielding Provo.

At the briefing earlier that morning, their captain shared an array of mugshots of the usual suspects and a few unfamiliar faces. He drilled them on being vigilant, as they'd have to report back on any issues, sightings of suspects, or vehicles of interest. 'Expect the unexpected,' he'd said.

Up to this point, the army's Aden and Cyprus experience offered little help in fighting this guerrilla war on home soil. At first, the men found it difficult to grasp the dangers of patrolling a city filled with hate. To outsiders, it appeared like any other UK city, with people shopping and going about their business day to day, yet it was a deadly war zone. Tragically, some of the younger recruits hadn't learned fast enough and fell victim to either a bullet or a bomb.

As he walked along the narrow road, Rob checked for loose bricks in the walls of the two-tone houses. Small, deadly devices were notorious for being tucked in and hidden behind them. They also avoided burned-out cars and empty containers that might contain remotely detonated explosives, ready to blow as they walked by.

Carefully studying the litter-strewn area, he focused on some burned-out houses adjacent to the demolished remains of others. They made a perfect hiding place for snipers. He paid even more attention to the movements of the adults and children as he inhaled the scent of burning coal from what seemed like hundreds of chimneys, reminding him of home. The air was thick and heavy and caught the back of his throat.

He was relieved to see lots of people about the place. It was worse when things were quiet. He watched little girls swinging on long ropes tied around lampposts, their bottoms cushioned by coats, whilst others played hopscotch or skipped using old nylon washing lines or rope.

Boys kicked a deflated football around as a few lucky ones played with yo-yos, frustrated by their failed attempts to do tricks. The children had nowhere else to play, a result of the daily riots that ruined most of the city's playgrounds. Even with everything going on, the youngsters acted as if nothing was wrong, laughing and playing.

The troops intentionally used the children for protection. They'd stay close and hunker down to the kiddies' height. It allowed them to rest, take in their surroundings, and hope the Provos wouldn't shoot.

A few of the lads, fathers themselves, felt guilty and attempted to talk to the smaller kiddies, who were, so far, none the wiser. The older ones taunted, mocked, or cursed them, but were ignored and left alone.

By now, Rob had recognised a few 'Dickers' from mugshots. Dickers were teenage men or women who watched the patrols and mapped out their routes for potential attacks. They'd gather the intel and feed it back to the Provos. It was a constant game of cat and mouse, and to rile them, Rob gave one a knowing *I'm onto you* wave.

As he proceeded along the single-file footpath, Rob passed the many apron-clad women who stood straight-backed and proud, their arms folded defiantly, on recently washed doorsteps. When they caught wind of the patrol, some retreated inside their houses but quickly reappeared, brandishing steel dustbin lids. The approaching soldiers were met by the women's frantic banging of bin lids on the ground, a signal of the Brits' arrival.

A deafening clang of lids filled the air with surreal intensity, leaving Rob breathless in the violent atmosphere. Within seconds, the children stopped playing and rushed to the safety of their homes. The clamour continued as Rob, with a hammering heart, tried his best to ignore the racket.

As he got near the last woman, his heart raced when she gave him a look of pure hate, stopped what she was doing, spat at him, and yelled, 'Brits out now!' Others joined in, and Rob's heart continued to race like the clappers. He didn't understand this hatred and doubted he ever would.

He kept walking, even though they taunted him, and reminded himself that he was a professional soldier. As his Lance Jack urged everyone to remain calm, Rob wiped the woman's saliva from his face using a gloved hand. The deafening clatter of bin lids kept echoing, now joined by outraged older children blowing hard on plastic whistles.

Rob scanned the area, every nerve on edge. A sniper's shot could come, he knew it. They all knew it. His fear peeved him, but he pushed it away, trying to focus. When he reached the corner, he heard his Lance Jack whisper from behind.

Rob turned and watched as the corporal gestured to the riot gun. 'Be ready to use that thing, Sallis I don't like this.' Confused, Rob looked to where the corporal was looking.

On the other side of the road stood a group of forty or so women and youngsters, jeering and screaming at a crying teenage girl. She was tiny, no more than 16 or 17 tops, with mermaid-length, flowing black hair. Dressed in a brown and white smocked blouse, an ankle-length cream skirt, and scuffed flat shoes, her condition drew a gasp from Rob – she was expecting!

Her bump held up some sort of makeshift sign, propped high on top. A torn sleeve revealed a bare shoulder, while tape covered her mouth, and her hands were crudely bound behind her back with rope. Three masked women, all dressed in black jumpers and A-line skirts, manhandled her toward a lamppost across the road, right beside the stunned patrol.

'Easy gentlemen,' advised the Lance Jack.

Rob remained kneeling, eyes glued to the mob, unsure of what they'd do next. Then, the girl turned, revealing a large homemade sign reading 'Turncoat Sanger Banger.' *What in the world?*

Shock paralyzed Rob; his insides were screaming. The victim's head hung low in defeat, her lengthy hair falling around her like a veil.

'Don't anyone move,' the Lance Jack told them gravely. 'Stay alert.'

The procession edged closer, step by step, until it stopped dead in front of the patrol, a wall of black bodies squaring up to the soldiers. Rob caught the teenager's choked sobs, raw and guttural, as she took in the lamp post for the first time.

Her muffled screams tore through the air as she shook her head from side to side. 'No. Noooo!'

He watched as she placed her hands on her tummy, shielding her unborn child. He was flabbergasted. These people must know her, for Christ's sake. Friends, neighbours. Surely, they wouldn't... couldn't... hurt her, or the bairn!

Like an animal caught in a trap, she screamed and thrashed, kicking out wildly, desperate to break free. One woman kicked the poor girl's legs. Swiftly and brutally, they hauled her closer, bound her hands, and secured her feet to the post.

Next, the ringleader removed her mask. She then reached into a black sack, producing an enormous pair of steel shears, and lifted the blades for the shrieking crowd to approve. In a shocking turn of events, she cut the expectant mothers long, dark hair into thick chunks and threw them into the cheering crowd. The group roared with approval, and a voice called out.

'Traitorin' bitch!'

They laughed in return as it went on, 'That'll show ye to keep your knickers on, won't it? Brit lover!'

The Lance Jack swore under his breath, trained his eyes on his men and repeated his instructions.

'Don't move an inch. We can't do anything for her.'

A mass of jagged tufts had replaced the girl's once beautiful locks. Tears streamed down her face as she continued to moan and sob, her tears falling onto the broken pavement.

Rob was lost for words, overwhelmed by it all. He desperately wanted to go to her, to help her, but couldn't. Where the hell was the RUC? It didn't make sense. He'd heard stories of locals punished for fraternising with soldiers, but witnessing this firsthand was soul-destroying. This was organised brutality.

For the first time since landing in Northern Ireland, something dark stirred in him. A hatred he didn't want, a hatred he didn't recognise. This wasn't what they'd signed up for. He hadn't trained to stand by and watch this kind of cruelty. But this was getting to him. Eating away at him. What happened to these people? Medieval. And women, no less. Neighbours, wives, mothers, sisters, doing this to one of their own? He felt sick. The Lance Jack noticed Rob's dazed look and shook his arm.

'With me, Sallis,' before turning to the others. 'Listen up. Move back on my count. Be ready to follow me.' The others acknowledged the order, and Rob waited.

By now, the crowd was clapping and cheering as the ringleader poured a gluey black liquid from a steel bucket over the teenager's sheared head. The dense fluid oozed onto her shoulders and arms, pooling thickly on the pavement.

Eerily still, she stood motionless and silent to protect her baby. White and brown feathers plastered her head and upper body, completing her humiliation as they stuck to the tar. Loose feathers drifted around her or floated away like dandelion seeds on a gentle breeze.

With a pompous grin, the ringleader stood back and watched, hands on hips. This woman had presence, no doubt about it. Her toughness was legendary — admired by some, feared by many.

Then, she barked, 'Showtime's over!' Like a ringmaster closing the circus.

'Let's leave the bitch here. It's about to lash, and I've gotta make me man his tea.'

Her audience, clapping, laughing and chatting in obvious satisfaction, soon dispersed in all directions. As she watched, the woman's cruel, sardonic smile remained, while the patrol rose and made to leave.

The Lance Jack hushed his men, instructing them to ignore her, leaving the soldiers shocked and speechless.

'Move out, there's nothing we can do here,' he ordered.

Chapter Fifteen

A Bucket of Piss

Hours later, the unit reversed their departure and zig-zagged back into the safety of Fort George.

They detested that final hundred-meter sprint, especially when exhausted. Like it would never end, each step carried a huge risk, leaving them open and exposed in no-man's-land. With a bit of luck, they'd soon enjoy a shower, some grub, a beer, and after that, lights out. Another day down.

Once inside, the haggard men walked to a sandbagged corner, where they unloaded their arms, checked their ammo, all followed by a debrief in the ops room. They remained solemn as they talked about what they'd seen that day.

Later, on the way to their bunks, Val squeezed his hand on Rob's shoulder.

'You okay? I'd nivver believe we'd see something like that on a British street, eh?'

Rob let out a low grunt. 'Can you believe it?' In frustration, he threw his gloves up onto his bunk.

'I mean, she was expectin', Val, and a proppa wee lass too. This godforsaken country is mad... They did that to her because she was with one of us.' Val nodded. He couldn't agree more and tried hard to cheer Rob up.

With a chuckle, he made a suggestion, 'Howay, lad, let's get into our civvies and grab a few beers. Put this shitty day behind us.'

Rob was knackered but knew he wouldn't sleep. Why not have a drink? To distract him from their 'shitty' day.

After getting changed, the friends left for the games room. Unfortunately, they encountered Billy Morris, pacing up and down the hallway outside the showers. He shouted and cursed at the empty corridor, spun around, then, eyeing them, let out a piercing scream.

'I'll kill them. I swear I'll kill all'a them, the dirty Fenian bastards! Do ye know what they did?' He pointed at himself as he continued to shriek.

'Some wee Taig threw a bucket of piss out the window right on me. Crisp packets full of dog shit, too.' He paused, uncertain. 'I think... Anyway, can ye believe it? And that dickhead of a corporal wouldn't let us go after 'em.'

He lifted his shirt and sniffed. 'Bloody hell, I'm mingin'.'

Rob and Val didn't dare look at each other as Morris waited for some sign of empathy.

Poker-faced, Rob replied, 'That's a *pisser*, Morris, right *shitty*, that is.'

Morris was too angry to pick up on Rob's innuendo and snarled, 'You're right. Just watch. I'll get 'em. I know the house.'

A boyish-looking private emerged from the shower room, sniffed, and took in Morris, who glowered back, daring him to speak. The lad was streetwise enough to sense the Irishman's mood and half ran down the corridor to safety.

Morris gave a snort and dragged his foul-smelling self inside for a wash, leaving Val and Rob in the corridor. They both just cracked up laughing like crazy.

Val gave Rob a good thump on the back. 'Magic, Robbie lad! Windin' him up like. "Pisser" and "shitty" – dead canny. Bummer that dimwit doesn't get it!' Still taking the *piss* and joking, they made their way to the games room.

The converted room was impressive, with its high, cornice ceiling. It was barely carpeted and contained four snooker tables. Cigarette smoke filled the air, and at the far end, next to a barred window, stood a long, crude bar offering cold drinks and light beer.

Randomly placed around the walls were sofas and chairs filled with men and a few women reading or watching a small black-and-white TV. A group in one corner played cards and concentrated on their game, Union Jacks and pictures of the royal family hung alongside lopsided posters of beautiful semi-nude women. Rod Stewart's latest hit, *You Wear It Well*, blared from a timeworn record player.

Val headed for the bar while Rob sat on an empty sofa and watched the nearest snooker game. He sighed as his mind traced back to the young mother, wondering whether she was still there, all alone, attached to that lamppost. He was sick to the core. If they could do this to their own, what else could they do?

As he tried to relax, a man approached. Rob had seen him about, recognising his distinctive cropped, stark-white hair. In his mid-twenties, he was short but well-built, with a solid upper body and rippling muscles that stretched his shirt sleeves. He smiled as he looked down at Rob.

'This seat free?' He pointed to the empty spot next to Rob, who nodded and shifted across the decrepit sofa.

'Yeah, sure, go ahead.'

The man sat, sighed, then sank deep within the couch. He watched the snooker game too but wasn't paying much attention.

'Heard about that tar and feathering. Imagine. Turns out they only shot the father a while back. Seems he was from here an' all. Joined up years ago, decided to come home. Provos warned him not to. Stupid git. Him Catholic too.' The stranger said.

'No way.' Rob was shocked. The white-haired man offered his hand, and Rob shook it.

'Steve North.'

'Robert Sallis. *Rob*. Who you with? I've seen you around.'

'Felix.' Steve replied.

'Felix?' Rob was confused.

'Yeah, Felix, like the cat – nine lives. Bomb disposal.'

'Aaah. Right,' Rob replied. That explained the white hair then. Bomb Disposal. Some job. Rob didn't know how they did it. None of them did. Took some nerve.

'You guys are legends.' Was the only thing Rob could say.

'Not really. Seems I've got steady hands. Can't understand it, they're as big as dinner plates.' He raised his hands for Rob to inspect. He was right: they were mammoth.

'They are an' all. Wanna drink?' Rob offered.

'Nah, thanks; back on duty tomorrow. But ta anyway.'

Val returned, carrying two beers. Seeing Steve, he flashed Rob a 'who's that there then?' look with raised eyebrows.

Rob did the formalities. 'Steve, Val. Val, Steve. Steve is with Felix.'

'Felix?' It was Val's turn to be confused.

'Yep, bomb disposal. Felix, it's our call sign.' Steve explained.

Well impressed, Val passed Rob a drink and whistled, wiping down the front of his shirt, which had somehow acquired a long trail of brown, sticky beer. He was a slob, but a slob Rob trusted with his life.

He smiled as Val, who'd given up trying to wipe off the dark, wet stain, turned to Steve. 'Bomb disposal. How'd ye hack it? Is that what happened with the hair?'

Steve had a good chuckle at Val's straight talk and took to him. 'Nah, went white for some weird reason – overnight – one of life's mysteries. Only been here a month. Some vets say they've seen nothing like it. That security brief they gave us before we left didn't prepare me for this shite. We're at three scares a day. *Three*. I've already had enough practice to last a lifetime.' He dropped his head.

'Bad day today, though. Lost a good pal. No chance. Report came in about suspicious-looking milk churns hidden on the side of a country lane outside the city. The RUC had to cordon it off and push back the locals. Some of them wouldn't leave, but stood there gaping at us.' He paused.

'Others gave us aggro, started stoning the crew. Madness. Anyway, went off before he'd a chance. Annihilated him. Twenty-five, and bang. Pulp now. Here one minute, gone the next.' He lifted his arms, dropped them onto his head and exhaled, before letting them fall away.

'Good mate, too. Know what the crowd did? Started singing some rebel song or the other. Can you believe it?' Steve's face emptied as the images came flooding back, blood, fire, the leftovers of a friend he'd had breakfast with that morning.

'Fucken' heck,' Rob cried. 'Sure, you don't want that drink?'

'Nah, thanks. Had to get away from the crew. Switch off. Not doing a great job, mind you. Need to lock all this shite in here.' Steve half-laughed, tapping the side of his head with his finger.

Rob and Val were speechless, staring at each other. It'd certainly put their day into perspective until Val came up with another brainwave.

'Tell you what, Stevie boy, let's switch that brain of yours off for a while, eh?' Checking out the room for a free snooker table, he soon found one and cheerfully ruffled the young man's white hair.

'How about I beat your ass with a game? A pint for the winner, eh?'

Steve smiled back in appreciation – anything to get rid of the haunting, bloodied images swirling around and repeating before his eyes.

'A pint it is. You're on,' he challenged, reaching for a snooker cue.

Chapter Sixteen

Mark of the Devil

C ontented, Honey remembered Kieran's recent spate of spending on her. He'd been so kind.

They'd gone to the pictures a few times too, always sitting at the back, cuddling, kissing, and giggling as they watched the latest films, like *The Mark of the Devil*. She hated it – it'd scared the living daylights out of her. But with Kieran holding her close, she felt brave enough to watch it through her fingers.

He'd been shopping, turning up with more clothes and make-up. She thanked him, touched by his kindness, though all the thank-yous were starting to feel a bit awkward. Honey was skint and couldn't return the favour, not even close. When she said as much, he only shrugged, like it didn't matter. Maybe to him it didn't, but to her it did. Sadly, she couldn't do anything about it, and loved him all the more.

At first, she found it strange when he offered to do her make-up. What man in his right mind knew about make-up? Yet, to her astonishment, he was brilliant at it, worked miracles, and before long she left it to him.

It was time to show off another new look. As she stood with her eyes closed in front of the mirror, Kieran's hands rested on her upper arms, and he excitedly whispered in her ear, 'Don't open them yet. Let me tuck your hair in a bit first.'

He spent a minute or two fixing some loose curls firmly in place, so close she could feel his breath. The intimacy of it made her shiver.

'Right. Done. After three, open up. One, two, three...' he counted.

Upon three, Honey peeked, then gazed in shock at the standalone mirror. The attractive woman smiling back was barely recognisable.

Kieran's latest shopping spree had been fab – a few short, flowery dresses that clung in all the right places, a slinky black cocktail dress, some cheap-looking pearls that somehow still looked classy on her, and a pair of shiny black patent shoes. But it was the boots that did it – three-quarter length, lace-up, tough but stylish, that matched perfectly with the dresses. They were her favourite by far. For the first time in her life, she looked... pretty. Sophisticated, even. Almost like she belonged somewhere else. Somewhere better.

Tonight, he'd worked his magic on her hair, every strand perfect. Her makeup was natural, with a hint of trendy pearlescent eyeshadow to finish the look. She felt out of this world.

'Oh...my...God!' she cried. 'You're something else! Is that *really* me? Can we go out now?!'

He agreed with a laugh. As soon as he'd showered and changed.

Honey was really surprised at first when they went to his flat. How the heck could he afford this place?

Later she found out it wasn't his, but some friend off backpacking in Australia. After she sank into the soft suede sofa, she let herself think about him while waiting for him to shower. The magician who'd miraculously transformed her into this new version of herself.

He was hesitant, but bit by bit, he started to let her get closer. He didn't talk much about his past, not really, but he did tell her about his ex-girlfriend. Two years together, then out of the blue, gone. Ran off with his best pal, no warning, no explanation. Just like that.

He said his girlfriend left over a year ago, and he feared being hurt again. Said he needed time before he could trust. That was fine by her. She'd wait. No questions, no pressure. She was in now, well in. Heart, soul, the lot. As far as she was concerned, there wasn't a person alive who could hold a candle to Kieran Kelly. What they had was extra special, invincible. She was head over heels in love, and if the rest of the world just keep its bloody nose out, all the better.

This wasn't a short-lived romance. This was the real McCoy. Their love was genuine, a timeless romance, like the films she watched as a child.

For the first time she was living her own Happy Ever After and she loved it.

Chapter Seventeen

Patrick Comes Home

Patrick McLaughlin finally came home. His body had been released by the hospital early that morning.

Caitlin stood beside the brass-handled pine coffin that dominated the centre of their living room. She inspected the corpse and blessed herself. Patrick lay in his best suit and tie, his only pair of cufflinks fastened to the cuffs of a specially bought crisp white shirt. She hated his coffin, lined with garish, cheap blue satin. His face expressionless, bearing the vacant look of the dead.

She bit back her emotions while she regarded his thick, freckled fingers intertwined with rosary beads, remembering how often she'd held his hand as they walked uptown before he got sick.

It had been a running joke between them until she turned sixteen, when he'd tease her and refuse to hold it, saying, 'People'll think you're me girlfriend.' It wasn't funny; holding his hand made her feel safe. Passing cars would pump their horns, and Patrick would wave back. Over and over, she'd ask who it was in the car, and he'd laugh – hadn't a clue!

Ever since he came home, a steady stream of people had been in and out of the house with its curtains drawn tight. They brought food and flowers, murmuring condolences. As they gathered around the coffin, whispering prayers, everyone remarked, 'Och sure, doesn't he look grand?'

Their words were ludicrous. Her daddy was anything but 'grand.' That body in the box wasn't him. It was a hollow, lifeless shell, a cruel mockery of the man she'd loved. Anger burned through her grief, bitter and unforgiving. How could he leave her like this? How dare he? He was supposed to be here. Always.

Tommy placed a large hand on her shoulder and caressed it. Today, he wore a dark suit, a black tie, and a white shirt beneath a long black leather coat. His hair was tousled and uncombed, his eyes shadowed and puffy.

'Love, I need a moment,' he said, drawing nearer. 'Can you come into the kitchen?'

With a nod, she followed him, moving through the overpowering scent of flowers and tobacco. People dipped their heads and grasped her hand as she passed, murmuring, 'Sorry for your trouble.' Most of them were strangers to her.

In the kitchen, Caitlin found her heartbroken mother, slumped in Patrick's chair. The doctor had increased her medication; it was working. She wore a dark dress – not black; she didn't have one, and her hair was pulled back into a ponytail, framing her pale, tear-streaked face. Heavily sedated, she sat there, listless and indifferent to everything around her.

Tommy gently ushered a few mourners out of the kitchen and closed the door, leaving Majella, Caitlin, Maggie from next door, and himself.

'Sit down a minute,' he said, guiding Caitlin to a chair. I need to ask you somethin'.'

Caitlin stared at him across the table, piled high with sandwiches, biscuits, and hot stew. People had been so kind. How bitterly ironic that they had so much food now when they'd struggled to scrape some bits for Martin only a few days ago. Tommy gestured sombrely towards his sister.

'Caitlin, look at your ma. She's not fit to lead today. Please, love, you need to take her place. The boys have offered, out of respect, if they might escort the funeral and place a Tricolour on your da's coffin.'

He watched as Caitlin jumped up and cried. 'What the hell! Are you serious? Respect Tommy? Daddy wanted nothin' to do with them. Tried to warn us to keep out of it, and God love him, look where he's ended up. Dead! So no, Tommy, no way. They're not going to use him as another martyr!'

Tommy could see her answer was a big fat no, but tried again anyway. 'Think about it, love. You don't turn these guys down just like that, and most likely, if your Martin were here, he'd do it.'

The Prison wouldn't release Martin for the funeral, and Caitlin was angry that her uncle was using him against her with his subtle threat of upsetting the Provos. She loved him, but now she was as angry as hell.

'Well, Martin isn't here, is he? And I'm certainly not worried about them ones, those Provos. I'm here for Mammy and Tina. Martin made his choice. Besides, I blame him for this—' She flung her arms wide, as if the whole kitchen had to see. 'He's the reason Daddy's dead!'

Tommy sighed and caught Maggie's eye. She shook her head, knowing he was right and Caitlin was wrong. His niece was close to breaking point, and he had to play his cards carefully.

'Right, love, if that's what you want. Though I still think you're wrong. Believe it or not, this nightmare is important for the Cause.'

Caitlin saw his concern and took his hand. Poor Tommy was caught between a rock and a hard place, and she knew it.

'No, Tommy. The answer's no. The minute Daddy died, I decided, fuck the Cause and all those with it.'

Depressed, Tommy inhaled and got up from his chair. The boys won't be happy. As for Martin, he'd be furious.

Frustrated, he quickly left the house of mourning and crossed the street towards a darkly dressed figure who sat on a wall, smoking and waiting for an answer.

He gave a nod as Tommy reached him and said. 'Sorry, it's a no. They're upset, especially the eldest girl. Our Jella's off her head; couldn't make a decision to save her life. She's so away with it. If it was up to her—'

Not the answer he wanted and pissed at the news, the man grunted, flicked his cigarette to the ground and rose to leave.

'Right then,' he said.

Meanwhile, Caitlin stayed in the kitchen, watching Majella, who sat unnervingly still. Maggie bustled about, busying herself with making more tea as the house filled once again with an endless stream of mourners. As Caitlin rose from her seat, she saw through the kitchen door visitors subtly sharing whiskey, secretly adding shots to their tea.

Today, Maggie wore another of her floral aprons over a black woollen dress, thick black tights, and flat, well-worn shoes. Without her infamous rollers, her blonde hair was brushed back from her face in a mass of rigid waves, set with a copious dose of hairspray.

'Thanks for all your help, Maggie,' Caitlin murmured. 'I had a word with Granny earlier. She still won't come. I don't get that woman.'

Maggie smiled. 'People are strange creatures, Caitlin, and sometimes families are the worst. It's no problem to me helping, love. I'm sorry Patrick's gone. Your da was a good man. Did you know we were in the same class at school?' Her eyes filled. 'I'll miss him.'

Caitlin knew Maggie had a soft spot for her da. 'I know. Daddy liked you too.'

A memory of Patrick passed between the two. Caitlin took Maggie's arm and linked hers through. She shook her head despondently and looked around.

'I'm not sure I can handle this on my own, Maggie. Mammy might as well be a zombie; Tina never speaks to me, and as for our Martin... I swear. I'd kill him if I had my hands on him.'

Maggie unlinked their arms and hugged Caitlin, who took comfort in the familiar scent of her Fleurissimo perfume. As a neighbour, she'd been a steady presence in Caitlin's life for as long as she could remember.

She whispered words that eased the tightness in Caitlin's throat: 'Listen, I'll be with you every step of the way. Sure, I love you like me own. And don't go frettin' over your Tina, you know what she's like. A day at a time, okay? Let's start by sortin' your ma out first. How about we try to get some food into her, bring her back to us, eh?'

Caitlin pulled herself back from the comfort of Maggie's arms and wiped her eyes. 'You're right. Sorry.'

Maggie looked down at Majella, 'Why not take her upstairs?' She suggested with a gentle nod. 'As soon as the kettle boils, I'll bring up a potta tea and a wee bite to eat.'

It was a good idea, so Caitlin led her mother out of the kitchen. Despite the staircase being only a few feet away, they struggled to navigate the sea of people who offered their sympathies. Caitlin had to thank each one and shake hands as she passed.

At long last, they reached the top of their staircase and went into Majella's bedroom, with its double bed adorned, as usual, with its threadbare pink candlewick bedspread. The room had little furniture. A fabric-topped stool sat opposite a three-drawer dressing table. On top, a series of black-and-white family photographs were proudly displayed, amongst some makeup and a few near-empty toiletries.

Majella sat on the stool, and Caitlin knelt beside her. 'Mammy, listen to me. We need to perk you up a bit. We're going to be leaving the house soon. The crowd will be massive, so let's get you sorted.'

She took her mother's much-loved hairbrush from the dressing table and released her hair from its loose ponytail. Brushing it, she carefully styled it into a neat bun. Finished, she opened the single wardrobe and searched for Majella's only decent pair of shoes.

Maggie soon knocked on the bedroom door and came through. She set a tray containing a teapot and a couple of cups on the floor, accompanied by a tomato sandwich, smiled warmly, and left. From the treacle colour of the tea, it was strong and likely dosed with sugar.

A little while later, Tina joined them and sat on the bed. She wore a black top and trousers, her fiery red hair tangled and unkempt. Her tear-stained face said enough. Caitlin reached out, wanting to hug her, but stopped, certain she'd be pushed away.

Instead, she sat next to her and, with a wavering voice, said, 'Please don't cry anymore, Tina. We have to make Daddy proud and keep it together. I'm not sure what to do here and—'

With a pained grimace, Tina jumped up and exclaimed, 'If Martin were here, he'd fuckin' know what to do!'

Caitlin was livid at her sister's outburst – especially in front of their mother. She stood up and pointed her finger right into Tina's face.

'Don't you dare use that language with me, young lady. And will you forget about big, perfect Martin? All I hear is our Martin this, our Martin that. Well, he's not friggin' here when we need him. Is he?! Today's about getting Mammy through this shit, that's all. Go to hell and get outta my sight!'

She readied herself for a row, but Tina was already off in a strop, slamming Martin's bedroom door after her – *same old story.*

Tina knew she'd gone overboard, sitting slumped on the bedroom floor. She shouldn't have cursed like that in front of her mammy. It wasn't right. But her heart was broken, and she was scared. She reckoned her sister was hurting too, trying her best like the rest of them. Even so, deep down, Tina couldn't take it in. Her daddy was gone – dead. And seeing him, the colour of him, lying there in that coffin, scared the absolute crap out of her. If only Martin were here...

After pouring the tea, Caitlin handed Majella a cup and a corner of her sandwich. She gave Caitlin a weak smile and waved her off. 'Go on, love. Get dressed. I'll be fine after this.'

Caitlin wasn't convinced, not really, but nodded and disappeared to her bedroom, feeling miserable. It was a cramped room, with old Holly Hobbie posters half-hanging from the walls, held by yellowed, brittle Sellotape. Her single wooden bed was strewn with clothes after Tina had rummaged, without permission, to find something to wear for the funeral.

A black dress hung on a steel hanger over her wardrobe door. She took it, dressed, and cursed herself as she remembered she'd put her finger through her last good pair of tights. With no choice but to put her bare feet into her polished black shoes, she decided no one would notice. Anyway, the way she felt, she couldn't care less. There were more important things to think about now than a pair of lousy tights.

A short time later, the family gathered in Blamfield's darkened, candle-lit living room to bid Patrick goodbye. Majella sobbed as she bent over to kiss her husband, placing a single white rose alongside the rosary beads intertwined in his hands.

Tina was sobbing and trembling, she froze for a moment, and then took a step back. No matter how much she cared for him, she couldn't go near his corpse. Majella understood and pulled her youngest aside, allowing Caitlin to take her turn.

Over the coffin, hot tears stung the insides of Caitlin's eyes, but she forced them shut, willing herself to keep strong. She'd cried so much over the past few days, it seemed impossible she had any tears left. Her throat tightened, each breath becoming harder, shallower. After swallowing the lump that wouldn't disappear, she leaned over and kissed Patrick's forehead just as she always did, and in a low, trembling whisper, she whispered her last words: 'Bye, Daddy. Love you.'

God, it hurt so much; the grief was biting, deeper than anything she'd ever known. She stepped back, casting one last glance around the room, biting her lip hard to keep the tears at bay. Nothing would ever make sense again; the world could never be the same.

Before stepping forward to bid farewell to Patrick, Tommy, sensing her misery, took her hand and gave it a firm squeeze.

The black-suited, hatless undertakers stood outside in the hallway respectfully waiting for the family to finish. It was time now, and Caitlin watched as they gently placed the lid on the coffin with prac- tised skill. She was the last of the family to leave and saw the men screw the coffin lid down. It was final. So very, very final.

Tommy waited in the hallway alongside her mother and Tina. As Caitlin came out, she could smell whiskey on his breath. Until now, she'd never had a drink, but at this moment and dreading the next few hours, she'd welcome anything or anyone who could ease or take this wretched pain away.

In silence, the women put on their coats and made it to the waiting black funeral car. Tommy was to be one of six pallbearers, along with Big Charlie and some of her father's school friends.

No surprise it was raining heavily, and with the estate's chimney smoke hanging so low, the sky looked almost dark. Caitlin scanned the street as she tightened her black scarf. The place was heaving with people as far as she could see, some holding umbrellas, black flags, or Ireland's tricolour raised high above their heads on wooden sticks.

She looked up at two hovering, glass-fronted British Army scout helicopters monitoring the crowd below. The noise was ear-splitting – they were so low – and with it brought back horrible memories of the night Patrick was lifted.

Along the streets, armed RUC and army patrols formed tense lines. Fully kitted out, they stood ready, hard hats dull under the grey sky, gripping shields, guns, and batons. In grim silence, they waited beside their steel-clad jeeps and hulking APCs, or Armoured Personnel Carriers.

Countless reporters, photographers, and camera men clustered at the front of the crowd closest to the house. As soon as they saw the family, they raced forward like a pack of starving wolves, holding out their microphones and cameras, barking out question after question.

'Mrs McLaughlin, have you insisted on an internal enquiry into the death of your husband?'

'Have you seen an autopsy report yet?'

'Are you angry, Mrs McLaughlin?'

'Do you condone the rioting and deaths last night in Londonderry and Belfast?'

'We understand you've refused to allow a tricolour on Patrick's coffin. Is this true?'

The questions continued until some local men pushed the media pack back and roared, 'For Christ's sake, get back! Let them be!'

Through the commotion, the women struggled to get to the funeral car. Caitlin was in front and turned back to ensure her mother and Tina were close. She reached out to grab their hands and pulled them closer until all three were inside the black Mercedes.

The noise outside was ridiculous, and Majella shook with rage. 'Jesus, Mary and Joseph, what's happening? What was that? Did you see those people?! Your daddy would've hated this, Caitlin.'

'I know, Mammy,' she replied. 'Tommy had a feeling it'd be bad, but I didn't think it'd be anything like this. We'll have to wait a minute. Then we'll go.' She twisted round, peeked out the rear window and saw Tommy, Charlie, and the pallbearers carefully bringing out the coffin through the black crepe-adorned door before placing it inside the hearse. They positioned the family's white roses and flowers on either side of the coffin before closing the rear door.

Through the rain, Tommy ran to the family car and climbed in. His coat was soaked through, and he was shivering.

'I knew there'd be a crowd, but I swear to God, that's one hell of a turnout,' he said, rubbing his hands for warmth.

Caitlin stretched over and placed her hand on his, squeezing it. The poor man looked like he'd sell his soul for a drink. It was her turn to reassure Tommy and it felt nice. His eyes acknowledged her gesture. They were good again.

As confidently as she could muster, Caitlin whispered, 'Let's make Daddy proud. All of us okay? I can feel him. He's here.' No one came back, but they smiled sorrowfully and nodded in agreement.

'Good.'

The Mercedes engine rumbled to life as two undertakers, in black-ribboned top hats and fitted Crombie coats, stepped to the front of the hearse to lead the funeral procession. As they moved forward, the crowd parted like the Red Sea, making way for the cars to pass. A hushed murmur spread through the gathered mourners as the gap closed behind them, and they followed the cortège towards St Mary's.

During the short drive, Caitlin noted the crowd hadn't dwindled. If anything, it'd increased. People were everywhere, including a few brave teenage boys who'd climbed the lampposts adorned with black flags for a better view, holding on for dear life. Men, women, children, and mothers with prams stood solemnly in the rain and blessed themselves as the hearse passed. There was little traffic, but any cars they encountered pulled over in respect, switching off their engines and waiting in silence.

The family car rolled up the short slope to the church entrance and stopped beside the hearse. With a quick nod to the women, Tommy stepped out to take his place as a pallbearer. The women fussed over each other, straightening coats and fixing hair, as Caitlin's voice cracked while she tried to speak.

'Right, here we go. Remember. Remember Daddy's here, watching us.'

Chapter Eighteen

A Colour Party of Four

M ajella was the first out of the car, met by Maggie, who popped up from nowhere, her hand outstretched and ready.

Caitlin and Tina followed closely behind. Together, the undertakers removed the flowers from the hearse. Then, the six burly men pulled out and lifted the coffin onto their shoulders, finding their balance. Next, the undertakers carefully placed the family flowers on top of the coffin. The pallbearers ready, they climbed the few steps to the entrance.

Caitlin studied the granite building. It wasn't a traditional church, far from it. Cruciform in shape, it had been built on a two-acre triangular site in the late fifties. Most times, she would have taken comfort from it and enjoyed the magnificent view from its entrance over the city and Foyle Valley. But not now, not ever again.

Maggie guided Majella between her two daughters, who took her arms, ensuring she was supported. They followed the coffin.

Inside, the church stretched wide, its arched columns soaring to an ornate two-tiered ceiling. The women moved past rows of packed wooden pews along the long flagstone aisle.

As a girl, Caitlin had dreamt of walking here with her father on her wedding day. Now the dream was gone, replaced by a nightmare. A choir sang as the procession reached the white marble altar. Father

McGuire, who'd known Caitlin all her life, stood waiting beside a new parish priest. McGuire looked older, drained, his white robe heavy against the purple vestments. Incense thickened the air as an altar boy swung a thurible back and forth.

An undertaker readjusted the wet flowers on top of the coffin after the pallbearers eased it off their shoulders and placed it on a stainless-steel gurney.

As the choir sang, Caitlin recognised the hymn *Here I Am, Lord* – one of her Daddy's favourite.

The church continued to fill as they waited. Caitlin later learned that the crowd had spilled out of the church car park into the nearby streets. Someone had set up loudspeakers outside so that as many people as possible could hear the Requiem Mass. When the time came, it began, and the McLaughlin women clung to each other.

For the first reading, Tina looked shellshocked as she rose and walked to the altar. Her voice shook as she began the psalm, but halfway through she broke down. Father McGuire stepped in quickly, guiding her back to the front pew and into Majella's arms. His eyes found Caitlin's, pleading, and she understood at once – he wanted her to finish.

She gave a small nod, stood, and walked to the pulpit without pause. Turning to face the congregation, she saw the church was full to bursting, people lined along the walls and pressed into the aisles. Women in the pews wept, each with their own reasons. Their soft sobs rose around her as Caitlin drew a breath and picked up where Tina left off. At the psalm's end, the congregation joined her, voices as one: 'The Lord is my shepherd; there is nothing I shall want.'

In his sermon, Father McGuire spoke of Patrick's life, how he'd known him, and assured the congregation that Patrick would not have wanted his death to lead to more violence. His voice, strained with tiredness, carried an appeal to the crowd.

'It's like this. Every man, woman, boy and girl, please listen to me. Go straight home today and find it in your hearts to forgive. Patrick's death is a tragedy, an awful tragedy. Let it be that. A tragedy. No more of this violence. Please.'

The church was quiet, out of respect, but the old priest knew his words had fallen on deaf ears. Trouble was already brewing in the city and Belfast. He ended the Mass, and the pallbearers removed Patrick's coffin.

A massive crowd followed the family car and hearse to Derry's Eighteenth Century walled cemetery nearby. The Merc drove past several burned-out and overturned vehicles on either side of the road, along with the waiting RUC and army vehicles parked by Stones Corner.

Once in the cemetery, the family were led to a freshly dug grave on the far side of the sprawling grounds. The women crossed the rain-slicked grass toward the open pit, while Caitlin, bare-legged and shivering, trembled with cold.

The crowd stood in silence as Father McGuire prayed. As he finished his final blessing and the coffin was about to be lowered into the rain-soaked grave, almost like magic, a colour party of four darkly dressed men, their faces concealed, emerged from the crowd. In perfect unison, they stepped forward and stood to attention in pairs on either side of Patrick's coffin.

The crowd gasped when one of the armed men, carrying a folded Irish tricolour, threw it over the coffin. Then, within seconds, a volley of gunshots resounded across the cemetery. As mysteriously as they arrived, the gunmen ducked and disappeared into the crowd of mourners. An instant wave of applause and cheers erupted.

The McLaughlin women could only stare at the coffin, now adorned in its green, white and gold shroud. Caitlin felt Tommy's eyes on her as he waited for her reaction. With grief weighing on her heart, she gazed down the hill toward Derry's infamous city walls, where a beautiful, vibrant-coloured rainbow hung in stark contrast to her sorrow. No longer did she pay notice to the draped coffin, the noise of the cheering crowd, or even the loud helicopters that searched above for the vanished gunmen.

To her, the rainbow was a sign. Tommy felt a wave of relief when she smiled at him. She'd no fight left, only a sudden, calming peace.

Daddy *was* here, holding her hand, not giving a hoot what age she was.

Chapter Nineteen

Making Ulster Safe

James had spent the last few days getting organised between home and the factory, where Caitlin – when Mrs Parkes, in her usual crabbit mood, allowed – helped him get things started. He followed that with a long weekend in the Victorian seaside resort of Portrush with a couple of friends, certain it would set him up for the coming months.

The beaches amazed him, especially the long stretch of white sand at Benone, pounded by roaring, white-crested waves. He also visited the world-famous Giant's Causeway, which always left him in awe. The entire Antrim coastline took his breath away. Wrapped in warm, waterproof clothing, he'd prepared for the rain and had walked for miles.

He loved being outdoors and laughed whenever people moaned about the Irish weather. This was Ireland! His friends commented on his good humour and teased him, asking what was making him so happy. A small part of his good mood came from the prospect of working with Caitlin, but he shared little and told them he was excited about his new job and the opportunities it offered – though it was still early days.

Having had a haircut the previous Friday, he studied his reflection. He was excited and, without realising it, took extra care when dressing. Today, he decided on his favourite dark grey suit, a Rocola white shirt, and a grey-and-white-striped tie. To finish, he slipped on his black leather Church shoes and splashed a little Eau Sauvage Dior aftershave on his face.

Over breakfast, it was his father this time who warned him to be careful driving to work. There'd been a wave of riots whilst he'd been away, resulting in several deaths across the province – something to do with a local man dying in police custody. Several RUC men and soldiers were injured, and a substantial number of arrests made. James half listened but assured him he'd be fine, so, with a hurried goodbye, left Melrose.

As he drove towards the Craigavon Bridge checkpoint, the traffic slowed to a crawl. From a distance, he read a giant handwritten blackboard fixed to the bridge's superstructure.

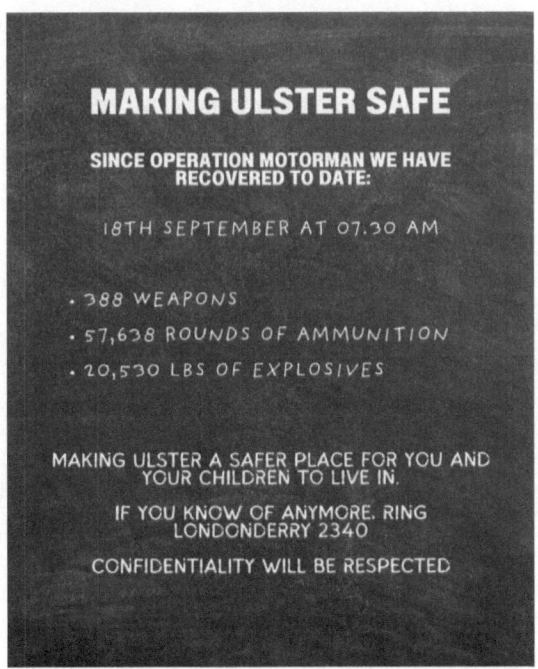

Fascinated by the numbers, he wondered if anyone ever called, hoping or believing their one phone call could 'Make Ulster Safe'... He didn't think so.

In a world of his own and not paying attention, he didn't realise that he'd allowed a wide gap to form between his Jaguar and the car in front. When he realised it, he swore, put his foot down and sped towards the car in front. It was a dangerous and stupid thing to do, and now he was driving too fast. *Shit!*

A newly arrived soldier to the province grew wary as he eyed the black Jaguar speeding towards him. Quickly raising his hand, he shouted at a colleague to be on guard as the car grew closer. Not knowing the vehicle or its driver, the squaddie remained alert, positioning himself a few paces back as James slowed and rolled down the driver's window.

To the private's relief, someone from behind yelled, 'He's okay, mate. Let him go.'

The soldier blew out a quick breath and walked towards the car. He peered inside, trying to look confident, but there was something in his eyes that said he wasn't angry. He was furious. *It'd bloody well terrified him.*

Without hesitation, James handed his licence over with an apologetic smile.

The soldier didn't bother to look at it but let rip, 'Sir. In future, keep your eyes on the road, will you? That was a foolish thing you did, speeding up like that. I could've shot you!'

James nodded, offering a half-smile that barely concealed his irritation – it had been foolish, and he knew it. Nonetheless, he didn't appreciate the soldier's attitude.

'Name?' the squaddie asked, his eyes narrowing as he scrutinised James.

'James Henderson.'

'Date of birth?'

'It's there on my licence,' James replied, his tone tight, holding back his impatience.

'Where've you come from?'

'Home.'

'Where's that then?'

James tensed up as he replied, 'Prehen.'

'And you're going where?'

'Work.' Keep calm, James told himself, clenching his jaw.

'And where's that?' The soldier tilted his head, his gaze fixed on the licence, his expression indignant.

'Rocola Factory, Blighs Lane,' James told him, his words clipped.

The soldier dawdled with the licence, flipping it over, his eyes fixed on James, who gripped the steering wheel a little tighter. *Didn't someone just say he could drive on?*

'Blighs Lane, eh? Isn't that the one by Stones Corner in Creggan?' The soldier asked, newly suspicious, and again, his eyes searched the inside of the car. A brave – or stupid – driver tooted his horn from the queue behind.

'Is there a problem?' James asked. He wasn't used to this kind of grilling and didn't like it. Sure, he'd screwed up, but this guy was a proper bawbag.

'Not so much a problem. Only you've a Scottish licence, not one issued in Northern Ireland. Why's that, sir?'

James blinked in bafflement. *A licence was a licence, wasn't it?*

'I'm Scottish. Moved here with work.'

'Ah. You're a Scot,' the soldier replied flatly, the words carrying a weight of disdain. James picked up on it straight away – no love for Scotland then.

'Landed here recently, have you?' James snapped, his irritation finally bubbling over.

'Beg your pardon?' The soldier's expression darkened, not liking the driver's attitude.

'You. Arrived in Northern Ireland recently. From England?'

'Yeah, why?'

'Figured,' James muttered with a dismissive tut, his glare fixed on the soldier.

'Oi, mate! I told you. Let him go!' A voice shouted again from the sidelines.

The squaddie, miffed at having to let James off, threw his licence back with more force than necessary.

'You'd better get yourself a Northern Irish licence. Away you go.'

James snatched it up, bit back another criticism, and drove off, his knuckles now white against the steering wheel. He was agitated, the soldier's attitude needling him, bringing to mind the uncomfortable conversation he'd endured over dinner the week before.

One guest was an RUC man, Bonner, who answered to Shalham. It didn't take James long to realise the man was a complete nuisance – rigid in his views and quick to brush off anything the other guests had to say.

Like Charles Jones, Bonner insisted that the British Army had been overly soft on the Roman Catholics. It was a disgrace that for eleven months, they'd had their own 'no-go' areas, giving the Provos the chance to hide terrorists and build up their stocks of guns and bomb-making equipment.

Operation Motorman had come remarkably late, in his opinion. And it was now the British Army who 'policed' Londonderry with little or no help from the RUC. He'd told them of the infamous three-day Battle of the Bogside, from which he still bore scars, and how he openly despised Roman Catholics.

For the first time since arriving in Londonderry, James was troubled. This man was a policeman, someone who should act as a peacekeeper, a protector, yet he was an unashamed bigot.

Afterwards, James spoke to his uncle and father about the policeman's behaviour. His father could only suggest that James attend a meeting of the Waterside Apprentice Boys, one of the Protestant Loyal Orders. He thought it might help him gain a better perspective on the Troubles, the complex history of the city and, indeed, Ireland. It was, he argued, an excellent way of meeting other Unionists — 'our own kind', in his words. James didn't want to take sides, but agreed to think about it, if only to pacify him.

The Jaguar continued moving along Foyle Road and past the city cemetery. A vast redevelopment programme had begun on the West Bank. Long rows of terraced slums around the Bogside and Brandywell had been demolished, and gangs of children, serious-faced and intent on their games, had taken over the resulting open space.

As he continued driving, he watched two boys aged nine or ten drag a steel-framed single bed towards a poorly built barricade. Their attempts were futile; it was exceptionally heavy, but almost comical to watch. Most schools were closed to coincide with an ongoing rent and rate strike in protest against internment.

He passed a makeshift memorial, no more than a metre high, standing forlornly in the middle of the road – a stark reminder of another civilian shot dead by the British Army. White scaffolding poles, anchored by grey breeze blocks, formed a crude frame, like a tent protecting the tribute. Inside, a framed photograph of the victim took pride of place, surrounded by Mass cards, holy statues, and wilted flowers.

Four yellow arrows had been painted around the base, marking the spot where the victim had fallen. A black flag hung from one post, near a waist-high wooden Celtic cross. Beside it, a man and a woman stood shoulder to shoulder, their heads bowed in prayer. The woman wept, pressing a handkerchief to her face.

It was a heartbreaking sight, so James sped up and switched on the radio to divert himself. The announcer informed the audience that it was nine AM, and the news report began with an account of the weekend's disturbances.

There have been full-scale riots and several deaths throughout Lon donderry and Belfast over the weekend in response to the death of forty-two-year-old Patrick McLaughlin, said to have been beaten up while held in custody following Operation Motorman. The SDLP have denounced McLaughlin's death and have called for an independent inquiry, not only into this case but into all those where beatings and torture have been reported.'

The announcer continued with other updates and finished with the sports news.

Because of the increased security risks for visiting football teams, Derry City FC has withdrawn from senior football in the Irish League—

James switched it off. This place was starting to affect him.

When he finally arrived at Rocola, the last stream of latecomers rushed past and through the doors, heads lowered, desperate to clock on in time and not be seen.

The lift remained broken, so James climbed the stairs and, slightly out of breath, opened his office door.

Mrs Parkes stood to attention when she saw him. 'Morning,' she said with a tight smile.

'Morning,' James replied. He removed and shook out his coat before hanging it on a carved oak coat stand, half-hidden in the corner.

Given his bad mood, he didn't want the woman hovering about. 'Caitlin starts full-time today. Unfortunately, my uncle tells me you'll have to share out her workload; we won't be back-filling her old job.'

The news seemed to perturb Mrs Parkes. She'd known Caitlin would be going, but not that she couldn't back-fill her. It would mean more work for her and that useless pair of dimwits. She grunted and waited for him to say more, but he didn't.

'Well, I'll need to check that with Mr Henderson first—' You'd think the fella had been here years, not weeks, with that attitude.

James, already pained at finding the old bat lurking in his office and still agitated from his journey, was enraged when she talked back, forever invoking his uncle whenever he gave her orders.

'Enough said, Mrs Parkes. Not a word to my uncle.' An unspoken battle of wills followed, their eyes locking like two swords crossed in a duel.

'But—' she began.

'Is Caitlin in?' James's voice cut her off, leaving nothing more to be said. *Bloody cheek.* Mrs Parkes thought, adding him to the top of her hate list. She was prone to evening the score with those on it.

In an icy voice, she replied, 'Aye. I've sent her to get some stationery. She'll be sittin' outside your office. By the way, there's something you need to know. She isn't well, she isn't—'

This time, James really lost it, 'What is it, Mrs Parkes? What's the Papist, as you so cruelly call her, done now?!'

Mortally offended, Mrs Parkes stared at the man's accusation. As usual, her neck and face let her down as she flushed a painful shade of pink. How dare he criticise her for trying to state a fact?!

James realised he'd overstepped the mark as the woman stuttered and stumbled over her words, desperate to explain.

'Wh– Wh– Why, no, M– Mr Henderson, no. My goodness, it's nothing like that! I wanted to warn you. You might've heard, but that man who was in custody, the one who died, Patrick McLaughlin – well, he's Caitlin's father. I was only tryin' to tell ye, that's all.'

Floored, James pressed his hands against the desk and bowed his head. He'd misjudged her. *Shit*. He owed her an apology.

Inhaling, he looked up at her. 'Sorry, Mrs Parkes, I made assumptions and was downright rude. Caitlin's father. How is she? Why is she even here?'

The woman realised she had the upper hand now and replied in a formal, controlled manner, 'I spent some time with her when she got in this morning. Told her to go home, but she's determined to stay and keep busy. Thought it might be good for her.'

James took a second to compose himself. 'Oh... I see. Well, good. Good for her. When she's back, send her in. Please. And thank you for telling me, Mrs Parkes.'

She gave a brief nod and took off right away. James had a feeling his put-down was something she wouldn't forget or forgive anytime soon.

Downstairs, Caitlin was collecting stationery from the store cupboard. Attending the funeral, arranging the food and drinks – on tick at a local bar afterwards – and finally getting her mother home had left her exhausted.

In the end, Tommy got well drunk and continued to apologise to her about the colour party. She'd told him time and time again not to worry, but he was wasted and wasn't for listening. Kept going on and on. It didn't matter. It was done. He was so good to them and she didn't want to spoil things. Not for a million pounds.

As soon as they got home, her mother disappeared to her bed with a glass of whiskey and sleeping pills. She stayed there, refusing to eat or drink, shutting herself off from the world. Caitlin was desperately worried about her. Tina stayed quiet and retreated to her room, leaving Caitlin alone in the messy kitchen, where she spent most of the night cleaning up after the wake, isolated in her thoughts.

Earlier that morning, Tommy showed up, hung over and looking like he belonged in the next plot in the cemetery. With him, he'd brought milk, bread, and, surprisingly, a pair of tights – having noticed her bare legs at the funeral and knowing she'd officially start her new job that day.

After such a thoughtful gesture, it was right not to stay angry. Instead, she offered him a drink, which he accepted with gusto. As the leftover whiskey worked its magic, restoring some life into him, he launched into a story to cheer her up, describing how some Republicans, before Motorman, had played a trick on a local character with a stocky frame, barely over four feet tall.

The Boys had ordered the little fella to man a barricade near Little Diamond, off William Street. He was overjoyed at being given such a grand responsibility. They'd told him to look for a specific car they were after, suspecting it was being used by undercover filth. Highlighting the car's model and registration, they couldn't over emphasise the importance of finding it.

Eager to prove himself, the poor lad spent day after day checking every car that came past the barricade. In the end, he gave up, only to be told – amid fits of laughter – that the car he was looking for had been right in front of him the whole time, burnt out and sitting proudly on top of the very blockade he was minding!

Caitlin couldn't help but laugh. Harsh, maybe, but a little funny. Tommy assured her the wee fella took it on the chin, and the story had already become legend.

Putting aside the thought, she grabbed some stationery, knowing she had to hurry back before Mrs Parkes went ape.

James looked up in response to a soft knock on his door. Caitlin. He motioned her in, and as soon as she entered, he couldn't help but notice the signs of grief etched on her pale face.

His heart softened, but he remained shy, unsure how to comfort her. Her damaged eye had yellowed, and her bruises were less notice-able. She seemed sad and frail as he pulled out a chair for her. Once she sat, he did the same and leaned forward across his desk.

'I'm sorry, Caitlin. About your father. I didn't put two and two together.'

'You weren't to know, Mr Henderson. But thank you.'

'Is there anything you need? Want to wait a few days before you start?'

'No, not at all. Please, I want to be busy. Prefer that.' He agreed that keeping busy was the right thing to do. Selfishly, too, he needed her and wanted to crack on.

'I understand. Well, if it helps, I do have a bit of good news. Uncle has approved your salary increase. Not a lot, but better than nothing I suppose. It seems I'm going to be in Londonderry for some time.'

Caitlin flinched when she heard him use the term *Londonderry*. It had always been *Derry* to her, but she was grateful. 'That's great Mr Henderson. Thank you.'

'And please, don't call me "Mr Henderson". No need. It's James, just James.'

'Okay, Mr—I mean... James.' She smiled.

He stood and carried on talking. 'If you want to be busy Caitlin, that I can do. Okay?' Caitlin nodded and quickly opened her notebook, ready to jot down her tasks.

'Okay, we'll need the names and addresses of all the political party leaders here, a list of senior personnel from the British Army, the RUC, and details of the church leaders. Every one of them. I want to know their backgrounds, family histories, likes and dislikes, everything, what makes them tick. Whatever you can find, but be careful, and talk to me first if you're not sure about anything.'

He paused, watching her as new ideas formed in his mind. 'Next, I need to familiarise myself with the local businesses. My uncle has some useful contacts already, but I'd like you to call the Chamber of Commerce and get a membership list. Perhaps I've left out some smaller organisations, like the independent traders on William Street. Uncle mentioned them. You know, small, medium-sized businesses. They're just as important.'

'Sure,' Caitlin replied.

When the time was right, she hesitated before saying, 'James. There is one thing. How do I contact the army or RUC?'

'Oh God, sorry, of course you won't! Uncle will see to that. Duh! How stupid of me.' James was mortified. After everything that had happened with her father, he's asking the girl to contact the security services. *You're a dick, Henderson!*

'No problem. Don't worry.' Caitlin said. She didn't hold it against him. He was new here and listened as he went on.

'Security's a priority for us, Caitlin. We need to make sure all our employees and goods arrive and leave in one piece. If they can't, we'll lose even more orders and, believe me, we've lost enough already. The continual rioting around that British compound next door hasn't helped, with lorries hijacked all over the joint. Worst-case scenario, we may have to close, and you can imagine what a disaster that would be.' He took a sip of lukewarm tea and carried on.

'Right... here's the idea. We get everyone round a table, and I mean *everyone* with any clout, not only in Londonderry but further out too, and come up with a plan to save Rocola. Find investors. Because if we shut down, trust me, it'll ripple right through this city. Businesses, families, the lot. And we're not about to let that happen.'

Caitlin sat back in shock. He was right. It would be a catastrophe, not only for her but also for Anne's family, and all the hundreds of others who depended on the factory. It was such a scary thought; it made her heart drop to her toes. *What on God's earth would they do?*

When he'd finished outlining the plan, James sighed. 'Given all that, Caitlin, remember this - everything you see and hear in this office stays here. Please. Keep it to yourself.' He mimed zipping his mouth shut.

'Goes without saying. It's frightening, that's all.' Caitlin told him.

'Frightening's not the word,' James replied. Things were a hell of a lot worse than Roger had let on. Rocola was bleeding cash as if there was no tomorrow.

Together they worked on until lunchtime, when James yawned, stretched, and said, 'Feel like grabbing something to eat?'

Caitlin couldn't believe she was hungry; food hadn't entered her mind for days, but funny enough now, she was.

'I'm starving,' she admitted. 'But I left my sandwich at home.' James laughed and admitted that he too was 'starving'.

'Don't worry; Mrs Parkes'll get us something.' Caitlin nearly choked.

'Mrs Parkes?! Are you serious? She'll have a fit. Her bringing me lunch. Sorry, James, but she'll go mental!'

'Well, we'll have to see, won't we?' James smiled mischievously.

She watched him leave in search of the dragon and couldn't believe her luck with her new boss. He was lovely, and extra money too. All the same, she was worried about what he'd told her, and since she promised to keep it quiet, she'd have to carry the burden herself. Just as predicted, Mrs Parkes was furious when James suggested she bring them some sandwiches from the canteen.

Fifteen minutes later, she marched in with the tray herself; her face like thunder, and all but dumped their lunch down in frosty silence. James and Caitlin had to bite back a giggle until she was out of sight. They ate while they worked, and Caitlin began to feel more like herself.

The day flew by, and before she knew it, it was over. She felt a touch guilty for feeling better, but told herself her daddy would be chuffed with what she was doing, that he was close by.

Feeling better had nothing to do with spending the day with James or getting lost in those sea-green eyes.

Nothing at all.

Chapter Twenty

A Honey Trap

Kieran Kelly had kept her sweet for long enough, but the pressure was on now, and the time had come to face the music.

With Honey at his side, he left the picture house and wandered down to the Rainbow, a small café further along the street, where they took a seat. She watched him closely, noticing how withdrawn he'd become, his silence unsettling, and from the look of him there was something not right. He wasn't himself at all, not in a way she'd seen before.

Taking his hand, she asked with concern, 'What's up Kieran? You've gone all quiet on me.' He looked straight at her, his eyes brimming before the tears flowed. *Jesus Christ.* She'd never seen a man cry like it!

Frightened now, she squeezed his hands, drew him close, and whispered, 'What on earth is it Kieran? Tell me. *Please.*' He tried to turn away, but she lifted his chin with her finger, forcing him to meet her trusting gaze.

'Tell me.'

He swallowed hard, then spoke. 'I'm in trouble, Honey. Big trouble, and I need your help.'

In their short time together, she'd never seen him so sad, those puppy-brown eyes full of tears and staring right at her. She'd do anything to make him happy.

'What kinda help? How?' she asked, gently rubbing the top of his hand.

The long-time café owner, Siobhan, known by nearly everyone in the city, brought their drinks, saw Kieran's tears and discreetly left.

Kieran began his story, his voice tinged with desperation.

'You can't tell anyone. Not a soul, Honey. Swear.'

'I won't. Swear,' she replied, crossing herself.

'I've been doing a couple of jobs for the Provos. Nothing major, low-risk stuff. But now they've given me something else. Time to step up. It's big, serious stuff — and they're not askin', they're tellin'. It's dangerous, and I don't know what to do. I'm bricking it.' He took her hand and moved even closer.

'They want me to set up a honey trap.'

Honey sat back, screwed her face up in confusion and asked.

'A what? How do ye mean?'

'Ye know. *A honey trap*. It's when a woman lures a man into a trap and then—' He didn't finish.

'Why? For what?' she asked, trying to make sense of what he was on about. She fell back in the booth.

'Intel. They want me to grab a couple of Brits so they can interrogate them.'

'But how can you do that? You'd need a woman for that.'

He stayed silent, watching her expression shift until the realisation hit her. It took a while, but eventually it hit home.

'Ah... ha! I get it!' she shrieked, sitting forward again.

She thought back to all the things he'd done for her, his generosity, the way he looked at her as if she were the only one that mattered. He had a way of making her feel special, seen in a way no one else ever had, and now, more than ever, she was sure he felt the same, that he cared for her too. The thought of not having him in her life scared the pants off her. She couldn't imagine life without him, and she didn't want to try.

Someone needed her for a change and smiling confidently, she chuckled, 'Right then. What d'ye want me to do?'

Kieran couldn't believe how easy it was. The stupid girl hadn't even tried to resist, just did what she was told. Pathetic, almost embarrassing. She was falling neatly into place, every bit of it playing out better than he'd imagined. For a moment, he almost felt guilty.

Almost.

Chapter Twenty-One

Hidden

S everal weeks went by, and payday rolled around again. Caitlin was pleased to see that the welcome raise in her wages had made a difference at home.

To date, around 26,000 Catholic households in the city had refused to pay their rates and rents in protest against internment, which was good news for the McLaughlins. They wouldn't have to pay anything for a while, allowing them to keep their heads above water. It helped, but Caitlin was worried sick about her father's funeral costs. The bill had arrived and lay untouched on the kitchen windowsill, ignored like the stack of red demands beside it.

Majella stayed despondent in bed, and when she did wake she grew frantic, crying hysterically and calling out for Patrick, with no one able to comfort her. She hadn't bathed in days. Tommy, worried, dropped by nearly every day, and as a last resort suggested they turn to his mother for help, but in the end they both baulked at the thought and decided against it. They agreed to give it another week and see if Majella improved without Caitlin's granny's far-from-tender brand of nurturing.

Caitlin, sitting in the kitchen noticed the time. Plenty of time yet. Tina, seated across the table, was subdued while she ate a small amount of cereal. She'd been quieter than usual over the past few days, another thing for Caitlin to worry about. Her sister no longer wore her braces, but her eczema had returned with a vengeance; the skin on her neck and face angry and sore-looking.

'How you feeling, Tina?' Concern crossed Caitlin's face. 'Never see you these days.'

'Why? What's it to you?' Tina shot back, flinging her spoon across the table. The anger in her voice stung.

'I'm only asking. I know I haven't been round much, but this new job's taking up all my time.'

'I said I'm fine. Leave it, will ye?' Tina snapped, her eyes fixed on the table. Caitlin swallowed her own temper, unsure what to say.

Even so, she tried again. 'Things any better with Emmett?'

'Still a moron,' Tina muttered, her tone flat. Caitlin felt the fight drain out of her. She finished her tea in silence and let it drop.

Tina gobbled her cereal, muttered under her breath, and clattered the bowl and spoon into the sink. She snatched her bag from the back of the chair and stormed upstairs, the thud of her feet carrying through the ceiling.

Caitlin looked up, cursed quietly, then flicked on the radio for a bit of peace. A loud, thumping song she didn't even know blasted out, and in a flash of frustration she snapped it off again.

As soon as Tina walked back into the kitchen with her coat on, she was off.

'I'm away.' And straight out the back door she went without another word.

Caitlin had had enough of her sister's moods and tore after her down the backyard, the privet hedges closing in on either side. The gate was still swinging when she reached it. She leaned into the lane, caught sight of her sister's back, and let out a scream that carried as far as her lungs would take it.

'Tina. Come back here!' But Tina ignored her calls and turned the corner, out of sight. *What in God's name am I going to do with her?* Caitlin thought as she wrapped her arms around herself.

It was so cold, in bare feet, she was wearing nothing but a light jumper over her nightie. She hurried back toward the warmth of the kitchen, but halfway up the path, she heard a slight rustle and stopped dead. She waited, listening intently, but nothing. Her vision wasn't great in the dim early morning light, but she knew someone or something was there. She was sure of it but wasn't scared – just angry – and demanded.

'Who's that? Who's there?!' Again, nothing, so she walked over to the thick, waist-high hedge and began prodding and pulling the leaves back.

She was right and stepped back, astonished, as a Brit rose from his hiding place. His face was painted as black as his badged beret, but she could make out his features – ordinary, unremarkable, except for his hazel eyes that met hers with a pleading look.

He held a rifle in his lower right hand and a Leica camera on a strap in the other. For a moment, she was torn – her instinct screamed at her to run, to shout, to give him up, but the sight of him, so young, so human, so afraid, stopped her. He was a Brit, could even be one of the Brits who'd taken her father...

'Please, miss, don't scream. Go back inside and shut the door,' he pleaded.

With a mix of fear and guilt, she hissed, 'I think it's you who should leave. Not me.'

Private Robert Sallis's eyes flickered, a brief flash of uncertainty crossing his face. He looked at the girl, then at the rifle in his hand, unsure whether to keep it low or raise it.

The suspense was mad as Caitlin's heart went ballistic. She still couldn't decide whether to scream, to run, or to give him up. She watched as he took a slow step back, his voice softer still.

'Miss. Listen. I don't want any trouble... just go back indoors.'

Her feet stayed rooted to the ground. She stared at him, unsure of what was worse – the danger of what he might do, or the idea of him disappearing into the shadows again, leaving her with the guilt of not giving him away.

Rob caught her hesitation and used it, pulling himself free of the hedge and hurrying down the path. In a few strides he was at the gate, peering over. From the top of the street came the low rumble of a heavy vehicle, and a weak crackle of static broke through the soldier's radio He muttered into it, then bolted, tearing up the street as if the hounds of hell were snapping at his heels.

'Stupid bastard,' Caitlin muttered, shaking her head as she stormed back to the kitchen. She should've screamed. Why the hell hadn't she screamed? Why should she care what happened to a bloody Brit?!

She slumped at the kitchen table, crying sore, feeling like the kitchen walls were closing in around her. Then, after a long moment, she looked up.

Majella stood in the doorway, groggy from a tablet-induced sleep, her mind still clouded. Without a word, Caitlin rose and pulled her into a much-needed hug, and they held on to each other, sighing together as Majella stroked her daughter's hair and offered soft, comforting words, giving Caitlin a brief sense of peace amid the whirlwind of her thoughts.

A short time later, Majella groaned as she surveyed the untidy kitchen. Caitlin had come home late from work the previous night and hadn't cleaned up. Deep inside, Majella heard a voice telling her she needed to pull herself together. Somehow, she had to try and be the mother she used to be.

'I've left you both in it, haven't I? I'm so sorry, love. I wanted to disappear. I'll try to sort meself out, promise.' They hugged again.

'I've got loads to tell you, Mammy.' Excited to share the latest, Caitlin's words came out in a rush. 'My new job. It's brilliant, more money and today's payday.' Majella wasn't even sure what day of the week it was. Friday and payday? Thank God. Maybe she could get a wee naggin later. She forced some enthusiasm.

'That's great, love. How about you tell me about it over a cuppa later?' She looked up at the clock. 'You'd better start getting ready.' Running a hand distractedly through her greasy hair, Majella hurried to find some aspirin – her head felt like it was about to explode.

On the way to work, Caitlin decided she'd set aside a little of her wages to buy some fabric and make a skirt and blouse on their old Singer sewing machine. With this meeting coming up, she'd need something decent to wear.

Anne, linking arms with her as soon as they met, ranted about some man she'd met who'd tried to slip the hand on their first date. Caitlin dutifully laughed but wasn't really with her, her thoughts running between this and that. Now that her mother was out of bed, she wondered if she might help with the sewing. She'd been a brilliant seamstress once, having worked in a factory before she married. She'd taught Caitlin loads about dressmaking, though Caitlin was nowhere near as good.

After saying goodbye to Anne in Rocola's main entrance, Caitlin headed up to the fifth floor, where she met James. He looked terrific and, as usual, smelled of expensive aftershave. The man's wardrobe seemed endless, with a constant rotation of smart suits, ties, and classic shoes that obviously cost a mint.

He smiled and opened the office door for her to pass through first. Caitlin had managed to cool down her swollen eyes before leaving the house, but James noticed her pale face and asked if she was okay. She assured him she was fine, maybe a little tired.

She watched him throughout the day, blushing every time he caught her, an amused look never far from his face. She was loving this job and, oddly enough, missed him whenever he wasn't around. Sometimes, he'd phone in while out meeting clients, and she relished the sound of his accent – reminding her of that lovely actor Sean Connery.

They were in his office later that day when she heard James cry, 'Caitlin. Earth to Caitlin!' He grinned at her mortified expression. He'd been talking away to her, and she hadn't heard a word he'd said.

'God, sorry, I was away there. What was that?' she asked, flustered. James was beginning to worry; from the sound of her she had a million plates spinning at once. She was clever enough, but with the pressure he was under he hadn't time to babysit, though he knew he'd need to keep an eye on her.

'I was saying, now we've got the invite list sorted. We need to set a date to meet.'

'Yeah, of course. Any preference on which hotel, and when?' Caitlin asked. For the first time, she sensed a flicker of impatience from James, and she knew she'd need to watch herself. He watched her closely as he considered his choices.

'City Hotel maybe? It's central and secure.' He then took a brief pause.

'Yeah, that'll do. Let's try to organise it for early next month. Call them. We'll need a private room for 40 or so guests,' then added, 'and definitely a round table. I want to look each and every one of them in the eye.'

That was all for now, and Caitlin was half way to her desk when she had an idea. 'James. I'm thinking, if I phone the hotel today, I can drop in and pick up more information tomorrow. I have to go into town anyway.'

'Perfect. Maybe they can show you a couple of conference rooms while you're at it. Thanks, Caitlin.' he said, offering her a smile.

James was fired up at how his plan was taking shape. He'd spent weeks meeting with as many businessmen and women in the city as possible. All were as keen as he was to be involved, knowing full well what was at stake.

To Caitlin's delight, her mother was sitting in the kitchen that evening as Caitlin got home and proudly showed off her payslip. 'I still can't believe it, Mammy. Look, £5 extra. That'll help, big time.'

Majella had kept to her promise. She'd bathed, washed her hair, and put on some fresh clothes, but a veil of sadness still clung to her. Caitlin suspected she might have taken some pills, but in reality, Majella had found some leftover whiskey well hidden and forgotten in the hot press. All the same, Caitlin saw it as a positive – at least she was trying. Wasn't lying in her bed. Wasted.

Majella picked up Caitlin's payslip with a wide grin. 'I'm dead chuffed for you, love, you're so good. Keep a bit for yourself and grab some material? We'll whip up something nice for work, eh?' Caitlin had told her little about the meeting but couldn't help mentioning that she'd soon be mixing with some VIPs.

'Funny you should say that, I was about you ask you the same,' she replied.

'Anne's coming to town with me tomorrow. Told her I'd treat her to tea and cake in Austins. I'll have a look at some fabric too.'

Majella smiled. The last thing she felt like doing was getting the sewing machine out, but the thought was there, whether it happened or not was another matter.

'Good girl. Anne'll love that. Oh, by the way, me mother rang. Full of excuses about why she didn't come to your da's funeral. Barely let me get a word in,' she added, shaking her head.

'Started giving off about your poor da, him not cold in his grave.'

At that moment, Tina walked in but paused at the kitchen door way. She gave Caitlin a warm smile, her eyes full of apology.

'Sorry for bein' such a pain in the arse this mornin'. You've been brilliant. I know you're doin' your best and I haven't helped, have I?' Her unexpected show of remorse took Caitlin unaware.

'Awe, thanks. Worried about you, that's all.' She reached for her pay packet, pulled out a few small coins, and handed them over.

'There you go. That's the money from your returns and a bit over.' Tina was chuffed, she hadn't expected that.

'Ah, great. Thanks! I'll go give the moron his share,' she called, already diving into the under-stairs cupboard for her coat. A moment later she shot out the front door, tossing a quick goodbye over her shoulder.

Caitlin and Majella exchanged a look and burst out laughing - relief more than anything. Tina's moods flipped like a switch these days, and you never knew which version of her you'd get in the morning. The rest of the night passed in peace, mother and daughter catching up like old times.

Chapter Twenty-Two

Blighs Lane Compound

V al came whistling over to Rob's bunk, grinning away despite the bandaged hand and gashed cheek – souvenirs from the missiles lobbed at them on a recent patrol.

They were worn out, fed up to the back teeth after eighteen-hour shifts with no proper kip. All the more reason Rob found Val's good mood suspicious. Standing there like a goon, right next to the bunk and grinning to himself, told Rob his mate was hiding something. He kept his own face straight, pretending not to care.

Val wasn't fooled; he knew Rob was dying to know what was occurring, could see the curiosity eating him alive. So he played it out, standing there in silence, letting him stew. *Smug sod.*

Rob kept his eyes on his book, but his curiosity irritated him, fierce and unrelenting. In the end he cracked, slammed the book down and grabbed Val, trying to spin him round.

'Go on then, spit it out. You're killin' me !' he cried, caught between laughter and frustration.

Val shrugged, playing dumb, and stepped back three or four paces, arms in the air as if innocent. 'Spit what out?' He couldn't help laughing either.

Rob jabbed a finger at him. 'Don't play daft. I know you inside out. You're up to something. What is it?'

Just like in a spy movie, Val dramatically glanced around to see if anyone was listening. He tiptoed back to the top bunk, leaned in close, and whispered into Robbie's ear in the worst German accent imaginable:

'It iz like zis... I haf ze *top secret informashun*... but 'ow can I be sure zat I can truzzt you, ja?'

The eejit was off his head. Rob picked up his book and smacked Val on the bandaged hand, laughing despite himself.

Val leapt back, clutching his chest like he'd been mortally wounded, outrage written all over his face. He thrust his bandaged hand in the air again and cried in his dreadful German accent, 'You dare torture me? I vill tell you nuzzing! I die first!' Then he staggered a step and slapped a hand to his heart as if the bullet had just struck.

They howled until Val moved back to Rob. Dropping the German accent; he nudged him.

'Listen, Robbie, you're not to take the mick, but I've gone and got mesel' a proppa lass. A date like.' Rob was gobsmacked. With all the hours they'd been putting in, how the heck had Val met someone and where?

Straightening up, he shuddered at the ache that shot through him from his run-in with the rioters too. Curious, he tossed his book to the bottom of his bunk for later. This was no ordinary thing. Val's usual cheeky self would bolt like the wind when a lass paid him any notice or, worse, tried to talk to him. Banter came easy till it didn't with Val - one minute confident, the next a right awkward sod. Rob had seen it a million times. His marra was hopeless when it came to chatting up women.

'Right. You've got my full attention,' he said, placing a hand on his heart. Val knew his marra should be chuffed for him, yet somehow, it hurt to see the look of surprise on his face.

'Don't look so surprised,' he said with a chuckle. 'Remember when we were all set to hit the Lighthouse for a few pints a while back, but you had to bail?' Rob remembered all right. The captain's last-minute request still peeved him off.

'Aye, I had to cover for that gobshite Morris.' Once again, their unpopular colleague had landed himself in bother, and Rob ended up stuck with his unit for a couple of weeks while Morris was under investigation.

'Yeah, well, since you left me high and dry, I headed off with a few of the fellas. Place was packed, and we were on the Guinness – pure beltas like.' It'd taken him a few painful days to recover.

'Anyway, next thing this gorgeous blonde comes over to us and starts chattin' me up.'

Val gave a playful shrug and pointed to himself, feigning surprise. 'I mean, seriously. She's all over me, right, like a rash. You've no idea. The lass. She's something else. The bazooms on her... Robbie boy. Nivver seen anythin' like it.' He opened and closed his fists against his chest and rolled his eyes. Rob laughed so hard it hurt.

Then, in a more serious tone, Val continued. 'Seen her a few times since. I'm takin' her somewhere special next. Maybe that fancy French place in the Waterside. I, my friend, have got it bad. She's nice. Genuine, you know? I like her.'

Rob recalled the teenager's tarring and feathering, and the officers' warnings about mixing with local girls. When the army first came to Northern Ireland, it riled the Londonderry men, furious at soldiers approaching and courting their women.

He didn't want to dampen Val's enthusiasm, so asked discreetly, 'She's from Londonderry then, is she?'

Val understood what Robbie was getting at and reassured him, jabbing his finger for emphasis.

'I know what you're thinkin'. Knew you'd ask. She's cleared security, no problem.' With that, he flew into his bottom bunk, cursing as he landed on his injured hand.

Not wanting to be a spoil sport, but with a note of caution, Rob reminded him, 'Gan canny, Val. Remember that poor lass. The one who got tarred and feathered?'

'Yeah, yeah, yeah, Mam,' came the reply from the lower bunk.

Val sighed, all dreamy-like, letting his imagination run riot. He was counting the days till he saw her again. The jugs on that girl! He near blushed at the thought.

Above him, Rob reached for his book and tried to read it but soon found it hard to concentrate. He lay back and closed his eyes. Good on ye, Val. He couldn't wait to check out the lass with the 'huge bazooms' and chuckled to himself.

It had been a shitty day. The 'aggro' weather hadn't helped. A clear sky with a warm autumnal sun meant there would inevitably be trouble. Fair weather always brought out the rioters.

In addition, Rob had received a phone call from his family the night before. As always, it took a lethal amount of energy and concentration for him to stay upbeat. Except, Tracey's voice sounded down this time. Not her usual cheerful self. He kept asking what was wrong, but she insisted she was fine. She wasn't; he knew it. The call had been a waste; he realised. Most of his ten minutes had gone on trying to suss her out, and he came off the line miserable and none the wiser.

After that, it went from bad to worse. That morning they'd been on their first mobile patrol as part of a supply run to the RUC's Blighs Lane compound- an armoured base crammed with nearly 115 soldiers just to protect and support two RUC men and a handful of Royal Military Police.

It made no sense to him or Val, and to think they'd two weeks of running back and forth to look forward to. The fortified site stood on a steep hill leading up to the notorious Creggan Estate, where gun law prevailed. To one side was Stones Corner, the scene of the worst riots orchestrated by the men, teenage boys and girls who gathered to throw stones or petrol bombs at the compound and patrols. To the right stood the main entrance to Rocola, a shirt factory.

The compound was ringed with four sangars, the army's eyes and ears, feeding back whatever moved in the 'real' world outside. Directly behind and too close for comfort, loomed rows of terraced houses – snug cover and perfect firing points for Republican gunmen. A sniper's dream.

Triangular concrete blocks and barbed wire ringed the compound. Inside, rubble, dead trees, and burned-out buses, lorries, and cars cluttered the space – a scrapyard of chaos, built from anything rioters could get their hands on to form barricades. Sappers from the Royal Engineers cleared it day in, day out with Centurion tanks, their cannons swapped for bulldozer blades. Dragged back into the compound, the scrap vehicles were left useless, the same relentless, demoralising cycle of destruction and cleanup playing out again and again.

The Stones Corner rioters were mostly bored youths, angry at everything and fuelled by the new curfews. They hammered the stronghold daily. Any barricade the army cleared was replaced overnight with another. Why? Because the Republicans were determined to choke off supplies to the compound. They didn't stop them often, but they sure made things difficult while trying.

At their usual briefing, Rob's unit was told to be extra cautious. With the schools shut, kids were bound to be on the streets, and only days earlier a five-year-old Catholic girl had been run down and killed by a Pig. Tensions were running high. It meant they couldn't tear through built-up streets, going slow made them easier targets. Either way, the risk was great.

When the flak-vested unit rolled out from the fortified maintenance base – once a submarine depot by the River Foyle – they braced for the ten-minute run and the inevitable hail of abuse, petrol bombs, and whatever else waited at the other end.

Soft-topped vehicles were useless, so the convoy relied on armoured carriers to haul the supplies. On one Pig, a private had daubed the word *Woodstock* across the front. It led the way, carrying everything from ammunition, riot guns, rubber bullets, and CS gas to boxes of food and drink. Whatever was needed.

The atmosphere inside the Pig was charged, stifling and claustrophobic. The sergeant did a radio check and raised the door visor to look around before he screamed over its roaring engine.

'Good to go. Okay, lads, let's get this over with.'

The noise had been deafening as the convoy approached the compound. Rob and Val sat side by side and held fast to their fibreglass shields. Their uncomfortable hard helmets with visors strapped under their chins added to their discomfort. No one tried to talk and it didn't take long before a torrent of missiles smashed against the half-inch-thick steel body of the armoured vehicle.

Instinctively, everyone ducked. Rob squinted through the slit on the side of the Pig and glimpsed the packs of youths throwing bricks and petrol bombs and screaming filthy abuse. The vehicle accelerated and sped closer to the complex like it wanted to get there too, quickly. In support, the riot guns from the fortified sangar above shot rubber bullets and CS gas into the angry crowd to push it back and allow the convoy to enter.

At the compound gates, the reek of cordite burned their eyes and throats. Rob and Val bailed out and sprinted forward to help force the heavy armoured gate open. Helmets and shields were all they had against the choking smoke and flying missiles. The moment the mob spotted them, the aim shifted. Stones and bottles came raining down, turning the two Geordies into soft targets. Shouts of rage rose as bare hands and bodies took the blows, the pair straining to heave the gates wide.

The moment they creaked open, Rob and Val fell back, letting the roaring Pigs thunder through. Once inside, along with a few others, they dragged the gates shut and quickly bolted them, heads low in case a sniper had the range. Breathless, and chests heaving, they crouched in the shadows and waited for the signal from the sangars to move. Only with the all-clear did they dare take a step.

The rest of the day was spent unloading and sorting the supplies until they left under the relative cover of darkness. They were met with some resistance and hostility at the exit, but it was nothing like before.

Val, with his usual sense of timing, tried to lift his mates' spirits over the roar of the Pig, pulling faces and cracking jokes as missiles clattered against the armour. The lads were worn out from the day, and they welcomed his efforts, glad of anything that might hurry the ride back to safety.

Tomorrow they'd face it all again, and if luck turned against them, they were fucked.

Chapter Twenty-Three

Shipquay Street

I
t was Saturday again, a welcome relief since Caitlin had tossed and turned all night. Recurring nightmares about her daddy's arrest and its aftermath had left her exhausted.

When morning came, she was thankful, said a quick, half-hearted prayer, and got up. These days, praying was tough. She didn't want to be angry with God, but she was. Extremely.

No doubt Anne would cheer her up. Caitlin loved their trips up town. She drew back the curtains to a bright, sunny morning – a welcome change. As she inspected the back garden, she remembered the hidden soldier and, becoming conscious that the house could still be under surveillance, swiftly closed the curtains.

That morning, the McLaughlin women cleaned the house from top to bottom. It needed it.

Afterwards, they grabbed some Campbell's tinned tomato soup for lunch before Tina skedaddled off to God knows where. Caitlin got ready to leave for town.

A few good shops remained in the city centre, along with the city's only department store. *Austins*. It was a lovely old building, with its creaky wooden staircase and rasping caged lift – the oldest independent department store in the world.

Caitlin loved walking through the main doors, greeted by the aroma of perfume. The girls behind the counters were always smart and perfectly made up. Unlike many, neither she nor Anne felt intimidated when browsing the store. They'd spend ages going through the rails, both well-known and liked by the friendly staff.

Another favourite of theirs was the tiny, dark-red-painted boutique, *She,* at the bottom of Pump Street, around the corner from Austins. Owned by two funky sisters who visited London to bring back the latest fashions to Derry. It was trendy, for sure, but well expensive for most, though they offered credit to the numerous factory girls.

Caitlin waited for Anne at the top of Shipquay Street, one of the four main roads within the walled city. In the sunshine, she admired the ancient oak trees on the steep hill and the small square at the top, known as The Diamond. Home to an impressive 1927 WWI memorial, designed by English sculptor Vernon March. Several bombed-out shops along the square were boarded up or lay in ruins.

Anne was uncharacteristically late, so Caitlin passed the time watching a load of Brits patrol the hill. Ignored by most passers-by, they moved along the street like ghosts. She eyed the patrol, thinking the Brit from her backyard might be one of them. He wasn't, but she was knocked out to recognise the Irish soldier who'd struck her.

He saw her, gave her a nod, then flicked his top lip suggestively with his tongue. Disgusted, she turned her back on him. *Creep.*

The sight of him made her skin crawl, and the wave of revulsion that swept through her brimmed with a vicious, simmering hate. For a fleeting moment, she even toyed with the idea of challenging him. But as her resolve hardened, a girl's voice rang out, cutting through her thoughts. Anne – *thank goodness.*

Caitlin watched her friend climb the hill with exaggerated breaths, playing the total gack. A right sight in her high red stilettos, full yellow skirt, matching turtleneck jumper, and a red scarf tied at the side of her neck. Classic 1950s.

As soon as she reached the top, she extended her hands theatrically and gasped, 'Jesus wept. That hill's gonna kill me one day!'

Accentuating her Derry accent, Caitlin laughed and said, 'It's them fags. Bloody Woodbines.' With a flourish she raised her hand, drawing on an imaginary cigarette as if it were the finest smoke she'd ever had, cheeks hollowing as she took in a long drag before blowing it out in a grand puff.

Anne knew she should quit, but sure, they helped curb her appetite.

'I know, I know, but where else do I get *any* satisfaction these days, eh?' She winked mischievously, hinting at her recent dry spell of a decent date and sex.

'Right then, smart arse, since you're in the money, where you takin' me? More importantly, I'm dyin' to hear about this Adonis boss of yours.' Her not-so-subtle nickname for James Henderson.

As Caitlin opened her mouth to speak, a blinding flash and a deafening boom absorbed her words. A volley of scalding hot air blasted into her, lifting her clean off her feet and throwing her against a boarded-up window of a nearby shop. Stunned, she lay still as a strange, numbing sensation crept over her. Then darkness consumed everything, once more.

Chapter Twenty-Four

The London Guests

James loved his weekends. A few friends from London had arrived at Melrose the previous night after a weary drive through the Sperrin Mountains from Antrim Airport, some sixty or so miles away.

Melrose, a beautiful house by any measure, had been turned into something more than grand, almost enchanting for a black-tie event. The hallway sparkled beneath its familiar strings of tiny white fairy lights, but with the addition of great vases of white roses and hydrangeas freshly cut from Aunt Jocelyn's garden, the air carried both fragrance and elegance that seemed to float in every corner. The housekeeper, joined by the hired help brought in for the evening, had shifted the dining table aside and set a buffet along one wall, and with the sliding doors thrown wide the room opened into a broad space where impeccably dressed guests drifted between the temporary dance floor or gathered in clusters to talk and laugh.

A lavish spread of food was laid out on silver platters, lobster, oysters, and crab piled high beside crystal wine glasses that caught the soft light and sparkled. Ice buckets brimmed with bottles of Dom Pérignon and white Burgundy, already chilled and waiting to be poured, while decanters of Châteauneuf-du-Pape were placed at intervals around the room, ready for the waiters and waitresses who moved quietly among the guests, topping up glasses without ever breaking the flow of conversation.

Before the party had even started, James heard a tap on his bedroom door. He brushed down his trousers and called, 'Come in.'

Looking elegant in his time worn black dinner suit, his uncle peeked around the door and entered, carrying a cut-crystal tumbler filled with a generous pour of whiskey. James waved him toward a chair. Roger sat and took a mouthful of Bushmills, his favourite.

'Nearly ready?' he asked.

'Yeah. You?' James replied with a warm smile.

'Tired and getting drunk. Don't know why I bother with these blasted parties, never enjoy them. There's fifty-odd down there, decided I'd get a few in beforehand. Dutch courage, 'suppose. Heard you've been working all hours.'

He chuckled, lifted his glass in a salute, and knocked back another slug of whiskey before adding, 'Well done.' James felt a surge of affection for his uncle as he sat on the edge of the bed and said.

'It's been a busy few weeks all right, but my biggest worry is the workers safety. We're sitting right between that humongous RUC compound and Stones Corner. The rioting's endless. It's time we came up with a security plan.' Roger was aware already and feared his employees getting caught in the middle of it all.

'I know, son. I've been thinking the same for some time.' James was eager to share his ideas.

'This curfew around the Bogside and Creggan worries me, too. If we change shifts, the women won't be able to get to or from work. I read today that the army closed the cinema for three months. I imagine half the problem is that the teenagers are bored stiff. What else is there for them to do other than riot? I mean, what if—'

'Bugger!'

Roger had somehow spilled a good slosh of whiskey on his trousers. He didn't give James a chance to finish, but kept talking as he dabbed at the stain.

'Mark my words, it's going to get worse, way worse, I don't see an end to it. The RUC doesn't trust the army, and the army doesn't trust the RUC. No pleasing either. I've said to George something needs to be done. No one trusts anyone these days.' Roger's voice rose as his outburst continued. James had never seen him so worked up.

'I love this country, but I'm at a loss. Do you know a bomb went off today on Shipquay Street? The UVF are blaming the Provos, and the Provos are blaming the UVF. Turns out it *was* the UVF all along. They've been deliberately carrying out bombings and blaming the Provos to stir things up. In my eyes, one's as bad as the other.'

James could see the whiskey was taking its toll on Roger, who slurred. 'And... and listen to this.' He peered into his glass and saw it was empty. 'Damn.' He rose unsteadily, hobbling towards the door before glancing back at his nephew.

'You remember that bomb that went off before? The one in the tea shop where that wee girl got killed? Know how they did it?' He paused, his voice lowering.

'Hid the explosives in a bike frame. Inside the hollow bit. Genius, but deadly. So many innocent lives lost, and for what?' He shook his head, a deep sadness overshadowing his eyes. 'Breaks my heart.'

James could see Roger was getting himself all upset and walked over to pat his shoulder. 'Come on you, try not to get upset.'

His uncle hung his head and murmured dejectedly, 'Can't help it. This Darlington conference is a washout too. No one seems to have the sense to sit and talk. It'll be civil war next.' James prayed it was the whiskey talking.

'Don't be thinking that way. It'll be fine. I know it's tough at the moment, but it'll be fine.'

Roger half-smiled and scoffed. 'I'll head on down. There is one last thing. I know the discussion is inevitable, especially after a few of our friends have a jar or two tonight, but let's keep politics out of it and have a good evening. I've depressed myself enough as it is. Can I count on you to smooth things over?'

'Course you can. Leave it to me,' James replied. Conscious of the time, he tried to steer his uncle towards the door, but Roger wasn't quite done.

'You're right about the factory. Security's more important now than ever. We've landed that Glasgow order and can't afford any more delays.'

James barely caught the next part as Roger mumbled, 'If we lose that, son, we're finished. All of us.' Then, as if something had only come to him, he turned to his nephew, wagging a finger.

'How's that wee girl working out for you?' Once more, James didn't get the chance to answer —'Och, and by the way. You've upset Mrs Parkes, ye know that, don't you? That, my lad, is not wise. Not wise at all.'

James knew that. The old bat was something else, watching him and Caitlin with those beady eyes of hers. One way or the other, he'd get rid of her. Soon as.

'I know. Doesn't like me much, does she?' He laughed.

'And the girl? Caitlin,' he added. 'She's doing well. Quick as a whip, but she's had a tough time lately. Turns out her father was Patrick McLaughlin. You know, the man who died in custody?'

Roger nodded. 'Ah, yeah. Sad that. Good man, I hear. Word is he wasn't involved at all. Poor critter's ticker gave up. Has a son inside, I believe. High up in the Provos. Dangerous fella.' He pointed a finger at James in warning.

'Careful with that girl, James. I'm all for fair play, but you're still green about how things work here. Londonderry's a far cry from Oxford.'

James was shocked. Caitlin had never once mentioned a brother, never mind one banged up, and a Provo at that. It threw him, yet lately she'd been slipping into his mind more and more. Running, driving, lying in bed – there she was, drifting through his thoughts when he least expected it. None of it made sense. He hardly knew the girl, yet...

Once dinner was over, James stood in the dining room surrounded by his London guests and, to his dismay, Charles Jones. To his left was the lovely widow, Mrs Kerry Brookes, an old family friend. James knew she'd been in love with his father for years, though James Snr remained blinded to her overtures. More than once he'd tried to tell him, but his father would wave him away in impatience. At times, James wondered if the old man still harboured hope that his mother might return. Doubtful, he thought, but then again his father never spoke about his private life.

John King, an ambitious, fresh-faced, up-and-coming Westminster politician, stood to James's right. Opposite him was the gregarious Marleen Fry, whom James adored. She was a year younger than he was and a great friend. Without batting an eye, his father and Roger said they would welcome her as a daughter-in-law. But alas, fate had other plans.

With that smile of hers and a glint of mischief in her eye, she'd once told James, 'Darling boy, you're simply not my type. Truth is, I've a bit of a taste for the fairer sex. If you catch my drift.' He loved her forthrightness, but sad to say, she wasn't far from the odious Jones –

his wine glass, as usual, filled to the brim. James watched as she spoke to Jones in an unapologetic English accent.

'Gosh, I do enjoy Londonderry, Mr Jones. Mind you, what's going on at the moment is absolutely dreadful. I can't understand what the fuss is all about. Could someone explain it to me, *please*?' She glanced around the group, all innocence, then locked eyes with James, waiting for him to step in. James remembered his uncle's earlier request.

Taking her arm, he suggested. 'Not tonight, Marleen. It's complicated and I've promised Roger we won't talk politics on such a beautiful evening. I'll tell all tomorrow. A walk on the beach, perhaps?' But Jones had other ideas.

'No, no, no,' he cried. 'Absolutely not!' He glared at Marleen, his eyes wide and him well-oiled.

'Young lady, I'll tell you "what the fuss is all about." It's all about control and keeping those Fenian bastards in their place.' James attempted to interject, standing before Marleen to protect her.

'Charles, please. Not now. I insist. You're a guest in my uncle's home, and he wishes that we all enjoy a relaxing evening by avoiding such sensitive subjects.' Astonishingly, Marleen pulled him back.

'Darling James,' she pleaded, 'please, I want to know. Let Mr Jones speak. I mean, people back home read the papers and watch the news, but we don't get it. *I* don't get it, and let's be honest, we see and hear about these ghastly things, and now that I'm here, I'd like to understand why.'

James' stare was met with a triumphant smile from Jones. Their eyes locked as the Ulsterman took a deliberate sip of his wine, savouring the moment before turning to Marleen.

'Well, it's a rather long story,' he began, his tone light but calculated.

'To make it clear, I'll explain the basics. By we, I mean us, you know, people like me and you. Loyalists, Unionists, Protestants. Call it what you will. Protestants who believe that Republicans and Nationalist Catholics are inherently disloyal to our queen and country. They're determined to force us into a united Ireland, whether or not we like it. And to do it, they're breeding like rabbits to boost their voting numbers. I must say, Rome hasn't discouraged them, have they? Always urging them to have more sprogs. Maybe they should be neutered!' He laughed, pleased with his own joke. Then he continued in a disgusted tone.

'Take this, for example, some of them women have up to fourteen or fifteen of the little brats. Revolting. And are any of their men working? No! But they're taking government benefits and the like. The same government they hate so much. Not only are they asking us to give them our hard earned money, they're asking us to build them free houses so they can fill them up with mini Papists.' He gulped more wine, oblivious to the reaction of the onlookers, who stood in stunned silence.

'And now... and now there's talk of power-sharing. Power-sharing, my arse! And talk of something like a Council of Ireland. I don't think so. Why should we share what is already ours with those southern Fenians? Sir Craig was right!'

Jones swung around as he theatrically recited, '"All I boast is that we are a Protestant Parliament in a Protestant state." The British government has failed us. Betrayed us! They are weak and should be ashamed. I say, No surrender!'

With that, the portly man thrust his fist triumphantly into the air. His wine glass slipped from his grasp, shattering on the parquet floor. Slivers of glass and remnants of red wine sprayed onto Marleen's immaculate silk white dress.

She searched for a napkin to wipe them off as the room went as quiet as a cemetery. James was furious at her for not listening, when he'd tried to head her off. He got even angrier at Jones for ruining the evening with his outrageous statements.

Aware of the abrupt silence, Jones coyly placed his raised hand back by his side. The other guests remained hushed and bewildered as a few waiters picked up the broken glass, and someone handed Marleen napkins to wipe her ruined dress.

Like everyone else, James stood still, stunned by Jones's sheer, unapologetic hatred. He'd always struggled to grasp the complexities of the Troubles. As a child, holidays at Melrose were nothing more than carefree days spent roaming the countryside, revelling in its beauty. Perhaps, he admitted, he had shunned political realities – a subconscious choice, since they had never affected him.

But Jones's venomous words had shattered that peace, dragging their grim realities into their home. His uncle's fears now felt tangible. With such deep-seated hatred festering among people, and men like Jones feeding it, Roger was right – civil war could be inevitable. John King came to the rescue.

'Charles, with respect, I find your tirade offensive, not only to Catholics but to our government. As a gentleman, I refuse to comment on your defamation of Catholics and Rome since we have ladies present. I will, however, add that I am a practising Catholic myself.'

James didn't know that. What an evening this was turning out to be! He listened as King continued.

'Nonetheless, you must remember that Direct Rule had to be enforced. It was, I admit, intended to be a temporary measure. However, with Stormont's failure to contain the security situation and the escalation of violence, we had no choice. As to the Unionists, they weren't prepared to allow the Nationalists to protest. Although I may add, they were well within their democratic rights to do so. Peacefully.'

Jones appeared stumped by John King's revelations. The politician continued, uninterrupted.

'The government first opposed internment. But again, you Unionists, well... you insisted. How many times has Stormont introduced internment over the years? Four, five? Maybe even more? And has it ever worked? No. What it has done, sir, is create a catastrophe for this country, which I believe will take years – decades even – to resolve. By the end of this year, they say nearly five hundred people will have died here. Five hundred. Think about that.'

King sighed. 'Now, I won't continue with this line of talk. We're guests in this beautiful home, and James here is, quite rightly, keen for us to enjoy the evening. Enough said, I think?' He noticed the flicker of approval in James's expression as the young man clapped him on the back and exclaimed.

'Well said, sir!' That'll show you, Jones, you bigoted bastard, James mused.

Charles Jones kept quiet in his fury, his eyes near to popping out of his red, chubby face, the picture of a man unused to being crossed. Perhaps he'd overdone it, he thought. This wasn't the Orange Lodge with its usual clapping and nodding audience, the place where his every word was taken as gospel. Still, he had plenty to get off his chest, and with the full confidence of a man who believed himself the most important in the room, he had just begun to lean towards King, ready to deliver his wisdom, when that upstart prick Henderson cut across him, raising his voice in a merry call to his blonde girlfriend as if Jones hadn't said a word.

'Right, that's enough of that,' James said, his tone light, a touch of mischief running through it.

'Time for some fun. Marleen, care to dance? Unless of course you'd rather slip away and change first?' She glanced down at the wine stain, then back up at him with a wicked little smile, as if daring him to care.

'Darling, it's only wine. Adds character.' She looped her arm through his and followed him onto the dance floor, both of them laughing like teenagers.

John King and Mrs Brookes drifted away from Jones, who stood rigid and smouldering, his eyes darting about in search of a waiter as he drained his glass.

'Oi, you, here — more wine!' he cried, grabbing the nearest one.

Chapter Twenty-Five

Apocalypse

After a few attempts, Caitlin opened her dust-filled eyes. Her head rang as she lay flat on her back, looking up. Dust swirled, filling the air, and the sound of screaming voices confused her. She couldn't understand what they were saying and touched her ringing ears to find them sticky with blood.

With great effort, she pulled herself halfway up against a wall. Torn leaves and branches from trees that once lined the street blanketed her body. She strained to brush them off, cringing as splinters of wood and fragments of glass dug deeper into her legs. Her bloodied, dusty, dry lips stung as she licked them.

Smashed and broken like a rag doll flung across a room, a ferocious pain overwhelmed her. Dazed, she took in the surrounding devastation. Her throat burned, and a relentless din, like the clamour of ringing bells, swirled in her head, leaving her on the brink of nausea. The noise was muffled, distant, yet somehow deafening all at once, the dull ding echoing in her ears. She wanted to cry, to move, to do something, but the strength simply wasn't there.

A fire raged behind the broken windows of the bank. Flames snaked in and out of the building's shattered windows and doors. White paper flew up like a stream of kites, drifting to the ground. Bikes once attached to railings lay further along the street, bent and twisted. A fireball blasted through a shop window with a loud boom. Disoriented, people wandered about observing the scene, shrieking in terror. It was an apocalyptic sight.

Soldiers with scorched hair and charred faces checked the motionless bodies that lay scattered across the square for signs of life. Ambulance crews and RUC men walked among torn limbs and other body parts like butcher's meat that lay scattered across the pavement and road amid deadly shards of glass. A small car had smashed into the gilded wooden windows of *Austins* and was jammed halfway into the shop, draped in rails of clothes and mannequins. Two lifeless bodies sprawled awkwardly, half inside and half outside the shattered windscreen of the car.

Caitlin couldn't believe what was in front of her – the body parts, the blood, the carnage. *Was she in hell?* Her hands shook excessively and her teeth chattered. The street was cluttered, with everything from window frames to office furniture. Curtains flew free and high from ruined apartments above the shops. Then she remembered. *Anne.* With great effort she tried to stand, but fell straight back down again.

Her eyes were so dry, they burned and in a rasping voice, she cried, 'Anne. Where are you, Anne?'

Caitlin scanned the debris and bodies for a glimpse of her friend, fortunately, after a while, she spotted something red and familiar. Though she gritted her teeth, she recoiled in horror from what she saw: a lone, blood-stained red stiletto.

She tried to heave herself into a semi-sitting position, then croaked, 'Anne. *Please.'*

The sound of ambulance bells and injured people screaming went on and on. This wasn't right. Light-headed and drowsy, she shook her head, fighting to stay alert. The pain throbbed, the ringing in her ears driving her crazy.

She forced out one last cry. 'Anne!' Her eyes grew heavier, and her head began to droop. She needed to sleep; her body taking charge. But then, by some miracle, she heard a faint voice.

'Caitlin, is that you?'

'Yeah, Anne, it's me. Keep talking!'

Silence. Panic rising, Caitlin yelled as much as she could, 'Anne!' An eternity seemed to stretch before she heard Anne again.

'Over here, Caitlin. I'm here...' Her voice was weak but steady.

Caitlin strained to listen, her eyes darting around until they locked onto a bloodied scrap of yellow fabric, close to Anne's shoe, jutting out from a heap of red bricks and twisted railings.

Suddenly, a hand grabbed her, and a shocked voice exclaimed, 'No way, Caitlin McLaughlin. What the heck?!'

After all she'd been through these past weeks, Caitlin had done her best to bottle it up, to keep sane, push on, but the moment she saw Kathy she lost it, the dam inside her gave way, and she broke, letting it all spill.

Kathy couldn't understand how her cousin survived being so close to the centre of the blast. Her coat and blouse were shredded, her jeans torn and singed. Heat had left her hair sticky, ensnared with paper and twigs. Yet, she didn't appear to have any life-threatening injuries. She was so shocked that her hands and teeth were going crazy.

'I don't believe this!' Kathy cried.

Caitlin smiled with heartfelt gratitude. She'd never seen her cousin so dishevelled, her clothes streaked with dust, but in that moment, she was nothing short of extraordinary. A miraculous sight.

'You're going to be okay, love,' Kathy murmured in a soothing voice. 'We'll soon get you outta here. I'm just going—'

'Kathy, no!' Caitlin grabbed her arm, her voice urgent as she gestured towards Anne. 'Over there. Anne's hurt. Look. There! See that
red shoe and that yellow bit?'

Caitlin pointed to the pile of rubble and screeched, 'Anne. Kathy's
here. She's coming!'

Anne burst into tears, half laughing, half coughing. 'There is a God!
Is that the light... Jesus, is that yourself? Is me time up?' she croaked,
forcing a laugh even though her voice shook. Neither of the women
could believe Anne could joke at such a horrific time. But then that
was Anne.

Kathy took in the devastation, then looked at Caitlin like she was
the luckiest girl alive. 'Someone up there's watching over you, love.
Take it slow,' she murmured. Caitlin knew who – her daddy.

'I'll go see Anne. But listen, my partner, Kevin, he'll be here any sec
and take you to the ambulance. Try not to move,' Kathy insisted.

'I don't think I can. I feel a bit sick. Go you to Anne. I'll be grand,'
Caitlin replied weakly, attempting to push Kathy away.

She watched as Kathy scrambled through the slaughter towards the
bloodied shoe, calling Anne. Kathy heard a weak response and stepped
away from the shoe and towards the voice. Ten or so metres later, she
stopped and stooped down.

Anne was nearly buried, only her face and one arm visible in
the rubble. Kathy tore at the debris, desperate to free her, until a
black-suited fireman in a white helmet spotted her. He leapt over to
help, dodging white hosepipes that twisted like sea serpents across
the sodden street. Together, they hauled away stone and brick, both
groaning as they uncovered the jagged piece of iron railing buried deep
in Anne's right leg.

By then, she'd passed out, slumped on her side. Kathy and the
fireman shook their heads and sighed. This wasn't good.

Kathy's partner, Kevin, arrived and went to help Caitlin. Feeling dizzy and nauseous, she stood up after wrapping an arm around his neck. Because she had no choice, she painfully vomited onto the street after pushing him away. Groaning, she steadied herself against a wall and wiped her mouth with the remains of her sleeve.

Kevin waited, then wiped her face with a handkerchief pulled from his silver-buttoned tunic. She assured him she was okay and leaned on him as he guided her to the white ambulance and carefully placed her on the ground against the vehicle's side.

She pushed him away as he tried to assess her, urging him to go, 'Find Kathy. I'm fine.'

The medic nodded. He could see the girl was okay, picked up a red canvas stretcher and left to find Kathy. Caitlin's eyes followed him until she saw the pair talking. Next, they placed Anne carefully on the stretcher. The embedded railing poked out from her bleeding leg, and Caitlin could see the injury was severe.

She trembled as she took in the ruins of the square. The statues on the war memorial lay shattered. Two soldiers were sifting through the debris. One clutched his jaw, blood on his lips – looked like he'd lost a few teeth. Even with his face dusted grey, she knew him. Her assailant. Aside from the missing teeth, he appeared fine. *Pity.*

Once the stretcher party came into view, she forced herself to her feet. A fresh wave of nausea hit and she hobbled out of sight, and by God did she retch, vomiting until her body ached. After a moment, Kevin was at her side, draping a blanket over her shoulders before helping her into the ambulance.

Anne was already on board, her pale face barely visible under a large oxygen mask. Two black straps were fastened over the red blanket that covered her torso but stopped where the railing protruded from her leg. She seemed so tiny and helpless. Kevin offered the girls a brief, comforting smile before pulling the vehicle's double doors shut.

The sound of the ambulance bells reassured them, taking them further and further away from the bloodbath. Every cell in Caitlin's battered body felt paralysed with fear and exhaustion.

Anne remained unconscious for the fifteen-minute journey. Fortunately, the ambulance was waved through any checkpoints. At the hospital, the staff assessed them and swiftly took Anne into theatre. With Caitlin shaking like a leaf, a waiting nurse took her as Kathy and Kevin vanished to drive back to the bomb scene.

Soon enough, Caitlin felt a bit better, and the nausea eased. Her ears had stopped bleeding, but her hearing was still dodgy. Following a quick once-over, the nurse placed her in a chair and said she'd be back in no time. Caitlin waited, but she never came back, and after a while, the need for the toilet forced Caitlin to shuffle to the nearest Ladies'.

Sore from heavy bruising, she used the loo and washed her hands. Her throat burned, prompting her to drink greedily from the tap.

In the mirror, Caitlin's reflection showed her torn, dust-covered checked coat, stubborn twigs and leaves clinging to the fabric. Ripped jeans revealed fragments of glass and bloodied splinters embedded in her legs. With trembling hands, she splashed water on her neck and face, trying to ignore the pain. Sick with worrying about Anne, Caitlin tried to tidy herself up.

In a cubicle, she placed the toilet seat down, carefully pulled down her jeans, and retrieved as many tiny splinters and glass fragments from her legs as she could.

It was the best she could do, so she stepped back into the emergency department and was swallowed by a sea of broken bodies and frantic relatives. Back in the thick of it. *Again*. After the tea-shop bombing and visiting her daddy, she'd never dreamt she'd find herself in this makeshift graveyard so soon.

She found a seat in a quiet corner, as far from the chaos as possible, and tried to make herself invisible. By now, she'd given up – more worried about Anne to care about herself, or anyone else for that matter. She had to close her eyes; they were so heavy. The clock on the wall read 2.30 PM. It felt surreal that she'd been laughing and joking with Anne such a short time ago, watching her taking the piss and breathlessly climbing Shipquay Street. A blur. A distant memory, as if it never happened.

As her eyes closed, a small voice inside wondered: How could life turn so shitty in such a short time? Daddy... and now Anne. Her beautiful friend with her beautiful shoes.

A loud crashing noise jolted Caitlin awake. Disoriented, she struggled to place herself until reality hit her like a train. Her eyes darted to the clock high on the wall: 7.15 PM! At first, her body refused to go anywhere. Hours had passed and she should have phoned home. Her hand searched for her handbag, but the memory of it being blown away in the blast returned. Along with the extra pay stashed in her purse.

Unsteadily, she found a public phone and placed a reverse charge call to the McFaddens. After several rings, Maggie, answered, her voice frightened with worry.

'Hello? Hello... Is that you, Caitlin?!'

'Aye, Maggie. It's me. Sorry, I've had to make a reverse charge.'

'Ah, hen, don't fret about that. Your mammy's been sittin' here with me for ages. We've been worried sick. Thought you were dead, love. Here, look, hold on, she's here,' Maggie cried.

'Caitlin... Caitlin, love? We're frantic here! For God's sake, Caitlin, why didn't you phone before? Where are ye?' Majella cried. Caitlin looked around and replied.

'I'm in Altnagelvin. We were right in the middle of it, Mammy, the bomb on Shipquay Street. But I'm okay. I fell asleep when I got here. A bit sick and shaky, that's all. It's Anne, though. She's caught a chunk of railing in her leg. Been in surgery for ages. Listen, I need someone to run to Anne's house. Tell them what's happened. Her ma'll be in a terrible state if she doesn't know already, and Anne will want her here. Get Emmett to run over, will you and tell them? I'll wait here.'

As she turned, she saw her cousin, Kathy, pointing at the phone and mouthing, 'Is that your mammy? Let me talk to her.' Reluctantly, Caitlin passed her the phone. She'd wanted to make sure Emmett would tell Anne's mammy straight away.

'Majella, it's Kathy. I'm here now with her. She's shaken up but fine. As soon as I'm finished, I'll bring her back. Okay?' Kathy listened for a few seconds and nodded. 'Yeah, right; I'll tell her. She's okay. Promise. Okie dokie, night, night.' Kathy replaced the phone in its cradle, looking like the life had been sucked out of her and drained of energy.

'You're to go right home as soon as Anne's mammy's here. I'll try to take ye. Hopefully, I shouldn't be much longer out there.' She pressed the back of her hand to Caitlin's forehead, scrutinised her eyes, and frowned.

'Has anyone checked you over yet?'

'Not really. I fell asleep over there.' Caitlin replied, pointing to the corner chair. 'Didn't want to be a bother. Even so, I've a cracking headache.' She cautiously rubbed the side of her head. Kathy reckoned her cousin might have a severe concussion and wasn't willing to take any chances – not after the day she'd been through.

She'd worked alongside the fire brigade and the police, helping to gather what was left of the dead. There had been up to ten of them, maybe more, torn apart beyond recognition. Blood soaked the ground, and pieces of bodies, arms, legs, and smaller parts she didn't dare name, were scattered across the wreckage. The screams had gone on for hours, fierce and unrelenting, and she knew those sounds would stay with her for the rest of her life.

This wasn't something she'd simply witnessed. It had wrapped itself around her, sunk into her skin, filled her lungs, and settled in her bones. No matter how much time passed, no matter what she did, it would always be there, deep inside her, refusing to disappear. Still, she had to pull herself together and get Caitlin sorted.

'You look like shit, Caitlin. C'mon, let's get that head of yours checked,' she suggested. Kathy went straight to the check-in desk, disregarding the grumbles from the queue.

Once she'd given Caitlin's details, she led her to the main seating area and asked, 'Can I get you anythin'?'

'No, I'm okay, thanks. What about Anne? I'll die if anything happens to her.'

Kathy sighed. 'I'll see what I can find out.'

She'd be as quick as she could, not wanting to leave her cousin alone, but now coming back, she slowed on approach, unsure how to break the bad news. Inhaling and then blowing through her lips she said.

'Right, I've seen the theatre nurse. The good news is Anne's injuries aren't life-threatening. The bad news is—'

'What? Kathy? Tell me! What—' Caitlin cried as she stood, wobbling from left to right.

Kathy waved her down. 'She'll be okay, but her leg won't. I had a feeling that rail was close to an artery, and I was right. Lost a lot of blood.'

She took Caitlin's hand. 'Sorry, love, but they couldn't save it. They've had to amputate.'

Caitlin sank back into the chair, staring at Kathy in disbelief. It could have been worse, she told herself, Anne could have died, yet the thought of her losing that beautiful leg was devastating for both of them. In her mind she saw her nutty friend again, laughing her head off and taking the piss, teetering about in her batty stilettos, and the image strangled her. A swell of sorrow rose so strong it nearly choked her, her chest heaving with the effort of holding back tears. She was tired of crying, sick of it, and the question hammered in her head - what had they done to deserve this?

What had any of them done?

Chapter Twenty-Six

Flower

When Honey promised Kieran she'd help him set up the soldiers, he'd pulled her into his arms, crying even harder.

At first, he tried to resist her offer, but she was firm – almost fierce – telling him he'd no choice. She loved him. After everything he'd done, she'd be happy to help. Whatever it took.

Things got even better after that. He was more attentive, showering her with love and affection, and couldn't do enough for her. She smiled when thinking of their precious time together. Someone needed her for the first time in her life, and it was magic. He'd changed her world in ways she'd never imagined. Honey was confident now, with a quiet inner strength she never knew she possessed, and her heart swelled with gratitude and love. Kieran had become her everything, her absolute all.

The first time was simple enough. She followed Kieran's plan to the letter, luring the soldier into the car park behind a bar known locally as a watering hole for peelers and Brits. Three dark-clad Provos pounced on him, dragged him away and she'd run straight to Kieran without looking back.

After that, things eased a bit. The next Brit was painfully shy at first but loosened up after a few drinks, and to Honey's surprise, she enjoyed his company. She couldn't persuade him to leave with her that first night; he was too careful. She wasn't going to give up – and she wasn't about to let Kieran down either. She'd kept at it, talking away to him a few more times until he finally asked her to dinner, his eyes leaving no doubt about what he wanted for dessert.

Honey laughed as she glanced in the mirror, her head running through the foolproof plan for the night. Kieran had done her makeup to perfection, and a new dress showed off her figure. It was something else – the soft red fabric swayed with every movement, making it impossible for her not to twirl around the room like a ballerina. Her happiness and feeling of being alive, being loved were so strong that she couldn't help but smile.

Kieran insisted that night that she look elegant and classy, so he carefully fastened a pearl necklace around her neck, his fingers slowly running down her skin. With a gentle kiss to the nape of her neck, he sent shivers through her, leaving her breathless with joy and excitement.

Honey adored his flat and had deliberately left a few personal bits and pieces about, praying to the Almighty himself that he'd ask her to move in with him. She especially loved the luxurious queen-size bed that occupied most of the bedroom. So far, they hadn't slept in it. She'd been careful not to push him, but that might change with how she looked tonight.

She crossed her fingers, closed her eyes for a second, then smiled again as she glanced at the lone black-and-red poster of Che Guevara above the bed. At the bottom, Kieran had written in bold black handwriting: 'In my son's veins flowed the blood of Irish Rebels.'

Ready to go, she slipped on her coat as the taxi horn beeped outside. One last glance in the mirror showed a woman she barely recognised – sexy, happy and smiling back at her. Time to focus. Time to get on with the job.

Val Holmes sat waiting at the bar, nervous yet excited to see her again. He got there early, so had a few beers to steady himself, and after three consecutive pints, was more than relaxed. He felt good, dressed in his only dark suit, a blue-patterned shirt, and a matching tie that had cost him a week's wages.

Honey walked in. Her eyes skipped the room until she found him, and her face broke into a radiant, open smile.

Val saw her, stood up and shook his head in awe. He couldn't get over how she looked. That red dress, that neckline, so deliciously low. Proper scorchin'.

The barman noticed, too, wondering how could such a lanky British gobshite pull a hot blonde like that. He turned back to wash another load of dirty glasses, sighing at life's unfairness.

Honey caught Val's appreciative look and next to him, noticed his bandaged hand. She took it gently and examined it closely. 'Hey, what've you done with that?'

He shook off her question, 'Ah, sure, it's nothin'. My God, Flower, but you look gorgeous.' He was forever calling her 'Flower'. She enjoyed the compliment and blushed as he kissed her cheek, and a little breathlessly, added.

'A-m-a-z-i-n-g.'

Touching his hand again and looking down, she said, 'Doesn't look like nothin' to me. What happened?'

'I'm good. Forget it now. Please. I've been looking forward to this all week,' Val replied. He gulped down the remainder of his beer.

'If you're ready for some scran, will we go straight in?' he suggested.

Honey nodded, wondering what he meant by *scran*. Was it food? Had to be. She was hungry and keen to get a glass of vino down her. She was still shaky despite Kieran talking her through their plan numerous times.

Hoping scran was food, she replied, 'Aye, please. I could eat a horse.'

Val waved to the impeccably dressed maître d', who accepted Honey's coat and hung it up. When he reappeared, he led the couple to an intimate corner booth, presented them with two black leather-bound menus, and offered aperitifs.

The restaurant was impressive. Honey had never been in such a posh place. Massive, dark, time-worn beams stretched above a grey flagstone floor, supporting walls of exposed red brick. She remembered hearing that the place had once been a mill. Candles glowed on each table, adding to the dreamy atmosphere. Determined to make the most of it, she eagerly picked up a menu, but within moments, panic set in – she hardly recognised any of the dishes.

Val noticed her hesitation, laughed, touched her arm, and reassured her, 'Don't worry, Flower. I'll order for ye. Do ye like fish?' Honey laughed with relief.

Once again, he'd surprised her by being so sweet. Val, in turn, was delighted with the chance to show off. She'd no idea he'd once spent a summer working in the kitchen of a fancy French restaurant in Newcastle, before he joined up.

A waiter soon arrived, and Honey watched Val place their order. She was impressed when the waiter smiled and said, 'Excellent choice, sir.'

They giggled together when he'd gone, and Val raised his glass in a toast. He beamed as she clinked her glass with his.

'To us,' he cheered.

'To us.' She felt surprisingly bright and happy.

The evening was fun, and the food exquisite – he'd chosen well. They both had sole with the tastiest vegetables Honey had ever eaten, and she found herself genuinely enjoying the Brit's company, realising she actually liked the fella. He was, by all accounts, a lovely guy. As well as being dead funny, there wasn't anything brash or snobby about him, and she saw in him a normal, kind human being.

But as soon as her affection rose, it curdled. Kieran's words came back to her: 'They're murderers, every one of them.' The thought struck hard - this 'lovely guy' was no more than a British soldier. Dining with the enemy.

Two bottles of wine later, plus a couple of brandies (mostly downed by Val), the novelty of the evening began to fade. Honey even wondered if he'd started drinking before she got there, the way he was carrying on – loud, intoxicated, and droning on about his family and friends. He rambled about his best marra – must've meant his friend Robbie, who he claimed was like a brother. He kept firing questions at her, but each time she neatly turned it back on him.

Thank God, she sighed as he finally paid the bill in cash. Leaning across the table, her voice dropped to a low, seductive tone.

'Fancy comin' back to mine for a coffee?' It sounded so sophisticated – especially since she'd never drunk coffee in her life. Couldn't afford it.

Val's face brightened as he sat back. God, yeah, he would. He was thrilled by the idea. All night he'd been hoping for this. It'd been forever since he'd had his leg over. A hell of a long time. He broke into a sloppy grin and slurred.

'Aye, Flower. I'd love one.' He giggled, 'A coffee, that is!'

Honey just stared, not understanding a word. By now he was so plastered she doubted he could stand, never mind walk straight. By now, she wanted rid, hand him over, and get herself back home.

'Grand. Gimme a sec. I'll scoot to the loo and call us a taxi. Won't be long.' She kissed him on the cheek and walked off towards the Ladies'.

Val stretched his arms along the back of the booth, leaned his head back, and waited eagerly for the night ahead. From the look she'd given him, he was on a promise, though he wished he hadn't had those few beers earlier.

As directed, Honey stopped at the public payphone and made the call. Two words were all she needed to say before hanging up.

'Five minutes.'

In the Ladies', she stared at her reflection and took a couple of deep breaths to steady herself. A faint tremor ran through her, and she fought to pull her composure back before heading to the table. She felt for the Brit - he was lovely - which only made her more nervous as she crossed the restaurant, unaware that half the men were gawping at her, to the annoyance of their wives and girlfriends. She smiled as Val drunkenly watched her approach.

He smiled lazily and mumbled, 'You're really lovely, Flower, ye know that?'

With a wide, relieved smile, she noted that he'd finished the glass of brandy into which she'd slipped the sleeping powder Kieran had given her.

It was time to get the Brit into the car. With all the booze he'd knocked back, he'd be out cold soon. She stood and offered her hand to help him up. With concern, she told him.

'I've got us a taxi, Val. Looks like that wine's hittin' ye hard. C'mon, let's get you back to mine.'

Val welcomed her words, he felt sick and battled to keep his expensive dinner down where it belonged. He swayed unsteadily, realising he was about to either puke or collapse, and clutched her arm, pulling her back into the booth. Nearby diners muttered among themselves, casting disapproving looks at the disturbance.

Fortunately, the maître d' appeared just in time to help as Val lurched to his feet, nearly toppling over. He slung a heavy arm over

Honey's shoulders, then gave the maître d' an exaggerated bow that almost sent him crashing back down again.

'I haf had zee most b-e-a-u-t-i-f-u-l evening, Flower,' he garbled, blowing a sloppy kiss into the air before breaking into the most ridiculous laugh she'd ever heard in her life. *What was that?*

She was so embarrassed; she kept quiet as a mouse as they virtually carried him through the dining room. She grabbed her coat from the attendant and offered an apologetic smile to the maître d', a true professional who gave a knowing smile – he'd seen worse over the years.

Outside, a blast of cold wind greeted them. At the far side of the car park, a taxi waited with its light on, and Honey strode toward it, struggling to keep Val upright and awake.

'Val – quick, love, please. I'm turnin' blue with the cold!'

The driver spotted them, flashed his lights, and steered the car in their direction. As it came to a halt, the window rolled down to reveal Kieran inside.

He let out an impatient tut, his glare set on Honey, and barked, 'Don't say a fuckin' word. Just get in!'

What the hell? Honey waited for an explanation, but Kieran roared at her instead.

'I told ye. Get him in the fuckin' car. Now!'

The atmosphere seemed to freeze. Kieran didn't lift a finger to help her, staying put as she somehow hauled Val into the back seat. The moment Honey climbed in, her date was out cold, and the taxi sped off at an unbelievable speed.

'What's goin' on, Kieran?!' Honey cried, trembling. 'Where's the others?'

Chapter Twenty-Seven

A Bottle of Jameson

Kieran ignored her and kept driving, incandescent with rage. He'd set everything up as instructed, but was so fuckin' annoyed now.

When she'd trapped that first Brit, the Provos hadn't kept their word; they hadn't, like promised, finished the bastard off. Wimps only gave him a good hidin'. A wasted opportunity. And now this. They hadn't even shown up! Well, tonight, he'd do it himself – the right way.

He kept driving, deaf to Honey's frantic demands. *Stupid bitch.* Did she honestly believe he'd ever wanted her for more than a tool? A pawn? He almost laughed at the thought, smug with how easily he'd played her. From the start she'd been hooked, wide-eyed and desperate, and he'd known it. Christ, she would've sold her soul for him, and he'd given her nothing but lies.

Half an hour later, he turned onto a narrow country lane and killed the car lights. Navigating carefully in the darkness, he drove toward a disused barn perched on a hill about a mile from the border. The farmer who owned it was sympathetic to the cause, and the Provos had used the site for this sort of thing before.

Still blinded with fury, he cut the engine, shot Honey a sharp glare in the rearview mirror, and cried, 'Get the fuck out and give me a hand with 'im'.

Honey didn't move; couldn't move, but stared back, defiant and silent. She pointed at Val, her response incredulous. 'On me own? Move him? No way. I'm not goin' near him!'

She cringed as Kieran lunged between the front seats, his breath hot and sour. Through clenched teeth, he snarled.

'Get off that fat arse of yours and do as I tell ye or I swear, I'll kill ye with me own hands!' He swung at her and missed, his fist slicing through the air.

She didn't wait for another chance. Heart pounding, she scrambled out of the car, stumbling in the heels she could barely walk in. Kieran was out after her in seconds, slamming the door so hard the car shook. He moved toward her, his face tense and eyes narrowed. Then, standing inches away, he looked her up and slowly curled his lip like he'd found something rotting.

'Well, aren't you somethin' else?' he sneered. 'See you. You're nothin' but a slag. Did you think I'd...?' He let the sentence hang, but she got the message loud and clear.

'Help us get him out?' he shouted.

Honey still didn't move. His cruel words had gutted her, and the way the night had turned out left an icy terror twisting inside her. This wasn't her boyfriend, the man she thought she knew. Not at all. She could only blame herself, it was her own fault that she was cornered, staring at the reality of what Kieran Kelly was - dangerous, merciless – and from the look in his eyes, there was no way out. She'd have to do what he said.

'Don't have a choice now, do I? You're talkin' to me like shit, Kieran... why's that? What've I done?' she asked, her voice shaking and terrified of his reply.

Kieran scoffed, letting his real feelings show. Christ, the act he'd put on for her. Made him sick thinking about it, forcing himself to play nice. Day in, day out. Nah, he couldn't be bothered to answer her.

She caught him looking back at the car. Her heart thudded so loud it hurt, and her legs trembled, her heels wobbling beneath her.

Swallowing her panic, she kicked them off, yanked open the car door, and bent to grab Val under the arms. He was friggin' heavy, a dead weight, and she dragged him as best she could, fumbling and awkward, until he slipped free and landed hard on the jagged gravel with a thud.

Kieran spat out a curse. 'For fuck's sake, I don't want ye to kill him. That's for after. Now help us get these rags off.'

Honey stiffened, an icy fear tearing through her. His words made no sense. Horrified, she whispered, 'I can't,' the tears already burning her eyes.

He looked at her with contempt. His silence more dangerous than his manic ranting and raving. Then he was right up in her face again, tilting his head with that disgusting smile - the kind that wasn't for real.

The whack came from nowhere as a flash of pain exploded at the side of her head. She stumbled back, clutching her temple.

'You'll do what I tell you,' he snarled. 'Ye hear me? I've no time for this shit. Not tonight.'

Honey's head was racing. She couldn't believe he'd hit her, that this was happening? What the hell had she got herself into? At this rate, and judging by the looks of him, he might finish her off as well as the Brit. Whoever this man was, he was a nutter – a fuckin' nutter!

'Didn't I say to help get his stuff off?!' he screamed.

Shaking, Honey knelt beside Val, unlaced his shoes and rolled off his socks. Deliberately taking her time, she noticed with a sigh of sadness that his bare feet were long and thin, his skin milky pale.

Meanwhile, Kieran rummaged through the Brit's pockets, finding a worn black leather wallet alongside a few loose coins. Grinning evilly, he dug through it, grabbed two fivers, and waved them around like a winner. 'Very nice!'

Honey remained quiet as Kieran pocketed the cash and continued searching. The wallet included a few receipts, which he glanced at briefly and shoved back inside. Next, he pulled out a small black-and-white photograph, scanned it, and handed it to her. It showed a fine-looking couple at a formal event, carefree and happy. Val stood between them, proud and smiling at the camera in his mess dress.

Kieran laughed and looked down at Val. 'Aaah, the parents. Shame they won't recognise ye next time.'

He ripped the photo into tiny pieces, stuffed the remnants into the wallet, and, without a second thought, drove his boot right into the Brit's ribs as he lay defenceless on the ground. Val groaned like a wounded animal. He stirred but quickly fell limp again. Honey took a few steps back and watched as Kieran began to strip the soldier.

Sensing her movement, he snapped, 'Where de you think your goin'? Get over 'ere and finish it!' He pointed to Val's trousers. 'I'll hold him up; you pull 'em down.'

With his arms under Val's, Kieran hauled him into a semi-seated position against the car. Val's head hung low as Kieran unbuckled his belt and opened his zip.

He glanced over at Honey, his voice menacing. 'Hurry up for fuck sake, will ye?'

'God forgive me,' Honey murmured, carefully peeling off one trouser leg at a time.

She stopped and looked at Kieran, but before she could catch her breath, he shrieked, 'For Christ's sake, are you that thick woman? His undies too. *Off*!'

Guilt ate Honey up as the reality of what she'd done sank in. Trapped in a living nightmare, she couldn't believe she was so naïve to think that Kieran Kelly loved her. The man had no heart. Her face burned with shame. He'd played her like a friggin' violin. But with no other choice, she grimaced as she removed Val's white Y-fronts, trying her hardest not to look.

Kieran snatched them up fast, and smirked - she looked so uncomfortable. He gathered the rest of Val's clothes and belongings, bundled them into a plastic bag as if they were contaminated, and tied it shut.

Terrified, Honey watched Kieran stride across the cobbled yard to a steel drum beside a milk bottle half-filled with what looked like petrol. He tossed the black bag in, splashed some petrol from the bottle, and struck a match. One flick, and the drum went up with a whoosh, flames roaring skyward. He laughed, jumped back, eyes locked on the blaze as it raged, burning Val's possessions to ash.

Honey looked everywhere except at the naked Brit.

Kieran, revelling in her humiliation, gave a low, mocking laugh and pushed her aside before nodding at Val's exposed body, his grin cruel, his finger jabbing toward Val's groin.

'So, Honey, what d'you reckon? I'd be generous givin' that a four outta ten,' Kieran spat, his face dark with anger. Honey's stomach hit the ground as she stepped back. It struck her there and then – the Derry man wasn't a nutter; he was evil, pure psycho.

He clapped his hands close to her face and shouted, 'Christ, but you're pathetic. Go grab me that stuff from the boot!'

Devastated, Honey walked to the car and opened the boot. Inside, a couple of open cardboard boxes revealed a chaotic mix of tape, black plastic bags, some tools and black coiled rope. In the corner, a smaller box held a handgun, half-covered by a green velvety cloth. She shook like jelly as she picked it up, leaving the rest untouched, and shut the boot.

Dragging herself back to where Kieran stood, she realised, for some absurd reason, she'd only brought the gun. He bit her head off.

'Where's the fuckin' boxes?!' Fear locked her in place, her body useless, her voice gone.

Cursing like a fishwife, he snatched the gun, sprinted to the car, hauled out the rest, and dumped it all in the barn.

Then he was back again, seizing her by the chin, hissing, 'For God's sake, Honey, pull yourself together and help me get him inside. Wise up, or I'll... I'll...'

His threat was obvious, but she could only stare back in bewilderment. Realising he needed her help, he softened his approach. Taking her icy hands, he rubbed them between his, his voice suddenly gentle.

'Can you do that for me, love? Sorry for losin' it. Wasn't supposed to be us doin' this. Boys didn't show. Honest.' He pointed at Val.

'C'mon, we need to get this one inside, quick. Try for me. All right?' He pulled the kind of smile that begged to be forgiven.

She stared at him, her heart leaping at the sound of his soft, familiar voice. For a moment, she forgot everything. It had to be a mistake. Of course it was. This was Kieran, her Kieran, not the cruel stranger who'd petrified her. This wasn't his fault - it was the Provos; it was their cock-up and they'd dragged him into it. He hadn't meant to be so horrible. He couldn't, *wouldn't* do that to her, would he?

When he saw the change in her face, he drew her into his arms. She melted, breathing him in, clinging to the comfort she'd been so desperate for. He kissed her forehead, tender as ever, and it was enough. Lovely Kieran was back. Relief washed through her in one long sigh, and she nodded. Yes. She'd help him. She'd do whatever he needed if it meant she could go home.

Minutes later, they dragged Val through the yard and into the barn, Kieran bearing most of the man's weight. Flashing her that same loving smile, it didn't even occur to her he'd reeled her in again. That he was thinking, how brilliant he was at it. She was putty in his hands.

'You're doing great, Honey. I don't know what I'd do without you,' he said. Honey loved the compliment and relaxed. She was right. It was going to be okay. Everything was going to be okay.

Sweat trickled down Kieran's face as he snapped on a few more lights in the barn. The nearest, a lone bulb swung from a cable on a beam, flickered to life. Grunting, he forced Val onto a chair beneath it. With steady hands, he looped the rope, binding the Brit's legs, torso, and wrists tight before slicing off the ends with a Stanley knife.

Honey, gobsmacked, watched as Kieran grabbed a handful of Val's hair, jerking his head back and winding the tape around his mouth twice. With a rough tear of the roll, he then secured a blindfold. Exhausted but pleased, he stepped back to admire his work and gave Honey a smug grin.

A spark of delight flickered in Kieran's eyes as the prisoner stirred, mumbling nonsense.

He rubbed his hands together, anticipation all over him. 'Wakey wakey. Looks like our boy's comin' back to us. Christ, I'm sweatin' like a pig.'

He shot Honey a satisfied smile. 'Wanna drink?'

She nodded, eagerly, anything to help, though doubt was eating at her again. Kieran saw it, grabbed her and kissed her, totally out of the blue. His tongue was cruel and suffocating as he forced it down her throat, making her gasp for air. The more she pushed, the deeper he pressed. Then he let her go, laughing hard, before striding out to the car.

Honey gasped, desperate for breath, and bolted for the door at the far end of the barn. She pulled it shut behind her, anything to block out the tragic scene inside. Panic clawed at her chest as she stumbled into the dark. She couldn't see, couldn't drive, didn't know where to turn. She spun on the spot, lost, trapped with no way out. Before she could think, Kieran was on her, dragging her back inside. He grinned like a deranged clown, holding up his prize - a bottle of Jameson.

'Get that in ye before the fun really starts,' he jeered, his eyes glinting with cruel delight.

All this time, she'd believed he was teetotal and watched in disbelief as he gulped from the green bottle, followed by a loud, disgusting belch. It was like watching a stranger. When he offered it over, she seized it. *To hell with it.*

She drank insatiably, allowing the numbing, magical warmth to course through her. Howling with laughter, Kieran yanked it back and took another swig. But Honey wasn't done. She snatched it again and tipped it up – one, two, three, four gulps – until her head swam and the world tilted, desperate to drown out the surrounding horror.

God help me, she prayed.

Chapter Twenty-Eight

A Blood Stained Hurley Stick

V al stirred again – slowly at first, then feeling groggy, his arms and legs felt heavy like they didn't belong to him.

It wasn't right. His head throbbed, his mouth was dry, and when he tried to move, a wave of **panic hit** him like a blow. Everything was black. *What the fuck?* A blindfold. His arms were pinned back, his legs wouldn't shift. He was tied up. And then he remembered.

The girl. *Flower.* Talk about sobering up.

Nooo... His thoughts thundered. The treacherous bitch! Robbie had warned him and he'd laughed it off. The girl – she'd played him, acting all along. What a fool. He clenched his fists, the shame burning through him like acid. A fuckin' honey trap. *Christ, what had he gone and done?!*

He tried to talk, shout, anything, but his mouth was sealed, tape tight across his lips. Blindfolded, gagged, helpless. He sucked frantic breaths through his nose, his nostrils flaring like some animal backed into a corner. The rope bit into his skin as he thrashed, desperate to break free, and then bang, he crashed to the floor, his injured hand smashing hard against the ground.

'Aaarrrggghhh!' he roared as white-hot pain tore up his arm. He bucked against it, wheezing, fighting to stay conscious. He strained to listen, desperate for someone, anyone who might help. Then he heard it – laughter, a man's voice somewhere behind him, chuckling. Rage and fear knotted inside him. He had to get away, *he just had to.* This was life or death. He screamed against the tape, his throat raw, the sound muffled and pitiful in the vast, empty dark.

No response, just a distant chuckling.

From outside, they heard him cry, and Honey ran to the car to hide. No way was she stepping foot in that barn again – no chance. Kieran muttered a curse and sprinted to the barn super fast.

A bitter wind blasted Val as the barn door opened. He shook with fury, bound tight like an animal ready for the slaughter. Footsteps drew closer, and he cried out for help, but his pleas were drowned out as Kieran hoisted Val and the chair upright.

An agonising quiet fell, leaving Val paralysed with fear, dreading what was to come. He shouted again – only for an oppressive silence to scare the daylights out of him.

What felt like hours, not minutes, later, a slow stream of Arctic-cold water was poured over his head and bare body, the shock of it so fierce it near took his breath away. The freezing cold was brutal, unyielding, as if it would never end, and with no choice he endured it, the Baltic water soaking him to the bone, until at last a savage boot smashed into his left knee.

Val howled as the cartilage tore, pain exploding through him in a blinding rush. His body writhed, every nerve ending begging for release, and then the blindfold was ripped away, a searing light stabbing into his eyes. He blinked and squinted, his head spinning as clarity came crashing back, scrambling to piece together where he was and who stood before him.

He found himself in an old barn, the smell of hay and damp hanging in the air, and whoever had stood there moments before was gone. The truth sank hard. Val Holmes was a dead man walking. Whoever had removed his blindfold, the one sure sign they no longer cared if he recognised them, wasn't going to let him leave this place alive. Determined not to go quietly, he strained against the ropes digging into his skin, refusing to give up. Then a voice, cold and merciless, spoke from behind.

'Well, well, well. Look who's back in the land of the livin'. Me wee party can start now our VIP's back with us.' With a quick yank from behind, the man tore the tape off Val's mouth so violently it brought tears to his eyes.

Val strained to twist around, desperate to see his captor, but couldn't, he was so tied up.

'Get off me, you sick Irish bastard,' he spat, each word laced with fear and fury. Kieran's voice dripped with mockery.

'Ah now here, Valentine, that's not very nice, is it? There was me thinkin', judgin' by that la-di-da photo of ye at some fancy do, you'd be sittin' here spoutin' the Queen's finest English, like some stuck-up public school brat.'

Had he been able to, Val would have laughed. The mad bastard couldn't have been more wrong – any talk of him having a 'la-di-da' childhood was miles off. His mam and dad worked hard yeah, but there was never money for the finer things in life.

As his captor stepped into view, Val's first reaction was surprise, followed quickly by disappointment. He'd half expected a brute, some hulking thug with fists like shovels, but instead what appeared was a lad a few years younger than himself. He was ridiculously good-looking, turned out to perfection in stonewashed jeans, shiny brown boots, and a smart navy coat with the collar flicked up, more like a model than the sort you'd picture dragging a British soldier into a barn, tying him up and God knows what else. Still, there was oddness about him, something that didn't sit right, a mannerism in the way he carried himself. A far cry from the usual down-and-out Provo – if indeed he was a Provo.

As the man came closer, Val found himself staring into a pair of dead, cold eyes, and his skin crawled. In that instant he knew, as sure as he'd ever known anything, that without a miracle he wouldn't see the night through. Yet even as the dread tightened in his chest, something deeper stirred, a fierce determination rising in him, the instinct to fight back, refusing to die.

He spat at him and snarled, 'You've no idea about me, man. What the fuck do ye want?'

Val's captor's smirk curdled into something darker. 'This isn't personal. Not really.' He waved a hand at the grim setup around the barn, then grinned.

'See you Val? You're nothin' but a minnow. Bottom-feeder. An ignorant British squaddie. Disposable, like yesterday's rubbish.' His eyes flared with hate.

'I'm sendin' a wee message to the top brass. Politicians. Tellin' them to get the hell outta Ireland. That's all this is, *man*.'

Val couldn't make sense of what the looney was rambling on about.

'What the hell are you sayin'? You're off your rocker,' he snapped, his anger boiling over.

Unfazed, Kieran loomed above him and crooned, 'Listen, Val... or should I call you Valentine?' He gave a low laugh, pure mockery.

'Seriously though. What kinda name is *Valentine*, anyway? Too poofy for my likin'. Val's better. Tougher.' He paused, pretending to think about it.

'Anyway, this message of mine – it's hardly rocket science.' And so Kieran's tirade rolled on, his usual venom against the English, the British Government, all of them.

A chill ran through Val. This one wasn't doing this out of duty. This mad fucker was enjoying himself – the whole bloody set-up. Then, without warning, his captor went silent and stepped out of view, though Val still caught his shuffling and low muttering a few feet away.

He strained against the ropes again, but they refused to budge. His feet were submerged in icy water now, his body convulsing with uncontrollable shivers. Fear had spiralled into basic terror, his heart pounding a frantic rhythm in his chest. The sound of footsteps grew louder until his assailant stood over him once more. Val gasped at the sight.

The man just stood there, stripped down to nothing but white undies and polished brown boots. A sly grin spread across his face, and Val's fear rocketed. The fucker looked ridiculous – almost laughable. But there was an undercurrent of hate, feral and dangerous, that couldn't be ignored. The cold didn't seem to bother him. He didn't move an inch, his icy gaze roaming over Val, dissecting him.

In his right hand, he clutched what appeared to be a hockey stick. Whatever he held in his other hand was well hidden. He raised the stick and leaned it over his shoulder. Val groaned when he noticed several long, sturdy nails embedded in the stick's brown-stained head and dimly remembered – a hurley stick. He closed his eyes.

At Val's reaction, Kieran's lips curled into a bitter smile. He placed the stick flat on the ground and shook open a plastic bag held in his other hand. From it, he pulled out an oversized white plastic apron, tying it securely around himself. His slow, deliberate movements terrified Val, who let out a scream like never before, thrashing wildly against his restraints. Defeated, he broke down, pleading with his silent, unmoving captor.

'C'mon, man, what the hell ye doin'? I'm just a soldier, followin' orders! It's a bliddy job, that's all — a bliddy job. They'll come for ye, they'll find ye!' he pleaded on deaf ears.

His response brought amusement to Kieran's face. He'd heard the same line before and hefted the homemade weapon, 'Following orders, eh? Isn't that what the Nazis said too: "Following orders!"'

In an instant the hurley stick smashed down on the soldier's thighs, nails tearing into flesh and sending waves of agony through him. His screams echoed through the barn as Kieran twisted the stick, ripping it free. Blood gushed from the jagged wounds. Kieran taunted his captive, wiped his brow, and swung the stick eagerly. He circled the chair, closing in, even felt himself harden as he neared his prey.

'Let me tell you somethin', Private Valentine Holmes,' Kieran scoffed.

'I bet you think I'm some ravin' nutter, bangin' on about my country, my people, and you Brits. Don't suppose you know a damn thing about our history, do ye?'

Val couldn't answer. Totally paralyzed.

'Naaah? Didn't think so. Youse bastards have done nothin' but torture and kill for your glorious empire. Well, Val, me man, I bet you're not feeling much glory now are ye?' With that, the hurley stick struck again in the very same spot.

Val reeled from side to side and wailed as the nails pierced deeper into his broken skin. Blood sprayed from the puncture wounds and painted his chest and legs red. Another blow fell down, then another, as Kieran fought to free the stick, shouting with glee every time.

Val's body just gave out. He was done.

Happy to stop, Kieran was knackered and desperate for a piss. He dropped his underpants, using the soldier's body as a wall, and relieved himself.

Laughing as he tucked himself back in, he looked down at his apron, splattered with blood like some mad piece of modern art, and reckoned it a nice touch, did the job. What bothered him was spotting a smear of blood on his boots at the last second, so he bent and wiped it off in a hurry. Even in the thick of brutality, he liked to keep himself neat, clean, turned out just right.

Meanwhile, Honey, his reluctant accomplice, lay slumped in the car. Even half-sloshed, Val's screams clawed at her ears, impossible to ignore. *Dear God*. What was he doin' now? She had to find out and with a groan; stumbled to the barn door, remaining half-hidden in the shadows.

Kieran, oblivious to her be, was crouched over Val, grunting as he yanked the hurley stick from between the man's legs. Tina winced at the sound, a thick, wet sort of rip, and something inside her turned cold.

She stared, horrified. Whatever he'd done, whatever he'd *been doing*, was beyond anything she could've imagined. This wasn't punishment. It wasn't even revenge. Pure terror made flesh. A kind of violence that came from a deep, dark place. A place she didn't want to be part of.

Val didn't scream anymore, but twitched and moaned.

Motionless, she could hear her own breath roaring in her ears. Kieran muttered something she couldn't catch and flung the bloodied stick aside like it was nothing. Like Val was nothing.

Honey swallowed hard, bile burning the back of her throat. In that moment, she knew that if she ever crossed him, really crossed him, she wouldn't be walking away either. And there she was, standing there, doing nothing, while her so-called boyfriend, half-naked, tortured a Brit with a hurley stick lined with nails. A fuckin' nightmare! His eyes were wild, Val's blood splattering across the floor. This wasn't the plan. It was madness. Pure madness.

Kieran Kelly was a complete *headcase*. No other word for it.

She wanted to scream but couldn't. Panic surged through her, and once more, she ran back to the car and collapsed inside. Curled up tight, she pressed her eyes shut, rocking slightly as she prayed. Desperate, broken prayers to a God she wasn't sure still listened. Whatever had happened in that barn, they were finished. There was no going back now. And nothing in her life would ever be the same again.

In time, Val regained consciousness and struggled to control the unrelenting torment. As mucus stubbornly hung from the tip, he breathed through his nose. With a loud sniff, he saw his attacker swig some whiskey. The man caught him looking and raised the bottle in mock salute. As he did, Val took in his kidnapper's scarlet-smeared apron, face, and body, then down to the crimson-headed hurley stick abandoned on the ground.

Kieran decided it was time for a smoke as he began searching for his pack of *Regals*, only to remember where he'd left them. With a nod, he walked off, reappearing moments later.

Opening the pack and pulling out a half-exposed cigarette, he offered it to Val, who, unlike most of his mates, didn't smoke.

'Wanna puff?'

Val ignored the offer and grunted.

His ungrateful response seemed to piss Kieran off. 'Suit yourself.'

He lit it, and took a slow drag, playing with the smoke and creating circles, one after the other. He glared at Val and confided.

'Tonight hasn't altogether gone to plan. Ye see, I wasn't supposed to be on me own. Sadly, means I won't have as much time with ye as I'd like.'

He took another drag and bent closer to Val, blowing the swirling smoke straight into Val's face and adding grimly.

'Sooo... let me tell ye how this is gonna work. Given the Professionals aren't here, I've found meself limited in tools and I'm having to use me imagination to come up with the worst possible way to kill you. *Your* murder, young Valentine, will be our message to *your* British government, to get-the-fuck-outta Ireland!'

To drive his point home, he ground the cigarette against the side of Val's face, stubbing it out with deliberate force. Val's cheek pulsed with agony as the man spat and screamed at him before smacking his burnt cheek with the side of his hand.

'That's for those poor fucker's you lot butchered on *Bloody Sunday*!' he yelled.

'And the photographer you threatened that very mornin', then murdered the same afternoon. Youse got him in the end too, didn't ye?' He swung again, cracking Val across the head.

'And for the wains, youse keep shootin' with rubber bullets!'

By then, the pain had ravaged Val's every nerve, and he could feel his body close to failing. As he watched his kidnapper pick up the hurley stick again, he was shocked to feel it smash down onto his thighs. The mad bastard fought with it and yelled, trying to pull it back out.

'And that's for the rest!' The stick released a sharp crack as it came loose, and Keiran threw it away. Then, on a roll, he hit Val right in the crook of his nose. It broke, and blood gushed out.

'And that's for that wee girl ye bastards knocked down in Cable Street,' he screamed.

Val's battered body was done, yet his heart fought on. He could almost hear its determined beat and was sure it was about to implode.

At last his assailant stopped, and through the haze of pain Val saw him rub his bruised hand. He prayed it hurt like hell. But it didn't seem to, for the man calmly lit another *Regal* and, with cool indifference, asked, 'Sure you don't wanna puff?'

By now, Val couldn't talk.

'Don't smoke? Let's see if this changes your mind, then.' He pressed the freshly lit cigarette hard into the soft flesh of Val's other cheek, once, then again, and again, counting each burn aloud until the cigarette was spent. Val stayed silent throughout, while Kieran ground the stub beneath his boot, irritation clear on his face. Even so, the sight of the Brit — beaten, soaked, trembling, and smeared in red — brought him a twisted sense of satisfaction.

'Not your thing then? Ah well... Maybe you're more of a cigar man,' he chuckled.

Val had given up, but not Kieran. So, with a final blow, he retrieved the hurley stick and slammed it squarely into Val's chest so hard his body rocked under the impact. The soldier screamed, then fell still. Kieran yelled in fury at the semi-conscious figure.

'And that's for Patrick McLaughlin – draggin' him outta his bed, and now the poor bugger's stone dead!'

With a double take, Kieran watched as his prisoner, stripped of control, involuntarily emptied his bladder and bowels. From the horror on the fella's face, he must've realised, somewhere deep inside, what had happened. Instinctively, he recoiled as the hot, yellow, bloodied fluid, along with watery shit, stung his wounds, trickling down his cut thighs and legs, darkening to red as it merged with the crimson pool at his feet.

Kieran tutted and giggled. 'Dearie me. We'll have to keep this one between us, eh Val? Man to man, like. I won't tell if you don't tell.'

If Val had been fully compos mentis, he'd have felt crushed and humiliated, but now, beaten down and barely holding on, he was close to finished. Even so, Kieran reckoned it was time to crack on. He glanced toward the doorway, sure Honey was nearby.

'You can come in now, Honey,' he called, then waited, but no sign. Silence. Likely she was hiding in the car.

Storming outside, he yanked the car door open and shook her awake, rough and impatient.

Val's vision blurred, but through the haze, he caught sight of his date hesitantly stepping into the barn. He'd nick-named her 'Flower', but she looked nothing like one now. Just wilted. A wreck. A far cry from the polished, sexy girl he'd been with earlier that evening. Her makeup was smudged, she was carrying what looked like a wig and it was obvious she'd been crying. And yet, despite everything, a ripple of sympathy stirred in him. The poor lass looked as frightened as he was.

On the way back to the barn, Kieran had suggested they play a game, but Honey wanted no part of it; she wanted to go home – right now.

She gasped the second she went into the barn. Val's face and neck were covered in angry red burns, each one a brutal mark of Kieran's cruelty. Blood crusted around his shattered nose, and his chest, thighs, and legs were riddled with holes, as though he'd been turned into a human sieve. Then the stench hit: a sickening mix of burnt flesh and something fouler. She gagged, realising with horror: the poor fella had shat himself.

She stepped closer and gave him a watery smile, reaching out to touch him, but with the last bit of energy he had, Val spat a big, bloody wad at her. It went splat on her face and in her hair, as he screamed out his words.

'Go to hell, you murderin' bitch.' Any feeling of sympathy for the girl, long gone.

Honey recoiled and cried out as she wiped his spit off with her hands in panic.

'What the fuck's goin' on 'ere?' Kieran yelled, as he stood next to her.

He tried to soothe her, pretending to be concerned. 'Your all right, sweetheart? Let me see.'

Honey sniffled, unable to bring herself to speak. The shame was too much for her, and she was terrified. This was her fault – if it hadn't been for her, Val wouldn't be here. *She* wouldn't be here. *This wouldn't have happened!*

'It's nothin'. I'm fine,' she breathed, staring at Val before falling silent. Her remorse poised like a shadow between them.

'Don't worry, we're nearly finished anyway,' Kieran assured her. 'Sure he can't hurt ye, love. Check him out.'

Kieran picked up the pistol from the box, carefully loading it with a single bullet. And in that moment, the Geordie soldier knew what was next. He made one last, futile attempt to get free.

Honey raced to the barn door and watched. *This was too much!*

Kieran sighed, looking like a butcher in his bloodied apron, as he spoke to his prisoner.

'I'm sure you know how this wee game works, Val. Six chambers, one bullet. That lovely wee girl over there and I are gonna play a game with ye – and guess what? Your brain's the prize. We'll take turns, nice and slow, until the winner, well, ye know...'

He turned to Honey and offered out the pistol. 'Ladies first.' Honey totally freaked out.

'No! No way. That's no game. That's sick!'

Coward, Kieran thought. He chuckled, went to her, put his hand on her shoulder and dragged her back next to the Brit. He'd make her watch and squirm.

'Och, come on, love, it's simple. Put it by his head, then 'bam'. Let me show ye.' He pressed the gun to the side of Val's bloodied head and clicked his teeth in mock execution.

Honey shrieked, 'You're insane! I'm outta here!' and bolted into the night.

Kieran laughed at her sudden exit and turned to his victim, 'Looks like it's you and me left, sonny boy. What d'ye say I go first, huh? See if it's number one,' he suggested, placing the pistol again at the side of the soldier's trembling head.

Tears rolled down Val's face as once again he closed his eyes.

'One, two, three...' counted Kieran, maliciously.

In the stillness of the barn, the only sound was the pistol's chamber rolling and a single click – nope, not this time.

Kieran clicked his tongue in disappointment as Val pleaded, 'Please, man, don't. Please...'

'Sorry. Needs must,' Kieran answered with chilling calm as he pulled the trigger again.

The blast from the shot jolted him backwards, sending a gruesome mass of blood, bone, and brains flying across the barn – the echoes of the gunfire filling the musty space with an eerie sound.

'That's that then,' Kieran muttered as he watched the Brit's body twitching and convulsing.

He tidied himself up as best he could, using glacial cold water from a barn tap to wash away the blood and gore. It was time to speed things up. Honey would have to play her part, whether she liked it or not. *Stupid cow.*

Rushing outside, he half-dragged her from the car and hauled her back to the barn. Inside, he pointed at Val's remains slumped in the chair.

'See what you've done? That's your fault, that is. You made me do that. You're in this now as much as me!' That way, the girl would have no choice but to keep her trap shut.

Honey stared, sickened and terrified, unable to process what she was seeing. Her tummy lurched at the sight of Val's mutilated body – a vision that would haunt her forever.

The sheer horror of it made her want to turn and run, but she couldn't, repulsed beyond words. With no control, the vomiting followed, and she wiped her mouth with her hand while forcing herself to look back at the soldiers battered and burned body. What little remained of his head hung limply to the side. Half his face gone. Kieran wrapped his arms around her and breathed into her hair. She shivered as it all sank in.

'I know it's hard, but I promise it'll be easier next time. Way easier. Now, let's get rid of it. We'll get ye cleaned up after. All right?' he said.

He lowered her to the cold, bloodstained floor where she sat, numb and shaking, as he peeled off his crimson-streaked apron and pulled on a fresh one. The barn felt stifling with the stench of death. It was everywhere.

With cold precision, he opened a black plastic bag, tossing in cigarette butts, bloodied rags, and even small chunks of flesh and bone. Once more, he burned the evidence in the oil barrel; the flames casting grotesque shadows that danced around the barn.

Next, he untied Val's lifeless body, its limbs limp and blood-soaked, and laid it flat with an unsettling tenderness. Blood pooled beneath the corpse, seeping into the barn floor. One by one, he placed black bags over what was left of Val's head, arms, and legs, the sound of plastic rustling mingling with the crackle of the fire.

After that, he split the remaining bags and meticulously wrapped the plastic around the body, trussing it with tape until the last trace of the young Geordie had all but gone.

Chapter Twenty-Nine

AWOL

R ob was dreaming of Tracey, his fiancée, and their last time together. They'd been camping in the Peak District with close friends, but the time alone with her, he'd never forget.

After a night of drinking and singing around the campfire like wallies, they'd got carried away, their laughter turning to passion as they shagged for the first time in the cramped backseat of his father's old green Ford Escort. It wasn't the most romantic or comfortable setting, but it didn't matter.

The memory of her – her warmth, her body, her smell stayed with him. Ever since that night, he found himself aching for her, craving her touch like never before.

He woke up to a hand on his shoulder and a voice urgently whispering, 'Sallis, wake up!'

Opening his eyes, he found his captain standing next to his bunk. The officer was deathly white, and his expression spooked Rob.

'Quick. Get dressed. Holmes has gone AWOL. My office, pronto,' he ordered.

Rob rubbed his eyes and sat up groggily as the captain walked off. It was still dark. He switched on his reading light and dangled his legs over the side of his bunk. Still half-asleep and hoping to prove his captain wrong, he peeked in at Val's empty bunk below. Even in his thermals, he shivered with cold.

He opened his locker and grabbed his black sweatshirt, tracksuit bottoms, and red tartan slippers. Dressed, his watch told him it was 4.10 AM. He needed to pee and dashed to the toilet before speeding towards the captain's office.

Val's words went round and round in Rob's head. His marra had met a local girl, and, with all due respect, she sounded too good to be true. Val's optimism had kept Rob back from asking more. Still, he'd warned him. Every briefing drilled the same message: the Provos' honey traps were for real, and none of them were safe. Be alert.

Even with the warnings, one lad had been led into an ambush by some girl and had the shit beaten out of him. He survived, but was sent him home to recover from his injuries. Rob desperately hoped Val's date had little, if anything, to do with his disappearance.

When he arrived at the captain's office, he was ushered inside, along with two strangers. Neither acknowledged his presence; but stood in silence.

Rob surveyed the room, having never been in it before. He'd heard it had once served as the head librarian's office. It was impressive, with its dark wood walls and a ceiling that stretched high, edged with some sort of fancy moulding. In the middle stood a pair of ox-blood-coloured leather Chesterfield sofas that faced each other at right angles to an ornate stone fireplace. A well-worn Turkish rug covered most of the floor. Behind a walnut desk hung a large colour portrait of the Queen.

The captain offered Rob and the men a seat, but they refused. From the visitors' demeanour, Rob sussed they were RUC Special Branch (SB). Uncharacteristically, his captain appeared agitated.

'Sallis, do you have any idea where Private Holmes might be?'

Rob paused. Shit – the girl with the... He could kick himself for not asking more about her.

'No, sir. Only that he had a date last night; there's not much more to tell, sir. He'd met a girl, told me she's been security-cleared. Worked as a receptionist in Belfast but came back to Londonderry a couple of weeks back.'

'Hmmm.' The captain paused and affirmed to his guests, 'It appears this girl used false ID. Did Holmes describe her at all, say anything more?'

'Nah, not that much, sir. All he told me was that she was good-looking.' Rob replied. He wasn't up to sharing Val's actual description of the blonde.

The two likely Special Branch men muttered to each other, but the captain, frustrated by the interruption, cleared his throat. He glared at them and turned to Rob.

'Sallis, we have a worrying situation here. Did he say at least say where he was going?'

Rob struggled to think. The captain stood and paced the room, waiting for an answer.

'I didn't see him leave, sir. I was in the games room. I remember he told me they were going somewhere expensive for dinner in the Waterside. I think the restaurant used to be an old mill, sir, but I can't remember the name. Sorry, sir.'

'Right, Sallis. Should you think of anything else, anything at all, straight back to me. You hear? Dismissed.'

Rob saluted and left, returning to his barracks as quickly as possible. He was exhausted, not from lack of sleep – but fear for his missing marra. His head was spinning, like he couldn't get his bearings.

They'd gone back to the Blighs Lane compound countless times, and it was always the same. Each time, they endured a relentless barrage as missiles pounded their paint-splattered Pigs. The compound sentries, fuelled by anger, retaliated, firing round after round of rubber bullets and CS gas in a desperate effort to disperse the rioters.

Rob felt certain that some of his mates were at breaking point, fed up and unsure how much more they could take. The story of a private trapped inside a burning Pig haunted the regiment no end. The poor guy had tried to put out the fire with an extinguisher, only to inhale the chemicals. Poisoned him. It was unbelievable.

And now Val was missing He couldn't help but wonder why it was always the good guys who got hurt, or worse. Why couldn't it be pricks like Morris? The lucky bastard had escaped a bomb blast recently, losing only a couple of teeth – making him, if possible, an even sorrier sight for sore eyes.

This shit wasn't what he and Val had signed up for, Rob reckoned, as he lay back in his bunk. Not this. Not to fight and die in the UK. He'd heard that the security forces planned another city curfew. All roads, bar one that led into the Nationalist Bogside, would be closed to traffic, including emergency vehicles, from eight PM to six AM.

It was downright stupid; the soldiers would only get more abuse and trouble at the lone checkpoint now. Someone's foolish idea was to cut off the Bogside population from the city centre and other parts of Londonderry. Supposed to make the city safer, but inevitably, it would fuel tension and make things ten times worse.

The riots were becoming more coordinated and way more sophisticated, given that the mob had little else to do or anywhere to go. The security services had cancelled all the social events in the city, and even the Catholic Church changed its Mass times. It made no sense to isolate these people, but then who was Rob to say?

Val's disappearance was seriously bad news, especially if those men in the captain's office were Special Branch. They'd all heard the stories about SB's dark, shady methods, especially their infamous interrogation and information-gathering techniques. All Rob could think about now was getting Val back in one piece, securing their leave, and going back to Byker. *Together*.

He tossed and turned in his narrow bunk, struggling to get comfortable. His body hadn't fully recovered from the battering at the compound. He thought back on the past month, including the girl who'd caught him in that overgrown back yard in Creggan. How was it she hadn't screamed? Why? he wondered. Hiding in that godforsaken hedge for hours, soaked to the skin by the rain and freezing – all because they'd been told a suspect had visited the address. He'd seen nor heard fuck all. His memory tried to take him back to the pregnant tarred and feathered girl, but he forced it away, obliterating the brutal images before dozing off.

The second he woke, he checked Val's immaculately made bunk, but still no sign of life. His watch read 06.00 hours.

Unsure of what to think, he leapt down from his bunk, grabbed his toilet bag, and headed to the unwelcoming makeshift shower room. After a pitifully tepid shower, he dressed and hit the canteen for breakfast.

Unfortunately, Morris spotted him and walked over with a phony, concerned look. The Irishman raised his eyebrows and asked. 'All right, Robert?'

Rob's guard went right up. Morris never used Rob's full name. Narrowing his eyes at the now gap-toothed man, he replied, 'Yeah. Why, why wouldn't I be?'

Morris frowned and whistled. 'Oh, shit man, ye don't know do ye? That pal of yours, Val... bad fuckin' stuff, that is. Right bad.' He smiled, thrilled that Rob hadn't heard the latest news.

Rob shook his head in confusion. 'What the heck are you on about now, Morris?'

Morris just stared at him, then a slow, smug grin took over his face and, without a care of the rules, Rob grabbed him by the scruff of the neck and forced him hard against the wall. Anger gave him an unaccustomed strength. Morris couldn't move as Rob raged and spluttered.

'Tell me, you slimy Irish bastard. Think it's funny, winding me up? Eh?' He aimed a punch at the man's nose and relished the loud cry Morris gave as it cracked.

Rob pulled back, and they both prepared to tussle before a commanding voice yelled, 'Attention!'

Both froze as their captain walked purposefully towards them. Morris touched his nose and stared balefully at Rob, who glowered back.

The captain's voice was fearsome. 'Morris, out of my sight and clean yourself up!'

He pointed at Rob and yelled: 'Sallis, with me!'

Neither of the men wanted to move, so in a deafening roar, he repeated his orders.

'Get out of my sight, Morris. Sallis, I said with me!'

Morris nodded and, for effect, didn't bother to wipe the blood from his face.

The captain glared at Rob and turned toward his office, oblivious to Morris, who sneered, shook his head, and raised a finger at his superior's disappearing back. Rob despised the Irishman, but he wasn't done with him yet. With no option he followed his captain in silence.

Once in the office, Rob stood at attention, hands clasped behind his back. The captain sat down with a weary expression, and Rob braced himself for whatever was coming.

His superior glanced up, tutting at the sight of blood on Rob's shirt, and sighed.

'At ease, private. Fortunately, I'm willing to overlook that incident with Morris. Between us, not a likeable fellow. However, under the circumstances...'

'Thank you, sir.'

The captain ordered Rob to sit before clearing his throat. His face was rigid as he stared gravely across the desk at the young soldier.

'Sallis, prepare yourself.'

Val was dead. Barely registering his captain's words, which came in a voice tinged with sadness, Rob remained composed.

'Early this morning, the RUC received an anonymous tip-off that a British soldier had been tortured and executed. The caller provided the location of the body. However, it took some time to recover, as there were concerns it might be booby-trapped – what was left of it, that is.'

The captain adjusted himself in his seat and inhaled. 'I've just received confirmation that the remains are that of Private Holmes.'

Rob gasped and turned away, barely keeping himself together as his body swayed. The colour drained from his face.

'You want some water, Sallis?' the captain offered. From his expression, Rob could see he too was struggling and hating this.

'No, sir. Thank you.' Rob pulled himself together and stood to attention.

'How, sir... How...?' he asked. The captain gave it to him straight.

'We don't have all the details yet, only that it was a cold, cruel execution – a single bullet to the head. From what we gather, Holmes was led to an unknown location – most likely by the girl. He was stripped and, from marks on his wrists and legs, tied up and tortured.

His body was wrapped in plastic bags and placed in the middle of a country road.'

The captain had to stop and clear his throat again. Rob waited for him to continue.

'Sadly, by the time the RUC arrived, a heavy goods vehicle had significantly damaged Private Holmes' remains. As we speak, the wretched driver is being questioned.'

Rob gulped; his throat felt like it was closing in.

'I can't believe it, sir. I told him. You warned us. All of us.'

The captain nodded and replied, 'I know. My condolences, Sallis. An obvious error on Holmes's part. However, we've still got a job to do. We need to find these monsters. There will, of course, be a full investigation, and I'll keep you informed. Now, if you'll excuse me, I have to call Holmes's family. Dismissed.'

Rob saluted and shut the door behind him. He walked into the corridor, leaned against the wall, and sobbed – like the little boy he once was, overwhelmed by loss and sorrow.

He couldn't take it in. Val was gone.

For good.

Chapter Thirty

An Unwanted Visitor

O n Monday morning, James sat in his uncle's study at Melrose. He'd needed the privacy and peace of the house as he worked through some sensitive documents and prepared his proposal for the factory's future.

Relaxed and comfortable in his black corduroy trousers, crisp white shirt and black cashmere V-neck, he smiled with satisfaction at his reflection in the window.

As promised, he'd taken Marleen to the beach the day after the unfortunate episode with Jones. They'd travelled to Buncrana first, stopping at the border security checkpoint, through customs and onwards into the Irish Republic. He'd chosen a beautiful stretch of beach at Lisfannon, only thirty minutes from the city.

From the wide bend at Fahan, the first view of Lough Swilly was something else. It helped that the weather had been kind. The air was crisp and fresh as they walked, and the sun shone warmly on the sand. The lough was still and peaceful as the waves lapped the shore. A world so far away from the Troubles back in Londonderry, yet so close.

Charles Jones's behaviour that Saturday evening cast a shadow over the following day. As promised, James did his best to explain to Marleen the political situation in Northern Ireland. She apologised for provoking Jones's outburst and felt embarrassed for ignoring James's request to steer clear of politics. He wasn't angry. James adored her, but he knew she wouldn't be visiting again anytime soon.

Last evening, after he'd waved her and his other friends off, he wondered when and where they might see each other again.

Over breakfast, he'd read the papers as usual and found them depressing. The situation was getting worse. Besides the bombing on Saturday, the news reported that the British soldier who the Provos had executed had his body unceremoniously dumped in the middle of a country road and subsequently mangled by an HGV. James sighed. *Shocking*.

Later, in his uncle's study, he stared across Jocelyn's rose garden, then picked up the phone, and rang the factory. He was surprised to hear Mrs Parkes answer. 'Good morning, Mr Henderson's office.'

'Ah... Morning, Mrs Parkes. Is Caitlin there, please?' He heard her gasp at the other end of the line before she cried down the phone.

'Oh my, Mr Henderson, I was about to call you. I've only heard meself. I mean, poor Caitlin. If it's not one thing, it's another with that girl!' James couldn't grasp what the woman was saying. In exasperation, he told her to repeat herself.

'What was that, Mrs Parkes? Slow down and tell me that again.' Naturally, James couldn't see how agitated Mrs Parkes was but he could hear it in her voice.

'Well, I've heard from one of the girls, Caitlin and her friend – Anne, I think her name is – well... They were in town when that bomb went off on Saturday. Across the street from it!'

James's heart took an almighty leap. He closed his eyes, almost afraid to hear the answer, and asked, 'Are they okay?'

'Oh, aye – Caitlin's all right. Lucky she is. A few cuts and bruises was all. Her friend lost her leg, mind you, but then I suppose she's alive. There's quite a few dead. I've heard body bits all over the place. Imagine?'

He sighed with relief and then replied solemnly, 'I'm glad she's okay, and no, I can't imagine. Do you have her number?'

Mrs Parkes was quick to answer. 'She doesn't have a phone. I've heard her say they use the next-door neighbours, but I've no idea the number.' Far from ideal, James thought. He heard an inner voice warning him not to get involved but dismissed it, justifying his concern as Caitlin's boss.

'How about an address?' He could almost feel the woman's shock vibrate down the line and imagined her sitting with her jaw hitting the floor. He smiled.

'You want her address? You're going to see Caitlin?!' Mrs Parkes voice gave away her shock.

He answered, 'Yes, Mrs Parkes, I'm going to see Caitlin. I am her boss, after all, and as her boss, I am duly concerned.'

Across the city, Mrs Parkes sat at her desk, stumped. There were unwritten rules, and this man was crossing the line. She'd have to speak to his uncle. James interrupted her by shouting down the line.

'Mrs Parkes. You still there? The address. Now, please!' She stiffened at the urgency in his voice, unsure of what to do. He could get hurt.

'Oh, dear. I don't know. Are you sure? I really don't think that's a good idea, Mr Henderson. You don't know what you'd be walking into. It's Creggan.'

James stayed silent, waiting until the office manager gave up, set the receiver down, and muttered to herself while searching for Caitlin's address. Noted, she picked up the phone, peeved but composed, and warned him in a tense voice.

'Your uncle's not going to be too happy. I'm warnin' ye. Caitlin lives in a right Republican area. It's not safe. But if you insist... You give me no choice.'

James felt a brief flicker of sympathy, 'It's fine, Mrs Parkes, and please, this is between us. The address.'

The woman recited it, and James scribbled it down. He thanked her and hung up the receiver before tearing the page from his notebook.

James drove through the usual checkpoints as he approached the city. However, as he reached the perimeter of the Bogside, he began to feel rather sceptical of his mission. Crowds of youths stood on either side of the street, and the atmosphere was tense. He put his foot down, then nervously drove down Blamfield Street to find Number 30, and slowed the car.

He didn't have any trouble finding it, and he pulled up to the McLaughlins' home. It was a dreary, pebble-dashed semi, the kind that looked like it had given up years ago, with a faded red door that had been patched over more times than he could count. The front garden was barely that, enclosed by what was left of a fence, the missing slats either kicked in or torn away perhaps during one of the riots. Not a flower to be seen, not even a weed pretending to be one. Just a lanky hedge, wild and untrimmed, guarding a patch of browning grass that looked like it hadn't felt rain in months. Empty crisp packets and torn newspapers flapped about near the porch, caught by the wind and forgotten.

He scrutinised the street and noticed some children playing. When they saw the black Jaguar, some stopped their games and ran towards it, laughing and screaming – a fancy car like that on their street was a treat!

A small, dirty-looking boy, who wore a black and white dia-mond-patterned tank top over a murky-white collarless shirt and street-stained trousers, cycled confidently on his battered Chopper towards James and yelled, 'Oi, Mister, what kind of car's that then?'

'An expensive one!' James answered and laughed as he suggested, 'What if I give you ten pee – will you keep an eye on it for me?'

The boy cycled closer, and James noticed a thick, lethal-looking stick attached to the back of the Chopper. A small grey mutt ran alongside, its yelps echoing up and down the street. It was filthy, its face, body and paws covered in mud, but it squinted up loyally at its young master and wagged its tail.

James smiled as the boy with the dirty face answered, a twinkle in his eye. He had a candy cigarette hanging from his mouth like he was Marlon Brando himself, red tipped like the real thing. He was some sight.

'No bother. Ten pee, but only for fifteen minutes, like. It'll be twenty pee after that!' He gave James a look that would melt butter – all innocent and angelic.

Cheeky bugger! James laughed, patting the boy's matted hair in agreement. He was impressed by the kid's hustle.

As James strolled toward the house, the latched gate resisted his attempts to open it. The net curtain in the front room twitched as he looked up. After several tries, the beleaguered gate gave way, and James strode up the short path to the front door. With no bell or door knocker, he hammered loudly on the letterbox flap.

Waiting, he glanced back at the Jaguar. The little urchin and his mutt circled the car, the boy now holding the stick in one hand and steering the Chopper with the other – like he was daring anyone to come near it. James, with a smile, shook his head. Grinning, the boy stopped his bike and gave a thumbs-up. James gave a thumbs up and turned when he heard someone coming inside. A zit-covered teen girl peeked through the door.

'Yeah?' she asked, her voice sullen and unconcerned.

'Oh, hi. I'm looking for Caitlin.' James said.

She opened the door wider and ran her eyes over him, from top to bottom. James raised his eyebrows, finding her stare rather rude.

She stretched her neck to look into the street, noticing the Jag, and, with abrupt curiosity, asked, 'Who's you, then?'

'James. James Henderson from Caitlin's work. Wanted to check if she's okay. Is she there, please?'

'Hmm. Maybe. I'll go see.'

With that, the grumpy teenager slammed the door shut, leaving James standing on the doorstep like a wally. This was a bad idea, and he figured it was best to turn on his heel and leave.

As he started down the path, the door opened again, but this time, Caitlin appeared, staring at him in disbelief.

'James,' she called, beckoning him back. 'What in God's name are you doing here?!' He gave an unsure laugh and walked back toward her.

'Sorry. Mrs Parkes told me you don't have a phone and I just wanted to see if you were okay. I heard what happened. Are you? I mean, do you need anything?' He rattled off his words fast, feeling like a gawky, stammering teenager. 'I was trying to explain to the other lady...'

Caitlin laughed. 'Lady? That's Tina, my sister! Don't worry about her, and no, I don't need anything. I'm fine, thanks. I was lucky. Mind you, I don't feel lucky today. I can hardly move.' James noticed the cuts on her face, neck, and hands. Her hands trembled as she held the door open.

She followed his gaze and smiled when she heard him say, 'Poor you, sorry about your friend – Anne, right? How is she?' Caitlin sighed and deliberately crossed her arms. Since the explosion, she hadn't been able to stop herself from shaking and didn't want him to see.

'Oh, she's heartbroken, miserable, and in a lotta pain. I know she's alive, but she's missing a good part of her leg. She's badly cut and bruised and lost a load of blood. It's going to take her forever, if ever, to get over it.'

They both stood on the doorstep, struggling to find something to say, until Caitlin remembered her manners. She opened the door wider, revealing a narrow hallway leading to a kitchen. James saw Tina, the rude teenager, sitting with a woman at a table, and he guessed she was Caitlin's mother. They both stared at him with interest until Caitlin, gesturing for him to enter, broke the moment.

'We're having tea. Would you like some?' He smiled and stepped into the hallway.

'Tea would be lovely. Thank you.' She took his raincoat, hung it under the staircase, then led him shyly into the first room they came to and pointed to a chair beneath a sizeable double-paned window.

'I'll be right back.'

Now alone, James could hear faint sounds from the kitchen – cupboard doors opening and closing, crockery clattering, and muffled voices.

As he sat down, he took in the living room around him. It was a large enough room, decorated with orange and brown hexagon wallpaper. Majella had placed a few framed photographs on the shelf above an open fireplace. He recognised Caitlin as a girl in white – her First Communion. With the fire not lit, the room was chilly. Long, feather-like dried flowers, nearly touching the ceiling, stood in a vase beside a brown corduroy sofa.

On a narrow wall next to the window was a rather scary framed image of Jesus, his hands open and heart exposed, with a small wooden crucifix hanging beneath it. Below that, a teak-effect TV with cream push-down buttons faced the couch.

The room exuded an aura of sadness. It wasn't homely – sparsely furnished for that – but it was clean, with polished surfaces, a vacuumed shaggy rug, and stark white net curtains. A small teak table stood in the centre of the floor, with one or two well-thumbed magazines arranged in neat piles.

Then, he heard footsteps pounding up the stairs, followed by blaring music – likely the sister, Tina, angry about something. He wouldn't forget that one in a hurry.

A short time later, Caitlin entered the room carrying a tray. James stood up to help, holding the door wide open. She carefully placed the tray on the small table, which held a blue and white willow-pattern teapot, along with two cups, saucers, and spoons. Milk was already in the cups. Caitlin poured the tea and handed James his. He searched for sugar but didn't see any. She knew he liked his sugar but had offered none, so thought it best not to ask.

Caitlin closed the door, took her teacup, and sat opposite him. She smiled weakly.

'Thanks for coming, but you shouldn't have. I told Mrs Parkes I needed a few days, that's all. With Daddy too, it's been one thing after another. I feel bad about missing work. Sorry.' James lowered his head sympathetically.

'That's all right. Take as long as you need.'

Caitlin sighed. 'Mrs Parkes'll be relishing this. She'll be glad this happened.' James laughed and set down his cup, smiling at her.

'Don't be daft! If anything, the old bat seemed worried. We're all worried. So much has happened to you. Aren't the Irish supposed to be lucky?' She smiled and dropped her eyes without answering.

'I know it's awkward, and we don't know each other that well, but I'd like to help,' James offered warmly.

Caitlin shook her head. I'm fine, thank you. Honestly, I find it hard to believe you took such a risk to come here. Do you know what the security services call this place? Bet you don't.'

He was clueless but figured it would be a good one, so he sat back and grinned. 'Go on then, tell me.'

Caitlin was half-serious. 'It's not funny. *The Reservation*. It's like the Wild West around here most days.'

James couldn't help but laugh again. He stood and pulled back the net curtain. 'I didn't know that. Suppose I've a well-paid brave watching my car then!'

Caitlin got up to look for herself, unsure what he was on about. Soon enough, she saw the boy on the Chopper and his mucky dog circling and guarding what was obviously James's classic car, parked across the street.

'That's Liam McFadden from next door. Cheeky wee dote. Nobody'll get near your car with him about - not with that killer mutt Lassie backing him up.' She grinned and, without asking, topped up James's cup.

They sat down next to each other on the sofa. James glanced at Caitlin, balking in sympathy at the cuts on her face. He could see how tired and worn she was. The physical cuts would heal, but he was worried about her head – psychologically. She'd endured more than her fair share of heartache in such a short time. Once again, a wave of protectiveness overcame him.

She wore no makeup, yet he found her breathtakingly beautiful. Disconcertingly, he couldn't help noticing she was braless, her nipples pressing through the white cotton T-shirt paired with dark flared jeans. Her feet were bare, save for soft pink polish on her toes. He knew he was staring but couldn't stop himself. He wasn't sure, but he sensed a sexual tension in the air. *Pull yourself together, man*, he chided himself. He hurried to break the spell, after regaining his composure.

'Not that I'm putting pressure on you, but when do you think you'll be back? It's quiet without you, and Mrs Parkes, well Mrs Parkes is Mrs Parkes!'

Caitlin smiled though she felt some kind of tension, too. Hadn't he been watching her with a funny look in his eyes – or had she imagined it? *Must have.*

'Wednesday or Thursday at the latest. I'm still shaky, you can see.' Without thinking, she put out her shaking hands. 'The doctor said I should take a few days.' He watched in silence, seeing her growing upset. Tears fell as she shared her guilt.

'I feel it's all my fault, James. This wouldn't have happened if I hadn't asked Anne to meet me. I was going to buy her tea and a nice piece of cake. That's all. I feel awful about it.' Her cheeks reddened with embarrassment at crying in front of him. James wiped them with his thumb.

'It is so not your fault. It's getting out of control here, don't you see? I hoped it would've blown over by now. But not anymore. It's scary.' He spoke so softly that she cried even harder as he passed her a starched white handkerchief.

'These bombings and killings are crazy.' He lifted her chin, looked her right in the eye, and told her determinedly, 'But listen. It's not your fault what happened to Anne. Sadly, you were both in the wrong place at the wrong time.' His eyes remained on her for a fraction longer than necessary, and he smiled the most dazzling smile. Tears streaming, she gave him a sad, longing look but couldn't answer.

The next thing he knew, she was in his arms, and he could smell coconut or something similar as he stroked her head.

'Ah, Caitlin,' he smelled her hair. 'What am I going to do with you?'

She sighed, breathing in his wonderful scent and noticing how safe she felt. Lips trembling, more tears welled as thoughts of her daddy surfaced, remembering how he, too, had made her feel safe.

They sat together, holding each other, until Caitlin pulled away with a twinge of sadness, but kept her eyes on his. No, it wasn't her imagination; there it was clear as day. He felt it too. A soft groan escaped as he kissed the tip of her nose, then trailed intimate kisses along her cut, tear-stained face before finally reaching her lips. She smiled, about to respond, when a tentative knock sounded on the door.

Majella semi-opened it and peeked her head around before entering the room. James could see how emaciated she was from how her purple dress hung off her thin frame. As if reading his mind, she smiled self-consciously and caught her daughter's eye.

'Sorry, love, but there's trouble at the end of the street. I think it's time your gentleman friend made a move.' Almost immediately, Caitlin jumped up and introduced them.

'Oh, right, sorry. Mammy, this is James. James Henderson, my boss, from the factory. James, this is my mother.' James offered his hand.

'Mrs McLaughlin, I was sorry to hear about your husband,' he told her solemnly. 'My condolences. And now this with Caitlin. You've had a tough time.' Majella acknowledged his words. Until now, she'd never told Caitlin she knew the Hendersons. *Jesus wept, but he's the spit of them!*

'I called to tell Caitlin to take as much time as she needs and to see if I can do anything.' James told her.

'Thank you, but you should be on your way now,' Majella replied bluntly – she knew exactly what the Henderson boy was after.

As she slipped out of the room, she reckoned her timing couldn't have been better. Thank God for that, because she knew fine well she'd walked in on something, and over her dead body would she be the one to put a stop to it.

'Bye then,' James called after her, but she'd disappeared.

After Caitlin closed the door, they waited before James pulled her in, kissing her with greater intensity and passion. Aware of his need for self-control, he broke away. Both gasped. Eyes closed, he shook his head and smiled.

Blushing, Caitlin was trying to get over how her body had responded to his kiss, the blood pounding in her ears. Excitement filled her, but the reality of their situation soon made an appearance. Confusion and fear crept in while James, eager and wanting, held her bruised face between his hands.

'Sorry, Miss McLaughlin, but I had to do that,' he said playfully.

Her face dropped as Majella shouted from the kitchen again, 'Caitlin! I told ye', time for your friend to skedaddle.'

'Your mother's right. I should go. Can I phone you next door, what's the number?' James asked. His words came out in a rush.

Mechanically, Caitlin recited it: 'Yeah, sure. 504341.' As James pulled a pen from his pocket, he jotted the number onto a scrap of paper.

Majella called out again. Mortified and growing cross at her mother's rudeness, Caitlin snatched his raincoat from under the stairs and shouted back, 'Right, Mammy, I hear you!' James stole another long kiss before Caitlin practically pushed him out the front door. He held up his hands in surrender and backed away down the path, laughing.

'Okay, I'm gone. I'm going.'

She watched him walk away, then chased after him, placing her hand on his arm to stop him. Her voice was barely above a whisper.

'Are you sure about this, James?' If anyone found out that they'd kissed, all hell would break loose.

He nodded. 'I get it, I do, but I don't care. I... will... see... you... soon,' he said, tapping the tip of her nose playfully.

She watched him retreat down the path, unable to believe how handsome he was as he waved to her from the roadside. She smiled, closed the door, and steeled herself before facing her mother.

Here we go.

Chapter Thirty-One

A Lethal Umbrella

Relieved, James found the Jag intact and handed over the promised fee, thanking its grubby guardian.

With the engine running, a mix of fear and joy filled him. It had been reckless and dangerous, kissing Caitlin. Yet the way she affected him, the way she reacted, made resistance impossible. He promised himself to be careful and from now on take it slow.

Determined to get off the *Reservation* in one piece and home quickly, he fired up the Jag and roared away. Within minutes, he saw trouble ahead. Mrs McLaughlin was right. Things were about to get ugly. He'd hoped to avoid the no-go areas, but failed. The earlier crowd had grown tenfold, and he watched plumes of black smoke rising in the distance. He drove as fast as he could, trying his best not to draw attention until he had to stop at a T-junction with traffic lights.

James waited nervously for the lights to change when out of nowhere someone flung open the driver's door. A rough hand grabbed his collar and yanked him out of the car. Pain exploded in his head as the hand gripped his hair and slammed his face against the rear passenger door. Strong arms rammed his arms onto the car roof, a kick forcing his legs apart.

He was patted him down as a ferocious voice snarled, 'Who the fuck are ye, and what the fuck are ye doing here, ye flashy git?'

Terrified, James didn't have time to answer before the voice screamed right into his ear, 'Did ye not 'ear me? Who the fuck are ye? I hope for your sake you're not a member of our beloved security services, 'cos that's what you look like, you fucked up prick, eh?'

The hijacker delivered a brutal crack to the back of James's head as his coat was yanked off and tossed onto the filthy ground. Across the car roof, James caught sight of another man, his face hidden by a black balaclava with slits for dark, unblinking eyes. In his hand, he gripped a Browning pistol, its barrel aimed squarely at James's face.

Hands rifled through his pockets, pulling out his license, wallet, and cash. They spun him around to face the man with the hateful voice. Armed with a pistol too, he wore a green hooded jacket, faded jeans, scruffy black Doc Marten boots, and a customary black balaclava.

James felt dwarfed, as he was towered over by someone at least six foot six. After raising the license, the giant sarcastically shared the details with the onlookers.

'Well, well, well, we've got ourselves a 'James Henderson' from bonny Scotland? I bet he's a right Orangeman, too, a definite Proddy with a name like that. Well, Mr Henderson, since you're a'visitin' our lovely city, and since we don't see cars like that much 'round here... we'd like to borrow it, take it for a drive. Hope it doesn't cause ye too much inconvenience.' His voice was laced with sarcasm.

The crowd went ape until a sudden commotion broke out. A small, round, elderly woman burst out of the mob and ran over to the Jaguar, armed with handbag and umbrella. James recognised her as a canteen lady from the factory. She showed no fear as she approached the giant gunman, shouting and waving her umbrella in his face. For such a puny woman, she had a right set of lungs on her!

'You leave that young man be, you big eejit, do ye hear? Do you know who that wee fella is? If it weren't for his kin, most of us women, including your ma, would be outta work!'

She turned and pointed the umbrella at the other stunned gunman, continuing her tirade with fury.

'He's a Henderson from Rocola and don't ye dare be touchin' him. I know who you are, you big gacks, and I'll be straight on to your mas if you don't let him alone!'

The crowd watched in awe as the granny took on the two gunmen. Most of them wouldn't dare cross Mrs Connolly; a tough old bird, and not one to mess with. The woman was lethal!

It was like a scene from a bad movie, and James might've laughed under different circumstances. But he watched in shock as the gunmen eyed each other in confusion. At a loss, they kept it shut for a few seconds before releasing him. The green-coated hijacker gave a crooked grin as he handed James his license, emptied his wallet of cash, and growled.

'You're blessed the day, Mr Henderson. I suggest...' – he poked James back against the car – 'ye get the hell outta here pronto and don't come back. You're a wanker for drivin' that 'round here in the first place. So, before we change our minds, jobs or no jobs, get the fuck outta 'ere!' James bent down to pick up his dirtied raincoat when, out of the blue, he was kicked in the ribs by an enormous boot.

He fell to the ground, winded and struggled to stand as his rescuer's voice cried out in rage, 'Get off him. I'm telling ye. I swear on this day, I'll be in both your houses no sooner than!'

The giant man laughed and told her, 'Sure, it's all right, Mrs Connolly. We hear ye; sure we're only having a wee bit of fun. No harm done!'

James somehow stood, clutching his ribs. He took a final look at the gunman, who returned his stare through his ominous slit hood and reminded him, 'You've been warned, Henderson. Hear me?'

James nodded and painfully climbed into the Jag. His hands shook, and the car almost stalled as he attempted to start her. He'd never been so shit scared in his life. Dear God, if it hadn't been for that brave woman, who knows...

He drove carefully and reached the checkpoint on the Craigavon Bridge, where the Jag, as if it felt sorry for him, gave up and died. Sweat poured down the sides of James's face as he shook and shivered. At the last possible moment, he thrust open the driver's door and vomited hard. His ribs clenched tight, the pain tearing through him. When it was over, his head and body stayed slumped over the car's sill until he spotted a pair of black military boots just below his face. An English voice broke the silence.

'You all right, sir?'

James stared up at a soldier and croaked, 'Just been hijacked. I'm okay... a bit shaky.' As he tried to rise, he dry heaved as a wave of pain consumed him. His ribs had to be broken.

The private hurried towards the checkpoint, waving and shouting, 'Oi, lads, quick! Grab us some water over here!' When he got back, James was still hanging over the side of the car. The drivers behind them were staring, super curious about what was happening.

'Where and when, sir?' The soldier offered the water, saying, 'Here you go.'

James wasn't exactly sure where, but tried to explain. 'Not far from those big flats on Rossville Street, I think. Five minutes ago.'

'With respect, sir, why on earth would you be so naïve as to drive a car like that through the Bogside?' the soldier asked. James felt like a right twat and nodded.

'I know. I know, but there was something I needed to do.' James replied.

He downed the cold liquid. He didn't mind the pain of drinking, rinsing and spitting again. The soldier slowly helped him climb out of the Jag. Another gunner, who'd recognised the car, jumped in and drove it to the side of the bridge, allowing the waiting traffic to move on. James held his ribs protectively and walked over to the railing of the blue-and-white iron bridge, relishing the fresh air.

'I hope whatever you had to do was worth it,' the private muttered sarcastically from behind. 'Looks like they've had a good go at you. Tell me, how the heck did you keep it: the car? I don't get it.'

'It's a long story, don't ask,' James replied weakly.

The soldier shook his head. 'Fair enough, but I'll need some ID.'

James gave a dry grunt and handed over his licence to the bemused soldier, who figured the Jock must've been off his head. Taking a beaut like that into the Bogside.

If it were his, he wouldn't have brought it within sniffing distance of the place. *Typical Jock, flash car, no brains.* He smirked to himself.

Wanker.

Chapter Thirty-Two

A Mother's Warning

Caitlin could hardly believe it - James Henderson had kissed her, and God, it was incredible. She shook her head, still dazed, unable to take it in.

When she woke, she'd felt downright miserable, as though she'd never find the energy to get up, let alone face the world. Her body ached, especially her hands, continually trembling. She hadn't had a decent sleep since the bombing. The wee hours dragged, long and cruel, her mind stuck in those final seconds before the blast... the torn bodies, the screams. Anne's bloodied shoe flashing up in front of her eyes – she doubted she'd ever sleep right again.

After James's surprise visit, after that kiss, she wasn't sure of anything anymore. *Astonished* didn't even cover it. What he'd said, what he'd done... she was all over the place. Her heart, her head. *How could it've happened?* She didn't give a damn; it was a few minutes of total happiness.

And now, with him gone, she walked into the kitchen and found her mother sitting at the table. Majella barely managed a smile when she looked up. Tina had stormed off upstairs to her room in a huff after Caitlin, while making tea for James, had suggested she might lend a hand around the house. No sooner had the words left her mouth than Tina was gone – stomping off, moody cow.

'What's going on, love?' With a tight grip on the kitchen door, Majella closed it firmly after Caitlin sat down.

'Why's someone like him callin' here?' she asked.

'Checking to see if I was okay. I'm as surprised as you are.' Caitlin fidgeted with her hands as she faltered.

'Ah, Mammy, what a mess. I don't know. I really don't. First Daddy then Anne, and now this... James, I mean.'

Majella gaped at her daughter. *James?* Right again. Something *had* happened and in her bloody house too! Caitlin's face gave her everything she needed to know and Majella went ballistic.

'Ah, for Jesus' sake! Where's your thinkin'? The man's your boss! Our Martin'll murder you if you get involved with the likes. I mean, it's bad enough he's a Proddy, Caitlin! He's not your typical Proddy. The man's from a different world, a different friggin' galaxy!' Caitlin was stunned by her mother's outburst and turned on her.

'Don't you think I know that?!'

'You've only started workin' for him. Don't ye realise? He's takin' advantage. That's what he's doin'. Thinks he can take what he wants. Are ye that thick?!' In a burst of temper, Majella slammed her fist on the table.

Caitlin jumped as her mother shot up, her chair fell back and marched to the kitchen window, fixing her eyes on anything but her daughter's stricken face. Hadn't she been killin' herself this past while to keep things right - the house spotless, the nets washed, the windows shining - and now this? This sorta carry-on she did not need.

Caitlin was frightened because Majella was furious; she'd never seen her so angry. She tried to explain the unexplainable.

'No, Mammy. It's not like that. It was a kiss, that's all! First time. I swear. I'm nineteen, for goodness sake, don't you think I deserve some happiness?' Majella turned and stared blankly at her daughter's flashing eyes and red cheeks as Caitlin let rip.

'Our Martin's caged up. Me daddy's dead. And you, Mammy? You're in friggin' cloud cuckoo land, whether you're up in your bed or not.' A pause. 'As for our Tina... none of us know what's going on in that stubborn head of hers. Don't I deserve a life and a chance of happiness? Don't I?!' A stony silence filled the kitchen. Until, feeling calmer, Caitlin whispered.

'If anyone understands love, Mammy, it should be you.'

Majella tutted. 'Hmmm. Don't be holdin' back now, Caitlin, go ahead. Speak your mind, why don't ye? I didn't realise you were so angry with me. Let me tell you one thing, young lady, we were different. Your father and me, we knew each other for ages before we got together. Both of us from the same street: the same friggin' religion, for starters!'

Caitlin grabbed her mother's arm, refusing to accept her denial. 'Think about it, Mammy. Granny went up the wall with you for seeing Daddy, but you chose him. Loved him. You've gotta understand!' Majella pushed her daughter away and shrieked.

'For God's sake, wee girl, grow up will ye?! Don't you get it? He's a Protestant, a Unionist. I'm warnin' ye: this will end badly. Martin might be out sooner than we think. Even more reason for you not to get involved with the likes of your bloody boss. I can hear the street talkin'. We'd be thrown outta Creggan!'

The kitchen door opened, and there was Tina. She wore a red scarf and a long red woollen coat Caitlin hadn't seen before. It didn't do her any favours, clashing with her hair. Completely ignoring Caitlin, she looked at Majella contemptuously.

'What's goin' on? I could hear youse two upstairs, even with me music on. What is it?'

'Nothin'. It's nothin', love,' Majella replied, shrugging slowly.

'So why's the kitchen door shut? We never shut it. And who's that fella in the posh car? What's he all about comin' here?' She finally glanced at Caitlin.

'He's my boss,' Caitlin muttered.

Tina, as suspicious as a detective, remarked, 'A bit snobby, isn't he? Some nerve showin' up in a car like that. Strange though. Well weird.' With her mind working like clockwork, she grinned mischievously.

'*Aha*, I get it. Fancies ye, does he?! Bit outta your league though, isn't he Caitlin?' Her words were wicked.

Caitlin blew up and cried, 'Tina, forget it, all right? Mind your own flippin' business!' Tina scoffed.

'He has to... fancy ye though, comin' here like.' She stepped back and put her arms up in surrender.

'Just sayin''

Indifferent to Caitlin's love life but enjoying winding her sister up, she went on, 'I'm outta here, anyway. Bet ye I'm right though, probably wants into yer knickers,' she ribbed, getting one last, spiteful jab at Caitlin. She laughed and hurried from the kitchen with Majella crying after her.

'Where you off to now? You can't go out! There's riotin'. Get right back here. I mean it Martina McLaughlin!' Tina slammed the door in response.

Majella groaned. What a day and they weren't near finished yet. God for a drink or the chance to close her eyes. Sleep. She needed sleep.

'I don't know what's got into her lately. Always bitin' everyone's head off. Windin' them up.' Yawning, she realised Tina couldn't be right in the head. Come to think of it, none of them could be after all this shite.

'She's upset about Daddy, that's all. It's going to take time. Mammy, sit, please. We need to sort this out. We never fight. I hate it,' Caitlin replied, her voice near breaking with sadness.

Majella didn't trust herself to speak. Like Caitlin, she couldn't cope with bad feelings either. But still...

The radio murmured in the background while they sat together in uneasy quiet, and Caitlin kept herself busy making tea. When she passed the mugs across, they each took their turn to stir in powdered milk, the very last drops of fresh milk going to James. She nearly keeled over when she realised there wasn't a grain of sugar left in the house. He couldn't bear tea without sugar, yet, bless him, he never said a word and drank it down. She tried with her mammy again.

'I'm not sure how I feel about anything, so please try to understand Mammy. Him turning up and kissing me was as much a shock to me. I don't want us hiding anything from each other. We never have secrets.'

Majella shook her head. She wasn't having it. Caitlin had no idea what she was getting into. It wasn't right. She'd get hurt – so hurt. Seen it happen before with his type.

'I'm scared for ye, love. That's all. It's nothin' like me and your da. It's dangerous. It has to stop, Caitlin. Before things go too far. I'm warnin' ye.'

A big hole seemed to open up in Caitlin's chest. The suffocating grief hit her harder than ever. She never would have disobeyed her mother, but, this time, she'd no choice but to lie.

'Okay, I'll stop.' Her voice was low and forlorn as she ended the conversation. 'I'll stop. But only for you.'

Majella's eyes narrowed, it couldn't be that easy, surely, and although a faint surge of relief crept through her, she reminded herself that she'd need to keep a watch on her eldest no matter what.

With relief came a promise, the same empty one as before. She still had a naggin of whiskey tucked away in the back of the hot press, and she'd take a sip today to steady her nerves, then swear blind she'd start afresh in the morning. She'd cut back on the tablets too, or so she told herself, though deep down she knew her promises were worthless, as fragile and broken as the last.

Trying to get things moving along, Caitlin asked, 'What about Brendan, anything?' The family had insisted on a public inquiry into Patrick's death. Their solicitor, Brendan Doherty, had requested copies of the paperwork and witness statements from the security services.

Majella took a deep sigh and then replied, 'Not a word. It'll take years to get anythin' from the peelers, if ever. At the end of the day, won't bring your daddy back, will it?'

'Suppose not. Knowing Brendan, he won't let it go. The same boy's a human Rottweiler,' Caitlin replied, trying to make light of it. Majella smiled at Caitlin's efforts to cheer her up.

'Aye, I know. Poor man's had some sorry cases this past while. He's a hero is what he is,' she replied.

Caitlin stood, gathered the empty mugs, and said, 'Listen, I need to go see Anne. I'm dreading the journey, but I have to.'

Majella gave her head a strong shake. 'No way, love. I'm not lettin' ye outta me sight. Ask Maggie to use the phone, call the hospital. There's trouble out there now. And look, you're shakin' like a jelly. Best leave it for the day.'

Caitlin should go see Anne but, after her argument with Majella, she felt whacked. Things outside were getting tense, and she didn't want to piss off her mammy by leaving.

'You think? I'll phone the hospital, then.' She reached into the cupboard under the stairs and pulled out Majella's old mac. Her own had been ruined in the blast, and though this one was too short and hopeless against the weather, it was better than nothing. She'd ordered a new one from Maggie's Littlewoods catalogue and was waiting on it, though God alone knew how long it'd take to come..

At the McFaddens' doorstep, Caitlin knocked hard, then folded her arms and glanced up and down the street. In the distance black smoke curled into the sky, twisting in the wind, while two helicopters hovered above, circling slow and persistent, keeping watch over whatever fresh chaos had flared nearby. She found herself praying James had made it home in one piece. *Where are you, Charlie?*

She bent and peered through the letterbox. The McFaddens' telly blared at full pelt, a sports presenter's nasal voice carrying through the house as he droned on about his next big racing tip. She straightened, knocked again, and waited.

At last the door scraped open, and there stood Charlie, bleary-eyed and in no rush, a dirty string vest clinging to his gut and a pair of wrinkled, stained pyjama bottoms hanging off him. A thick gold chain with a crucifix caught the light at his throat, the only thing on him that shone. His stubble was days old, the can of beer in his fist failing to mask the sour staleness rising off him, and a roll-up sagged from the corner of his mouth as he split into a wide, careless grin.

'All right, love? Come in, come in.' He said, ushering her inside.

'Thanks, Charlie. Could I use the phone to call the hospital? See how Anne is.' Caitlin asked.

'Aye, no bother.' He signalled her to follow him down a hallway like Caitlin's, but way better decorated, thanks to Maggie's hard earned cash.

While Charlie searched for the key to the flat-roofed shed in the garden, Caitlin waited. He fumbled about, trying to remember where he'd left it, then looked at her.

'Whose posh Jag was that outside yours? Bit flash. Our Liam says he got twenty pee for mindin' it. Told me some man with a weird accent asked him to.' He found the key and displayed it in his hand, but before handing it over, he waited for Caitlin's reply.

'Och, him. Just my boss. Wanted to see how I was after... you know.' Charlie nodded.

'Aye. That's nice. Needs to be careful, mind, drivin' a car like that 'round here. He'll be lucky if he's not hijacked.' He laughed and handed over the key.

'There you go, love.'

'Thanks, Charlie.'

Caitlin crossed Maggie's spotless kitchen and slipped out the back door to make the call. The sky looked angry, all grey and cloudy, like a storm was about to roll in.

Her call lasted less than a minute - polite, perfunctory, and a complete waste of money. All they'd say was that the patient was asleep, and they weren't for waking her. She asked them to pass on a message, to let Anne know she'd phoned, that everyone was thinking of her and sending love. She didn't believe they'd actually do it, even as she spoke. They'd enough on their plates. Still, she'd tried. She locked the shed behind her and stepped back into the warm comfort of the McFaddens' kitchen.

Back in the sitting room, Charlie lay sprawled on the sofa, one leg dangling as he stared at the TV. The air reeked, like lingering, stale smoke. Caitlin handed him the key with a quiet thank you, but as she turned to go, his voice rose behind her.

'Hey, love – wait a sec, will ye?' he asked.

She stopped in the doorway, closed her eyes for a moment, and sighed through her nose. Ah, Charlie. *What now?* With no choice but to humour him, she stepped back into the smoke-filled room, the stale air wrapping itself around her like an old coat she'd never shrug off.

Charlie was a slob through and through, there was no denying it, yet his heart was huge, all kindness and gentleness; he'd do anything for you. She often thought back to the night he'd driven her to the hospital to see her daddy, a memory that stayed with her because it showed the measure of the man, and she knew it was that same goodness which made people so fond of him. Slob or no slob. He was lovely.

For that reason, she forced herself to be patient, even though every part of her longed to be outside, breathing in fresh air instead of choking on stale smoke.

'Bet they wouldn't let you talk to her?' he asked.

'Nope, but they'll pass on a message.' Caitlin replied with a half-smile. He shuffled his vast body around, faced her, and took her in properly.

'You sure you're all right, love? You're right pale. Been through more than most lately, haven't ye?'

'Suppose so. A bit beat, Charlie, that's all.' Another half-smile.

'Aye, well, no wonder. How about a drink? Might help.' He offered her a can, but she smiled back graciously.

'Don't think so, Charlie, but thanks. I'll be off.'

As if he didn't want to part with her, he exclaimed, 'Ah, Caitlin, wait a minute, give us a sec. Have to tell ye this one. This'll cheer ye up... You remember that wee critter Tommy was tellin' ye about. The boyo who'd been told to wait and watch for that "special" car that was right in his face all the time? Wait, wait til' ye hear this one. Miles better.'

It took all of Caitlin's willpower to look interested as Charlie paused for another slug of lager. It dribbled down the sides of his mouth, and she copped he was smashed. *Poor Maggie.* She sat through it, listening as he rambled on, the story a muddle of slurred words and giggles.

'He's in a right huff.' Another slug of lager.

'So... he's manning a Provo checkpoint, right? All decked out in his black balaclava and everythin'. Same as before. Anyway, there he is, stoppin' all the cars goin' into the Bogside, asking the driver's questions, all professional-like. Well, sure, they can't help but burst out laughin' and shoutin' as they drive past and don't stop, "See ye later, Stevie boy."' And another slug, 'The wee man were ragin', roarin' after them and mad as a volcano, 'cos they knew who he was! Him in his balaclava an' all... I mean, Jesus, Mary, and Joseph, don't ye get it, Caitlin? He's a feckin' dwarf. The only one for miles 'round here. Sure every man and his dog knows Stevie!'

'That's a sin, Charlie McFadden. A mortal sin.' Caitlin waved him off with a hand, though smiling. It was as bad, if not worse, than the first yarn. 'Thanks for the phone,' she said gratefully, getting out before he'd the chance to call her back.

She made it inside just as the rain came down hard. Standing in the living room, she thought of James as she picked up the tray holding their empty cups. Her mammy was still in her chair in the kitchen and looked up when Caitlin walked in.

'Any luck?' she asked.

'Wouldn't let me talk to her.'

'Aye, well, not surprised. Maybe tomorrow.' Majella said.

'Hope so. Saw smoke, though. Helicopters are out. It's started.' Caitlin told her. Majella sucked the last of her cigarette and stubbed it out in a yellow and red Double Diamond ashtray. She stood and sighed.

'Don't think it'll last. There's a bad storm comin'. Been on the radio. They won't want a soakin'. Mind you, I'm gonna kill our Tina when she gets back.'

Caitlin watched her, then had an idea. 'Stop worrying about Tina, you know what she's like. Martin's the same. Two peas in a pod. Come into the front room. I'll light a fire and we'll watch some TV.'

The living room was freezing, and the women huddled together while Majella sat fiddling with the TV, waiting for it to warm up. It'd take a while before Caitlin's fire made any real difference, so she ran up to the linen cupboard and pulled out a couple of old flannel blankets.

Back in the room, Caitlin dropped a blanket over Majella's lap and planted herself onto the sofa, tugging the other around her own shoulders. The two of them snuggled in close and quiet, the cold still nipping at their noses. She leaned into her mother and asked.

'Better?'

'Aye, love... better. Thanks,' Majella said with a small smile, reaching out her hand. Caitlin took it, and for a moment, mother and daughter sat in silence, fingers intertwined, a quiet kind of reconciliation. The screen had lit up, and the black-and-white images had formed.

'By the way, you'll never guess what I got in the post,' Majella moaned. 'Another reminder from the undertaker, chasin' their money. I don't know what I'm gonna do. Suppose I'll have to talk to Tommy again.'

They couldn't pay it, and Caitlin prayed Tommy might come up with something. Still cold, she tucked the blankets in tighter.

'Come on, Mammy. Forget it now, yeah? Let's just watch this,' she said with a soft reassuring smile, nodding at the TV as Morecambe and Wise came on.

The storm broke in no time, and Caitlin leaned at the window while Majella slept. Rain hammered the pavement, leaping in the orange glow of the streetlights until the road itself seemed to shimmer and heave. Water rushed along the gutters, swirling at the drains, and the wind tore down the street with a low, eerie howl. Lightning flared, bleaching the houses bone white for a heartbeat before darkness swept back in, the steady thrum of the storm never letting up.

'Bring me sunshine, in your smile, bring me laughter, all the while...'

Chapter Thirty-Three

A Gooner

'How long have you known?' Rob's voice was low and steady over the phone.

'A while.' Grasping the handset, an awkward silence hung in the air as he tried to control his anger.

'And when were you gannin' tell me?'

Tracey sighed. 'I was waiting 'til you got home. But after what happened to Val, your mam insisted I tell ye. I didn't want you to worry.' Rob couldn't believe she'd kept such news from him.

'I think I should've known first off. I mean, I am the da. I've been worried sick about you. You haven't sounded yourself for weeks. There's me thinking you were about to call the wedding off. I love you, Trace, and I'm sorry if I don't sound over the moon. But with all the shit that's going down here, I'm surprised. It's the last thing I expected.'

Tracey had wanted to tell all, but Rob's mother insisted she wait. These days with his mam, it seemed she couldn't do right for doing wrong.

'I know, Robbie,' she said with a sigh. 'I'm sorry. I didn't think it fair to tell you over the 'fone. Aren't you pleased a bit?'

'Course, I'm pleased. I am. I'm only sayin', it's a bit out of the blue. What about the wedding... the honeymoon? I hope we're still on for that?' Tracey let go of her breath at the change in his tone.

'Course we are. Now, calm doon. Leave it to me and your mam. It's not long 'til you're home, and we'll celebrate proper... *And* we've got your twenty-first. I can't wait for that either.'

A sudden thought hit her. 'Shit! A bairn means I'll have to give up the drink and fags. Bugger that.' She laughed happily.

A few moments passed before she ventured delicately, 'How are feelin' with Val an' all? Have they got anyone yet?' He could still barely bring himself to think about it, no matter mention it.

'Trace, I swear, I can't understand this place. No one yet, and the lassie who led him on seems to have disappeared off the face of the earth. You don't want to know what they did to him, especially in your condition.' He sighed, 'I spoke to his da. Will you go to the funeral for me? Buggers here won't give me leave.'

Tracey didn't want to. She hated funerals, but she'd go. *For him.* The fear it could be Rob next haunted her, day in, day out. 'Course I'll go,' she replied, feeling less brave than she sounded.

Rob was nudged by another private, who stood close by, impatient to use the phone. He pointed to his wristwatch as Rob wrapped up the call.

'Time's up, Trace. I'll call you soon. Look after yourself and don't worry about me. Love you to bits, both of you.'

She was hurt he couldn't talk for longer. 'That's it? Can't you talk more, hang on a bit longer?'

'Nah, love, I have to go.' Rob said, 'Love you.'

'Love you too. Bye then. I'll tell your mam you know.' Her voice seemed to go quiet towards the end until the line was cut, and Rob, feeling depressed, was about to put the handset down when the impatient soldier grabbed it from him.

'Sorry, mate, didn't mean to hurry you. Just landed and need to check in with her indoors,' he said.

'No probs,' Rob replied, half smiling, as he surveyed the eager squaddie. Little did he know what he was letting himself in for. Rob only hoped he was better prepared for this than he and Val had been.

As he made his way back to his quarters, Rob struggled to take in the news, hardly believing the words even as they circled his head. *A da.* A father.

The thought should have filled him with pride, and in a way it did, but it also came with a responsibility he wasn't quite ready for, because aye, he wanted children, just not now, not like this. It must have been that camping trip, the pair of them half out of their minds, careless, plastered, never giving a second's thought to what might follow.

His first instinct had been to tell Val and head out for a few bevvies to mark the occasion, to laugh and celebrate, but reality came thundering back, the same way it always did, his best marra was gone, and nothing would ever bring him back. No matter how many times he tried to block it out, the truth of his murder was forever crashing down on him, persistent as ever.

He stood there, looking at the empty bottom bunk, the rolled-up mattress a sad sign Val was gone. His belongings, what little was left of his broken body, were on their way home, a waste of life packed into boxes. With a groan, Rob pulled himself up onto his own bunk and lay back, his eyes staring at the familiar cracks in the ceiling, his mind turning over and over the earlier conversation he had with his captain, trying to find sense in it.

'Sallis. At ease. Take a seat.'

Rob sat on a visitor's chair and stared at the serious-faced officer, who talked quietly and sympathetically. For a Rupert, he wasn't a bad sort.

'I appreciate the past few days have been difficult and that you've been in contact with Private Holmes's family.'

'Yes, sir. Had a word with his da yesterday.'

'Good. Good. I did too. Sometimes, one can't find the words... A tragedy. Bloody awful. However, as I'm forever saying, we've got a job to do here and ultimately we're all aware of the risks.'

He paused before continuing. 'As for you, Sallis, I hear good things. Word is you keep calm under pressure, aside from that run-in with Morris, which I've chosen to overlook.' He offered the faintest smile, then clapped his hands once and rubbed them together.

'In any case, I'd like to see you put that composure to good use in a new initiative we've rolled out.'

He sipped his coffee from a huge mug with a portrait of the Queen on it before he went on.

'Our role in Northern Ireland has evolved, and we recognise the need to change our strategy towards more covert operations. The government has agreed that to win this "war", as our Republican friends refer to it, we need to play them at their own game. To date, our intel has been lacking and, frankly, has caused us more trouble than it's worth. Therefore, we need to get our hands on highly reliable and trustworthy information.' Rob didn't know where this was headed, but he politely listened anyway.

'To date, several courageous men and women have applied for this programme, which requires deep undercover work. They come from all walks of life and bring with them a wide range of experience. So far, we've accepted sixteen candidates.' He picked up a file from his desk, then tossed it back down without looking.

'The induction process is deliberately demanding. Rigorous enough that many don't make it. Candidates are trained in a range of disciplines: breaking and entering, advanced close-quarters combat, local dialect, and firearms proficiency.'

He gave Sallis a brief, appraising glance. 'You're an exceptional marksman, I'm told. Multiple inter-regiment awards to your name.' By this point, the captain had Rob's complete attention. *This was the big league.*

'This assignment is hazardous. Extremely dangerous. Our aim is to identify the enemy, confront and, if required, eliminate. In exceptional circumstances, and strictly off the record, the Yellow Card or standard rules of engagement need not apply. A free hand if you like.' He let his words sink in before continuing.

'The unit will help to unearth individuals like those responsible for the torture and murder of Private Holmes. We've already seen what one effective undercover operative can achieve. So far, it's been hugely successful. The impact can match that of an entire company of a hundred and twenty men on the ground. Something to think about.' He watched for a reaction, but Rob remained silent and focused.

'All in all, and cutting to the chase, Sallis, I believe you have the necessary mindset, skills, and abilities to apply. Therefore, I'm recommending you. The decision, of course, is yours.'

Rob didn't budge. He could see what the captain was doing. Dragging up Val's murder to mess with his head, and Jesus, he was good. Rage burned in him like a fuse lit at both ends. The more he heard about what they'd done to his marra, the worse it got. He wanted revenge. But applying for something like *that*? A covert op? He'd never even thought about it. Not ever. All he'd ever wanted was to do his job, keep his nose clean and pay the bills. Especially now, with a bairn on the way. That changed everything.

'Sir, you say the failure rate is high, and I've done nothing like this before. Let me assure you, I'm not annoyed. I'm beyond furious at what happened to Private Holmes and what they did to him.'

He hesitated, struggling to keep the lid on, his emotions taking over. 'It's more than anger I feel. I can't even put it into words, sir, but Val... Val was like a bruv to me. I would've taken a bullet for him.'

The captain answered Rob's outburst objectively. 'Don't you see, then? It's simple. You're a professional soldier. It's time to either turn this justified anger of yours around and use it positively and effectively, or allow it to fester and eat you up from the inside. Holmes's death was calculated and pitiless. If anyone has good reason to catch and stop these bastards, Sallis, it's you. And now you have an opportunity to do just that.'

The boss was right, but Rob wasn't sure undercover work was for him. He'd be well out of his comfort zone.

'Would I have to go back to England for training, and what would I tell the family?'

The officer rose from his chair, drawn to the window by the great oaks of Brooke Park, their sturdy limbs arching over lawns that had long offered quiet in the heart of a city at its most brittle. A history buff, he thought how odd it felt, that a place of such gentle grace could stand, unchanged, when all around had been smashed by chaos.

He knew the park's tale: how it rose from the grounds of Gwyn's orphanage in the mid-19th century – thanks to John Gwyn – and was gifted to the people when James Hood Brooke's will set it aside as a green haven for ordinary people back in 1901.

He remembered, too, that monarchs had made their mark here: King Edward VII and Queen Alexandra planted trees in 1903, King George VI followed suit in 1945, and the newly crowned Queen Elizabeth II in 1953, each planting with the same trowel as if stitching themselves into the city's memory.

Now, as he watched children weaving between the tree trunks and soldiers stationed just beyond the iron railings, he felt that same jolt again - the contrast of innocence so close to harm. He turned and answered Rob.

'No, Sallis. Training will happen at an undisclosed location. The first phase lasts up to six weeks. If you get through, we'll send you on a medium-risk surveillance operation first. After that, you'll receive intermittent training in specialist skills. We'll also tell you how to deal with your family.'

Exhaustion wasn't the word for how the captain felt. He hadn't slept right for weeks and had hoped to be finished here by now. It was his third, and fingers crossed, last tour of Northern Ireland. He sighed heavily and turned to face the private and said.

'I'll need your decision Sallis. Tonight.'

No pressure then. Rob thought. He was baffled. His head spun until another consideration struck him – the most compelling reason not to go for it.

'There is one thing, sir. I'm due leave at Christmas. It's my twenty-first, and I've only found out I'm going to be a da. If I apply, would my leave be cancelled?' The captain extended his hand and shook Rob's warmly, smiling.

'Congratulations. A father, eh?' But his smile faded as he lowered his hand. 'Ah, right... yes. I'm afraid it would. Time is of the essence.'

Rob's heart sank. 'In that case, sir, I'll have to think about it. Thank you.'

Both men knew what Rob really meant. Most likely a big fat, disappointing, 'No,' with a capital 'N.'

Lying back in his bunk, his eyes, as usual, staring at the cracked ceiling, Rob's thinking swam until he felt sick, the timing circling him like a curse he couldn't escape.

Of all days for this to happen, with Tracey carrying his bairn, it was a cruel blow. If he went for it, he could see her face, clear as day, the fury in her eyes, the way her temper would erupt, and he was near certain that if he told her he wasn't coming home, she'd walk without a backward glance. What cut deepest was knowing he couldn't give her the real reason, not even the smallest part of the truth, nothing she could hold on to. All he could say was an empty line, *I can't tell you*, and those few words alone would send her ballistic.

He tried to picture it. See himself applying. Covert work, undercover, the training, all that came with it. Was he cut out for it? Brave enough? Hard to say. He didn't have answers, only questions. But think about it... the captain selected him. It had to mean something.

He was relaxing and mulling over his next move when some heavy footsteps stomped in and stopped by his bunk. He heard a cough.

'Scuse me. You Sallis?'

Rob sat up and found a teenage-looking private standing like a pleb at the end of the bunk. He was tall, around six foot two, excruciatingly thin, with cropped jet-black hair and a face covered in acne scars. He couldn't have been over eighteen. Rob groaned. They were getting fresher by the day.

The skinny kid hesitated, then repeated himself. 'You Sallis?'

'Yeah, why? Who're you?' Rob replied with a nod. The youngster looked relieved.

'Ah, great. I'm Fraser... Anthony Fraser, but call me Tony. That's my bunk.' He pointed to Val's old berth before tactfully adding, 'Is that awright wiv you? 'Eard about your mate. Sorry. Rough that.'

'Aye, thanks,' Rob answered, lying down again to avoid further conversation. He listened as the youth unpacked his gear and made up the lower bunk. Once finished, it grew bloody awkward as Tony sat on the edge of his bunk, quiet as a mouse. Minutes passed like hours, and soon enough, Rob felt bad. *Poor bugger.* He knew he should give the fella a break and jumped down off his bunk.

'London, right?' he asked, grabbing a sweater. The youth stood up so quick, he nearly took his head off, whacking the side of the bunk.

Rubbing it, he groaned, 'Yeah, East End. Bethnal Green. Tell us this, I ain't eaten nofink since this mornin'. Travellin' all day like , and I'd kill for a Rosie Lee and a bitta grub.'

'A Rosie Lee?' Rob's brow furrowed. *He'd never heard of a 'Roise Lee'.*

'Oh, sorry, mate. Cup of char... Tea, like.' Rob liked him straight away and laughed, giving him a playful smack on the shoulder.

'Fair enough lad, let's get you your Rosie Lee.'

The two men chatted about football on the way to the canteen. Dinner was still a while away, so the place was reasonably empty. They took a long rectangular table by the window at the far end of the hall.

The storm was rolling in, making it dark and rainy, the wind and rain really slamming against the windows. Rob wasn't hungry, but sipped at his coffee while the Eastender tucked into a doorstep sandwich like he hadn't eaten in days. Rob cleared his throat, ready to listen as he asked.

'So Tony. What made you sign up so young?'

Tony mumbled through a mouthful of bread, 'Had to, like.'

'*Had to.* How d'you mean?' Rob probed. Tony stopped eating half-way, looking baffled, and replied like he'd just been asked the most ridiculous question in the world.

'Runs in the family, don't it? Me old man, his old man, and his old man before... And then me bruv, see?'

Rob understood. 'Military family then.'

'One hundred per cent.' Tony laughed. 'It's aw right though. Wanted to play for Arsenal, I did, but I 'ad to join up, din't I? Always a Gooner.'

Rob was genuinely interested and said, 'And here you are in Londonderry.'

He noticed sadness creep into the boy's open face, and a glassy look come over his small, dark eyes.

'Ad to, for me old man, see. Me bruvver 'Arry – daft muppet only went and got 'imself shot in the head, din't he? Sniper up in Divis Tower, them big flats over in Belfast. Poor sod never knew what hit 'im. Thank fuck.' He paused, rubbing the back of his neck before going on.

'Me old man's broken over it, like – 'ates the Irish, can't stand the sight of 'em. Felt I 'ad to do somefink, y'know, try an' put it right somehow? 'Cos end of the day, we're meant to be the same country, ain't we, all part 'a the UK. I still don't get why we're at each other's throats. So I signed up, wound her indoors up, big time. Barely spoke two words to me or the old man since.' He smiled thinking of his mother's smile and said, 'she'll come round, always does.'

Rob whistled. 'Whoa. So what I'm hearing, Tony, is you joined the British Army to sort out the Irish, did you? Well, I hate to tell you this, bonny lad, but there's fuck-all chance of that. No power in the world can sort this lot out.' He drank more coffee, saddened by the youth's naïvety. But Tony wasn't about to be put off.

'I 'ear you, mate, I do, but someone's gotta try, ain't they? They can't just keep on killin' us one by one like it don't matter, cos it ain't right, not by a long shot. I mean, I heard about your pal an' what 'appened to him, an' it's the same story all over, innit? Shit like that. They're shaftin' us every chance they get, blowin' up kiddies an' all, and I don't care what anyone says, it's outta order.'

Tony waited, staring at Rob, and they both just went quiet. He didn't say anything right away, but something came over him that he couldn't understand. Got to him with a clear, fast, and decisive understanding.

'Ye' know what, Tony? You're so right. So bloody right,' he muttered, voice low.

'It is a God damn mess. And aye, we do need to do something.'

He stared off for a moment, cracking his knuckles as his thoughts tore through him, knowing deep down that this wasn't just about following orders or playing out tactics on a map. It was personal, and no one could tell him otherwise. Okay, he'd signed up because he needed a job, but him and Val believed in what the army was meant to stand for – service, discipline, pride in his country – and even after all the filth and violence he'd witnessed, that part of him stayed. He still believed.

Now Val was dead, taken from him in the most brutal way imaginable, was Robert Sallies just going to sit back and swallow it, let it go as if Val was just another casualty, another statistic on their charts? Not a chance! Every time he shut his eyes he imagined a pool of Val's blood spreading across the barn floor as they tortured him, heard the sneers of the bastards who'd done it, and knew now he wasn't walking away from it.

He was going to do it, no question. For Val. For the army. For the country he'd sworn to protect. For his family, whatever it took.

'I gotta go, mate. You keep yourself safe, I'll be gone the night,' he said, playfully patting Tony's head.

'Make sure you keep that head of yours down, hear me? I'll get someone to look out for ye. You're sound.'

The young Eastender couldn't understand what he'd done to produce such a reaction and watched Rob with surprise. With his mug of Rosie Lee still raised in the air, he cried.

'What'd I say? Why you leavin'? Crap, I only got 'ere. 'Ave you 'ad enough of me already then?' Rob laughed, and everything felt as near okay as it could be.

'You've done me a big favour, lad. A big one! I'll see ye in a bit.' A new lightness entered Rob's step as he rushed to tell the captain his decision.

This is for you Val, this is for you.

Chapter Thirty-Four

Caught Out

RUC Chief Constable George Shalham sat opposite James as they ate supper with Roger later that evening.

James's father had been invited to stay with Charles Jones in Belfast and had yet to reappear. Much to James Jnr's dismay, his father was getting remarkably close to the Belfast bigot.

The chief constable had been on duty when the call came through about James's near-hijack. Unusually, tonight he was in full uniform. A deep green tunic and matching trousers, the cut acute, cinched with a silver-buckled belt. His rank was unmistakable, marked by ornate epaulettes decorated with silver braid, red piping, and the RUC insignia. The red-trimmed lapels were edged with six tiny shamrocks, stitched in green and gold. The whole ensemble carried more than a whiff of comic opera, but Shalham's fury as he challenged James about his earlier behaviour was anything but theatrical.

'It was downright stupid of you, James. Why, for Christ's sake, were you in the middle of the Bogside, and in the Jag too? You would've stood out like a sore thumb, and you nearly gave Roger here a heart attack!'

James understood why Shalham was angry. He did. It was he who'd ordered for the bloody Jaguar to be driven home and James brought back to Melrose. Now, besides Shalham's fury, James felt even more of a wally.

The policeman who had dropped him off in the back of the Hot-spur Land Rover hadn't spoken a word the entire drive, the silence thick and awkward. So when they finally pulled up outside Melrose, all James could muster was a sheepish, 'Cheers,' as he slid out, his face burning – he must've looked a right tool.

The other policeman brought the Jag to a halt with all the care you'd give an old runabout, jumped out, climbed into the jeep, and roared off, their laughter trailing behind as they disappeared down the driveway, no doubt having a grand old go at his expense.

When James stepped into Melrose, he found Roger had already heard from Shalham and wasted no time in calling for Dr Harris, who now stood in the hallway with his bag in hand. The doc gave James a fast once-over, taped his ribs pretty roughly, then left, muttering to himself.

Three ribs were badly bruised, the pain fierce enough to force him to move with care, and as he sat at the table, holding his sides and trying to disguise the odd wince, he felt every pair of eyes on him. Roger said nothing, but his steady gaze across the table was worse than any tongue-lashing, a look that left James feeling like shit. A good blasting he could take, he deserved it, but this cool appraisal was harder to bear. He wanted to finish his supper in peace, sneak upstairs, sink into a hot bath, and let the water soothe what nothing else could.

'All right, George. I feel a perfect fool, but I had an important meeting, and I got disoriented. Next thing, I'm in the middle of a disturbance. It was stupid, and I assure you it won't happen again. It was—'

'Important meeting, my arse!' Roger yelled at his nephew before James could say another word.

He turned to his influential friend, exasperated. 'I don't get this idiot, George. I've warned him time and time again.'

George ignored Roger and instead turned to the injured and embarrassed young man facing him. He wasn't finished with him yet.

'No, James, it won't happen again. It would be best if you remember these are dangerous times. The Republicans won't tolerate Loyalists or the like coming into their areas. Droves of Unionists are moving out of here and Belfast to the Republic, some even further. And here you are, landing yourself in the middle of the Bogside, and near hijacked!' James knew of the Unionist exodus but made no comment as Shalham, whose uniform seemed to add gravitas to his words, finished his lecture.

'You need to wise up James. And Roger... most, if not all, of your management team are Unionists. It's increasingly likely they won't be able to work at the factory and remain safe. You need to think about improving security or relocating.' Roger wiped his mouth with a napkin and looked at his friend.

'Funny you mention that, George. James and I have been talking about the same. We've been doing a lot of number crunching, and, unsurprisingly, moving would cost us a small fortune. Money we don't have, regrettably. If we were to sell, I guarantee no one is gonna touch that site with a bargepole, given its proximity to your Blighs Lane compound.' Shalham wasn't surprised but listened as Roger continued.

'If we close now, we can't even pay redundancy. The only option is to sit tight and pray. Our order book is relatively healthy for the time being. But, we have to consider the workforce. Rocola is responsible for the livelihood of nearly three thousand people in this city, mostly women. So yes, security is one of our many priorities if we want to stay above water.'

George groaned. 'Goodness, I hadn't realised so many.' Roger nodded.

'Fraid so. We're the only big gun left. The women are predominantly Catholic and live in and around the Bogside and Creggan.
Another reason for us not to move. They can't afford to travel far, and
we can't afford to lose their skills.'

The men shared some bread from a basket offered by the housekeeper, who left quietly. As soon as she'd disappeared, Roger piped up
again.

'A few of our managers are already complaining about intimida-
tion. They're understandably scared, and we've had some resignations.
I've assigned James to find ways to raise capital and enhance our
security. The safety of the workers is our top priority, but without
securing additional funds, we might not survive. Quite the challenge,
I'm afraid.'

A grimace crossed James' face as he moved in his seat, and a sharp
pain shot through his side, making him grunt. The spasm persisted,
but he was relieved the two men's tirade at him had ended. Hopefully,
the matter was closed. Soon to be forgotten.

'It's a challenge for sure,' James said, adding, 'Still, we have a plan.
We're planning a series of one-day meetings with the city's key business figures from the chamber of commerce, the city council, even senior reps of both churches. Hoping – fingers crossed – we can generate
ideas to attract investment and, as you rightly pointed out, George,
improve security. After all, it's in Londonderry's wider interest to keep
Rocola open.'

It made perfect sense. It'd be an unmitigated disaster for the city if
the factory closed. He took a sharp breath and said.

'Thousands of jobs being lost in such an impoverished area would
be catastrophic. If it means getting these decision makers in a room
together, no matter religion or background, we have to make it hap-

pen. Someone will come up with a solution, even if I have to lock them in there myself!' James laughed. It hurt.

Roger and George smiled as they listened, seeing a glimmer of light at the end of the tunnel. By now, James noticed he had their full attention.

'George, this is where we need your experience, especially around security. Your presence at these meetings would add impetus, and your reputation would help allay any fears people may have.' George was flattered but warned them that not all would welcome his presence.

'I think it's a novel approach, James. A brave one, too. Go for it, but be wary.'

'Aye, I know, but I'm glad you think so. It won't be easy, but we have to try, don't we? Quite frankly, I can't think of any other option.' George was impressed by James's passion.

'I agree in principle,' the chief constable told him, 'but if it's okay, I'd like to run through the invitation list. You'd be amazed at the complicated personalities in this city, and I know the troublemakers.'

Shalham stood and wandered over to the fireplace, warming his hands and backside as he sighed and rather candidly filled them in.

'For this to succeed, gentlemen, you need to make sure there's a fair balance of reps from both sides of the divide. Last month, a chunk of Catholics withdrew from public bodies in protest at internment, and anti-Unionist councillors walked out across the province. The right people have to be there. All the same, it's going to take some persuasion. Provided I see the guest list, I'm more than happy to help.'

James was delighted. 'Of course. Thank you. I hope to hold the first session in the City Hotel within six weeks at the latest. My secretary will arrange the logistics, and I've already drawn up a draft invitee list. We can go through it together.' George nodded in agreement.

As an afterthought, James paused before continuing. 'Actually, given what you've said, am I right in that we definitely need to invite a top dog from the British Army?'

The chief constable scoffed, doubt flickering across his face. Relations with his British Army counterpart were strained and unlikely to improve.

'Hmm, that's an awkward one, but, aye, I suppose we should try. I'll see what I can do.' He moved back to the table and sat down.

The three men continued eating and discussing the plan until they moved on to lighter topics. The wine flowed freely, washing away any tension and pushing aside thoughts of the Troubles and Rocola. Shalham finished his glass of port and announced it was time for him to go.

'My carriage awaits,' he remarked, referring to his protection bodyguards. 'It's unfair of me to keep these men out so late from their families.' George was most likely number one on the Provos hit list, a fact that hadn't fully registered with James until now. It made him admire the chief constable even more.

As they were leaving, George pulled James aside, out of earshot of his uncle, and warned him in a low, earnest tone.

'By the way, James, I know *exactly* where you were today. Don't ask me how, but I know. Stay away from Creggan, for Roger's sake. And don't get involved in something you'll regret, especially with the girl. Trust me. Thank you for dinner and good night.' No sooner had he finished than he vanished into the night. Perplexed, James leaned against the door frame, staring out as the bulletproof car's rear lights disappeared down the drive.

In time, he stepped back inside. The hallway greeted him with its cold, chequered tiles and a silence that somehow felt accusatory.

Roger was waiting, standing under the stairwell with a cigarette lazily burning between his fingers.

'You all right?' he asked. James gave a half-hearted shrug and nudged the edge of a rug with his foot.

'Not really,' he replied. 'Nightcap?' he offered, moving towards the library.

'No, thanks. Tired now. I'll come in with you though, but head up once I've finished this,' Roger replied, lifting his cigarette with a slight flick of his wrist.

'You get one. Might help with the pain.' They walked into the library together, but as soon as they were through the door, Roger challenged him.

'I'm standing here thinking. Why can't you be honest and tell me the real reason you ended up in the Bogside today?!' Before James could so much as blink in reply, Roger pulled again on his cigarette and barrelled straight into a rant.

'So we're clear here, son, I've a good idea already, only I hoped you'd be man enough to tell me yourself. Mrs Parkes rang me in hysterics, said she'd heard there was trouble near the Bogside and wanted to know if you'd come home safe. Now, it's rarely that I agree with that woman, but this time she was bang on. Told me she warned you not to go near Creggan!'

James could feel his anger rising, hot and fast. Wasn't he entitled to any privacy? First Shalham, now Roger, and that old crow, Mrs Parkes, poking her beak in too. Refusing to let his frustration show, he kept his voice even.

'Yes, she warned me. And yes, I didn't listen. How many times do I have to apologise?'

'You really are, at times, James, downright stupid when it comes to this country. And to visit that girl – *your secretary* – in the middle of a Catholic ghetto is simply foolish. You could've been killed,' Roger replied, angrily, stubbing out his cigarette. He shook his head and looked at his nephew with disappointment.

'I just pray to God "secretary" is all that girl is to you: a *secretary*. Because if I find out otherwise, I assure you, your father'll be the first to hear. And he'll have you in the army so fast your feet won't touch the ground. Don't tempt fate. Don't do something stupid, not only for your sake, but for hers too.' Roger looked at him, exasperated. It wasn't like him to lose it with his beloved nephew.

James, hoping to calm things down, gave his usual reassuring smile, even though he was worried.

'Och, Uncle, Mrs Parkes loves to dramatise - you know that. Did she not tell you I asked for Caitlin's number first? Bet she didn't. I'd no intention of going anywhere near Creggan. Honest. It's only that... well... she doesn't have a phone.'

Roger's continued silence didn't help. James shifted slightly, then added, more quietly, 'I was showing concern for a valued employee, nothing more. She's been a great help to me so far, and her father died recently. Remember? On top of that, she was hurt in the Shipquay Street bomb. Her best friend lost her leg, for God's sake! That's why I went. It was the right thing to do. Anywhere else, it wouldn't have raised an eyebrow.'

He met Roger's gaze, forcing calm into his voice. 'Trust me, the girl means absolutely nothing to me.' Roger shook his head slowly, his eyes tired.

'Problem is, James... This is not "anywhere else," this is Northern Ireland. And I don't believe you. Wish I could.' With that, he gave a curt goodnight and walked away, leaving James alone.

James poured himself a large Glenfiddich, turning his nose up at ice like any decent Scot. He threw the drink right back, fell into a red leather chair by the fire, and stared into the glowing embers. Lying to Roger didn't sit right. He hated himself for it. Not about the lie, but how easily it'd come to him.

He sighed. How the hell had Shalham known about Caitlin? Were they being watched? If so, they'd need to be more careful, smarter. Wasn't it his life to do as he pleased? He shouldn't be drinking, not with the painkillers, but the way he felt right now, he couldn't care less. Defiant, he topped up his glass and swallowed another mouthful of the deep golden liquid. Punishment came quick – he choked, and a fit of coughing tore through his ribs. Pressing both hands against his side, he swore under his breath.

Fuck, but what a scunner of a day!

Chapter Thirty-Five

Martin

'Are you feckin' serious?! Have ye any idea what you're doin'? And what about your mammy?' Anne hollered. She folded her arms across her chest, unimpressed by what her best friend had just told her.

Caitlin perched on the end of a hospital bed, watched Anne's face darken. She'd been on the ward for weeks and was finally going home in a few days. Her lower body was under a green cotton bedcover, and Caitlin's eyes traced it up to where Anne's right leg should've been – it was missing, the absence stark and impossible to ignore. She went to see Anne whenever she could, even though it was tough with work and her days off after the blast. Thankfully, James made sure she wouldn't get docked pay, which was nice.

Majella's good intentions of keeping off the drink and the tablets hadn't lasted long after her and Caitlin's cosy evening together. She was worse than ever now, drifting through her days in a perpetual diazepam haze that left her with little interest in life itself.

Caitlin hadn't seen much of Tommy either, he seemed to be up to his eyeballs with his own troubles, while Tina was out doing her own thing, either at the tech or hiding away in her room. What had once been a happy home now felt soulless and hollow, every corner filled with a persisting heartache, and Christ, how she missed her daddy.

Until now, Caitlin hadn't told Anne much about James, but Anne, being Anne, knew Caitlin was hiding something and pestered her until she'd no choice but to tell. And, boy, was she sorry.

'How long has it been goin' on then?' Anne snapped.

'Since your accident,' Caitlin replied, repeatedly glancing at her friend's missing limb and cowering inside.

'It wasn't an *accident*, Caitlin. It was a feckin' bomb those UVF bastards planted!' Anne wailed.

'I know, I know. God, I'm sorry. I keep thinking it's my fault!' Caitlin cried. Out of nowhere, Anne gasped loudly and screwed up her eyes.

'Sweet Mother of Jesus.' She held her breath until the pain subsided. Feeling tired and perhaps guilty for being so crabit, she took Caitlin's hand.

'Don't be silly. It's not you. I'm miserable. Been bitin' the head of the nurses, me ma even, bitin' the head of everyone! Tell me then. I'm listenin' now, tell me everything' and I'll keep me gob shut this time.' Caitlin smiled, relieved.

'There's not a lot to tell. As soon as I got the job, we hit it off. He's tough to work for Anne, but he's committed. He's kind and funny. I mean, he's a bit of a snob, to be honest, but I like him a lot. Mrs Parkes, the old bag, told him what happened, and he came straight over to our house. Can you believe it? He couldn't phone, could he? She doesn't have the McFadden's number. Just got in that flashy Jag of his, and the next thing, he's standing like a gack at our front door!'

She paused as she recalled that afternoon, 'We were in the living room, having a cuppa, I got upset, you know, talking about it and before I knew it, we were kissing. I see him at work, but we're hardly ever alone. Mrs Parkes, the old bat, is forever snooping.' Anne nodded in understanding and listened.

'And then I go and tell me mammy,' she scoffed. 'Well, she goes absolutely ballistic and warns me to stop. Kept at me for ages, going on about her and me daddy and whatever. Doesn't matter now though, she's back in la-la land. Wouldn't care if I was dead or alive — you should see the shape of her.' Caitlin had finally found the nerve to tell Anne what was really going on with Majella and her drinking. She had to tell someone, but Anne gave her a look to kill.

'Don't be horrible, Caitlin. Remember, she's only lost her hubby, and your Martin's locked up. Ye can't blame her for taking those pills. Half the women in Derry are walkin' round, high as kites. It's the only way they survive this shit.' But Caitlin wasn't having it.

'I know, I get it. It's just that she's on *Planet Majella* most days, doped up to the eyebrows. It's hard enough with Daddy gone. I can't even talk about our Tina or Martin. I feel like it's only me that's keeping that house going.'

With a fed-up sigh, she pulled her hand away from Anne, slid off the bed, and moved over to the window. She took in the housing estate surrounding the hospital, with open fields stretching beyond. Anne had a point about Derry women – it was common to rely on medication. The only way they could cope with the endless jail visits, early morning raids, and the crushing poverty they faced with no husband at home to support them.

Angry clouds outside darkened the ward, allowing Caitlin to see her reflection in the window pane. She'd run up some clothes herself and wore a homemade short black-and-white floral skirt with a chunky cream-coloured wool jumper. Her hair was parted in the middle and tied in twin bunches that rested on her shoulders. She took no joy in the new outfit – too much had happened and turned back to face Anne.

Anne's body had all but disappeared. She was mega thin and frail; her face almost hidden in a mass of hair that badly needed washing. She'd done nothing to tidy herself up, and Caitlin sensed her friend's mood sinking further into a deep depression. Like Majella, her will to live seemed stripped away. The vibrant light and energy that once made Anne, Anne, had died.

Caitlin walked back to the bed and clutched her friend's hand. She wanted the old Anne back – she *needed* the old Anne back. Trying to sound bright and breezy, she talked excitedly.

'Listen, let's not talk about him anymore. Let's plan something for us. Something for you and me to look forward to. What do you say?'

'We'll see,' Anne replied, her voice tinged with anger and sadness despite trying to keep her spirits up.

'I can't help being so fed up. I mean, why us Caitlin? Sure, we were only goin' for a cuppa, for Jesus' sake! They had to pick a crowded Saturday afternoon to do it.' Anne pointed at her injured leg, shook her head and said, 'I mean look at me, Caitlin!'

'There goes me beautiful stilettos, the only things I loved wearin', gone. Who's gonna look twice at the likes of me now, with half a peg missin'?' Her voice cracked as she tried to make a joke of it, as if she could laugh it off, but the truth bled through, and before she knew it her pent-up tears broke free, drowning whatever bravado she'd been holding on to. Caitlin hugged her hard and kissed the top of her head. She murmured words of reassurance, telling her it'd be okay.

'I'm sorry, love. It was me who took you uptown,' she said. Her eyes welled until she cried too. The girls held onto each other both crying for a million and one reasons. No words could ease their misery. They stayed put until a nurse tapped Caitlin and said it was time to go.

Caitlin grabbed some boxed tissues and passed a handful to Anne, who wiped her face and said between wipes, 'I told ye, it's not your fault. I don't want to hear more of that talk. But, please, be careful with the Adonis. It'll end badly for all the reasons we know. Your mammy's right. You'll get hurt.'

'We'll see,' Caitlin answered, picking up her handbag.

'More importantly, you need to get better. I'm worried about your mood. It'll be nice to get home to your own bed. This place is mega depressing,' she said, looking around.

The nurse came back, raised her eyebrows at the sight of Caitlin, and gestured for her to go. Caitlin hurriedly put on her mother's mac, finding it a too small to button up. As she thought, her *Littlewoods* delivery had yet to appear – likely burned out in the back of some hijacked lorry, somewhere.

'I'm away then. See you soon,' she said through sniffles.

'Nice coat,' Anne said with an impish grin. She looked a state – her eyes red raw, her cheeks blotched, and her hair, well, her hair was a sight. Caitlin smiled.

'Don't start me,' she said, kissing her goodbye. 'Bye, you.'

'Bye,' Anne replied in a small voice.

The journey back to Blamfield Street felt endless, the notorious Craigavon Bridge checkpoint causing its usual chaos. Inside the bus the thick stink of cigarettes drove Caitlin barmy. She'd be reeking by the time she got home, so she leaned her head against the window and let her thoughts wander.

When she eventually got James alone and voiced her concerns over Anne's sad mood, he'd warned her that she couldn't expect her friend to be the same after such a traumatic experience. It was understandable for her to feel down.

Before the bomb, Anne would never have snapped at her, not in a million years, and Caitlin couldn't help but dwell on that. She'd tried warning the hospital staff how low her friend had sunk, but they only smiled politely and said they'd need to speak with family, which was a fat lot of use. Anne's mammy was pregnant again and too unwell to travel, while her brothers and sisters were either at school or working shifts, leaving no one but Caitlin. Walking away that evening had near broken her, for it felt as if the hospital itself was swallowing Anne whole, draining every trace of the happy-go-lucky girl she'd been and replacing her, bit by bit, with someone Caitlin barely recognised.

James and Caitlin had been wracking their brains, trying to find a way to be alone. She ached to talk to him, to feel his arms around her. Added to that, she'd been dodging Father McGuire, who'd unsuccessfully tried to check in on her mother. Caitlin hadn't attended Mass since her da's funeral, and she was sure the elderly priest wasn't best pleased. Missing Mass was a sin. In the old days, the family would never miss it. Guilt at lying to her mammy, missing mass and until now, keeping secrets from Anne, was doing damage.

Caitlin was at her front door, and after a bit of a search in her bag, she finally found her keys at the very bottom. She'd just pulled them free and was about to slip one into the lock when the door swung open, and there before her was a face she knew only too well.

'Hello, Sis.'

'Martin. When did you get here?!' Caitlin gasped, pulling the door wide, her bag slipping from her hand and landing with a dull thud on the hallway floor as her brother stepped forward and wrapped her in a hug, tighter and longer than anything she'd ever been used to from him. It freaked her out. Martin was never one for that sort of carry-on, not with her anyway. Any show of affection from him had always felt forced.

She stood stock still, her arms stiff at her sides, uncertain how to respond until at last he released her, and though she'd find it hard to admit, the novelty of it was nice. A small part of her, a tiny incy-wincey part of her, was quietly pleased to see him.

He shut the door, picked up her bag, and led her into the living room – another surprise. Tommy was sitting on the sofa, dressed in a smart black suit, white shirt, and tie. He stood up and gave her a peck on the cheek. She took a deep breath, inhaling the mix of booze, smokes, and her dad's favourite *Old Spice* cologne. It took her back for a second.

'Hello, love. How's you?' Tommy asked warmly.

'Grand, Tommy, thanks. Haven't seen you forever.' She removed her mac and slung it over the back of the sofa before flopping down.

'Just been to see Anne. In a word. She's crap.'

Tommy shook his head in understanding. 'I bet. Poor soul,' he said.

Martin sat across from her, and Caitlin gave him a good look over. A pang of sadness hit her when she noticed how much weight he'd lost and how badly he needed a haircut. His cheekbones stuck out and he was missing a front tooth. Obviously he hadn't shaved, so he was rough-looking, dirty, with stained trousers and a black jumper that could do with a good wash. He wasn't even wearing socks, his bare feet crammed into a pair of naff plastic slip-on shoes.

'I can't say you're looking your best, Martin,' she told him. 'When did you land? Does Mammy know you're here?' Martin said he knew he looked like shit. Felt like it too. The Special Branch really laid into him during questioning. He was a wreck, completely knackered and stumbled over his words.

'Got here 'bout half an hour ago.' He looked up at the ceiling, 'Me ma? She's out for the count, and from what I'm hearing, it isn't exactly headline news.' Caitlin ignored his comment but pointed to the teapot on the coffee table and asked.

'Any tea left?'

Tommy sat up and checked the pot. 'Might be enough.'

She jumped to the kitchen for a mug and hurried back to the living room. As Martin poured, his hands shook so badly the tea slopped everywhere. Tommy and Caitlin exchanged a quiet look. Martin noticed but pretended not to, passing the trembling mug across to his sister. She took it gently; her face soft with pity and concern, while he kept talking as if nothing was wrong.

'There's no sugar,' he laughed.

'When do we ever have sugar?' Caitlin chirped. The tea was lukewarm, but it didn't matter.

Her brother looked out the window, scanning the street. 'Where's Tina?'

'No idea. I've been working all hours. Hardly see her,' Caitlin replied. 'She'll be dying to see you, though.'

He grinned through broken teeth and joked, 'Aye, that's Tina, always on me tail. Heard you got yourself a fancy job. Good on ye.'

Caitlin smiled. Given her mother's warning, she wasn't for telling him *anything* about James. The room went quiet until Martin sniffed his shirt and let out a weak laugh.

'I'm mingin'. I put the immersion on, hope that's all right. Water should be hot enough by now. Want me to leave it in for ye?' There was a playful glimmer in his eyes as he looked at Caitlin.

Caitlin mocked, 'I don't think so thanks.' She could imagine what colour the water would be when he'd finished with it and hoped him being back might ease things a bit. But secretly, she thought he'd make things worse. Martin gave Tommy a nod of thanks for getting him home and disappeared up the stairs.

'Looks awful, doesn't he?' Caitlin moaned after he'd left.

'Aye, love, and no wonder. He won't talk about what went on. No doubt it'll come out over time what those bastards did, but it's aged him.'

Caitlin shook her head. 'Tommy, what's happening to us?'

'I don't know, pet. I'm strugglin' meself. If it's not one thing, it's another. Have you seen the state of your ma?'

'Not yet. I'll go up in a bit.' Noting his dark suit, 'You at a funeral?'

Tommy didn't hear her, so she touched his hand and repeated, 'Tommy, were you at a funeral?'

'Sorry, love. Away there for a minute.' He sat forward on the sofa.

'Aye, that wee fella the SAS murdered. On the news. Did ye hear?' Caitlin hadn't time to listen to the news, no matter read a paper.

'The poor father only rang the peelers to tell 'em the lad found a cache of weapons in a nearby graveyard. Told 'im they'd call back but didn't. Next mornin', his wee fella went back to see if the stuff was still there. Fuckin' SAS was waitin'. Thought him a Provo. Shot dead on the spot. No warnin', and him barely sixteen. Massive funeral. The father's a broken man. Him thinkin' he was doing the right thing. Shows ye, doesn't it?' Tommy finished.

Caitlin flinched. 'Jesus, that's brutal. I hadn't heard. And his da, his poor daddy. God love him.'

'I know.' Tommy shook his head. 'They'll charge no one for that either. Like the rest. Doubtless they never will.'

Tommy seemed off somewhere else, so Caitlin started gathering the used mugs. The clatter brought him back.

'Been meaning to tell ye, love. I've sorted that bill out for your da's funeral. Our Majella won't be pleased, but sure, it has to be done. The Boys covered it; at least, that's one less thing on her plate.' He took a sip of tea and spat it out. 'Shit, that's freezin'!'

Caitlin couldn't help but giggle. 'Wanna fresh one?'

Tommy hauled himself up. 'Naw thanks. Need to get movin'. Do me a favour, will ye? Don't talk about the Boys paying that bill. Say the community pulled together or somethin'. Your ma doesn't need to know, not yet anyway.'

Caitlin nodded, mulling it over with relief. The Provos' offer surprised her, especially after she'd flat-out refused to lay a tricolour on her daddy's coffin.

'Well, you can thank them for me. Hadn't a clue how we were gonna scrape it together. Maybe now, with Martin back, things'll ease up a bit.'

Tommy threw on his black leather coat and headed for the door. 'Don't hold your breath, love. So long as the same boy keeps his nose clean, he'll be grand. If not - well... who the heck knows?'

Chapter Thirty-Six

Always, Remember, Must...

'That's fine. Thank you, Mr Holmes... I'm really sorry I couldn't make it... Yes, yes, I understand. You, too... Thank you now. Bye.'

Rob sighed as he hung up the payphone on Val's day. The funeral was over and had even made the BBC news.

That afternoon brought a rare opportunity for Rob to contact the outside world for the first time in weeks. He'd called Tracey earlier, but she was in a right huff, barely answering him. When he first told her he wouldn't be home for his twenty-first or Christmas, as he'd predicted, she'd gone ballistic.

Half-hoping she'd understand that it wasn't easy for him either, he was disappointed in her reaction. There was no talking to her. Tracey's worst trait was her inability to see things from any perspective other than her own.

Sometimes, she could be downright selfish and he worried what kind of mother she'd make.

He felt relieved that he hadn't spoken to her until now. Tracey was hard work at times, though, fair play to her, she still went to Val's funeral like he asked. Their brief, frosty conversation hinted at the sadness of the day and the devastation Val's family must have felt.

Catching sight of himself in the mirror, he paused to take a look. One of the first things they were told to do was let their hair and beards grow. Rob wasn't used to facial hair – never liked it. His skin felt dirty and itchy as he gingerly touched an angry crop of spots under his effort of a beard. His hair had even curled a bit. It wasn't long, but he felt less and less like a perfect, clean-shaven British soldier every day.

After hearing the fresh-faced Eastender in the barracks tell his reasons for joining up, to 'sort Ireland out,' Rob went straight to his captain and accepted the offer to join the covert op.

From then on, his life had become a mix of intense briefings and training – some exciting, others terrifying. The training bombarded him and the five others with lessons on undercover tactics, surveillance, and interrogation techniques. Photography was mega important too. At first focusing on the fundamentals, they later transitioned to night-time infrared photography and how to hide cameras in their clothes and vehicles.

After that, they memorised the layout of Nationalist and Republican areas around Londonderry, and studied how to handle contacts, bug phones, and monitor weapons and vehicles using tracking devices. They even planned for the dreaded scenario of what would happen if they were caught. He'd memorised the mission statement and warnings that were drummed into the small team day after day:

ALWAYS assume your enemy is armed. **REMEMBER** to maintain your self-control at all costs. The Provos **MUST** be eradicated. We **MUST** minimise their activities. We **MUST** act like a terror group and play them at their own game. Let's root them out and **FINISH** them off!

At first, the physical side of the training had been excruciating. The assault course left Rob's body sore, and black and blue from bruising, but over time, it got easier.

In hindsight, the assault course was a breeze compared to the real-life forty-eight-hour interrogation sessions. The hopeful applicants were locked in lone dark cells, stripped, blindfolded, and sporadically doused with ice-cold water fired from a high-pressure hose.

During those endless hours of sluicing, kicks, and verbal assaults, Rob curled into a ball, seeking what little protection he could in the corner. Throughout the ordeal, his body trembled from the cold and shock. He had little to cover himself with and soon became confused and disoriented, losing all sense of time.

Periodically, sleep overtook him – curled up like a puppy – only for brutal kicks to jolt him awake, followed by relentless interrogation from unseen assailants.

The ordeal was insufferable, but he understood its purpose. He had to be prepared physically and mentally for the torture and beatings that would come if he were discovered by the Provos. Lives depended on his ability to endure all and stay silent. He mastered shutting down his thoughts, using the psychological tactics drilled into him day after day.

Eventually, an emptiness settled over him in that dark cell, leaving him close to numb - a state he welcomed. It shielded him, dulled the noise in his head, and let him push aside thoughts of Tracey's disappointment, his worry for her and the bairn, and the rage that still burned over Val's murder.

The sweet thing was, he'd rediscovered his passion for photography. But what really set his blood racing was the advanced driving course — high-speed chases, using the car as a weapon, smashing through controlled crashes, spinning out in skid recovery, and learning anti-ambush drills that left his heart thumping. It was wild, dangerous, and absolutely brilliant. Rob loved every second of it and knew Val would've been in his element too.

When he and the other recruits first turned up, Rob couldn't tell where the new training camp was sited. No one would say. The team were in a cordoned-off area made up of numerous Nissen huts. He guessed they might be near Bessbrook Mill, originally a Quaker village, but now the largest helicopter airbase in Europe, judging by the distant sound of numerous aircraft taking off and landing day and night.

There was no contact with the outside world. Only the applicants and their trainers worked and slept in these huts. They never saw any regular soldiers or civilian staff. Food, laundry, you name it, was prepared and laid out in advance.

Occasionally, Rob heard the sound of automatic rifles. If they were at Bessbrook, the Provos were probably shooting from the nearby Republic. Frustratingly, the army couldn't shoot back across the border, so the Provos had the upper hand and boy, they knew it. Leveraged it.

That night he washed his bruised body, brushed his teeth, and stiffly climbed into his hard as rock, single bed. Six of them remained – four men and two women - but by morning only one would be chosen, after a gauntlet of physical and written tests. Rob felt good about his chances. If he pulled it off, he'd be thrown straight into the thick of it, and the thought left him buzzing, caught between nerves and raw excitement.

Never imagining he had it in him, he was proud to discover otherwise. The entire experience had been transformative. Confidence and self-reliance replaced any doubts. Mentally, he felt strong. Physically, his body ached like hell. But he felt good. *Alive*. Alive and willing. Exhaustion prevailed, but the training had done its job. Ready to become an undercover operative in a perilous new world, Rob was determined to succeed for Val. With bitter relief, he'd given up trying to understand the Irish and their godforsaken country.

The next morning, the weather was comparable to an English autumn day, and Rob felt nostalgic as he walked through the thin early-morning sunshine to the main hut. Decision time. He and his casually dressed fellow applicants took their seats. Someone had set out six chairs in a semi-circle before a wooden desk with a single chair tucked underneath.

When they first set foot in the camp, applicants were instructed not to share personal information with their peers – not an iota. As a result, none of them became friends but kept to themselves. It suited that they were then given code names. Rob's was *Kentucky*. There was nothing extraordinary about the group. The kind of people you'd see any day waiting in line at a bus stop or having a cuppa in a greasy spoon.

One of the women, a girl with long brown feather-cut hair, was code-named *Iowa*. Today, she wore a white-collared brown floral shirt dress that hung well below her knees. Oddly, she'd paired it with checked bell bottom trousers. Even for someone as casual about his own wardrobe, it stood out miles that fashion wasn't the girl's strongest suit.

She spotted Rob at the far end of the row and met him with a look of pure contempt. He'd never taken to her from the start, and her expression left no room for doubt, a clear warning to back off, to stay away. Rob got the message and avoided her like the plague.

The fella sitting beside her was stocky, with greasy mid-length brown hair and a pair of sideburns that put Rob's to shame. He wore a thick, woollen fisherman's jumper and jeans, and waited, staring at the ground like it might speak to him. Rob had the feeling this wasn't his first time round. He had that look about him.

The hut door banged open, and the training coordinator strutted into the cold room. Sporting his usual look: a spotless white T-shirt, black joggers, and trainers, he called himself 'TC' because it kept things simple, as confirmed by the security pass dangling from a chain around his bull-like neck.

Again, they knew little about him except that he had a Welsh accent. TC was a wiry, bald man but ripped, like a classic sergeant major from an American war movie, minus the accent. He populated the room with such a forceful presence and confidence that Rob had come to respect him. Tough but fair. Rob kept his eyes on him as he sat at the desk and let out a low, deliberate *ahem* before addressing them.

'Morning all. First to say is that the British Army appreciates your dedication and commitment throughout these trials. This process has been challenging. The training intended to enhance your survivability, and we make no apology for taking you to hell and back.' He then pulled a sheet of foolscap from a file, gave the group a fresh once-over, and added.

'Second, it's been noted that the calibre of this intake is exceptionally high, and you've all put in an outstanding performance. So, for that very reason, we're selecting two candidates instead of the usual one.'

The surprising news drew an unmistakable intake of breath.

'The British Army's presence in Northern Ireland has often been described as "the meat in a sectarian sandwich." This perception must change. We must prove our ability to address the ongoing security situation here. For the two selected candidates, the unit's objectives will be clarified in the coming months. Be warned: if captured, you will doubtless face torture and execution. We operate in one of the most dangerous environments in the world, and this is a wartime scenario. Covert operations require absolute discretion.'

TC pointed outside and said in a harsh voice, 'There is malevolence at large. Remain vigilant at all times, no matter the outcome of this selection.' He paused, taking a sip of water before continuing.

'I'd better get on and put you out of your misery.' He gave them a rare smile.

'The following candidates have been unsuccessful: *Ohio, Kansas, Arizona*, and *Washington*. Despite your commendable efforts, you have been passed over on this occasion. Please vacate your quarters, collect your belongings, and report to the designated meeting point at 13.00 hours. Transportation will be provided to return you to your respective barracks. Thank you for your participation, and best of luck in your future endeavours.'

The four who didn't make it gave TC a quick handshake and left.

By now, Rob's heart was doing somersaults. Hell yeah, he was in! It'd been a challenging ride for sure, but he'd made it. He fought to keep his cool. *We nailed it, Val; we nailed it!* Iowa remained silent, her anger simmering just below the surface. TC addressed the pair with their new orders.

'Iowa, Kentucky, congratulations. You are to be partners. Our first male and female operatives. Your accommodation in Londonderry has been arranged, and you will proceed there tonight. Report here at 17.00 hours to discuss your op, including your new identities and logistical arrangements. We will also cover the protocol for communicating your absence for the coming months with your families.'

Rob thanked TC, who shot him a small smile before heading out. Iowa didn't speak – she didn't need to. Her face said it all: she was livid. Maybe this wasn't what she'd bargained for, Rob thought. From the way she'd been carrying on these past few weeks, she was a loner, a weirdo through and through. A weirdo who wanted to fly solo, not be lumped with a partner.

He hung around anyway, waiting for her to congratulate him or say something, anything. But all he got was the cold shoulder. Done with her, he shrugged with a wry smile and got ready to go – to hell with her.

'I wanted to do this alone!' she snapped at his back. 'The last thing I needed was a bloody "partner!"'

Rob spun around. 'Oh yeah? Well, I'm not exactly thrilled to bits about teaming up either, especially with a right mardy mare like you. Ye don't see me whining about it, do ye?!'

Iowa had no idea what he meant, but she threw him another filthy look, hoping to put him in his place. It fell flat. Rob didn't bite. He simply turned away and walked out.

Back in his hut, he packed up his few possessions, stuffing his army gear into an over-sized, clear plastic bag with a label left by his door. His civvies went into his old, battered sports bag. He took off his dog tags and placed them in a small red velvet box, next to the engraved gold watch his parents had given him for his eighteenth birthday.

Carefully, he tucked the box into the plastic bag, along with the sports bag and the rest of his belongings.

Iowa and Rob arrived back in the meeting room at 17.00 hours to find TC waiting at his desk.

The room had been rearranged: two empty chairs were now positioned in front, each accompanied by a small brown cardboard box. TC motioned for them to take their seats.

'Iowa, Kentucky, I trust you've packed all your personal items into the provided bags.' They nodded.

'For your security and operational effectiveness, you are not to keep any possessions that could link you to the British Army or your family.'

He stared at them expectantly, and again they nodded to acknowledge the order.

'Excellent. A vehicle has been arranged for your use in Londonderry. Only use it when necessary. Otherwise, you're to travel by foot or by public transport. Your contact is a local man who owns a mobile laundry service. He's well-regarded and trusted in the Republican community. He may come across as evasive or unhelpful at first, but like the others, I guarantee - once he smells the cash, he'll fall in line.' TC took a breath before continuing.

'Your first op begins tomorrow and will run for four weeks, with the potential for extension depending on results. You'll accompany your contact during his daily runs through the Creggan and Bogside estates, collecting and delivering laundry in his van. Iowa, you're the less conspicuous of the two, so you'll drive. Kentucky, you're good with a camera - you'll photograph and film any persons or activity of interest from the back of the van. Keep any interaction with the locals to an absolute minimum. I suggest you re-familiarise yourselves with the area and review the mugshots provided.'

Rob kept listening, jaw tight.

'Laundry retrieved from a suspect's residence will be passed to forensics for immediate analysis - we'll be testing for explosives, gunshot residue, and other relevant traces. To speed things up, we've established a temporary lab next to the laundry facility, close to the city. Based on any findings, we can move fast, and without question, conduct searches or make the necessary arrests.'

Iowa's anger rolled across her face like a dark cloud until TC dropped yet another bombshell.

'Since you're to act as a couple, shared accommodation has been arranged at a local bed-and-breakfast.'

Iowa actually gasped. TC shot her a warning glare before carrying on.

'The proprietor is reliable. We've used her before. Everything you'll need, funds, clothing, new ID, is packed in these boxes. There's also a written brief inside. Read it carefully and memorise it. Once you've done that, return it to me.'

The pair took their boxes and, along with TC, spent the next hour going over the finer points of the op. TC explained how to tell their families, which was key.

'You'll tell your next of kin you're being deployed overseas on an advanced training programme. It's the line we use - helps settle nerves. You'll be safe, but out of contact for the foreseeable.'

As soon as TC was out of sight, Rob didn't hang about. He brushed past Iowa, who looked like she'd swallowed a wasp, and made straight for his hut. He needed to write his letters.

First was Tracey. He poured everything into it. His heart, his guilt, how sorry he was for letting her down. He wrote about the bairn, the hope that he'd soon make things right, he'd come home and they'd be a proper family.

The next one was harder. His parents. It might be the last they'd ever hear from him if things went south. He tried to keep it light, reassuring, but honest enough to bring them some comfort if the worst came. As soon as they were both finished, he sealed them in the plastic bag, ready to leave.

Late that evening, TC drifted about his office, filing papers and waiting for the next load of candidates to arrive. He stopped at the window and let a crooked smile tug at his mouth. Outside stood Iowa and Kentucky. They looked the part, no question. Two youngsters, hacked off with life and each other, standing there like a couple who'd already had enough of each other. The girl wore a face like she'd just ate a lemon, and the poor fella looked guilty for drawing breath.

'Perfect,' TC muttered, dry as a bone.

They were perfect.

Chapter Thirty-Seven

A Perfect Idea

Caitlin returned to Rocola, and James was overjoyed to have her around.

He'd almost forgotten how captivating she was. Her wounds had near healed, and she wore an outfit he hadn't seen before, a short black skirt, a white blouse, and a matching black jacket. Her hair was tied back in a loose bun. Impeccably professional, he felt a surge of pride as he greeted her. Silent smiles passed between them, speaking volumes.

With Roger watching him like a hawk, the hours dragged for James without Caitlin, and he hated the hollow feeling it left behind. What unsettled him most was his uncle's warning that he'd tell his father about the trip to Creggan. The thought irritated him. His father had never made a secret of wanting his son in uniform, following the family line into the army, and that made Roger's threat all the more dangerous.

While Caitlin was off, James burned the midnight oil on the talks proposal. George Shalham had been glued to him, going over the guest list and, after a lot of back-and-forth, finalising it. Mrs Parkes had sent out the invitations and, when Caitlin returned, she'd start with follow-up calls to lay out their aim and answer questions.

RSVPs were trickling in, including one from Charles Jones who accepted. James was seriously not happy about the invitation. He didn't want Jones anywhere near the room, but for some bizarre reason, Roger stubbornly pushed for it.

Uncle and nephew almost had a showdown over it, but with James already skating on thin ice, he backed down. Jones would be nothing but a nuisance, unlikely to contribute anything meaningful to the conversation, and was sure to stir up trouble. The man was an outright fanatic.

Mrs Parkes was buzzing around James's office like a fly to sugar. When Caitlin came in, she was there, acting as if she was looking for something while listening by the door.

In the end, James lost it. He stood up, shot her a vicious look, and shut the door in her intrusive face. *The woman was insufferable.* He then turned to Caitlin with a genuine smile.

'How are you? Feeling better? You look fantastic,' he remarked, nodding in approval at her outfit. He then gestured to a leather visitor chair for her to sit in.

'Thank you. Been busy sewing. Glad you like it.' Thrilled by the compliment, Caitlin's face went beetroot.

James was impressed. 'Made it all yourself, eh? Clever you.'

She glanced at him sideways. 'My mother was supposed to help, but she's not well.' Her face reddened further. She was nervous; he noticed.

'James, you, me, this thing... I mean, what happened was so far out – I never saw it coming. And now it's the only thing that's keeping me going. I'm scared.'

It wasn't the right time for a deep discussion, so James explained how Mrs Parkes had grassed to his uncle that he'd been to Caitlin's house, and how both his uncle and George Shalham had reacted. He wasn't for saying a word about his near hijacking.

That was it then, Caitlin presumed. Over in a flash. She wasn't going to be responsible for James losing his job or his home – and over her dead body would he be joining the army. She braced herself, thinking she might be out of a job at this rate, but he leaned across the desk.

'Caitlin, no one was more surprised than me when I kissed you. But I had to.' He chuckled, adding, 'My head's all over the shop.' Her heart sank.

'I get why your uncle's upset. Once you know this place better, you'll understand. Think about it: you and me. We come from worlds that never mix. Never have, never will. That's how it is.' James refused to accept it.

'I don't care where you're from. It's only you I want,' he said, getting up and wincing.

'Are you hurt? What did you do?'

'I'm fine. Overdid it with the running.' They noticed Mrs Parkes's silhouette once again outside the door.

Caitlin got up. 'Let's think for a minute. I love it here. At least we've got that for now, but we need to get on. Mein Führer is outside again.'

James laughed. 'I don't care. I need to see you. Alone. We'll talk later, all right?'

'All right,' she agreed, smiling radiantly. James opened the office door so fast, surprising Mrs Parkes, who almost fell through it.

'What is it now Mrs Parkes?' he growled.

'Oh... nothing. Nothin' at all, Looking for my favourite biro. Lost it somewhere, that's all, Mr Henderson,' she said, scurrying away.

James gave Caitlin a smile as he watched Mrs Parkes scurry off. 'Right, time to go to work, yeah?'

Caitlin gave a smirk, went to her desk, and grabbed James's spiral notebook and a pen before rejoining him. This time they left the office door wide open, making sure *they* could keep an eye on Mrs Parkes.

The day flew by as they hashed out the meeting itinerary and presentation. The City Hotel had confirmed the rooms and accommodation, and James floated the idea of having a casual dinner afterwards. He envisaged it'd be a great way to get everyone to relax. However, special attention and sensitivity were a must for the seating arrangements.

A good number of prominent businessmen and women from different community sectors had committed to attending, including the weary traders of William Street, who'd fought hard to keep their businesses open during and after the riots, as well as city councillors, bankers, and politicians.

At first, the army had been reluctant to get involved, but Shalham had convinced them to compromise and show up. To Roger's delight, representatives from the Catholic Church and the Free Derry Presbyterian Church had agreed to join, which was a rare thing considering their history of hardly ever being under the same roof.

James and Roger knew they needed to get a chunk of investment for Rocola and soon. They were under pressure from their Glasgow clients, fed up with the delays caused by the riots and hijacking. He'd spent hours on the phone trying to talk them out of cancelling. Although it was a struggle, he was happy with the results so far. He and Caitlin kept at it until Caitlin picked up her notebook.

'Want a cuppa? I think there's some biscuits lying around if you're lucky.' James rubbed his belly and laughed.

'Nah, I'm good. Haven't been running for a while. Keeping off the sweets.' She closed the door behind her, a faint, knowing smile tugging at her lips.

James exhaled deliberately slowly. Too close. He couldn't be sure whether Caitlin had caught the lie in his story about his ribs, first claiming he'd hurt them running and then contradicting himself by saying he hadn't been. He'd have to watch it. The last thing he needed was her catching wind of what really happened with the hijacking.

Thankfully, the office phone rang and he grabbed it. 'Henderson.' He knew the voice straight away. *Roger*. Only the fifth time he'd phoned that day.

James leaned against the windowsill to look out and listen. He never grew tired of watching the factory at work. An eight-foot-high steel fence surrounded the site, with one gated entrance next to a security guardhouse.

The car park lay behind a single-storey red-brick block with a weather-boarded white apex roof. It housed quality control, which Roger had built onto the original factory, developed in the Victorian era and bought as a derelict site fifteen or so years ago.

It was an ornate building with large white ferrous-framed windows set in a stone and polychrome brick façade. Goods In and Goods Out were on the ground floor. The first floor held the cutting department; the second was decked out with bench after bench of sewing machines. On the third and fourth floors, hundreds of workers made collars, fronts, and cuffs for shirts and other garments. Not only did Rocola produce shirts, but they made underwear and nightwear for several Scottish and overseas clients. James had only been half-listening to Roger when his uncle cried.

'Hello? Are you still there James?! Did you hear me?'

'I'm here... And yes, I heard you. If you insist, I'll be back for dinner with Harris... Yes, I know, he's not the easiest... Okay. Right, see you at seven... No, I won't be late. Bye now.'

James hung up the phone, dreading yet another dull, all-male dinner. He never had much time for Doctor Harris.

As a child, James had come down with chickenpox, and it was Harris who treated him, leaving the boy disturbed in a way that never quite went away. Over the years, little about the man seemed to change. To James he was always the same peculiar, odd-looking fella, with far-right views not unlike Charles Jones. Shockingly thin for a doctor, he had the off-putting habit of scratching at the dry, flaking skin left by his diabetes. His clothes were no better, often shabby, sometimes edging into downright filthy.

Much like Jones, James could never understand why Roger kept him around. His uncle's choice of friends, more often than not these days, was downright baffling.

By lunchtime, James looked up to find Caitlin standing at the threshold of his office, cheeks flushed, eyes bright. She knocked on the open door.

'Can I have a quick word?' Intrigued, James gestured her in.

'Sure. Come in. Close the door.'

She walked gracefully into the room and stood before his desk. She'd removed her jacket, and he could see the curves of her breasts through her sheer blouse and the outline of a lace bra. His eyes moved downwards to appreciate the slimness of her tiny waist and boyish hips.

'Mr Henderson, *please*,' she joked, noticing his naughty expression and reading his mind.

'This is important. I've had an idea.'

'Okay. I'm listening.' James clasped his hands behind his head, leaned back in his chair, and waited.

'Well, I've been invited to a twenty-first party on Saturday week at the Malin Hotel. I've told them I'll go, but... I was thinking. I could use it as an excuse for us to spend some time together instead. What do you think?'

James held his tongue, pulling a face as though scandalised by the very idea. Caitlin's brow creased, worry creeping in.

At last, James couldn't keep a lid on it; a big grin broke loose, and he pointed at her, teasing, 'Fooled ye!' Her eyes narrowed.

'That's not funny,' she said. 'I nearly died then.' Her protest only made him laugh harder. He thought it was a perfect idea.

'Aye, that'll work. I'll say I'm meeting some friends. You tell your mother you're off to this birthday do, and we're covered. When is it again?'

Caitlin was still answering when Mrs Parkes came sweeping into the office without so much as a knock. She paused at the sight of Caitlin's flushed cheeks and the charged air between them, then thrust a stack of invoices towards James.

'I need your signature on these.' When he handed the papers back, she fixed them both with a long look that said. *'Don't think you can make an eejit outta me.'*

Then, without another word, she stepped away, quiet as a shadow, her lips moving in a frenzy she kept to herself.

James jotted the party date in his diary, but after that he couldn't concentrate. His thoughts were elsewhere, fixed on the idea of time alone with Caitlin. Mrs Parkes had surely picked up on their excitement. *Shit.*

He'd have to find a way to manage her. But how? Then either a very bad idea or a great idea crept into his head: he'd ask Caitlin to make a weekend of it. A whole weekend! Donegal Town tempted him, far enough from the city, far enough from curious eyes; no one would know them there.

Caitlin wasn't like other women. He'd have to remember that. He couldn't just blurt out and ask her to go away for a weekend. She stirred feelings in him like he never knew, that was what set this thing apart. If he wanted to make a weekend of it, and he did, he'd need a gentler, slower, considerate approach.

Otherwise...

Chapter Thirty-Eight

Mortified!

Her plan was flawless. Caitlin started by casually mentioning the birthday invitation to Majella, hoping to ease her into the idea – assuming she even noticed.

The thought of hanging out with James by herself made Caitlin nervous and thrilled at the same time.

They finished work on time that night, and since Mrs Parkes had left early, they said goodnight to the admin girls, who giggled when James gave them a smile and cracked a joke. He told Caitlin, not too thrilled, that he was going home for dinner with his family and Doctor Harris.

The mere mention of the man who'd neglected her father, and likely helped send him to his grave, knocked her for six. Although she'd told James all about Harris's role, she felt hurt and surprised when he insisted he couldn't get out of the dinner. He did admit, however, he'd never liked Harris and said the man gave him the creeps. No matter the circumstances, his hands were tied. He had to go.

James knew better than to annoy Roger, but his explanation calmed Caitlin down a bit. Then, he blurted out the one thing he promised himself he wouldn't: he asked her to spend the weekend with him!

'Caitlin, about us getting some time on our own... let's make a weekend of it, just us. A bit of time away together – you'll love it.'

His words landed wrong, nothing like he'd meant them to. He'd thought a weekend away might cheer her up, ease the disappointment of him being with Harris, but the look on her face said it all.

'Ah no! Caitlin,' he blurted, springing up and grabbing her hand. 'I didn't mean it like that! I meant separate rooms, separate rooms! I only wanted to give you a longer break, that's all.' She said nothing, her gaze sliding past him to the window, the light paling across the glass.

Softer now, he tried again. 'Listen. All I meant was, we'd go for a drive, get dinner, walk the beach, talk. Honestly. Two rooms. That's what I meant.' He was beginning to sound like a broken record. Her face relaxed, but her voice cut through.

'I wasn't expecting that. It's you, James – the way you said it so casual, as if I'd jump at the chance. Like you were doing me a favour. I'm nothing like the women you've been with before.' She turned from him, sure enough of the sort he'd been with. They were nothing like her, she'd stake her soul on it.

He scoffed and shook his head. 'You've got me so wrong. Caitlin. Not casual, *never* casual. Not with you. I probably shouldn't have brought it up.'

Mortified, this time Caitlin shook her head, gathered her things, and left without another word, leaving him standing there, red-faced, coffee cup in hand, looking every inch the wanker that he felt.

She didn't have Anne to talk to, and the walk home felt super long. She missed her friends' jokes and straight talk, the way she could turn dark into light with a laugh or a quick one liner. She wanted to tell her about James, but she chickened out because Anne would be furious. Caitlin could almost hear her yapping: *'Told ye, didn't I? His sort's only after one thing!'*

As Caitlin reached her front door, she did what she always did, fumbled around in her bag for her keys. But before she found them, Martin had yanked the door open. This time it was different. No welcome, no hug. Decked out in a second-hand Army and Navy coat, a beat-up grey turtleneck with grey trousers over scuffed boots caked in dirt, he was quite a sight. The minute he saw her, he lost it, exclaiming he was going mad.

'I can't take me ma. Keeps callin' me fuckin' Patrick! She's off her fuckin' rocker, Caitlin. Should be in Gransha with all the other loonies! I'm outta here.'

He stormed past Caitlin without a second glance, causing her arm to smack painfully against the corner wall, then slammed their rickety gate, which somehow didn't fall apart.

'What's going on?!' Caitlin called after him. Without answering, he waved her off and continued walking instead.

'Nice to see you too Martin,' Caitlin mumbled.

Inside, the cold air hit her hard through her thin coat. The house was an ice box. She pulled her coat in tighter and hurried up to Majella's bedroom. The room was almost pitch black and freezing, a grim reminder that they couldn't afford to keep the heat on.

'Mammy. You awake? It's me,' Caitlin whispered.

She sat on the edge of the bed and turned on a small lamp with a shabby shade. Stained bedcovers, marked with God knows what, caught her eye as she carefully pulled them back, revealing a frail, skeletal figure. Because Majella wouldn't eat, they had to call the doctor. Caitlin was hoping he'd send her to a psychiatrist or put her in the hospital, like Martin said, so she could get the right care. Majella quickly pulled the covers up and burrowed herself under them.

Caitlin placed her hand on her shoulder and said. 'Mammy, it's me.'

'Go away, please! I'm so tired, Patrick. I'll get up in a while.' Majella mumbled from underneath the blankets.

In the end, Caitlin gave up, tucked the blankets in further and turned off Majella's bedside light. Drained, she groaned as she reached her room and cast aside her new coat. There were no tears left to give. She threw her work clothes across the bed, pulled on a sweater and jeans, then went to the landing to fetch fresh sheets from the linen cupboard. After that, she sorted Majella out and, though she could hardly think straight, managed to change the bed.

Things were getting out of hand. Somehow, she had to get Majella moving. It was plain the doctor hadn't called, despite Martin's promise to see to it. So much for her hoping he'd make life easier.

She couldn't believe her eyes when she went into the kitchen. Dirty plates, glasses, cups, and overflowing ashtrays covered every surface. The smell of something rotten was all over the place. Her mother's once-immaculate countertops were smeared with sticky brown cup rings, spilled beer, and mystery leftovers. Martin had thrown another party with his so-called friends.

Caitlin cursed. Unlike most, she never swore, but dear God, she was fed up. 'For fuck sake!'

Any happiness she felt that morning was long gone. Thinking of James only made it worse, for he'd hurt her too. Her patience was being tested, ready to give at any moment. She sank into a chair, shut her eyes, and let herself dream of a time when the house had been filled with happiness and some sense of normality.

A nudge on her shoulder woke her up some time later. Tina stood there, looking worried. 'Why ye sleepin' in the kitchen?' she asked.

Caitlin stretched and made to get up. 'Awe, Tina, where've you been?'

'Next door. Take it Mammy's still in bed?' She removed her red coat and went to hang it under the stairs.

'Yeah. Zombied out. Our Martin's a bastard, Tina. He flew outta here as soon as I put the key in the door. Has the doctor been?' Caitlin replied.

Tina shook her head, taking in the disaster zone that was their kitchen. Normally it didn't bother her, but this was well bad.

'Not that I know.' she told Caitlin, sitting down.

'Pay no heed to our Martin, he's all over the show.' Caitlin groaned. She always found it hard to ignore Martin.

Tina waited as Caitlin explained. 'He ran right past me, ranting and raving, almost took the gate off. I come in here, Mammy's away with it, you're MIA, and the kitchen's a friggin pigsty!'

'Aye, I have to admit, it's bad in here all right. Tell ye what.' Tina's voice was tense. She shifted nervously, as if on the brink.

'Forget Martin. Let's sort this, then get some food. I don't know about you, but I'm strugglin'. This close to breakin' point.' She snapped her fingers, as if the sound alone would show how close.

Caitlin gave her a smile. Tina was finally confiding in her, and for the first time, she realised they were both struggling to cope. They surveyed the mess and then gave each other a look. Small smiles crept onto their faces, growing wider as an idea passed between them. Memories of Majella, singing in the kitchen.

Tina wandered over to their old tape recorder and pressed the sticky 'play' button. The room soon filled with the poorly taped music from Radio 1's Countdown show.

With the music up loud, the girls started cleaning and laughing; it was like second nature to them. Lost in the music, they snatched up wooden spoons, belting into them like microphones, spinning and dancing until their sides ached.

They needed this, the craic and the laughter, a spark of what life used to be. For a while it almost felt like the old days, before Martin's internment, before Patrick's death, before Majella had hid herself away from them, and before that bloody bomb on Shipquay Street.

After failing to persuade her mother to eat, Caitlin stepped into the living room later that evening. Tina lay sprawled on the sofa in front of the TV. The fire burned low, but the room felt warmer. Eddie Waring's voice filled the space as he presented *It's a Knockout,* Tina's favourite.

'No Luck?' Tina asked. Caitlin sighed and flopped down next to her.

'Not a bite. It's those pills. Her mouth's dry and coated in some sort of white stuff. What are we gonna do?'

Tina patted the sofa, signalling Caitlin to move closer. 'Leave her be. Better she sleeps it off,' she advised.

Caitlin was chuffed Tina was here. They'd had a good laugh earlier, and Caitlin felt closer to her than she had for some time. Could this be a new beginning? Hopefully, they'd become close. Support one another. Especially now.

'You've been great today. Thanks, Tina. I'm struggling too. I—' Caitlin began, but the words were cut short as the front door burst open with a bang that startled them both.

Martin.

He stood there swaying in the doorway and gave his siblings a filthy look. Then he snorted before heading for the kitchen. Both girls jumped up and followed as he switched on the main light.

At Caitlin's angry face, he flung his coat across his chair after clumsily taking it off.

'Who died?' he sneered at her.

She watched on as he plopped a brown paper bag on the table, opened it, and took out a bottle of white lemonade and a big bottle of cheap vodka. He cackled loudly for no reason, then grabbed some glasses and raised the vodka in the air.

'Who wants a drink?' he cried.

Caitlin gave him a look of disgust. Pissed as a newt, he reeked of the stale moth-eaten clothes he wore like a bad memory. She'd been leaving early and returning late from work, barely catching a glimpse of him for days. Now that she stood there, she noted his lifeless skin, his greasy hair, and unshaven face. Her brother was a stranger to her, an old man – a mere shadow of the teenager she once knew.

'C'mon, don't let me be drinkin' on me own!' he declared, faking a sad clown face.

'I've got friends comin' in a minute. For a wee party.' Smiling from ear to ear, he looked like he'd won the lottery.

Jesus Christ! Caitlin couldn't believe he'd the nerve to think he could throw a hooley now, in their freshly cleaned kitchen. *No way.*

'Martin, you're plastered and there'll be no parties in here. We've spent the evening cleaning up after *you*!' Caitlin yelled. She shot Tina a look, hoping for some backup, but to her utter dismay, Tina retorted.

'Jesus, Caitlin, get a life! Didn't I tell ye to pay no heed to him?' Caitlin was mortified and completely speechless. She shook her head and bit her lower lip.

Tina chirped in with a soft smile and a wrinkled nose and sat down next to Martin, 'Right then, Martin, I'll have a drink with ye since you're askin'.'

'You will NOT, Martina McLaughlin. Over my dead body!' Caitlin shrieked as she tried to grab Tina's outstretched hand.

Tina rolled her eyes to the heavens. 'For Pete's sake, Caitlin, will ye stop it? You're drivin' us up the wall. Martin, hurry up and pour us that drink, will ye?'

Caitlin knew what Tina was thinking because of her smirk and how happy she looked. She was pleased. She didn't want Caitlin there. Pleased that, for now at least, she had her precious brother to herself.

Caitlin shook her head. And there was her thinking, she and Tina had a chance. *Would she ever wise up?*

Martin squinted, struggling to focus on Tina. His head wobbled from side to side.

'See you wee girl. You're a diamond, Martina McLaughlin. Know that? A carat diamond.' He turned to Caitlin, pointing a finger at her with a sneer.

'But see her. You're not like that stuck-up cow in that there corner. Her with her fancy job and Goody-two-shoes act   you're a waste of space, Caitlin McLaughlin. You're a p...p... pompous, p...p... pretentious p...p... person!'

Deliberately stuttering, both he and Tina burst out laughing, like a couple of spoiled brats who'd got away with nicking something from their mother's purse.

Hurt, Caitlin had no words, but watched on as her younger sister poured out a heavy measure of vodka with a splash of lemonade. She and Martin lifted their glasses, cried, 'Sláinte!' then knocked them back, shaking their heads before letting out a wild, 'Yeeesss!'

Caitlin's life had become a rollercoaster, up one minute and crashing down the next. She fought back tears while the partygoers knocked back shot after shot.

Intense she hissed. 'Go to hell!' Then ran to her room.

All night, she pressed her pillow over her head, desperate to block out the noise from downstairs. The racket only got worse as the poorly repaired front door slammed with people coming and going. She couldn't believe it. If she went down and complained, they'd start her again. That she could not handle.

Between the carry-on below and Majella, drugged and snoring so loud Caitlin reckoned her daddy in the cemetery could hear her, she knew it was going to be a long night. She'd never forgive Martin for this, nor Tina either. Small wonder then that sleep refused to come.

As for James Henderson... huh

Chapter Thirty-Nine

The Rainbow Café

O kay, it hadn't gone to plan, but Kieran told himself he'd done well enough under the circumstances.

The soldier's murder had got pretty good TV coverage, but in true BBC fashion: they never told the whole story. He'd bet most Brits didn't know why their soldiers were even in Ireland, fighting this bloody war. Probably didn't give a shit.

Bigotry, gerrymandering, internment, *Bloody Sunday* – to name but a few - that was why. It was all one-fucking-sided. The British media were turning a blind eye to the cold, calculated murders of Catholics, the brutal interrogations, the illegal internment happening right in front of them. Should be ashamed.

The night after the Brit's execution, Kieran had slept like a baby, but now his head was busy with what came next. Honey did okay, but that's about it. She was terrified by what he said while he drove her home.

'Breathe so much as a fuckin' word about tonight or the other and I'll kill ye. You first, then the rest of your lot slowly and painfully. You're to blame. Just you.'

He gave her a cold, hard stare before continuing, 'Remember, it was you who picked those bastards up. If I'm lifted, I'll say it was you. Your idea. Your word against mine,' she'd nodded, understanding she was well and truly screwed.

'I'll need you again, Honey, so when I call. Run. Do-not-refuse-me. Otherwise...' He didn't have to say anything else, so she'd kept quiet and got out.

Bare-chested, Kieran was lying in bed, finishing a spliff. The room smelled strongly of weed, and it was stuffy. Sweat was rolling down his torso and he laughed softly as a hand appeared and gently wiped the moisture away. He watched as fingers gracefully moved up, then went into a full-lipped mouth and playfully sucked. A suggestive smile suddenly appeared on the most beautiful face Kieran had ever seen.

With a giggle, he jumped on the perfect body and whispered, 'I know a few things those fingers could be doing.'

'I bet you do,' came a wicked voice. But I gotta go to work, my love. I've a lot on my plate today.'

The couple shared a long, steamy kiss before Kieran was left to chill in the quiet of their bed. He kicked back the bedclothes, finished his joint, and watched as his lover showered and dressed. What a beauty. God had been overly generous.

Following a passionate kiss goodbye, he found himself alone and groaned with contentment, replaying their steamy night and morning together. He had a chuckle then leaped out of bed to see what the weather was like. *Hmm, not bad.*

Later, in the Rainbow with a coffee and the *Derry Journal*, Kieran felt someone lurking nearby. He looked up and saw Martin McLaughlin staring daggers at him. High up in the Provos, today he was barely recognisable - looked like a total yob. Word was he'd been hammering the drink since he got out, and looking at him now, Kieran reckoned they were right.

The guy had red-veined cheeks, a busted-up nose, a missing tooth, and heavy, bloodshot eyes. As he walked over, the stench of stale booze sealed the deal. Kieran thought he must have crashed out in his crumpled second-hand military gear. For a high-ranking Provo, McLaughlin was an embarrassment. He now looked and smelled like a bum, like something you'd see at the bottom of Waterloo Place, a local haunt for the down and outs.

Kieran, who was fanatical about his hygiene, drank more coffee as he tried to ignore the stench wafting from McLaughlin, who'd sat down uninvited across the booth. He watched as he grabbed a salt shaker, emptied a load on the table, and, playing with it, asked Kieran, in a raspy, hung-over voice.

'What ye up to Kelly?'

'Nothin' much,' Kieran replied, folding the paper and setting it aside.

Martin set the salt cellar down, then with a flick of his wrist sent the grains scattering across Kieran's lap. He searched the café until he spotted Siobhan, the white-haired owner, who came straight over. She knew Martin McLaughlin and understood that the same boy warranted fast service.

'Right, Martin? What can I get ye?' she asked with a smile.

'I'll have a full Irish and a strong black coffee. Cheers, Siobhan.' Martin grinned.

'And he's payin',' he quipped, pointing at Kieran who nodded, grumbled, and ordered himself another coffee. Martin slumped forward across the plastic tablecloth, inching closer to Kieran, who recoiled. Christ, the guy really did reek.

Martin gave a weak laugh, knowing Kelly wasn't happy. Without asking, he plucked a John Player Special from Kieran's half-empty pack on the table. First smoke of the day, he said, and with his stomach growling and a hangover brewing, he needed it. Kieran struck a light for him, slow and reluctant, and watched as Martin took a deep drag, then blew the smoke straight at him, letting it drift into his eyes.

'So your op went tits up. Weren't your orders clear – if there was a no show, you had to pull back. A couple of volunteers got lifted on the way to ye.' He dragged hard on the smoke, eyes locked on Kieran like a hawk.

'You, Mr Kelly, have landed us in the shit. Fucked it up. The Brits are crawling over us like a rash. Did you see that BBC report? Pure shite, the lot of it. Absolute shite!' Martin kept going, huffing and puffing, while Kieran just listened. Inside, though, Kieran felt no shame, no regret. He was glad. He'd done exactly what he wanted.

'So here's the deal.' Martin continued. 'Get outta Derry, go somewhere over the border and lie low – *pronto*. Personally, I think you're a lightweight, a weasel. I seriously do not like you. We're told you've been up to some shady shit with a certain individual, and that has got me disturbed, very disturbed. You know what I'm on about, right?'

He waited for an answer, already feeling his annoyance spike at the sight of Kelly's polished look. The cocky bastard bugged him, made him even more conscious of his own scruffy state. Something about the poser felt off. He could feel it in his gut. Nevertheless, he'd wait. Play along. Didn't matter, he had the wanker over a barrel, thanks to a piece of juicy intel. Once the time was right, and it would be, he'd take it and relish every second.

Siobhan brought the coffee, spilling some on the table as she hurried away. She'd normally have wiped it up, but today she rushed off. The atmosphere in that booth was thick enough to cut with a chainsaw.

Kieran knew what McLaughlin was on about but shrugged and played dumb.

'Haven't a clue what you're on about, Mr McLaughlin,' he said. Martin wasn't surprised by his response. *Figured.*

'You're a down-and-out liar, Kelly. You know exactly what I'm talkin' about. Yet, you're still at it, playin' with fire. Keep it up, and I'll take you out. Finish it for ye, along with the rest of your choirboys. Metaphorically speakin', that is.' Kieran wasn't an idiot but acted like one.

'Honest to God, I told ye, Mr McLaughlin. Swear on my mother's life.' He shook his head like crazy, 'I don't know what you're on about!'' Martin couldn't take blatant lies and grabbed Kieran by the collar. His voice was like ice when he spoke.

'Listen to me, ye sleazy piece of shit; do ye want me to lay it out right here, right now in this wee café run by the lovely Siobhan over there? That woman knows everything, except for your recent shenanigans. 'Cos, If I do, it'll be in the front page of the *Journal* in minutes. I'm warnin' ye. Cut it out or else!' Kieran caught sight of something unhinged in McLaughlin's eyes. He recognised that look. He saw it in the mirror every morning.

Martin fell back, hoping the creep would ignore his warning. That way, he'd take care of it himself. He never liked Kelly, couldn't stand him in fact, and was ready to give him a serious hidin' or worse.

Anyhow, he'd said what he needed to, and judging by the racket coming from his insides, he'd better move on, get some serious grub in him, then run for the nearest bog. Once again, he caught Siobhan's eye, and with a small wave she signalled she'd be right over.

'By the way, we need the gear back. Where's it at?' Martin asked. Kieran was told to hide a few pieces and a chunk of explosives, but after McLaughlin's threats, he wasn't going to give them up. If ever. He'd use them for something better.

'They're safe,' Kieran told him, 'and well hidden.' Martin was good with that and when Siobhan turned up, ordered a massive Irish breakfast. The second she was out of sight, he brushed Kieran off with a wave and said.

'I'll be in touch. As for now, pay for my friggin' breakfast and get outta me sight.'

Kieran split and headed back to his flat, muttering a curse as he pulled his jacket tight against the drizzle. To anyone watching he looked cocky, handsome, without a care. And that was just how he liked it. Let them buy the act. He knew what was really going on.

The Provos were doing the dirty on him. The very ones he'd sacrificed so much for, and it felt like a poisoned arrow through the heart. He thought of his beautiful mother, ravaged by cancer, who'd adored him. She'd pleaded with him not to get involved, but he hadn't listened. He'd hurt her, and she'd never forgiven him. She even refused to see him on her deathbed, and now they were threatening him, telling him to run and hide like a... well, fuck them! Wasn't he the one who knew where the stash was? He'd figure out how to use it and get back at the bastards.

He jumped when a hand grabbed his arm just as he opened the ground door to his flat.

'What the fuck!' It was Honey. Holy Christ, but she was the last person he needed to see.

'What the hell do you want?' he snarled. Honey wished she hadn't come as soon as she saw and heard him, but she had to talk to him. Sleepless nights were haunted by Val's cries and the memories of so much gore and blood. This had to stop. Tears streamed down her face as she cried.

'I need to talk to ye. You've gotta listen to me,' she shrilled. 'I'm outta this. It's over. All of it. I'm done!'

'*Et tu, Brute?*' Kieran sneered. 'You betrayin' me, too? I don't think so, sunshine. This ain't over 'til I say it is!' His icy stare pinned her where she stood, making the hairs rise at the back of her neck. He was actually more frightening when he was like this. She didn't or couldn't move until he grabbed her by the hair and yanked her through the door. She fought against him as he dragged her up the stairs to the first floor.

Her screams grew louder as he shoved his hand between her legs and yelled, 'You want some of this, do ye? Okay then, you're gonna get it. You've been nothin' but a thorn in my fuckin' side, so I suppose I'd better give it to ye. Get it over with.' He held her hair with one hand while juggling for his key, then unlocked the flat door and kicked it open with his foot.

'Get that fat arse of yours in there now!' Honey went down hard on her knees as Kieran slammed and locked the door, terrifying her. He tossed his keys in a bowl, took off his wet jacket, and hung it on the chair.

'Okay, you've got my attention.' Honey tried to get up, but he stopped her.

'Take them off. Your clothes. All of 'em.' She was frozen with fear as Keiran slowly and deliberately repeated himself.

'Take your clothes off. All of 'em.' He figured nobody could hear him, the flats were usually empty during the day. Honey stood wide-eyed looking at the boy she used to love. He was so angry, so bloody scary. She was shaking.

She knew he'd hurt her if she didn't do as he asked. So, giving in, she slowly and carefully removed her coat and dropped it. She felt dizzy. She barely had time to think before he pushed her to the ground, his hands turning into shears, ripping off her blouse, tearing away her bra. Her skirt and panties followed, shredded in a violent blur. Somehow, he had her hands pinned above her head. She tried to shake him off, but he was too strong.

Kieran laughed when she went totally limp. Surrendering. He looked at her with vacant eyes, then stopped. He wasn't into her. Not at all. He'd made his case. He lowered his voice next to her ear.

'Don't worry. I'm not gonna hurt ye, Honey. Just makin' sure ye know not to fuck with me. Right?'

The sudden change in his tone confused her, and she wondered if it was another one of his tricks. She couldn't tell. To her astonishment, he left her on the floor and walked around the flat, undoing his shirt. He even offered her the bathroom like she was a guest, all friendly. Feeling the lowest of the low, Honey crawled across the floor to collect her torn clothes and, weeping, shuffled into the small bathroom, locking the door behind her.

While she was tidying up, Kieran stripped off his trousers and shirt, grabbed his jacket from the back of the chair, and carefully hung it up. He neatly put the rest of his clothes in the cupboard and then changed into a grey tracksuit. *What the hell was she doing in there?*

He shouted, losing patience. McLaughlin hadn't even let him grab a bite, and the fridge was near bare. With no real choice, he pulled out two beers, cracked them open, and let the foam spill over before dropping onto the sofa. It felt like an age, but at last the bathroom door opened and Honey stumbled out, a mess, shaken to the core, tugging her clothes together as best she could. Seeing the message had sunk in left him with a strange mix of satisfaction and unease.

He offered her a can with a forced smile. 'Here you go. Have a beer?'

'Don't want one,' she mumbled. He smiled in a twisted way.

'Ah, come on now. Get over here. Could've been worse. I didn't hurt ye, did I?' He patted the seat next to him. He might still need her and told her to sit.

'Pretty please?' he said. She sat, squirmed when he held her hand, then yanked it back and listened.

'My fault. I didn't mean anything bad by it. Sometimes us fellas mess about for a laugh. No harm done.' He waited for a response, but none came.

'C'mon. Take me hand; talk to me.' Ignoring him, Honey reached for a beer and took a big gulp to calm her nerves. He ran his fingers along her leg.

'There now, isn't that better? We'll try another time, but slowly. Make it nice. Sure look at ye, you're beautiful, Honey, and you're mine. All mine.'

She gave him a small smile.

'I love ye, don't I?' he continued, laying it on thick and lying through his teeth. 'You're me special girl. Always. Now come on, cheer up and trust me, will ye?'

Honey's resolve began to crumble. He'd told her he loved her, *loved her!* Said it out loud. Here was the nice Kieran back, not the other, horrible, nasty one. The old Kieran, the one who'd just confessed his love, coming back to her as she watched him. Her heart skipped a beat and she sighed gently when he ran his fingers through her hair. *Thank you Jesus, Kieran's back.* He hugged her, laughing, and said he was sorry, promising things would be even better.

Kieran knew he'd aced it, and was thrilled. Piece of cake. Crazy, really, the power of three little words, and fuck it, how easy was it to say: *'I love you.'* She'd do what she had to do, one last time. After that, he'd get rid. Make it swift and for always.

'I love you too, Kieran Kelly,' he heard her say as she snuggled in. A big grin spread across her puffy, ugly boot of a face.

Chapter Forty

Lux Laundry

R ob was already bored, claustrophobic, and feeling downright miserable, and they'd only been at it for a near fortnight.

He recalled the fury and disappointment in Tracey's voice when he'd told her about him being away - indefinitely. Their last call had shaken him up, no end, and she'd threatened him with all sorts.

This op was pure hell: same crap, different day. Iowa drove the van while their tout, a fat, sweaty, cracked-out laundry owner named Thomas Deeney, slogged up and down the neglected garden paths of Creggan and the Bogside, banging on doors. He'd gossip while waiting to pick up or drop off the weekly laundry. A few lucky families had washing machines, but most didn't.

Deeney was a massive man, bald as a cue ball and seriously obese. Rob saw him for what he was - a nasty, mean son of a bitch. More than once, they'd had to listen to him rant about why he was working with them, like he wasn't getting paid and was doing it out of the kindness of his heart. Didn't help that his mouth was pure filth. His cursing was off the scale - nothing like Rob or Iowa had ever heard before.

They'd learned from their briefing, and Deeney himself, that he'd been born in Londonderry. His mother had raised him alone in a condemned two-up, two-down terraced house close to Cable Street, one of the worst slums in the Bogside. When she couldn't handle him, she often sent him to the local Nazareth House orphanage.

He'd never known his father, only that he was part of the old IRA and had to flee to America. His mother never forgave him and raised Deeney to hate not only his father but the Cause that had stolen her husband away. She became a recluse and never left the house until recently, when she fell down the stairs, died, and ended up in a solitary, pitiful grave. Deeney rarely met women socially and had never married.

Lux Laundry was his family now. His pride and joy. But the truth was, the business was going down the shitter fast. Working for the Brits had been a stroke of luck, the best he'd had in years. He hadn't even blinked at what he was doing. It was for money, plain and simple. No loyalty, no cause, no bleeding heart. Just cash. Hard cash.

As their day ended, Rob watched through one of the van's rear windows as Deeney's portly frame accosted another unsuspecting customer. No doubt he'd bounce back soon and, in his foul language, tell them about the householder. Unbelievably, the man could list who lived in which house, who they were related to, who they were shagging, and who – most pathetically – went to Mass each Sunday, even those who didn't! The hold the Catholic Church had over these people never ceased to amaze Rob. For some unexplained reason, people trusted Deeney. Much as Rob disliked him, he'd proved himself capable as mole and informer.

They were sitting in the heart of Creggan, or 'Stony Place' in Irish. It was a massive but poor council estate. Most men couldn't find jobs and spent long days in the pub or at home looking after their many children. The air around the estate was filled with grey smoke from the numerous coal fires, often producing an inert low cloud that shrouded the hillside.

He'd heard through the grapevine that other covert operatives and lookouts had blended in with the estate's inhabitants, some disguised as council road sweepers, phone engineers, or even meth drinkers loitering on street corners. Rob was convinced the bastards who'd murdered Val were out there, somewhere.

Working with Iowa was bloody disheartening. She was so quiet, especially with him. Their pad turned out to be nothing but a shabby bedsit. Certainly not a bed-and-breakfast. He couldn't figure out how the military had come to trust their ancient, near-blind landlady. She'd squint her weak eyes on the rare occasions they met, trying to focus. Next to her, her breath was appalling - rotten teeth and all. The woman could only be described as horrid.

The four-storey townhouse was filthy and permanently dark. It was eerie, filled with Catholic relics, pictures, and statues lining the walls and hallways. Worse than that, she had cats. Rob hated cats. There were millions of the blasted things, and the smell of cat piss and everything else was overwhelming. The place was rotten, and he despised it. Convinced they were the only 'guests', he understood why.

On the day they'd arrived, Rob muttered that the place was like something out of a horror film, but Iowa ignored him.

The old woman had led them slowly up the stairs to an L-shaped bedsit on the third floor. Both gasped when they saw a small double bed. Fortunately for Rob, a shabby sofa stood in the corner. His relief at not having to share a bed with Iowa was beyond words.

A small kitchen was half-hidden around the angle of the room. It was unwelcoming and rank, too. Rob couldn't find any mod cons, no TV, electric kettle, and on closer inspection, not even a radio.

Snapped back to the present, he watched Deeney struggle to lug a large, labelled cotton sack back to the van. He quickly scanned the street before yanking open the rear door and carelessly hurling the sack into the back, slamming it right on top of Rob who let rip.

Deeney slammed the door shut, paying no heed to Rob's anger, and shuffled back to the front passenger seat, sweating and panting as he hauled himself in. Rob was seething, and his anger just flew out.

'For fuck's sake, can't you watch where you're throwing that? That's the fourth time today, you useless bastard!' he shouted. Deeney laughed.

'Ach, don't be such a fuckin' pussy. My orders were, ye eejit, to get the fuckin' stuff in and out. Fast. You're fuckin' holdin' us back, now time to get a move on.'

Rob struggled to make sense of Deeney's words. The man possessed the thickest Londonderry accent he'd ever heard. Something about getting the stuff in quick? Was he joking? Him that size! He was a total Warlus!

Rob got super angry and yelled, *'Get this stuff in quick!* Are you kiddin' me? For goodness' sake, man, you stand there talkin' for hours while I'm stuck in here. Don't you realise how exposed and vulnerable we are? We'd get through way more if you kept that trap of yours shut!'

Deeney could only turn his vast body a quarter of the way around to face Rob. Iowa kept her gaze straight ahead.

The large man snarled, 'Listen to me, you English prick. I'm doing me bit here, ye know. If I don't talk to these people, one, it'll look strange. They know me; they've known me for years. They expect me to talk. Two, and fuckin' more importantly, you bastards want me to find out stuff, don't ye... Don't ye?!

He paused. 'So if I don't talk, they don't talk. Can you fuckin' stop buggin' me about takin' so much time? And three, by the way, I'm doin' what you Brits pay me to do, aren't youse usin' me van 'an everything? All you've fuckin' done is fuckin' complain since you got 'ere. Your woman over there, she's grand, doesn't say a fuckin' word!'

Iowa cringed, pressing her head against the steering wheel as Deeney's words battered her, each one landing like a stone to the gut. She'd never heard language so vile – like an overflowing sewer.

Her mother always said using vulgar language was a sign of being thick. Maybe that was why it made her skin crawl, why every filthy word spilling out of the man's slobbering mouth felt like grease slicking into her ears. Swearing was like a national sport around this place: every sentence stitched together with a curse.

Deeney turned to face the front again and muttered something under his breath. Rob hated him even more now but knew he was probably right. After all, the laundryman was coming up with the goods.

He watched Deeney pick up a list from his lap and, mockingly like a chauffeur, told Iowa where to go next.

'Drive on Charles, Blamfield Street. Straight ahead and second right.'

Iowa started the van, and they took off. Rob settled at the back, grabbing his favourite Leica 35mm camera with its telephoto lens. Leaning forward to look out the window, he spotted a crowd of hoods gathering around Stones Corner. Excited, he raised the camera to his eye, focusing the lens for some close-ups.

Shouting to the front, he called, 'Slow down a bit, will ye? I'll get some good shots from here.'

The van slowed, and Rob took numerous images, one after the other. *Click, click, click...*

In an instant, the van stopped. 'Why are we stopping?' he cried out angrily. It was dangerous to stop. Iowa had spotted two RUC jeeps and a Saracen who'd halted the traffic.

In a controlled voice, she told them, 'RUC checkpoint. Sit back, Kentucky.'

Deeney mumbled under his breath, 'I hope to fuck these fellas know youse. Otherwise, this could be fuckin' it.'

The van inched forward until it was forced to stop again. Iowa was spot on; it was the RUC, which couldn't have been worse. Little, if any, information about the covert ops was shared between the army and the police.

Iowa wound down the driver's window. Rob couldn't see what was happening but heard a man's voice.

'Morning, miss. Driver's licence, please?' The policeman bent down to look in the passenger seat and laughed heartily.

'Is that you in there, Deeney? You don't normally do the rounds. Where's wee Russ?'

Deeney responded nervously. 'Who... Russ? Sure, did ye not hear? Got himself involved,' he babbled. 'On the run. Of all people, youse should know! Business is bad enough without this shite going on. Just tryin' to make a livin'. You know what it's like. I mean, we all have to work, right?' He continued talking about how unfair and difficult life was.

The peeler couldn't get Deeney to shut his gob and soon looked bored out of his mind. He threw a questioning glance at the girl, but Deeney jumped in before she could even open her mouth.

'This is me wee niece from England,' he blurted, grinning way too much.

'Bless her heart. Her mammy thought it'd be a grand idea to send her over. Keep the fellas off, y'know what I mean?' He let out a loud, snorting laugh. 'Silly moo thinks it's safer 'ere.'

He winked at the officer, who nodded eagerly. With two teenage daughters himself, he understood.

'Wee girl's been nowhere and doesn't say much. Mind you, she doesn't have time to get a word in with me. Dead pleased, she's here so I am... I mean, you can't trust anyone these days, sir, but at least she's family. You can trust family. I'm a lucky man.'

Rob squeezed his eyes shut, fists clenched, wishing Deeney would shut the hell up. Both the policeman and Iowa were thinking the same.

Iowa handed her licence to the officer, who barely noticed it but commented solemnly, 'You are that, Deeney, a lucky man. Family is what it's all about. Thanks, miss. Can you open the back a sec, so I can take a look?'

The officer laughed. 'Never know what you could be up to, eh, Deeney?'

Adrenaline surged through Rob, his heart hammering against his ribs. Convinced it was all over, he sat still, the dead silence so thick he swore he could hear his own watch ticking. Deeney, teetering on the brink of collapse, let out a coughing fit to steady himself. They were seconds from disaster, praying for a miracle, when suddenly a thunderous bang cracked against the van's roof, shattering the tension.

The policeman yelled, 'Deeney, get outta here, quick! Christ, man, they're comin' for us. Get that wee girl of yours away!'

Rob cautiously peered through the window. It was like the 7th Cavalry had arrived. He never dreamt he'd be thankful to see a mob of rioters charging toward the police Land Rovers. The officer bound toward his jeep like a jackrabbit, and without thinking, Rob waved his arms and shouted at the top of his lungs, 'Iowa, go! Go! Now!'

The van sped off, and minutes later, they were on Blamfield Street. All three were tossed around as Iowa slammed on the brakes, bringing the van to a sudden halt. Deeney, gasping for air, burst into laughter. What started as a chuckle grew louder and louder until he lost control, his Buddha-like frame shaking like jelly in an earthquake.

Rob couldn't help but join in, laughter bubbling up inside him. Even Iowa, usually as stoic as a statue, had the faintest hint of a smile playing on her face.

Deeney wiped his eyes with his sleeve and exclaimed, 'Fuck me. That was close. Fuck me!' They sat silently for a few minutes, letting the tension drain away. Deeney glanced around to get his bearings, checked his list, and opened the van door. He stepped out and toddled toward the nearest house.

Rob's heart rate soon settled down. He leaned over to Iowa and congratulated her. 'Good work.' She didn't answer, like always.

Fifteen minutes crawled by as they waited for Deeney, who was deep in conversation with a mid-twenties bearded, scruffy-looking man dressed in second-hand military gear. He vanished inside the house, then reappeared with a load of laundry that they struggled to cram into a sack.

Rob quietly snapped numerous wide-angle and close-up shots of the would-be action man, identifying him from memory as Martin McLaughlin. A well known Provo. Rob had recognised the house immediately and remembered getting caught in the back yard with the girl. The girl who didn't scream. The intel must have been spot on if McLaughlin lived there.

Frustrated, Deeney snatched McLaughlin's leftover laundry and tucked it under his arm. He nodded at the young man, who waved him off with a casual goodbye and disappeared indoors.

Burdened by the bag's extra weight, Deeney struggled to the back of the van, where he dropped the sack and loose laundry onto the ground. He opened one side of the double doors, leaving Rob partially exposed. Exhausted and wheezing, the laundryman paused for breath.

Just then, the house's red door swung open again, and McLaughlin appeared with even more washing.

'Hold on, Deeney!' he cried. 'There's more. Here.' He ran to the back of the van carrying a small pile of bedclothes for Deeney to see.

'Me ma's messed up over me da. If I don't give you all the washin', our Caitlin'll kill me.'

While the two men continued to chat, Rob grabbed the camera and radio, shrinking back as far as possible from the door, burying himself deep in the stinking laundry sacks. Deeney, breathless and stunned, watched as McLaughlin cranked open the van's rear door.

Deeney thought fast and snatched the laundry from Martin. 'Sure, give us that, don't worry,' he assured him. 'I'll tag it when I get back.' He calmly piled the loose laundry on top of some bags at the front and shut the door.

Rob heard him mutter, 'That's you, Martin. Right. Sorry again about your da, and your poor ma. Look after yerself.'

As Iowa got the engine going and the van took off, Deeney let out a massive sigh. He was grey in the face. This malarkey was tougher than he'd bargained. Sweat poured down his football-fat, red face. He blew out his lips.

'You feelin' okay, Deeney?' Robert asked, from behind the purpose-built glass. On second thoughts, the man couldn't be that bad – he'd just saved their bacon.

'Didn't need that on top of everything else, did I?' Deeney exclaimed. 'Just feelin' a little weird, that's all,' he said.

He pointed at the house. 'See that boyo in there? Keep an eye on him - Martin McLaughlin. One angry fella. You lot and the peelers beat his da up, and then the old man died in custody a while back. Big fuckin' funeral. Loads of people still fuming 'bout it.' He took a much needed breather.

'His da' was a good man too. Kept to himself, never mixed up in anythin'. Fuckin' Martin was banged up when it went down. Ye blamed him for murderin' a Brit, but couldn't pin it on him. Let him out in the end. High up in the Provos, too. Isn't that what you're lookin' for.'

Rob made a mental note. *Just what the doctor ordered.*

Back at the launderette, all three unloaded the soiled laundry and carried it into the makeshift forensic lab. Deeney grabbed an unused sack and threw in McLaughlin's extra laundry, neatly labelling it.

'That's it,' he announced. 'I'm away. Can't handle all this fuckin' excitement for one day. I'll leave you to it. Night now.'

Rob watched him shuffle off. 'You sure you're good, mate?' Deeney kept walking, tiredly lifted his arm in a wave, and vanished.

Iowa shot Rob a look and shrugged. He still couldn't get over her fashion sense. Today, it was like she'd been pulled straight out of a charity shop window, going out of her way to look as ugly and unattractive as possible. She looked ludicrous, no sense of style at all.

One of the white-coated lab technicians approached them. All the time they'd been working with Deeney, neither had spoken a word to Rob or Iowa. *Geeks.*

In a deadpan voice, the woman said to Iowa, 'We found a good amount of gelignite on some of the stuff you two brought in a couple of days ago. Here, have a look at the report. Nice work. Leave it there when you're finished.'

Rob shot a look at Iowa and grinned. Was that a flicker of satisfaction in her eyes? He wasn't sure.

Pissed off by his attempt at friendliness, she quickly turned away and picked up the report to read.

Chapter Forty-One

A Hissy Fit

Once again, James was at Melrose's dinner table, feeling totally fed up. He'd made a colossal blunder with Caitlin and dreaded the evening ahead even more.

The diners were gathered at one end of the long table, and he watched in disgust as Dr Harris devoured his guinea fowl like it was his last meal before a hanging. Harris raged about the McLaughlin 'incident' between gulping down his wine and chewing his food.

'I was only doing my duty, you know. No one told me the man had a dodgy heart. You've no idea the pressure they put me under. No idea. They send me in to examine these people, then put me on the spot. Before I know it, they say, "Sign there." I never get a chance to do a full medical. It's a production line. So tell me, what am I supposed to do?'

James stared at his father in desperation. This was what he'd been afraid of. He didn't want to hear Harris's tirade, especially since he didn't believe a word of it, and his feelings for Caitlin made him view the man with renewed disgust.

He remained silent and listened as Roger answered forcefully, 'I understand, Harris. However, I've said it before, and I'll say it again: internment has been an unmitigated disaster. George Shalham is my friend, I know. But it appears the intel the RUC gave the Brits for the first round of arrests was so outdated it included the names of dead men, for goodness' sake. And now the government has insisted Faulkner add known UVF terrorists to their lists, and he won't! I'm ashamed. The whole thing is shameful.'

James sighed. *Here we go again.*

Harris paid no attention, having heard this rant from Roger many times before.

Roger was furious at Harris's silence. 'Not one Loyalist has been arrested, and we know they're committing atrocities, too. It's ridiculous - stupid. Then *Bloody Sunday*, fourteen dead, and *Bloody Friday*, twenty-two bombs in Belfast in one day. And what are we left with? An angry, divided province. Our beautiful country is now one of the most dangerous places in the world!' The doctor looked at Roger with a blank stare.

But Roger wasn't finished. 'Turns out that man McLaughlin you saw was another innocent and had nothing to do with the Provos, or anyone like them, for that matter. Internment has backfired. It's a catastrophe. Always has been, always will be. After *Bloody Sunday*, seems to me it's the Provos who're benefitting the most in attracting world attention and volunteers.'

At night, Roger was forever absorbing the news, flicking between the BBC and RTÉ, and it left him where it always did, depressed, with little to hope for the days ahead. He felt tired and fragile tonight, older than he should. As for Rocola and Charles Jones, he couldn't bring himself to think about it, not after what he' done, not after the papers he'd signed in a moment of foolish necessity and hidden at the back of the bureau, as if tucking them away might erase the deed. Not tonight. He wouldn't, couldn't let his mind go there.

Instead, he prayed that his nephew James's investment plan would bear fruit, that it might yet steady the whole venture and spare him the need to tell the truth about what he'd done.

James's father had just come back from Belfast after a stay with Charles Jones. He'd listened to Jones and started seeing things his way, finding a cold, hard logic in his views on Northern Ireland. Everything just clicked for him, and he even won at blackjack! Jones was a great host who was generous with cash and compliments -a winning combo.

Roger heard James Snr talking and felt anger bubbling up. He couldn't stand the sureness in his voice, and it made him stand up. His brother spoke over him before he could answer, louder than he meant, his ridiculous words snapping out, one by one.

'I agree with you, doctor. I've said it before and I'll say it again. Shoot all the Provos. The lot of them. If I had my way, I'd take them out, one by one, and put a bullet to the back of their heads myself. That'd put a stop to your "production line", doctor. What's happening to Ulster is contemptible. See what they've done? Sod their civil rights!'

Roger fixed him with an icy glare, barely recognising the man in front of him who'd come out with such hate. His temper surged, rare but unstoppable when it came.

'How ridiculous James!' he shouted. 'I'm disappointed in you, brother. That's got to be one of the most idiotic things I've ever heard you say!' He could barely hold it in. Without a second thought, his brother, his own flesh and blood, had clearly been taken in by Jones's narrow, blinkered bile. Roger made it clear he was disgusted. He was done with Jones's hateful rants at his table.

James Snr grunted but remained quiet as Harris stopped eating. In frustration, Harris shook his head and slowly put down his knife and fork. Disappointed, he tutted and let out a deep sigh.

'Well, Roger, it's clear whose side you're on.' He paused. 'Tell me, how long have we been friends?' Harris waited for an answer that wasn't forthcoming before continuing.

'Twenty-five years. I come to your home for moral support... And what do I get? You on your soapbox lecturing your brother and me. Tell us then, whose side *are* you on?' Disappointed, he glanced at James Snr, searching for support, but found none. He then whipped back around to face Roger.

'Let me tell you something: I know what's happening in this country. *Why*? Because I'm in the heart of it, day after day. I see it. Don't you understand? I've been threatened, man! Told to get out or I'll be shot. They want to kill me! I love this country, and I'm the one being told to get out!'

The Hendersons were unaware that the Provos had threatened the doctor, and for a split second, James almost felt sorry for the unsavoury little man. Roger sat motionless, quite stunned at such news.

Someone had to say something, so James tried to appease their guest. 'Doctor... we'd no idea. No idea at all. Can we help?'

But Harris wasn't having any of it. 'No. You can't, James. I'm past help.'

Dinner was quiet and uncomfortable afterwards, and soon the subdued doctor complained of fatigue. He thanked Roger and took his leave under a dark cloud.

Back at the dinner table, downcast and silently moving to take a seat by the fireplace, James Snr shrugged as his son refilled their glasses.

'That was an unmitigated disaster,' he remarked. Roger nodded. He was still bewildered by the evening's events, especially his brother's tantrum.

'Fraid so, didn't help with that outburst of yours either,' he agreed. James took a good look at his uncle, who was ashen and had bloodshot eyes. He'd aged a lot, lately.

'You okay?' he asked. By now, his father had gone quiet.

Roger nodded and took a sip of wine, feeling quite tipsy. 'I'm fine thanks. Know what, son? I'm strangely relieved Harris has gone. He was good to your Aunt when she was dying, and I've stayed loyal 'cos of that,' he said.

Surprised at himself, he then joked, 'I'm not gonna lie but I've never liked him, more iguana than man!' James was stunned, and as the brothers laughed, any bad feelings faded away. They made small talk for a while, though Roger's thoughts drifted back to Harris.

'Still, serious business, a death threat,' he said, staring into the candle flame. 'Not much we can do. Poor bugger.'

'Not really our remit, no,' James replied.

James Snr stayed silent, a little sorry for what he'd said, but glad Roger had dropped it. Important to stay on his good side. Plus, he needed a roof over his head.

'Ah well,' Roger went on, 'he'll be back at some stage.' James hoped he wouldn't have to see Harris anytime soon and, keen to steer the talk elsewhere, offered some news.

'You'll be pleased to hear we've completed the invitee list. I make it thirty-seven now. We've some top guns coming, just as we wanted. Forgive the pun.' He let out a laugh.

'George has worked miracles. He's got an army official coming too. Can't do any harm if we're talking about security. You're thought a lot of, Uncle. When I mention your name, everyone agrees there and then, no hesitation.' Roger waved off the compliment.

'Don't be silly. It's you who's doing all the work. No need to butter me up.'

James smiled. Still, it was true; Roger was well-respected – he'd heard it more than enough times when talking to invitees and employees. Somehow, as if James's compliments had upset him, James Snr stood, muttered a lazy goodnight, and retreated to his room. Perplexed, Roger shook his head as he watched his brother leave.

'I'm not sure what's going on with that father of yours James. I'll try and get to the bottom of it tomorrow.' He groaned. Things were going from bad to worse, and he wasn't sure what to do about it. Christ, he was tired. He half-listened as James continued.

'I know. He's been a bit odd tonight, hasn't he?'

Roger nodded, 'I'll talk to him. Go on now, what were you saying?'

Sitting forward, James came back. 'I was just saying. None of the political parties are prepared to talk about peace, but somehow, we've got them into a room for a day. All of them. In one room. It's a giant step forward. I know it looks like we're meeting them to find a way to protect and invest in the factory, but it's bigger than that now. This model could help bring peace here. Through talking. Talking to the right people. People who want change for the good.' James's words went deep, and for the first time, Roger acknowledged the scale of his nephew's undertaking.

'It's quite an achievement, son. But believe me, we've had countless summits and 'talks'. Promises made left, right and centre, but in the end? Very little to show for it. Be warned. You could be bitterly disappointed.'

He took a moment to think. 'Best to stick to the agenda. No talk of politics or religion. Trust me, those two'll poison the air in that room faster than anything.'

James nodded emphatically, reassuring Roger that Shalham had taken a personal interest in who was attending and ensured airtight security for the day.

'That's good. He'll keep the troublemakers out,' Roger replied with relief as he stood up. 'You've brought up some important points so far: workforce security, the need to outsource locally, apprenticeships, cross-border trading, and more.'

He patted James's shoulder. 'I admire you, son, and I'm proud of you. These people will be tricky. Maybe, old man that I am, I need to dig deeper and have a tad more faith, huh? Come now. Call it a night. Don't know about you, but I'm beat.'

James had a terrible night, dreaming all sorts of crazy stuff about Caitlin, the factory, the carjacking, and then Harris.

When morning finally broke, he dragged himself out of bed, raking his hands through his hair. He needed to speak to Caitlin. He needed to set things straight.

Today.

Chapter Forty-Two

Feel Good Friday

The day after James suggested they spend the weekend together, Caitlin noticed how tired and, unlike him, how dishevelled he looked.

He'd stayed in his office all day, not even taking a lunch break as his meetings ran back to back. She was wiped out after Martin's party, which went on all night and kept her awake.

Fortunately, Charlie from next door, came to her rescue by knocking loud on the door, telling Martin and his so-called friends to pipe down, or he'd punch their lights out. Drunk as they were, they knew better than to mess with him. Even though she heard Charlie giving off, Caitlin stayed in bed.

She kept to herself as much as work allowed. James spent the rest of the week on the road, and any talk between them was strictly professional. Things with her mother weren't much better, and she'd only seen Tina once. Caitlin hadn't forgiven her for taking Martin's side and drinking with him. She was so done and in a terrible mood that she even yelled at Mrs Parkes, who shot her a look that said, 'Don't push it.' Caitlin nearly died.

By Friday home time she told herself to pack up, another lonely weekend ahead whether she liked it or not. The bombing was more than a month behind them, yet it remained with her, fresh as yesterday, as if the dust had only just settled. No one had been charged, not a word in the news or in the papers, and that silence bugged her. As if it had never happened. Her hands still shook, on and off, the sort of tremor that made the key slip past the lock or a cup clink too loud on a saucer. She hated that it showed.

She was still upset at James for asking her to stay the whole weekend. One minute she thought cheek of him — did he really think she was that easy, a slag? The next, she felt like some prudish convent girl, too straight-laced for her own good. It was 1972, not 1872, for God's sake. Her face burned, a mix of mortification and temper, and she couldn't make her mind up what way to feel. She was all over the place, a walking disaster.

Ready to walk out the door, she was startled to see him standing on the threshold of his office. The last person she expected to see. No one was around, and from the way he looked, she could see he was as fed up as she was. It'd been a long, crappy week for both of them – no other way to put it. James hadn't had a moment to himself between meeting after meeting, dinner after dinner, and couldn't find the right time to phone her and explain.

'Caitlin,' he said. His voice, she noted, sounded so sad.

'Mr Henderson,' she replied. He winced. *Mr Henderson.* She wasn't for making this easy.

'Everyone gone?' he asked, glancing up and down the corridor. Caitlin didn't know where to put her eyes.

'Yeah, just me left. I'm about to go.' The sight of him left her weak; her legs felt ready to give way and her trembling hands betrayed her. She clumsily buttoned her coat and hitched her handbag bag higher on her shoulder, ready to move, but James didn't move. He filled the doorway, watching her, daring her to meet his eyes. He wasn't going to budge.

'James. Please. I need to get home.' She tried to move again, but he stopped her with the lightest touch to her hand. Such a small touch, and it felt like fire. He ran a hand through his hair and sighed. His voice heavy with remorse.

'Ah, Caitlin, I'm glad you're here, but you've got me so wrong. When I suggested... you know... it came out bad, and I'm sorry. I'd never take advantage of you. I wasn't asking you to sleep with me, us together, I mean... I'm not explaining this very well, am I?' He was making a total arse of himself. With a low groan, he set his briefcase on the floor and took her by the arms, lightly, so she knew she could shrug him off if she wanted.

'All I meant was that we could use the party as an excuse to spend time together. In separate rooms, of course. I never meant for us to, you know, be together, *together*. Believe it or not, I am a gentleman.' He placed a hand on his heart and gave her a huge, warm, but repentant smile. Her cheeks flushed. Perhaps she'd read the whole thing wrong. Made a mountain out of a molehill. She'd jumped to the worst conclusion without even letting him explain. What a waste of time and energy.

'It was more the way you said it. Just blurted it out, all expectant like. Like you were doing me a favour,' she admitted. He shrugged. She was sort of right, in a way.

'I didn't mean to. I was hoping to cheer you up after Harris. You were so annoyed, and, boy, did that backfire.' He gave her a beautiful smile. How could she resist that?

She felt bad, but smiled and said playfully, 'Have to admit, it wasn't the most romantic way to ask for a first date.'

He arched his eyebrow. 'First date, eh?' he smiled again, 'Can I try again then? Start over.' She couldn't say no.

'Go on then.' He double-checked to make sure they were alone, then spread his arms wide.

'Caitlin McLaughlin, will you *please* spend a weekend with yours truly?' She gave him a stern look, pretending to think about it, then her face softened into a smile.

'Now that's better. I'd love to. Separate rooms, mind.' She laughed, pointing a finger at him. He let out a goofy cheer and, just to be sure, pulled her into a quick, reassuring hug. Caitlin was so over the moon she nearly burst into tears.

James loved Fridays, but this one was exceptional. They'd planned it all with great care, and tonight, they'd be driving away for the weekend. He wasn't sure his uncle believed him when he'd said he was meeting more touring friends in Donegal Town. Just a feeling he had. Roger was still keeping a close eye on him.

His father had only snorted when he told him he was going. Ever since he got back from Belfast, he'd been in a terrible mood and wouldn't talk, no matter how hard James tried. James threw in the towel.

The drive to work that morning passed without incident, though the news bulletins were worse than usual. That week alone, five dead in separate incidents, and in Dublin Jack Lynch had closed the Sinn Féin office. Grim, and no mistake. Yet James felt a current under his skin, a steady charge of excitement that he couldn't ignore, and he knew the source of it. Caitlin. He felt his heart race just thinking about her, and suddenly he felt alive and free, like he'd been cooped up and could finally breathe. The days had been hard of late, all malice and bad headlines, but not with her. With Caitlin there was a difference, a transparent truth to her, the kind of honesty a man could trust.

And now, with a weekend to themselves drawing near, a quiet flow of excitement ran through him.

When he arrived at Rocola, he found Caitlin working away. Mrs Parkes was off sick, and with her gone the whole building seemed to let out a sigh of relief. The atmosphere was carefree, and the smiling workers kept at it without her baleful presence hanging over them.

He had to suppress a smile when he saw Caitlin. She looked lovely. Her eyes were bright, her wounds had healed. She was radiant.

'Morning, Caitlin,' he said, hanging his coat on the stand.

'Morning,' she replied, a beautiful, open smile on her face.

'I've a feeling this is going to be a good day,' he said as he walked to her desk.

'That it is, Mr Henderson. I'll bring you a coffee in a sec.' The look she gave him said everything. She was excited too.

'No hurry. Thanks,' he said, offering another of his cheeky winks.

James spent most of the day on his presentation and storyboard for the City Hotel meeting, keeping his head down and barely speaking to Caitlin.

When he did catch her, she seemed skittish in a good way; he felt it too, so he let the work keep him distracted. By the end of the day, he'd pulled together an impressive set of numbers.

In the outer office the girls were laughing, squeaking with excitement about the upcoming birthday party. Their happiness floated through his door, a nice change, since Mrs Parkes wasn't there to sour the mood.

Once everyone was gone, James signalled to Caitlin that she could go too.

'See you at Pennyburn Church. I've hired a car, less obvious. Seven by the gate. Quick, before I take advantage of you. Go, go, go!' He let out a low, throaty laugh.

'Okay, okay. I'm away!' she cried. Giggling and with clumsy hands, she tidied her desk and locked her papers away.

James grabbed her coat from the stand and held it open for her. He smoothed her collar and his hands settled on her shoulders. She shivered at his touch, goosebumps rising along her back.

With a warning look she whispered playfully, 'See you soon,' both giddy and a little afraid at the thought of having him to herself for a whole weekend.

'You will indeed,' he said excitedly. 'Can't wait.'

Chapter Forty-Three

Donegal Town

Anne was finally home from the hospital, but Caitlin hadn't managed to see her. She'd tried knocking on her door, talking to her sisters, but the message always came back with the same line. 'She's not in the mood. Not herself these days. Doesn't want to talk to anyone.'

Caitlin begged to be let in, but Anne's exhausted mother, cradling a newborn, could only apologise before closing the door and leaving her standing on the doorstep, embarrassed and disappointed. In the end, Caitlin gave up thinking it might be best for Anne to come to her first; when she was ready.

Meanwhile, Majella lay in bed, oblivious to the world. Tommy called by, worried for his sister, and told Caitlin they had no choice now but to ask his mother for help. What else was there to do? He also confided that Martin was mixed up with the Provos again; hardly a shock. Guilty about lying, she told him she'd be at a party that weekend. He perked up and hugged her, saying it was about time she did a bit for herself and had a good night out.

When she left James to go home and pack, she opened the front door to be met by loud shouting. Without taking her coat off, she walked to the kitchen and found a raucous exchange between Tommy and Mary, Caitlin's granny.

Tommy's face was turning red with anger. 'Because I'd no choice, Ma. Who else was gonna' to pay, eh?' His yelling freaked Caitlin out. He was so angry.

Her granny pointed at him. 'Have you any idea what you've done? It means we're committed to 'em. Don't ye see? She'll kill ye when she hears!'

Mary sat in her daughter's chair, wearing a floral crossover pinafore dress wrapped tightly around her frail body. Her steel-grey hair was pinned in a bun, accentuating her long, drawn face. She'd changed for the worse since the last time she'd been in Blamfield Street.

Caitlin took a second before asking, 'Who'll kill you Tommy? What's going on?' Tommy stood beside the dish-filled sink, still in his flat black cap and long raincoat. Red-faced and fuming, he jabbed a finger at his mother.

'She's giving out 'cos the Boys paid for your da's funeral, and I haven't told Jella. I mean, who else was going to pay, huh? I don't have it. There's just enough money in this house to put the electric on. So tell me this, Ma, where were you when Patrick died, eh? You've got a few bob on ye, yet you didn't offer a penny to help. Ye didn't even bloody turn up! So don't being goin' all righteous, comin' here and fuckin' giving off about what I've done. Right or wrong!'

He grunted. 'I'm away! I can't listen to her any longer.'

Infuriated, his mother retorted, 'You've no right to use that kinda' language with me, Tommy O'Reilly!'

Tommy had enough of her and threw his cup into the sink. He growled, readjusting his cap, 'I'm tellin' ye Caitlin, I'm not listenin' to any more of this shite!'' Smiling, he touched her hand.

'Hope you enjoy the party, love. You deserve a break, it's you that's been keepin' this feckin' madhouse goin'.' His hatred was obvious as he stared at his mother and, without another word, he stormed off.

He didn't look back - afraid he might say something he'd regret. The inevitable slam of the front door told them he was gone. Mary pulled a face and turned to Caitlin.

'Off to some party then, are ye then?' She asked, nodding toward the ceiling where her sick daughter was.

'And now I'm supposed to handle all of this meself?' She moaned, glancing around like the cluttered kitchen. Caitlin took the place in - a tip, thanks to her siblings. She wasn't rising to her granny's hostility, not today, not now. She was getting out of there, quick. Just like Tommy.

'It's a twenty-first. I already told Mammy.' Was all she could say.

Mary rolled her eyes, got up, and went to the sink full of dirty dishes. She turned on the tap and muttered, 'Do what ye want. As if I give a shite!'

That's what Caitlin did. She did exactly what she wanted. She ran to her bedroom, packed a couple of warm jumpers, a pair of jeans, her new red dress and her best shoes. She had tights set aside, since James had said they would go somewhere special for dinner. She could hardly wait. Having freshened up, she changed into her favourite jeans and a soft pink V-neck jumper. The suitcase waited on the bed, an old brown thing with scuffed corners, a frayed handle and dented clasps. No one knew where it'd come from; it just appeared in the house one day and stayed. She set in her toiletries and her best underwear and closed the lid with care.

She checked on Majella before heading downstairs. Her grand-mother's handiwork was evident: a fresh bed, a clean nightie, hair brushed and neatly plaited. Caitlin felt bad; Granny's presence was already making a difference. It was the carry-on that came with it, the sharp tongue at times, though she'd seen the better side too, the kind side, and wished there were more of it. She pushed the thought to the back of her mind and looked down at Majella. Her face was puffy and pale. Caitlin touched her arm, a gentle nudge, and Majella's grey eyes opened and found her.

'Hello, love. You okay?' she asked, weakly.

Caitlin was thrilled to hear her voice. 'I'm fine, Mammy. You?'

'Grand. The old battle-axe is here. Made me eat and won't give me any more tablets. You're away for a birthday thing in Malin tonight, aren't ye?' Caitlin nodded.

'That's good. I'll be better when you're back. Promise.' Majella said, closing her heavy eyes again.

'Love you,' Caitlin said softly.

'Love you too, sunshine.'

Caitlin felt another wave of guilt from the lie as she quickly returned to her room. She pulled on her coat, grabbed the suitcase and took the stairs down two at a time. There was no point calling out to her Granny, so she opened the front door and found Martin on the step, key raised, about to come in. He had a sour face on him, clearly fed up with the world. With all of it.

'You away, then?' He sneered. His face broke into a terrible smile.

She gave him a quick nod and moved to pass. He was a worse sight than before, hair slick with grease, unshaven, a reek of booze and fags coming off him like sweat. He grabbed her arm and pulled her back into the hallway as she passed, the pressure of his grip making her skin crawl.

'Well, you have a nice time, missy. Don't be worryin' about us. We'll be fine,' he said sarcastically.

He threw his hands up in the air, and she pulled herself free. Then he gave her a lopsided smirk before staggering off towards the living room. The door slammed shut behind him, and seconds later, the TV was blaring loud enough to drown out the rest of the house. Because of the racket, Mary stormed out of the kitchen, wiping her hands on a tea towel.

'Is that your Martin?' Out of all her grandchildren, it was him she despised the most. Ignorant git. The sight of him shamed her. Him a Provo. Oh, she knew all right. *A bloody disgrace.*

Caitlin nodded and watched Mary march into the living room. Curiosity got the better of her, and she followed. Martin was sprawled on the sofa, coat open, legs splayed. He glared at his granny while she flicked the tea towel at his shins, quick and stinging, again and again.

'Martin McLaughlin, get those filthy boots off that sofa now. Who do you think ye are? You might have people on that street out there scared of ye, but not me, fella. So, quit messin' about. Feet off. *Now!*'

Mary wasn't having any of her useless grandson's crap, Caitlin could see that.

Having mumbled a quick goodbye, she grabbed her case and hurried to the bus stop. The bus was about to pull away, so like a bat out of hell she went for it, scowling as the suit case thumped hard against her legs. Fortunately, the kind driver spotted her and waited. Thanking him after a quick climb up, she hurried to the back, dropping herself and her case onto an empty seat. She'd done it. She was out! A huge smile took over her face.

On the way, Caitlin's excitement soon waned, and she began to freak out. James might be all gentlemanly and polite, but let's face it – regardless of his "not taking advantage" talk, sooner or later it'd have to come up.

Sex.

Her stomach was going bonkers. She'd tried it with Seamus, telling herself it made sense, that it was natural and the right time. But she was only fooling herself - she didn't want him, not like that, so in the end, she sent him packing. He'd been cut up at first, sore even, then turned angry, accusing her of leading him on. After that he went quiet, and before long he was off to America.

Anne, on the other hand – well, Anne was in a league of her own. More experienced, more laid-back, and fond of sharing all the juicy details. Honestly, the girl could write a manual. She wouldn't stop going on about how great shagging was, making Caitlin wonder if she should take notes! They'd crack up laughing whenever Anne told her about the variety of 'extras' the barber would throw in for her older brothers after a haircut – especially if it was a Saturday special. Anne understood men and their primal games, while Caitlin sat on the sidelines like a lost sheep.

After a few stops, she watched a young, glum looking couple step on board the bus. The girl appeared shabby and miserable as she hauled a small, well-worn suitcase alongside a plastic bag full to the brim with books. Apart from her dress sense, Caitlin thought her pretty. Shame she seemed so sad and immune to her appearance. She assumed the guy with her was her other half and studied him closely. There was something about him. She knew him... She was sure of it... But from where? He gave a small smile when he saw her watching, then sat with the sad girl and put a sports bag on his lap.

The bus rumbled on, and soon enough, Caitlin forgot about the couple. Her mind was back to the weekend ahead, and by the time her stop came, that flicker of excitement had returned. She practically bounced off the bus, trying to play it cool. She looked down the road and then spotted a black Cortina near the church gates. James sat in the driver's seat, waiting.

She crossed the street, tossed her suitcase in the car, and slammed the door shut. Then, she grinned and hopped in the front seat with James.

'Sure it's closed?' He chuckled having heard the door shut with an almighty bang.

'Oh, God. I'm always doing that. Sorry!' she laughed.

Caitlin glowed with happiness. James felt the same and allowed himself a small, private smile. With his eyes on the road, he chatted about simple stuff – directions, the weather, a new song on the radio, and just let the weekend happen. He'd take it easy, give her space, and do what he said he'd do. Two rooms. No rush. Great food, a stroll, and a chat, no Parkes or phones!

They approached the army border checkpoint, where, unsurprisingly, there was a long queue for a Friday night. Those lucky few with caravans or holiday homes across the border liked to escape to the safety of the Irish Republic, aka *Free State*, for the weekend.

Caitlin shared what little she could remember from school about the history of Grianan of Aileach, a sixth-century stone ring fort standing proudly on a hill as they passed. The drive was a breeze, and the car was super comfy and smelled fresh. They traded stories about growing up and talked about what they hoped for, especially Caitlin's big travel dreams. Ireland was great, but she really wanted to see the world.

James couldn't believe it. He didn't know Caitlin was into traveling, but he enjoyed learning more about her. Christ, she was extraordinary. Sure, there were moments when a voice in his head would pipe up, reminding him this whole thing was risky. Madness, even. He just shrugged it off.

Although he'd grown up comfortable enough, he'd lately found himself dogged by a nagging loneliness, craving something real. Something genuine. A trustworthy, steady relationship. And this girl? So unlike anyone he'd ever met. The more he listened to her, the more he found her funny, intelligent, and authentically kind. And to top it off, she was gorgeous. He finally saw that she was beautiful on the inside too.

It soon grew dark. The landscape no longer visible, but James assured Caitlin it was magical and promised she'd see it for herself in the morning.

They pulled up at a fancy hotel, once a grand manor house. The entrance hall gleamed warmly; its polished terracotta floor glowing under soft lighting. Tall, black double doors stood at the far end, framed by elegant, minimal decor. Near them, a middle-aged receptionist sat at a stately Georgian writing table. The overall atmosphere was simple yet luxurious, with every detail thoughtfully arranged.

With the most ridiculous fake names, *Jack Pointer* and *Hilda White,* James smiled as he confidently filled out the registration cards. A porter arrived and escorted them to their rooms, starting with Caitlin's. He smiled, opening the door, knowing the girl would love the room.

Caitlin stepped into what felt like Wonderland. Something out of a dream – unlike anything she'd ever seen. A majestic four-poster bed with rich red drapes took over the space, resting on a bare oak floor. A stunning stained-glass window shimmered with jewel-like colours, and an open fire crackled in an iron grate set inside an ornately carved wooden fireplace with a fluffy sheepskin rug.

She clapped her hands in delight, taking it all in, and then spotted a doorway. Curiosity killed the cat as she opened it carefully and gasped at discovering a fabulous roll-top bath with gleaming brass taps. The floor tiled in a cream-and-black checkerboard pattern was perfect, like something from a swanky magazine she could never afford.

The porter, grinning, placed her case on the luggage stand and handed her the key before heading down the corridor with James. As soon as they'd gone, Caitlin squealed with delight and dived head first onto the soft, luxurious four-poster. God, but it was bloody massive! *If only Anne could see it.*

Her mind raced, full of deliciously wicked thoughts about James. At last, Caitlin McLaughlin was living the dream!

Chapter Forty-Four

Aunty Kay

He was well aware his Aunty Kay didn't like him much, probably wouldn't give a toss if he got hit with a bus.

Most days he didn't much like her either. Two faced. The same girl could be holy as a saint one minute, playing the good Catholic, and the next, she'd be weak at the knees and wet the moment that leech of a priest, Father McGuire, walked in the door. The thought of it turned his stomach. *Yuck.*

Kay was a world away from his elegant mother, as different as night and day. His aunt was about as unattractive as they come - short, fat, not easy on the eyes, busty, and a real pain in the hole. No surprise she never married. You'd have to pay someone to take that on.

Nonetheless, Kieran was her only living relative, and, painful that it was, he'd deliberately kept in with her. The house had to be worth a few bob by now, and that antique crap she'd hoarded a bit, too. He hated having to ask her outright for a loan, but needs must.

Tonight, they sat in her large kitchen and ate the dinner she'd prepared. He'd tuned out of her familiar whining as she lectured him. It was the same old stuff – blah, blah, blah.

'Know what you need? A job. I've got three now. How about that, eh? Three.' She used her fingers to make her point.

'There's the canteen at Rocola's, cleaning St Peter's after school... and now the City Hotel. Hmm, what is it they say? "Without hard work, nothin' grows but weeds." That's it. That's right. "Without hard work, nothin' grows but weeds." That's what you are, Kieran Kelly, a great big lump of a weed!' She chuckled and looked affectionately around her sparkling, meticulously organised kitchen. Kieran never took his eyes off her. A weed, huh? He had to admit it was funny and fair play to her; she did work hard.

He laughed inside as he allowed her to make more jokes at his expense. Keep working hard, Aunty Kay, 'cos one day this will all be mine without me having to work a stroke, he mused. He pretended to take a genuine interest in job number three to stop her from yapping. 'What ye doin' at the City Hotel, then?'

His aunt sounded excited. 'Well, it's only for a few days to start. They've overbooked themselves for some top-secret meetin' thingy and two big posh weddings the week after next. Need extra help. Maggie McFadden says the hotel can't afford to turn down the business. Just cleaning, mind.'

By now, she'd his full attention. 'How d'ye mean, a "top-secret meetin' thingy?"' Kay instantly regretted her loose tongue after being sworn not to say a word.

'Can't say. Maggie told me I had to keep it shut.' She mimed zipping her lips closed, then topped up Kieran's tea and walked around the kitchen, praying he wouldn't ask any more. She should've kept it shut, but she'd been so excited.

With the extra cash, she could finally buy those bedroom curtains she'd been wanting from Hills on John's Street. But, of course, typical Kieran, nosey parker that he was, he wanted to know more.

Telling his aunt to sit down, hoping she'd say more, Kieran joked, 'Ah, come on Aunty Kay, everyone knows Mrs McFadden's got the biggest gob in Derry. She'll be blabbing it to the *Derry Journal* next.

Go on, spill the beans.' He crossed himself and added for reassurance, 'Cross me heart and hope to die. I won't tell a soul.'

She slapped his hand and scolded, 'Honest to God, Kieran, I can't say. They'll sack me if I do. I haven't even started!' She let out a thin, awkward laugh. Kieran poked at his food and put on a show of disappointment.

'Ah, all right. I was only askin',' he pouted, as his brown eyes took on a pleading look.

Kay knew what made her nephew tick. That fella was such a pain, always mooching for money and not returning it. She hardly ever said anything good about him, but he was still her flesh and blood. These days, only Father McGuire kept her company, God love him. Whenever Kieran was off gallivanting, doing whatever he did, Father McGuire would pop by. He was a good man; great at listening.

Eyeing her nephew's wishy washy act, she decided she ought to show some Christian compassion. When she kicked the bucket, the cheeky chancer expected her to leave him everything, the money, the house but the poor eejit was in for a right shock. It was Father McGuire's: all of it.

Kieran sat and sulked, continuing to toy with his food. Ah sure, what harm would it do to say more, Kay thought. She was never great at keeping secrets. The gobshite didn't have any friends, so it wasn't as if he could blab it to any old Tom, Dick or Harry.

With him huffing and shifting in his chair, she gave in. 'All right, you win. I'll tell ye, but don't ye dare speak a word.' He flashed her a big, childish grin, looking all pleased with himself.

'There's a special meetin' comin' up, right? A bunch of bigshot businessmen from Derry and God knows where else. The bishop'll be there. That Scottish fella from Rocola, the factory up by Stones

Corner, is organisin' it. He's only gone and roped in the RUC, the Brits, and a few church types *from the other side. Protestants.*' Her face changed as she whispered her last few words with distaste.

'All under the same roof at the same time. Can ye believe it? Security'll be tighter than a duck's arse. They're scrabblin' for money to keep the place open, so the poor women don't end up out on their ears. Aye, very dignified altogether.' She heaved a sorrowful sigh for saying too much, then took a dainty sip of her tea, which, unbeknownst to the lad, had a good old splash of Jameson's doing laps around the cup.

Kieran's mind raced into first gear. This was precisely what he'd been looking for. His next op! Keeping a straight face, he played it down.

'That's it? Seriously, Kay? You'd me all excited there for a minute. Who gives a toss about some factory? That's about as borin' as paint dryin'.'

Kay was disappointed by his uncharitable response. 'Ah, come on, son. What about those poor women if they lost their jobs? If those jobs go, half the town'll go with them. Think about that.'

She had a point, though Kieran couldn't really give a shit. To keep her sweet, he replied, this time apologetically, 'Well, aye. I suppose when you put it like that.'

He barely listened as they picked at dessert, Kay nattering about parish gossip. His heart hammered, not at her words but at an idea gathering pace in his head. This could be a serious play, one that would do the Brits real damage, hurt them. This time he'd be in control, do it his way. He hadn't heard a peep from Martin McLaughlin since he threatened him at the café, and after this, he wasn't going anywhere now. Him lie low, slip over the border? Not a chance in hell. He started to reckon he could string out his stay at Kay's a bit longer and set the plan in motion with no one breathing down his neck.

By the end of dinner, Kay was feeling merry, having had a fair share of *tea*. She'd convinced herself she'd enjoyed her nephew's company and – out of the blue and to her own astonishment – made a suggestion.

'Why don't you stay here this weekend? I'm on a last-minute retreat with Mrs Boyle. Say nothin', but she's got a wee problem with the old drinkie-winkie. Needs some spiritual help.'

She hiccupped and went on. 'The fridge is half-full. It'd be a sin for that good food to go to waste.'

Kieran was floored. 'God Almighty, Kay, I was just about to say that! Me landlord's painting the building, and there's decorators all over the shop - noisy gits.'

Kay suddenly realised what she'd let herself in for and groaned inwardly, always doing silly things when she'd had a taste of the poison. Kieran in her house, poking around her stuff. She pictured it and decided she needed another drink. With her back to him, she slyly topped up her tea with the whiskey hidden behind the kitchen curtain, flinching and squeezing her eyes shut when she heard his next words.

'Don't suppose you could ask Maggie if there'd be anything in it for me? A job like. You're always givin' off at me.'

Kay sighed. It never ended with him, did it? Always something. She took a long swallow of her whiskey laden tea, gathered herself, turned back and, with a forced smile, reluctantly agreed to ask.

'I'll ask.' Kieran gave her the cheesiest smile. Put him in front of Maggie McFadden and he'd have her soft as putty in his hands in no time.

The following day Kay, blithely ignoring the fact she'd had far too many cups of *tea* and was now a walking hangover, convinced herself she must have eaten something dodgy. Shuffling towards the bus stop, she let Kieran trail behind, dragging her battered suitcase and burning with humiliation to be seen with her.

She wore a hideous black lace scarf draped over her head like a cheap veil, mercifully shading her muggy face. A moving streak of black, he thought, like some Mafioso widow. Along with the scarf, she wore a black coat, tights and shoes, and for what? To look like a virginal nun for Father McGuire! Hypocrites; all of them. Every Holy Joe on that bus, pretending to be better than the rest of them.

As she climbed aboard and shuffled down the aisle looking for a seat, he kept to the footpath, hands in his pockets, grinning like he knew a secret they didn't.

Once Kay sat down, he knocked on the glass and bellowed through it, loud enough for the whole bus to hear.

'Oi, Aunty Kay! Don't forget to say a prayer for me soul. Loads of 'em. You have a ball now and behave yerself. I've heard what goes on at those retreats!' Almost dying with embarrassment, Kay waved him off impatiently, and turned her cherry-red face away.

Kieran was still laughing as he walked back to Kay's house and made the call. He waited until a voice answered and the usual old biddy told him to hang on. He grinned as he looked around the fully stocked kitchen, twiddling with the phone, until he finally heard her voice.

'Hello?'

'Bet you weren't expectin' to hear from me so soon?' he joked.

On the other end of the phone, Honey's heart hit the floor. She wouldn't have gone near the phone if she'd known it was him, and for a split second, considered hanging up.

'Don't even think about it, ye hear me,' he warned, as if reading her mind.

'Remember what I said, 'cos if you hang up, I fuckin' swear, I'll do it. I'll do you and the rest of your lot this very day. I mean it!' Honey was too worn out to argue, so she went along with it. 'I hear ye,' she whispered.

'Good girl. I'm at me Aunty Kay's. I need you to come over.' He gave her the address. She hadn't known he had an aunty, but then, after what he'd done, she didn't know him at all. If she had, she'd never have looked at him, let alone spoken a word to him. Reluctantly, she told him she'd get there as soon as she could and hung up.

Kieran had convinced himself that Kay would get him a job. She'd known Maggie McFadden for centuries. He laughed as he recalled her beamer on the bus when he'd wound her up. Serves her right.

By lunchtime, Honey and Kieran sat together in Kay's kitchen. It hadn't taken long for Kieran to make his mark - the house was already upside down. He handed her a shopping list, which she limply accept-ed. From her expression, he needed to soften her up – one last time.

'What's up? You look as miserable as sin.'

Honey shrugged. 'Nothin'.'

Raising his arms and waving them around, he jibed, 'Did you know me auntie's going to leave me this place? One day, it'll be mine. Bet you'd like a kitchen like this, Honey?'

Not with him, never with him. In that moment Honey hated him with a fury she had never known and, for feck's sake, what galled her even more was how good he looked in that tight blue denim shirt and jeans. She kept quiet as he hauled a black sports bag onto the table and eased the zip, but her breath caught when he drew out a handgun and set it down.

Memories flooded back, stripping Val, his milk white feet as she pulled off his socks, the tortured screams, the blood, the plastic they wrapped him in. All of it.

Then, to her horror, he lifted out two automatic rifles, terrifying to look at.

'For God's sake, Kieran, what the hell are you doin' with those?' she screamed. He placed his hand on her arm, but she jerked away.

'Relax, Honey. Those eejits that didn't show - well, they haven't picked their gear up yet, that's all. I've been holdin' onto it for them.' He removed some soft cloths and a bottle of oil and began to expertly clean the guns.

Honey peeked into the bag. At the bottom lay a couple of small ammunition boxes and a medium-sized packet wrapped in clear plastic, like a mustard coloured putty. It didn't take a brain surgeon to work out what it was.

'Seriously, explosives, Kieran? What are you up to now? You're scarin' me.'

He shot her a dark look, then steadied himself and said quietly, 'Take it easy, baby. Trust me. Sit there, keep it shut, and give us some peace. For a minute. *Please*. I need to think.'

She obeyed and scanned the room, taking in the photographs: Kieran as a boy with a tall, fine-boned woman who had to be his mother, his image, and another with a short, dumpy woman. All three shared the same chocolate brown eyes, so the second had to be his Aunty Kay. There were other pictures of her too, in her garden, at a social that looked like St Mary's Community Centre, The Vatican, St Peter's Square, and gathered at a country shrine with a group of women and a priest.

Honey couldn't stop staring at the man in black. She knew that face inside and out.

She turned to Kieran and watched as, one after another, his deft hands stroked and rubbed each part until the gunmetal shone. Slowly, carefully, he reassembled the weapons. When he was done, he wrapped them in a soft cloth, tucked them back in the bag and closed the zip. Satisfied, he met her eye.

'Listen, I've the best plan in the world, and you, missus, are gonna help me.'

She didn't want to know, didn't want to hear it, and yet her body wouldn't budge. Rooted to the spot, he laid out what she was to do, each word driving her pulse higher. Fear tightened across her chest like a vice and her breath almost stopped. It was mad. Completely mad. No way on this earth would he get away with it!

Kieran watched the panic gather in her eyes. He gave her a small, cold smile.

'Aye,' he said softly. 'You'll be grand.'

He lifted the bag up and added, almost kindly said, 'If you breathe one word of this, I'll know.'

Chapter Forty-Five

Abandon Ship

It happened so fast, but looking back, Rob wasn't surprised. The laundryman's massive body couldn't handle the physical side of the job, let alone the mental, especially after yesterday.

Early the previous night, Deeney had keeled over from a fatal heart attack while eating his dinner and watching TV. A girl from the laundry had found him. Unusually, the big boss hadn't phoned first thing, and she needed to speak to him urgently. Eventually she gave up and went to his place, where she peered through the front window when he didn't answer the door. She found him, sprawled out on the living room floor, his body covered in discarded food and beer. The sight scared the living daylights out of her. Panicking like fuck, she took off to the neighbour's house and, after some frantic convincing, finally got him to smash a window and climb through to unlock Deeney's door from the inside.

It was a real kick in the teeth, that's for sure. The night before, Rob and Iowa received a message that briefly lifted their spirits and confirmed what the lab technicians had discovered. All that tedious work had paid off, and several arrests were imminent. Their current orders were to stay put until further notice.

Rob decided to grab a bit of sleep, but the lumpy sofa offered no soft spot. He shot a glare at Iowa, sprawled out on the bed with her books. She wore what looked like a pair of men's striped pyjamas that drowned her slight frame. It had been a long night, not for the sofa but for him; the woman was forever crying out in her sleep. Best not to say a word otherwise he'd be dealing with the fallout. Yawning, he went to make a hot drink, filled the kettle, turned on the stove, and grabbed two mugs.

'Wanna cuppa?' he offered.

'Yeah,' she mumbled.

'What's the magic word? Yeah, what?' Rob asked, playfully holding the mug up.

'Yes, please,' she replied, firing him a sardonic look.

'Good.' *Progress at last!* Rob thought.

He made the tea and topped hers up with sugar. She liked a ton of the stuff, which, given the size of her, astounded him. He placed her cup on a worn pine bedside table next to her. The woman seemed to be permanently surrounded by books. He wasn't sure where she'd got them, but six or seven thick novels lay scattered between the floor and the bed. He waited for a follow-up 'thank you.'

And waited and waited until at last: 'Thank you.'

'You're welcome,' he snapped. 'Christ, Iowa I'm sick o' yer attitude.' He snatched the book she was reading, but she grabbed it back, glared at him and screamed.

'Stop it! Just 'cos you made me a cup of tea changes nothing. Why don't you mind your own bloody business and leave me be?!' Rob grimaced. He'd had his fill of her foul temper and swinging moods; if she'd been a bloke, he'd have her on the floor by now, beating the shit outta her. Instead, he hissed.

'Fuck you, Iowa. I don't know what your problem is. We're meant to be in this together. It's called teamwork, ye know. You've got my back, I've got yours.' She stared at him; outburst or not, it wasn't what she expected. *Teamwork, my arse*, she thought.

Rob wasn't through. 'Is it because I'm a man, Iowa? Are ye a man-hater? You into girls? No problem. You're already rocking that dyke look!' Balking at his cruel words, Iowa placed a bookmark in her book and slowly closed it. She set it down next to her untouched tea and turned her eyes to him.

Kentucky was good-looking, sure, but he irritated the hell out of her. From the moment they met, an intense dislike for him had settled in. Being assigned as his partner had been the final straw. The last thing she wanted was to be responsible for anyone but herself. By dressing in pathetic, unstylish clothes, she hoped to avoid attention of any kind. Her only goal was to kill as many Provos as she could and nothing, not even this wally in front of her, would get in her way.

Deeney's death brought relief. The op was over. It'd been hell, sitting next to his stinking lard arse day in, day out, and listening to his vile language. She shivered at the thought. Hopefully, they'd ship her off somewhere else now – ideally Belfast. *Alone.*

'Typical man,' she remarked in response to her partner's snide comments. 'If you don't understand something, pin a label on it till you do.'

Rob took a step back, regretting the 'dyke' comment. He watched her swing her legs over the side of the bed and stare down at the floor.

'Look,' she said, 'I told you I wanted to do this alone, right? Solo. I don't have the time or energy to sit and listen to your petty tantrums. For now, we're stuck in this godforsaken dump, so please quit huffin' and puffin' like a child, get out of my face. Get lost.'

She'd spoken to him for longer than usual. No messing. She'd got under his skin, and he'd lost it. If she wanted to go solo, fine by him. He'd stewed over her moods for days, weeks, and now that she'd spoken her mind, he hunted for his coat, found it, and threw it on. He wanted nothing to do with her.

'Right then. I'm outta here!'

She grabbed his arm and yelled, 'We've been ordered to stay put, you idiot. Don't be an even bigger wanker! We stay put. Together.'

Rob spat, 'What? You think I'm gonna sit here in silence with that miserable face of yours the only thing to look at all day?!'

He gestured to the window and scoffed, 'I'd rather take me chances out there.' They stared at each other, both frustrated and unhappy. Rob knew she was right about staying put, but her dark mood and the cramped, gloomy room was getting to him.

He shook his head and dropped onto the sofa, buried his face in his hands, and pleaded, 'Iowa... We have to—'

Without having time to finish, there was a loud knock on the door. The two soldiers jumped into action, grabbing their weapons. Each stood on either side of the doorway, guns at the ready.

Rob pressed his face against the door. 'Hello?'

Nothing.

He tried again. 'Hello. Who's there?'

They heard some shuffling from the other side, and soon enough, a shaky voice replied.

'Ah, hello. Mrs Mulligan here. I've a wee envelope for ye. I'd slip it under the door, but I can't because of me back, ye see. It nearly killed me climbin' those stairs. I shouted up, but you two were busy yellin' me house down.'

Rob nodded at Iowa and opened the door. He kept his gun out of sight as the old crone squeezed the envelope through the crack in the door. She muttered something that made no sense and shuffled down the stairs, clutching the rail, terrified that she'd fall. If he were a gentleman, Rob should've helped her, but today, he couldn't be arsed. He locked the door and skimmed the note inside the envelope.

Abandon ship. Pier F1
Black Sabre 19:00 hours.

At last! They were to ditch this hole, leave the car where it was, and return to Pier F1, code for Fort George. It sat at the bottom of Pennyburn, on the other side of Londonderry. The password was Black Sabre, and they were to report in at 7.00 PM.

The next few hours were a blur of cleaning until the bedsit was unrecognisable. Likely it hadn't been so clean in years, but they couldn't afford to leave any trace of being there.

They cooked in silence, ate in silence, washed the dishes in silence, and waited – in silence – until it was time to leave. It would take at least thirty minutes to get to Pennyburn. For Rob, it felt like the longest afternoon of his life. For Iowa, his sulking silence was a godsend.

A little after 6.30 PM, they left. Each carried a suitcase, and Iowa had her most precious books stuffed in a plastic bag. At the bus stop, an elderly couple gave them a warm smile. But the soldiers stayed silent. Luckily, the bus came early, and Rob jumped on to pay.

Iowa followed him down the aisle toward some empty seats. Out of habit, they scoped out the passengers as they passed. To his surprise, Rob spotted an all-out, stunning-looking girl sitting alone by a window. She felt his stare and he stared back, looking puzzled. Then he remembered that face and tried to suppress a small smile as he sat down and placed his case on his knees. His heart raced. She too was probably trying to figure out who he was. Not a chance in hell could she remember him – she couldn't. It was dark in that backyard when she found him, and anyway, his face was decked in camo paint.

A while later, Rob nudged Iowa. It was their stop. He pressed the bell and waited as the bus slowed. The girl rose and gave him another puzzled look. Rob spun around and, grabbing Iowa's arm, got down off the bus and dragged her toward Fort George. After a couple of steps, he turned to see the girl crossing the road toward a black Cortina and relaxed.

Iowa knew something was going on. 'What's up? Who's that?'

'Some girl,' Rob muttered.

Iowa wasn't having it and stopped, whispering harshly, 'Some girl? What girl?'

'I've seen her before, that's all. Think she might've recognised me.'

She couldn't believe it. 'That's all? Are you serious?!'

Rob whispered, 'It's fine, Iowa. Leave it and don't raise your voice with me.'

'I'm not raising my voice.' She was, and she forced herself to stop. 'Don't you realise what that means?' Of course, Rob knew and only half-listened as Iowa raged until they reached the fort's gate, where Rob gave the password. Within minutes, they were shown to a small meeting room and ordered to wait.

While she still had the chance, Iowa warned him, 'You've got a choice, Kentucky. Either tell me who that girl is, or I'll report you.' Rob didn't like where she was going, not one bit, but deliberately played it cool.

'Relax, will ye? I was holed up in her garden doing surveillance when she caught me, she didn't squeal. There's no way she'd recognise me. I mean, it was well dark, and I was all camo'd up. Drop it now. You're getting on my tits.'

His attitude infuriated her, and she was on the verge of losing it when the meeting room door swung open and a man dressed in civvies stepped in. Neither of them knew him.

He was in his late fifties, medium height, with thin, greying hair. Dressed in an off-the-peg navy three-piece suit and white shirt, a red-stained tie hung untidily around his neck. A cigarette dangled from one corner of his mouth and he reminded Iowa of how her father had looked when he'd come home after a rotten day at the office – miserable and short-tempered. The man barely acknowledged them, sat down, and introduced himself as their new handler. Both soldiers sensed his senior rank as he complimented them in a strong Belfast accent.

'I hear you've done excellent work for your first op. Shame that big lump of shite cut it short by dyin' on us.' He stood up, prowled around the room, and flicked his cigarette ash onto the floor with a hint of a grin.

'We've got some solid intel and updated mugshots from your stint, which is good. You'll hear more about what's next in the morning at the debriefing. Same room, 09:30 hours. You'll likely move into the next phase of training and stay together since—'

'But sir!' Iowa broke in. She shot up from her chair so fast it fell back onto the ash-strewn floor. Its steel frame made an almighty crashing noise as it hit the concrete. The handler gave her a look as sharp as a razor, undoubtedly not used to being interrupted.

Iowa knew she'd cocked up and slowly picked up the chair. She eyed him and nodded an apology. Rob watched on with little pity. She was met with the handler's cold stare.

'As I was saying... before I was rudely interrupted.' He paused while he stubbed out his smoke.

'You will remain together since it appears you have done remarkably well in such a short time in Londonderry. Until 09:30 hours then. Goodnight, both.'

Chapter Forty-Six

Bubbles

James was on cloud nine, and Caitlin was thrilled with her room. It cost a lot, but it was worth every penny because of how she reacted.

He found out way more about her on the trip than he had before, and now they had a whole weekend together. From what she said, she cared deeply for her family. She talked about losing her dad and the effect it had on her heartbroken mother. On all of them.

It was hardest when she spoke about her brother, Martin, how he had gone from a fun loving teenager to an angry, bitter young man. He'd changed beyond recognition, and she could scarcely take him now. She laid her father's death at his door. Such talk faded after that. James sensed there was more she wasn't ready to tell, and he let it go. She went on, half laughing and half crying, telling stories about her best friend, Anne and their calamities. She got teary talking about the bombing and Anne's leg, but then smiled when she talked about her childish love for those crazy, multi-coloured stilettos. Either way, they were both still messed up.

Whole swathes of youngsters like Caitlin had been through hell here, and too many had taken the boat or the bus out and not come back. The shirt factories were thinning out, work was quiet, and the dole queues bent round the corners in the rain. Caitlin talked about doing the same one day, leaving, her eyes set on somewhere she could work and breathe without waiting for the next blast or gunshot. It made perfect sense. However, he was more troubled than expected by the idea of her leaving Londonderry at all. He hadn't known a feeling could hurt like that, quick and clean, right under his already painful ribs. He wanted her to have a life that was safe and whole. Of course he did... but here. With him.

They had rolled in late, grabbed a quick bite in the bar - the dining room was shut - then dropped into the snug. By the fire they settled down, the heat of the turf easing the cold from their bones. They sipped hot whiskeys, watched the flames, and let the quiet do the talking. No awkwardness. Just easy smiles and a low hum of excitement for the few days ahead.

James studied Caitlin out of the corner of his eye. She was flushed but seemed relaxed. *Good*. He wanted her to forget all the trauma she'd left behind. She caught his eye and smiled lazily at him.

'I believe, Mr Henderson, I'm a little tipsy.' He couldn't understand how. She'd only had two small glasses of wine with supper and had hardly touched her whiskey.

'Well, Miss McLaughlin, it appears it doesn't take much to get you tipsy.' She hiccupped.

'Told you, I don't drink. Ever, ever. Not 'til now anyway.' *Hiccup*. James appeased her, pointing to her unfinished drink.

'Then why don't you leave that, and we'll get to bed? I've got a full day planned for tomorrow, and we're out in the evening. It'll be another late one.'

Caitlin sat up, placed a hand on her chest, and mock-scolded him, '*Bed*? Mr Henderson? Are you propositioning me already?' He wasn't sure if she was serious until she shrieked with laughter and directed a finger at him.

'You should see your face. I'm jokin'!' *Hiccup.* 'I think you may be right about bed, though.

She moaned, 'It's only that this place is so lovely. I want to make the most of it after these past few weeks. I never dreamt I'd feel so good again James, and to be somewhere like this. It's like something out of an ad on the TV.' James let out a breath of relief, laughed to himself, and knocked back the rest of his drink. *Touché.* She nearly had him there.

His eyes met hers as he held out his hand to help her up. She smiled, swaying a little as she stood and fell in towards him, their faces almost touching.

'I can't thank you enough,' she murmured, kissing him.

'You're welcome. Let's forget about the rest of the world, okay? Just think about us,' he suggested.

Like the gentleman he was, he walked her to her bedroom. It took no small amount of self control to part after a long goodnight kiss. With a quiet sigh he turned on his heel and made his way back to his own room, the bed there big and empty.

The following morning, he found her waiting at the breakfast table. The sun was shining, so they took a long stroll around Lough Eske. It turned out to be a cracker of a day. They sat on a park bench for lunch, soaking up the winter sun and munching fish and chips wrapped in newspaper.

Dinner was an entirely different story. Caitlin came down in her new red dress that caught the light, and James met her in one of his classic Donegal tweed jackets with jeans, casual and smart all at once. They headed for a posh fish place at Castle Eske, outside Donegal Town.

Inside, the linen was crisp, the glassware bright, and the room held a soft murmur that made James feel he'd chosen well. Plates arrived that looked almost too amazing to touch, the food fresh and clean on the tongue, set down with a care that made them giggle like children at each other. Course after course was a delight, the presentation neat as a picture and the flavour to match.

They talked in low voices, shared forks across the table, and let the pleasure of being together warm them, both of them certain they would remember this night. *Always.*

Afterwards, they got roped into a wedding party, enjoyed the traditional Irish music, danced, and got very Jameson-merry.

When they returned to the hotel, they staggered down the corridor towards Caitlin's room.

For James, it had been an unbelievable day, God Almighty, it had flown by. It felt as if they'd only just had breakfast and now the day was nearly over. Caitlin looked stunning. Her hair was loose, she wore barely any makeup, and her flowing dress with black shoes only added to her appeal. Without a hint of airs and graces, she chatted with anyone who crossed her path. The way she was so open and friendly made him feel alive and carefree. And proud.

As the night wound down, he smiled when she tried to unlock her door and kept missing the keyhole. After a few attempts, he took the key and opened it for her. Unsure what to do next, he turned stone cold sober. This was delicate. The last thing he wanted was to spoil the night, so he stood there like a spare part, waiting at the doorway, hardly believing it when she said, almost shyly,

'You want to come in?' His whole body screamed yes, but he didn't want to risk upsetting her.

'I don't think so. I'd love to, but I promised, didn't I? To be a gentleman.' She felt warm, fuzzy, and truly happy. If she had too much to drink, she didn't care. Today had been the best day of her entire life.

'You did, but I trust you. I don't want this day to end. Please, James. Come in.' Caitlin ached for him. The booze had washed away any inhibitions, but a flutter of nerves remained.

James attempted to refuse again, but she took his arm and tried to pull him inside. After a playful fight, he gave up, following her in without another word.

Almost afraid he couldn't control himself, he ordered a bottle of Chianti Classico from room service as a distraction. He planned for them to sit together, have a nightcap, and chat. Nothing more. After putting the phone down, he looked over at her. As he watched, she stood up and turned off the main lights. She stood right in front of him, close enough to touch. His fingers brushed one of the small, round pearl earrings she always wore and looked deeply into her sparkling sapphire eyes, eyes full of trust. He stood still, not wanting to do anything to spoil things. But as if reading his mind, she reassured him with a small smile.

'It's okay. I'm okay.' In answer, he kissed her. It began gently, and then the heat rose, his eagerness pressing against the restraint he made himself keep. At last he drew back.

'I want you so badly, Caitlin. But we have to take this slowly, as hard as it is for me. And trust me. It's *hard*! He joked.

'Give me a minute, okay? Why don't you take a lazy soak in that amazing bath in there? I'll call you when the wine comes.' Caitlin felt a little disappointed. He was sweet, a total gentleman, but she wished he knew she wasn't as clueless or as shy as he thought.

School had been a disaster for her. The nuns had talked about sex in such a dry, detached way that the whole class had shifted uncomfortably in their seats - redners all round. Later, when they all laughed, everyone said they were broke to the bone. The penguins were trying to teach them sex! Like they even knew about sex. The long lessons were gruelling, unpleasant even, and no one dared ask questions afterwards. At home, sex was still a closed-door topic. Anne was Caitlin's go-to for the sex talk.

With James, this felt different – nothing like with Seamus. She wanted him now. *It* now. All of it. She wanted to please him, but more than that, she wanted to show him she wasn't afraid. She took charge, grabbed his hand, and with a slow, deliberate breath, said, 'The bath can wait. I can't.'

She kissed him first. Then, without warning, he felt her fingers fumbling with his belt. He realised she was unbuckling it and wasn't going to stop. Bugger that for a laugh, he thought, there wasn't a hope in hell he was for stopping her.

'What *are* you up to, young lady?' he asked in a whisper. She'd remembered one of Anne's golden tips.

'Trust me,' she replied, 'Relax.' How the heck was he meant to 'relax'?!

She seemed to know exactly what she was doing as she tugged his trousers and undies down. He kicked them free and sent them flying. Caitlin slid her hands round his waist, down to the small of his back, and drew him in. Then her hands came round to the front and she took hold of him. He answered her touch, a tremor running through him as they kissed, hard. He was totally fired up in no time, fully aroused.

She led him to the bed and got him to sit on the edge. Her eyes burned with want, her hair falling across her face.

Once more, she seemed to read his mind and smiled mischievously before kneeling between his legs and taking him entirely in her mouth.

Lost in ecstasy, he groaned and leaned back on one arm while gently caressing the top of her head with his free hand. His head rolled back. His body was on fire, the sensations heightened by his pumping blood.

She teased him with her tongue, slow and deliberate, until he lost himself completely in the rush. A deep moan escaped as he came, his chest rising and falling. When he finally opened his eyes, he saw her crawling up from the floor, a small, naughty smile playing on her lips.

Anne was so right! That was something else, fantastic, but only with the right person, Caitlin reckoned. She relished seeing James so powerless and vulnerable and it excited her beyond measure.

A tingling sensation ran through her as she made him wait a little longer before cheerfully telling him, 'Time for that bath.' He nodded, taking a deep, much needed breath, and grinned like a boy let loose in a sweet shop as Caitlin disappeared into the bathroom, deliberately leaving the door slightly ajar.

He collapsed onto the bed, his heart racing, and listened as she ran the bath. Startled, he heard her singing, and barely recognised the tune – Patsy Cline's *Crazy*. His emotions were all over the shop. Where did she learn to do *that*? Lost for words, he shook his head and chuckled at her efforts. The poor girl couldn't carry a tune in a bucket! So bloody dreadful he could only laugh.

Minutes passed as the bath filled. James jumped off the bed, un-dressed completely, and grabbed a white towelling bathrobe from the wardrobe. Without a second thought, he sneaked a peek into the bathroom. She didn't notice him gawking as she stripped off her dress to reveal a red lacy bra and matching panties. She had a gorgeous, lean body, just like a ballerina's. He was watching when she dropped her underwear and turned.

'Oi, you! Cheeky bugger!' she protested, testing the water. He laughed, feeling like the luckiest man alive.

'Can you blame me? It's not often I see a sight like that. All right, I admit it, I'm no gentleman. I'm a horny Scot with a filthy mind! But more importantly, where did you learn to do *that?*'

'Learn to do *what*?' she replied, teasingly. She felt fantastic and wasn't shy about her nakedness, appreciating James's mix of surprise and delight.

'*That.*' He laughed, gesturing towards the bedroom.

'Ah, *that*. You wouldn't believe me if I told you. I'll tell you after. It's funny.' Anne had seen an article in a saucy magazine yonks ago. Something a girl had found near the Gents at the factory. A group of them had snuck into the Ladies' or the 'parlour,' as they called it later, to gawp at the baffling images. Of course, Anne tried it first, but she wasn't sold on it. Some of the lazy gits stank of piss, she said, but with the last fella; it was well good, and she loved it! At the time Caitlin had pulled a face at the very idea of it, but after *that* with James, well...

He couldn't fathom how Caitlin knew that stuff; he'd half expected her to be a vestal virgin, but honestly, after *that*, he didn't give a hoot. As sure as hell, he wasn't for complaining. He checked out the bath and cried.

'Caitlin McLaughlin, you're something else. But you'd better turn those taps off, or we'll be turfed out. It's about to overflow!' She screamed at the sight of the bubbly, overfilled bathtub.

'Oh nooo, I've put too much bubble bath in. Help!' She frantically tried to turn off the ancient taps, but the bubbles kept rising, and the two of them burst into fits of laughter.

With some effort, James grabbed the tap and stopped the flowing water. Soaked and covered in bubbles, they collapsed onto the slippery floor in tears, their sides hurting. James more than Caitlin's, his ribs were killing him.

A loud knock sounded at the bedroom door. James, after tightening his robe, opened the door to see the night porter there, looking worried and holding a tray.

'Room service, sir. Is everything okay in there?' he asked, doing his best to peer over James's shoulder into the bedroom.

James laughed. 'Aye, all good. Bit of a mishap with the bath that's all. Sorted now. Thanks.' James tried to close the door, but the porter's foot stopped it.

He wasn't entirely convinced. The fella in the doorway, wearing a bathrobe, was sopping wet and covered in bubbles. What the hell were they up to in there? When he saw their fake names, he knew they were a funny pair and likely up to something. He wasn't an idiot, but at least he'd have something to write in the log tonight - nothing ever happens around here.

Hearing another scream, he stepped forward. 'Sir, is the lady in trouble? Does she need help?' James put a hand out to stop him.

'Nah, we're fine, honestly. No need to worry.' He flashed a smile, took the tray, and shut the door in the porter's face.

Caitlin giggled while spying from the bathroom door. Thank God the porter didn't come in. The place was drenched, like William Street swimming pool's changing room. It was soaking! She tied her hair up and sank slowly into the deliciously hot water. *Bliss*. So different from the freezing bathroom and lukewarm water back home. Her skin tingled with goosebumps as the heat soaked in.

After a lovely deep breath, she leaned back and closed her eyes. James wasn't expecting *that* from her. She'd even surprised herself. She felt a tiny bit guilty, but she pushed it away with a tune. Nothing was going to spoil this for her.

James popped his head into the bathroom, sat on the side of the bath, and squinted through the mound of foam. 'Still alive in there? How is it?'

Caitlin groaned. 'I swear to God, James, I don't think I've ever had a bath like it. We're always running out of water at home, and the bathroom's like an icebox most days. This is heaven. It's so warm and lovely.'

She lifted her hands and waved them like a conductor, singing: *Oh Mary, this London's a wonderful sight, where the people are working by day and night...*

James let out a belly laugh. He loved seeing her like this, so relaxed and happy, but dear God, she seriously couldn't carry a tune to save her life. As she hit a high note, he squeezed his eyes shut.

'I'd like to know, Caitlin McLaughlin, who I can blame for teaching you to sing like that?' he asked with a warm, teasing smile. She knew she was crap, but tonight, she felt like an angel. She was happier than she'd been in forever, and that was all that mattered.

'One of my many hidden talents,' she quipped. 'Do you think I've missed my calling?'

James chuckled, shaking his head. 'Let's say, I wouldn't give up the day job!' Her voice maybe God-damn-awful, but that face, that body? A piece of fine art.

Rather boldly, he grinned and asked. 'Any chance I can join that heavenly choir in there?' Gobsmacked, Caitlin blushed and sat up, her eyes wide and wondrous.

'What, us two, in here? Together?!' she screamed.

'Yep,' James replied, his face glowing, 'though you might want to let some water out first.' Any shyness died out as Caitlin reached for the bath plug. Bubbles clung to her back and slid down her pale milky skin, trailing over her breasts.

James found himself responding, but shot to the bedroom, calling over his shoulder, 'Not too much. I'll be right back.' He switched on the radio, and the smooth, velvety voice of Ella Fitzgerald filled the room. He was filled with a feeling he couldn't name.

As if silenced by Ella's magic, Caitlin stopped her banshee-like singing. Then, after pouring two glasses of red wine, James carried them into the bathroom. She chuckled when she saw the glasses, took one, and watched as he carefully sat on a stool by the bath and shrugged off his robe. She noticed the bruises on his ribs and how he winced as he gingerly climbed in. With soapy hands, she gently touched the sore spot.

'What happened?' He wasn't for telling.

'Och, that. It's fine. Got carried away at the gym. A bit of boxing, sparring, you know?'

She didn't buy his story. He'd blamed it on running last time. But she let it go. No one or nothing in this world was going to spoil tonight. She'd play along, so she sipped her wine, relishing the taste. Before this weekend, she'd never touched wine, but sampling it now, she liked it.

James had an impressive body, muscular, toned, and perfectly formed, as if a master sculptor had created him. Every muscle seemed to ripple with effortless strength and grace. She couldn't help but marvel at how life worked. One moment, it could crush you with grief, and the next, it handed you a glass of fine red wine and a body like this. And in a bloody great big bath, big enough for two!

He smiled, conscious of his effect on her. Those hours in the gym weren't a waste, he decided. Caitlin was eyeing him up like he was the last slice of cake, and he loved it. Tonight was turning out to be perfect. More than perfect. It'd gone way ahead of him, so far from what he'd imagined or hoped. Careful with his glass, he slid deeper into the suds, chuckling when he realised Caitlin was right: it was heaven – warm enough to relax but not hot enough to cook.

He raised his glass for a toast. 'To the weekend.'

'The weekend,' she replied with a dreamy smile. They sipped their wine and carefully placed their glasses on the floor next to the bath. They lay back, top to tail, and soaked up the heat and intimacy.

James began to play with Caitlin's toes, wiggling each like they were piano keys, then moved his hands up to massage her calves. Their eyes met as his hands wandered higher, sliding up her inner thighs, her waist, and , her back. He drew her closer, sliding her along the bath to face him.

She laughed softly as the water topped over the bath, then subconsciously wrapped her legs around his torso. His fingers traced her neckline before finding her breasts. She moaned as he teased her foam-covered nipples, gently cupping them while he kissed her. Next, he took a nipple in his mouth, giving it a lick before cheekily nibbling it with his teeth.

In no time, they were lost in each other as his hands drifted down again to her inner thigh, where he delicately stroked between her legs. Her breath quickened, her heart raced. Anne never told her about this! She half-wanted him to stop, but sweet and gentle Jesus, she totally didn't! Whatever he was up to, it was sensational.

He teased and tantalised her, whispering soothingly in her ear, 'Your turn to relax, my love. Enjoy.'

Caught up in the sensation of his exploring fingers, Caitlin felt like she was walking on a tightrope, wavering with each step, when suddenly – a wave of indescribable pleasure overtook her. She cried out in sheer, unrestrained joy, having experienced nothing like it before. James smiled, looking as smug as a cat who'd got the cream.

Shaking her head and dazed, she laughed, 'And you, Mr Henderson, where did you learn to do *that*?'

He laughed back 'Ah, now that would be telling. You've still got to tell me your secret first.' They kissed again until an almighty gurgling noise erupted from the bath.

'The stopper's come out!' James yelled. 'Quick, let's get out!'

He leapt out of the hot bath, grabbed a towel from the rail, and lovingly wrapped it around her as she rose. He kissed her shoulders and neck, drying her off slowly, savouring every moment like a sip of fine wine. Like a child, she spun around as he dried her back and bum, giving him a wide, radiant smile. Noticing a small round birthmark on her lower hip, he gave it a saucy little kiss and secured the towel.

As the bath emptied, they grabbed their glasses and made for the bedroom. James pulled up one of the soft chairs by the fireplace.

'May I refill your wine glass, madam?' he offered, trying to sound like a butler.

She nodded, handing her glass across. 'Why thank you.'

The clock on the mantelpiece told James it was almost 1.30 AM. *What a day! What a night!*

He settled into a chair, and Caitlin perched onto his knee. Before long, they cuddled and chatted like they'd known each other forever.

The wine was soon drunk, and as the coals in the fireplace glowed warmly, James took Caitlin's hand and pulled her down onto a sheepskin rug in front of the fire. He'd never wanted anyone so badly. When Caitlin was singing earlier, he'd discreetly slipped a small silver packet from his wallet and tucked it under the edge of the rug – just in case. It was a sneaky move, but a wise one.

They snuggled up, and James slowly took off Caitlin's towel, his eyes glued to her. Except for her birthmark, her skin was flawless: milky white and smooth, like a porcelain doll. Words weren't needed. They wanted this. Both of them. They kissed, the energy between them electric, and once more, both were lost in a whirlwind of passion. But there was genuine emotion, too. Their lovemaking was intense and raw, a mix of tenderness and fire.

An hour or so later, James lay wide awake on the rug. It was getting chilly in the room. Caitlin was fast asleep next to him. He was too scared to move, for fear of waking her up. He'd never felt this way. He was a shipwreck of feelings.

This beautiful Derry girl continued to surprise him. She was a natural at showing love and always wanted to please him. He was both excited and terrified. *Gordon Bennett.* Was he - James Henderson – falling in love? It didn't add up. He hardly knew her, if at all. Nevertheless, there it was. That feeling in his chest, like a little hum, and how he kept replaying her laugh and the way she looked at him, like he actually mattered. He wasn't designed for this sort of thing. Not until now.

Caitlin McLaughlin, what did you do?

Chapter Forty-Seven

How Does that Even Work?

Caitlin woke up, and for a split moment, she'd no idea where she was. Christ, but her head hurt! It throbbed, and her mouth felt like it had been stuffed with cotton wool.

As the memories of the night before came rushing back, her face turned scarlet. She covered it with her hands, half-laughing, half-mortified. Friggin' heck, what a night!

In the cold light of day, she groaned and turned to see James grinning at her sideways, looking best pleased with himself.

'Morning, you.' he said with a look of satisfaction. She realised she was starkers but found it didn't bother her.

'Morning.' she replied. It was all coming back to her.

He didn't seem the least bit fazed about being butt naked too, and chuckled, 'How's the head?' She felt as if a truck had hit her – her first hangover! How the hell did Majella cope with this day in day out? *God make me disappear. Please.*

She grumbled and whispered, 'Not the best. How much did I have?' He'd tried to tell her to slow down, but of course, she didn't listen; she'd been in fantastic form. Happy.

'Well... you downed half a bottle of red in record time, on top of what we had earlier. Shouldn't mix grape with the grain. Lethal.' Caitlin didn't trust herself to speak.

'By the way, young lady, you were something else. I'm still shell-shocked,' he teased with his usual cheeky wink.

'You passed out on the rug afterwards, so I carried you to bed. Have to say, you've left me bleedin' knackered.'

She was horrified. 'I did? I'm sorry.'

'Don't be! I had a whale of a time. Just wondering if you did?' he asked, cautiously.

Her smile said it all, and then she playfully hit his arm. He squeezed her, delighted that she was okay. No regrets. As she turned to face him fully, she admired how handsome he was in the morning light and noticed his apprehension. They'd shared an unforgettable night and still had the day ahead to look forward to.

'I had a wonderful time. Honest. Surprised myself.' She giggled and blushed.

'Surprised me, too, I can tell ye,' James quipped, 'but I'm not complaining!' He threw his hands up.

'Do we honestly have to get up? I mean, right now?' Caitlin pouted. He seized her and began to tickle her.

'If you're asking whether we have to get out of this bed, then no way. After last night, I'm not letting you outta my sight. I'm wanna pick up where we left off!' With a carefree laugh, she tossed the sheet over her head and let out a dramatic shriek.

Against the clock, they dragged themselves up for a late checkout, then filled their plates at the carvery and ate until they were full up. They took a short walk to clear their heads, and after that, it was time to go. Caitlin had to be home by teatime and she meant to be on time; her granny's wrath was not worth testing.

The car ride home was silent, with heavy rain and thunder, a complete contrast to the Friday night chatter. James kept his attention on the road and the spray from the lorries, while Caitlin let the rain-soaked hills pull her thoughts this way and that. A little bit of sadness tried to spoil her happiness, but she shook it off and looked at him. He seemed as grey as the sky, so she tried to cheer him up, and laughing, said as she touched his sleeve.

'Well, boss, that was some weekend. So much for you being a gentleman!' He smiled at her efforts, and soon they talked about all sorts until they reached the border, when a slow black cloud of reality suddenly descended on them. The queue made James feel worse.

'I don't want to go back,' he told her. Caitlin nodded.

'I know. Me neither!' Her heart skipped a beat. It was over. Their weekend was over.

The customs posts and army checkpoints were quiet and they passed through without fuss. Caitlin felt worse and worse as they got closer to the city, but she didn't want to ruin things after James had been so kind. She bit her lip and stayed strong, watching the road signs and the rain on the windshield. Seeing the rain, he offered to give her a lift home when he stopped the car near her bus stop at Pennyburn.

She gave her head a firm shake. 'I don't think so. James. Not after last time,' she said, thankful for his offer. He grabbed her hands and gave them a squeeze.

'I won't kiss you,' she told him quietly, her heart doing a little dance. 'No need to explain why. I'm going to get out now before I fall apart. Bye now, and thank you for the most amazing weekend. I'll never forget it James. *Never.*'

A wave of sadness crossed his face too as he replied, 'Bye, Caitlin. It was perfect, wasn't it?' A little smile played on his lips. She opened the car door and stepped out.

'See ya,' James whispered.

'See ya!' she said, and slammed the door, again not thinking. *Bang*!
James chuckled as the Cortina almost jumped, and she blew him a kiss,
standing in the rain like something out of a bad rom-com.

The second he was gone, Caitlin groaned and rushed to the bus stop.
As it was a Sunday, she expected a slow bus service, probably requiring
one or two changes. Under the decrepit shelter, she sat down and
reflected on the weekend, blushing several times as each moment re-
played in her mind.

It had been perfect, even with a hangover. How the hell did Majella
cope with the sickness, Caitlin didn't know? As it was, her tummy was
doing somersaults and her lunch was trying to make a comeback.

She understood why she felt so sad: she'd had a taste of the finer
things, the starch white Egyptian bed linen, room service, the turf fire
in the snug, the amazing food, and beyond all that the simple grace
of a day lived without fear or fuss, a day where she could laugh and
be herself and be seen, by James. The thought of going back to their
damp house and her granny's razor sharp words felt like it was trying
to squeeze her back into a life that she no longer wanted. She asked
herself, 'Did she regret this weekend? Do I wish we hadn't gone?' The
answer? Definitely not.

Yeah, she was sad, because once she'd breathed in air that was light
and carefree, it was hard to choke back on the murk and soot again.
No longer was she a gullible teenager from Derry. James Henderson
made her a woman this weekend.

The bus arrived, but the route took her the slowest way home along
the abandoned WWII warehouses of the River Foyle quayside towards
the Guildhall Square. The city was always dreary in the rain, and the

blown-out relics of once-proud Victorian buildings and warehouses didn't help.

Several army checkpoints hindered the journey. Caitlin pretended to be asleep as the caped soldiers walked up and down the aisle, mostly questioning the men and rummaging through the women's handbags. Luckily for her, she wasn't disturbed.

A feeling of dread hit her as she looked up and opened the rickety gate to number 30. She didn't mean to be ungrateful – this was her home – but she'd grown to hate it with a vengeance, even more so after this weekend.

It was a house of pain. The luxurious bedroom and bathroom of the hotel filled her with a longing to go back. She didn't need luxury; she wanted normalcy. Security. She didn't want to worry whether the electric would run out, if there was enough food on the table, or even enough hot water for a lousy bath. That would be luxury enough.

She hated this house's weather-worn, pebble-dashed facade. Hated its unkempt garden. Even hated the damaged pillar-box red door her father had painted last summer, with its crude, matching red-trimmed window frames. Had she ever been happy here? Somehow, she had to get away. But to where? And how?

As she walked over the threshold, the smell of cabbage and bacon hit her. A far cry from the delicious aroma of the food she'd enjoyed just hours ago. It only deepened her anguish as she placed her suitcase at the bottom of the stairs, removed her wet coat, and hung it up under the stairs.

Before entering the kitchen, she took a much-needed deep breath to calm herself, wiping the dampness from her face and tidying her hair.

Tommy was in his usual spot beside her granny at the ironing board. She was astonished to see him and, with that knowing smile of his, he wasted no time and asked, 'How was it, then? Did ye have a laugh?'

'It was lovely Tommy, yeah,' Caitlin said quietly. 'Great.' She didn't like how easily lying was.

She made a fresh pot of tea and offered it around. Tommy nodded and put out his cup. Somehow, he seemed more wound up than he had on Friday night.

'What's up?' she asked, settling into her chair.

'Listen, love,' he began, 'all hell broke loose here on Saturday night. Martin's been lifted again - lifted in Mailey's. Place went ballistic. Brits say there were traces of explosives on his clothes. Turns out that fat prick Deeney's a Judas, been grassin' for the Brits. Forensics have been testing half of Derry's laundry. Just as well the fucker's dead. Dropped like a stone with a heart attack. Should've suffered, if you ask me. Anyway, it looks like Martin's away for a good while now.'

Caitlin was startled by her initial feeling: relief. Martin hadn't been back long, but he'd been a feckin' nightmare. The relief didn't last – or show. Guilt moved in. He was her brother.

'Feck. Does Mammy know yet?' she asked, looking up. Tommy yawned before answering.

'Nah, none the wiser. We've told her nothin'. Your granny's worked miracles here, so we don't want her to know yet. Majella ate more in the last two days than in the past couple of weeks. Fair play to you, Mammy.' He raised his cup to his mother, who waved away the compliment. Caitlin watched her fold a newly ironed blouse.

Mary eyed her son and mocked, 'Well, she's me daughter, right? I'm not gonna let her lie up those stairs and starve till they take her out of this house in a box, now am I?!' Tommy winked at Caitlin and pulled a face behind his mother's back.

'No, Mother, you're not,' he answered dutifully.

Caitlin grinned at his antics and stood to leave. 'I'll go say hello.'

Her granny stopped folding the laundered clothes and said coldly, 'Suit yourself.' Thinking it best to ignore her, Caitlin walked out of the kitchen.

Tommy called after her, 'See you later. Glad you'd a good time. Like I said, ye deserve a bitta fun, love.'

Caitlin reddened as a little voice inside whispered, 'God love you, Tommy, but if you only knew...'

Blamfield Street seemed to zap her of energy as Caitlin climbed the staircase. Before checking on Majella, she tapped on Tina's bedroom door and waited. No one in. She groaned at the silence, stepped away, and entered her parents' bedroom, where the smell of fresh bed linen greeted her. Majella was pleased to see her and gave her a loving smile. She wanted a hug and tried to sit up, but she was too weak and fell back.

'Ah, Caitlin, love. Did ye have a nice time?' she asked.

'I did, Mammy. Lovely. Tired now, though. How's you?' Caitlin replied, sitting on the bed edge.

Majella gave her a weak smile. She felt like crap drying out but couldn't say so. Shivering like mad and with shaking hands, eating had been a disaster – every bite a battle. Nevertheless, she put on a cheerful face for Caitlin.

'Ah, grand. Better. I'll give the old bag credit. She's practically force-fed me. Even washed me hair. I might try gettin' up in the mornin', it being a new week an' all.' Caitlin was glad. To her, Majella appeared a hundred times better, until she caught sight of her trembling hands.

'That's good, Mammy, but your hands, they're shaking.'

'Only the cold,' Majella whined. Caitlin knew better but still tucked the blankets in around her and fluffed the pillows to make Majella warmer and more comfortable.

'You can tell me about your weekend after, love. Over breakfast. Where's Martin and Tina? They haven't been near me.' Majella asked.

Caitlin wasn't for breathing a word about Martin, nor would she dare mention her weekend with James. She'd find out where Tina was later.

'Don't know. I'm only in myself. Tommy's been. I think he's trying to get back into Granny's good books – boy but he lost it with her on Friday night.'

Majella knew all about it. 'Aye, I heard. How's work going? I've been spaced out, I know. I'm sorry, love.'

'I hope you're not still daydreaming about Mr Henderson, Caitlin,' she said with a warm smile and a gentle tone. She tried to sit up a little. 'You'd tell me, wouldn't ye?'

Caitlin lied, even though she didn't want to. 'Busy as ever. And nah, Mammy. No more daydreaming about Mr Henderson.' She sounded cool as a cucumber, but she was going mad inside.

Majella released a massive sigh and fell back. 'Good girl. Love you.'

'Love you too.'

Caitlin went to her room and hid away. She didn't want to talk to or see anyone. She took off her clothes, got into the chilly bed, and then pulled the covers up until she started to feel warm. The weekend returned in flashes, it'd been so wonderful. Was this love? If it was, it felt like the world was ending. She was a mess of nerves, but at the same time, unbelievably happy and heartbroken.

How does that even work?

Chapter Forty-Eight

White as a Sheet

K ieran had enjoyed crashing at his Aunty Kay's. The grub in the fridge was spot on, and the house was warm and inviting. Bigger and better than the flat.

Honey was really stressing out after that night in the Barn. All that sulking, the neediness, the constant looking for reassurance - it was wearing thin and fast. She was more hassle than she was worth, and he thanked Christ she'd be out of the picture soon. He'd see to it after this was over. That whole 'trying-to-please' thing just made her exasperating.

She was a stage-five clinger, a burden he didn't want and seriously annoying. Her family would be heartbroken when they found her dead no doubt. But he was okay with it already. It didn't bother him. Casualty of war. That's what he thought. No stress, no regrets. Doing it for the Cause.

His aunt returned from her retreat in a frosty mood, but Kieran soon won her over with his enduring charm. She told him she'd scored him an interview at the City hotel, and now, with Martin McLaughlin's re-arrest, he felt pretty feckin' pleased.

He'd got back to the flat the night before, and with nothing decent in the fridge, threw some cornflakes and milk in a bowl and sat in the dimly light kitchen with his thoughts. His head was ticking over, his idea coming together. Nice, simple and if things go his way, doable. Chucking his bowl in the sink, he wandered into the bedroom and fell onto the bed. Kay had said he'd have to buy his own uniform. Fine by him. He preferred wearing his own clothes, anyway. No second-hand rubbish, reeking of the dead.

His wardrobe door lay open, and he took a moment to admire the few perfectly pressed shirts and trousers inside, each colour co-ordinated and hanging on wooden clothes hangers. A bit of a snob, he was particular about what he wore. Always loved fashion. Maybe in a previous life, who knows what he could've been. A designer, perhaps. One day, he swore, when he got some real dosh, he'd buy nothing but the best. No knock-offs. No tat. His wardrobe wasn't vast, but what he had was quality.

He needed to learn more about this so-called 'secret' meeting. Kay had been vague, but his head told him he was onto something big. In his mind, he pictured the place packed with security services and, if lucky, some of those Proddy wankers who illegally controlled the city. What if he wiped them out? All of them. The mere thought of it...

He'd go it alone this time – no need to involve the Provos, especially after they'd fucked him over with the Brit, and sent McLaughlin to make idle threats. He could picture the front page of the *Derry Journal*: 'Wipe-Out at the City Hotel.' They'd remember him for that.

A soft knock on the door interrupted his day dreaming. It was too early for visitors, or deliveries, so he grabbed a sports bag from the bottom of a cupboard, unzipped it and pulled out a revolver. After checking that it was loaded, there was another knock – this time louder and more impatient.

He approached the door cautiously and called, 'Who is it?'

'Only me.'

Kieran's face brightened – chuffed to bits to hear that voice. *What a lovely surprise!* It was his soul-mate and the love of his life, Alex. Deciding to have a bit of fun, he opened the door, held the revolver up and pointed it right at his guest. Alex spotted the gun right away and jumped back, startled at first, then furious.

Kieran couldn't help but laugh as Alex exclaimed, 'That's so not funny Kieran Kelly. I nearly wet me knickers!' At such a reaction, Kieran realised he hadn't done himself any favours. Might have pushed his luck. He dropped the gun.

'You're as white as a sheet, *shit.*' Can't ye take a joke? Come in. Sit down. Quick,' he begged. Alex strode past him, back rigid and furious.

Kieran shut the door, unloaded the revolver, and stashed it safely back in the sports bag. He offered to make some coffee, but Alex wasn't interested, fervently pissed off. Nothing funny about having a gun stuck in your face.

Alex's hands shook as a bead of sweat was dabbed away with a crumpled tissue, and Kieran knew he'd better get this sorted, or else...

'What the heck are you doin' with that ?' Alex demanded.

'Nothin' for ye to worry about, my love. Just precautions, that's all.' Kieran explained.

'How do you mean, precautions?' Kieran was up to all sorts of shenanigans these days.

'What's going on? Tell me. What have you got yourself into now?'

Kieran shrugged and then, with a wide smile, brushed off the question and casually shared his news.

'Listen to this. I was at Aunty Kay's this weekend. And... wait 'til ye hear. Got me a job interview this mornin'.'

'About time we got some good news.' For a minute, Alex forgot about the sports bag and its contents.

'Where's the interview?'

'City Hotel.' Kieran explained how it'd come about. Alex flashed a wide congratulatory smile.

'Will ye give that thing back to whoever, love, soon as, will ye?' Motioning towards the sports bag.

'And get over here I wanna big, sloppy, wet kiss. To celebrate!'

'You're such a princess!' Kieran teased. He felt a huge wave of relief.

They were laughing and falling all over each other on the bed, kissing like crazy. The neighbour's loud bang on the wall, a sign to be quiet, just made them laugh harder, their giggles hidden against each other.

Kieran nipped Alex's ear and murmured, 'By the way, McLaughlin's been lifted again. Gone for a while this time. We're in the clear.' Alex smiled brightly.

'Thank goodness for that. Work's crazy right now. Everyone's going on about some flashy meeting that's coming up. Funny enough, it's at the City Hotel too.' Kieran couldn't believe his luck.

He sat up, all ears, and with a mock innocent expression, asked, 'What meetin's that, then?'

'Can't say, but I bet half of Derry's grapevine knows already.' Alex grumbled, playing with Kieran's fringe.

'I've heard a whisper or two meself,' Kieran wise-cracked, laughing at Alex's expression.

'Please. Tell me your jokin'. What'd you hear?'

'Some big-shot meeting's being run by a Scot from Rocola. Loads of VIPs expected. That's about it.'

Alex's arms went up in exasperation. 'See what I mean? That's my point. Who told you?'

'Only my gorgeous benefactor, Kay.' Kieran sneered – *gorgeous* was the last word he should use to describe his aunt.

Alex was really worried now. The meeting details had to be kept secret, below the radar.

'That's not good. I won't be there meself, helping with the setup. Sounds like the whole town's caught wind of it. This could screw things right up. I'd better let them know.' Kieran was even more curious now.

'Why? What's the big deal?'

But Alex wouldn't say. 'Nah, it's fine. Don't worry about it. C'mere.'

Kieran's internal antenna went into overdrive. He was right. This meeting could be exactly what he was waiting for! He'll worry about it later – right now, Alex was here.

Their lovemaking was frantic and intense, the kind that left marks. Exactly as they liked it. Sweat trickled down their backs as they moved in unison together, not with affection, but with purpose. It'd always been like this between them, from the start. No talking, no pretence, but raw instinct. Both wanted the same thing.

As Kieran pressed his face into the warm crook of a damp neck, Honey crossed his mind. He hadn't meant to think of her, but there she was. So careful. So eager to please. Always watching him, afraid of getting things wrong. The thought of her made him dig his nails in deeper, drawing a groan from beneath that he barely heard it.

Honey. *Jesus.* The girl hadn't a clue. All soft voice and needy, all hopeful eyes, hanging on to his every word like he was some sort of Prince Charming. Seemed like she was fumbling her way through some dreamy romance, looking for her 'Happy Ever After'. *Pathetic.*

With Alex, Kieran needed something else entirely. To get lost, to blaze through a world of their own making and come out the other side with nothing left but skin, heat and a delightful ache. To be torn down and built back up by hands that knew what they were doing.

This... this was what he needed. What Alex needed.. Their fantasy, their truth. The only thing that ever made sense to either of them. And Honey? She'd never come close.

With every change of pace, their low, raw moans grew louder. They didn't hold back. They never did. Hands roamed over body, sex toys pulled out from under the bed. Their rhythm was jagged, feral, built on pain and pleasure in equal measure. Again, the wall thudded from next door, but neither of them noticed. They weren't there. They were somewhere else entirely.

Much later, they lay in the mess of tangled sheets and bruised skin, their chests rising in sync. Neither spoke. They didn't have to. No one would ever understand them. No one could. And that's how it had to stay.

Kieran puffed on a cigarette while Alex slowly ran a hand across his rock-hard stomach. An idea popped into Kieran's head. Once the deed was out of the way, it could work.

'D'you know what?' he said, flashing a grin. 'We should take a wee break after this. Somewhere decent. What about America?' Alex shut it down right away.

'Can't. Not yet anyway. I've only been here a few months.'

But Kieran was dead set on it. He'd hit Aunty Kay for another loan, and if he picked up some work in the next few weeks, well... they could make it a killer trip.

'We don't have to go right away. It'd give us somethin' to look forward to. How about Miami? Picture us in that sunshine. I'll find the cash.' he said, near pleading.

'I can't, darling. Sorry, it's too soon. What'll work think if I head off into the sunset when I've barely been here?' Alex wailed. At this, Kieran leapt out of bed, stubbed out his cigarette, and exploded.

'For fuck's sake! I'm offerin' you a trip to Miami for free. Most people would jump at the chance!'

'Don't go losin' it, darling. I'll see what I can do, all right. Now come. Come and lie down,' Alex coaxed, patting the bed. 'Beside me, *please.*'

Like a sulking toddler, Kieran gave in and dropped onto the bed, grumbling under his breath, arms folded as he turned his face to the wall. Alex didn't rise to it, just reached out, calm as ever, and began to scratch the top of Kieran's head - slow, steady strokes, the way he liked it. Kieran's breathing soon calmed, his shoulders relaxed, and he dozed off lightly, something that happened more easily when Alex was near.

But lately, it'd been different. Subtle clues. A smear of lipstick on the bathroom sink that didn't belong there, a stranger's perfume hanging in the air, bits of clothing tossed carelessly over the arm of the sofa - all of it left out in plain sight.

Alex noticed, of course. Saw everything. Said nothing. Acted like it wasn't happening. Because it couldn't be. No chance. No one else could control Kieran, could pull him back from the edge. Could love him the way he wanted, the way he needed. Kieran knew it too. Had to.

The risk was always there, crawling beneath the surface. One slip, one whisper in the wrong ear, and it would all come crashing down. The scandal would ruin them both, maybe worse. But whatever this was - whatever name the world might try to put on it – they'd get over it. Doesn't love beat everything?

They'd made a promise, one neither of them had spoken aloud in months, and it held. Whatever happened next, however far it all went, they'd stick it out. *Together.*

Kieran woke to find the bed empty. He hoped he hadn't messed things up with Alex. Scratching his head; he sighed and searched for his watch. It was next to their used sex toys, which he quickly flung under the bed.

The bright morning light spilled through the curtains, catching him full in the face as he sat up, and for a moment all he could feel was a surge of anger, a bitter twist of disappointment that he couldn't show Alex to the world as he longed to. He was hopelessly in love, and he kept telling himself that once they made it to America, everything would be different, that they could be together openly, for real, without the prying eyes and poisoned whispers that dogged him, like Martin McLaughlin. McLaughlin knew. One day, Kieran thought, one day the bastard would let the cat out of the bag. But for now, he pushed the thought away and told himself to concentrate.

He stretched, rolled his shoulders, stood up, and already he felt the nerves buzzing beneath his skin. This wasn't just any day. This interview mattered. He needed this job if he was going to succeed. Not for the money or to appease his Aunty Kay, though both reasons were fair enough, but for the chance it gave him to get close to the right people, to hear the names. The VIP meeting was coming up, and if he was in the right place at the right time, he would finally learn who'd be there. That knowledge was worth more than any wage.

He strolled to the bathroom, splashed cold water over his face, shaved carefully, and washed until his skin was bright and clean. He leaned close into the mirror, checking his reflection as if he could read his fortune there, and for a second a worry caught him off guard- would Mrs McFadden see through him, would she sense what he was really after? He stood up straight, pushed that thought away too, and made his mouth into a firm line. What was up? He didn't usually doubt himself.

Back in the bedroom he laid out his clothes with care, meticulous as always, wanting every piece to speak well of him. A crisp white shirt, pressed flat and gleaming, a tie tied neat at the throat, dark trousers with a sharp crease, and the jacket he'd chosen specially, that fitted him perfectly. He ran a hand through his wavy hair, thick and unruly at times, but today combed and set, smart enough to impress but still young, stylish. *So good-looking.* Last came the shoes, black and polished until they reflected the light as he stepped across the room.

He stood before the mirror one final time, gave himself the long, deliberate look of a man who knows appearances can win or lose the day, and though his stomach knotted with nerves, he smiled. He had to believe. He had to carry this through. This job could mean everything. This job meant answers. The job meant access to the meeting — and the names. He paused, collected himself, and walked out into the bright morning, the world full of chances, his mind spinning, because today could be a game changer.

The clear blue sky made Kieran smile again. It was a perfect morning, and the hotel wasn't far away. He loved being outdoors on days like this and joined the security queue at Butcher Gate – one of the seven gates of the walled city. When it was his turn, he raised his arms and spread his legs as a no-nonsense soldier frisked him. Then he was quickly turned around for a search under his collar and another thorough pat-down.

As he waited, he watched the Brits and wondered if they knew Valentine Holmes. He chuckled as they went about their dreary duty, searching the men and making half-hearted attempts to chat with the waiting women, boys, and girls. No one bothered to answer – no one dared.

In time, he got the nod and moved on, passing the shattered remains of the war memorial in the Diamond, near the bombed-out
Austins store and bank. The once impressive steep street now resembled the aftermath of a battlefield, its formerly majestic trees reduced
to splintered matchsticks.

Kieran was searched again at Shipquay Gate, then turned to Foyle
Street and up into the City Hotel.

At the reception desk, he immediately disliked the fair-haired man
in a snug grey suit who, in a sing-song voice, asked, 'May I help you,
sir?'

'Flamin' queer,' Kieran mumbled, then barked, 'Lookin' for Mrs
McFadden.'

The receptionist looked Kieran up and down, sizing him up. 'Got
an appointment?'

Kieran gave a quick nod. 'Aye. Kieran Kelly.'

Much as Kieran Kelly was way too good-looking for his liking, the
receptionist wasn't impressed. From the moment Kieran Kelly walked
through that door, he'd felt *it* - that low simmer of disdain. He'd
caught it straight off. He'd known that kind of homophobia so much
in this dump of a city that it didn't bother him anymore. It didn't hurt
as much.

He just stood there, quiet, letting it wash over him, knowing full
well it wouldn't be for much longer. He was into his last month, and
then he was done with the lot of them. Gone for good. He'd only ever
come back if his mammy was on her deathbed. And even then, it'd take
a lot. San Francisco was waiting. And this time, he wasn't ever looking
back.

'What's it in relation to?' he asked, unfazed at Kieran's obvious
contempt.

'In relation to minding your own fuckin' business,' Kieran hissed, hoping no bystanders would hear. This one was getting right up his nose with his high-pitched, squeaky voice and gay ways.

The receptionist stood there, stone-faced, not budging an inch. They stared each other down until he finally gestured to an empty seat by the revolving door and instructed Kieran to take a seat.

Inside, Kieran was dying to give the knobhead a piece of his mind but forced himself back. Usually, he would have given him a proper talking to, or worse, for that attitude, but he couldn't afford to screw this opportunity up. After throwing himself onto a sofa, he gave the poof a frosty look, watched him phone Mrs McFadden, then schmooze and flirt with some new guests.

Maggie appeared, shook Kieran's hand, and motioned for him to follow. He fired one last glance at the receptionist, who, to his irritation, flashed an over the top saucy smile and give a little girly wave. Behind Maggie's back, Kieran gave him the finger.

'Thanks for coming in,' Maggie said cheerfully as she marched ahead. Your Aunty Kay must be prayed out after that retreat.'

Chuckling, she led him downstairs then through a door marked 'Staff Only' and into a bustling canteen.

Several hotel staff members dressed in various uniforms, were scoffing down breakfast and chatting away. Some peeped up at Maggie and the good-looking fella following her, but most kept eating.

Maggie found them a quiet spot in a corner. 'Wanna drink, Kieran?'

He shook his head. 'Nah, I'm good, Mrs McFadden. Thanks.'

She told him to sit while she grabbed a mug, filled it with hot water from a catering-sized urn and added a tea bag. Milk first, she began to swig the tea bag around the cup as she returned to the table and sat across from him.

'So, Kieran,' she began, cautiously, 'I'm not promisin' you the moon, but Kay mentioned you need some work. Here's the deal: I need some muscle for next week's shindig. We've got two weddin's and a massive business meetin' all on the same day. Four hundred people. Thinkin' about it makes me shiver. We'll need to turn the rooms around right quick, and that's where you come in. You'll handle the weddings, not the meetin' - that's sorted.'

Kieran's heart plummeted. Maggie, unaware, sipped her tea before going on.

'You'll have plenty to do before and durin' the weddings, believe me. Remember, security's gonna be tighter than a drum. You'll get an ID badge that ye have to wear at all times. That's about it. If you do a good job, we'll see if I can hook you up with something more permanent after.'

Kieran, ever the charmer, said, 'You're a gem, Mrs McFadden. That's brilliant. But what's with all this extra security? Is the Prime Minister visitin' or somethin'?!' Maggie laughed and put her hand to her heart.

'For cryin' out loud. Nah, nothin' like that. Thank Christ!' She seemed a bit unsure all of a sudden. Could the Prime Minister actually show up? She shot down the idea. Nah. *Ted here in Derry? No chance!*

'You'll get three quid cash in hand each day. How's that sound?' she asked, taking a good swig of her tea.

'Good. That's good. Thanks a lot. Great.' Kieran gave her his best smile, happy he'd snagged the job. But inwardly, he was miffed. He was still in the dark about the meeting and who'd be there. He needed to know more and soon. Maggie got ready to leave.

'Right then, I'll see ye 6.00 AM sharp, Wednesday. And, oh, by the way, you'll sort out the uniform yerself – white shirt, black trousers, black tie, okay?'

'Sorted already, Mrs McFadden.' Kieran assured her.

Maggie appreciated the young lad's good manners and initiative. Thank God he hadn't taken after his Aunty Kay in the looks department. Smartly dressed, polite, and glad of the work. He'd been brought up right and she liked him on the spot.

With a twinkle in her eye, she replied with a smile, 'Good boy. See you then. And don't be doin' anythin' I wouldn't do!' He flashed a wide, insincere grin – all pearly whites and no warmth. Beautiful, aye, but there was menace in it, a warning dressed up as appeal, and anyone with a lick of sense would know better than to trust it.

If only you knew Maggie McFadden, if only you knew...

Back upstairs, he glared at the receptionist and stomped outside, taking a big breath on the steps.

Busy, busy, busy.

Chapter Forty-Nine

Forty Percent

After leaving Caitlin, James dropped off the hired car, picked up his own, and hit the factory. He wasn't ready to face Melrose and needed time to clear his head.

When he reached the factory gate, one of the security guards, an ex-pro boxer, stopped him and stood next to the car. James rolled down the window. The guard, recognising the vehicle, showed surprise. It was uncommon for the Scottish fella to be here on a Sunday.

Rain pelted his face as he remarked, 'Mr Henderson, not your usual weekend haunt. Got you working Sundays now, have they?'

James forced a smile and replied, 'For my sins, Neil. Everything all right here?'

'Grand today, but last night, a whole other story. Mad it was. Well rowdy. With the rain on the day, I'd say it'll keep those rioters in their beds, and there'll be no bother tonight with the footie on the telly as well. Anyway, I'm here till the mornin' if you need me.'

James rolled up the window, saying, 'Thanks, Neil. See you later.'

He waited as the man swung open the tall metal gates before parking the Jag, climbing out and darting for cover under the partially sheltered entrance to the admin block. He searched for his keys, unlocked the double locks, and, once inside, shed his wet coat.

On a Sunday, the factory was like a deserted stage set. A weird, unsettling quiet replaced the usual clatter of machines, shouting voices, and loud chatter over radios. He missed the familiar noise and suddenly felt like a lone musician in an empty concert hall.

The lift, finally working, creaked its way up to the fifth floor. Once he reached his office, James grabbed a half-full bottle of whiskey from a teak sideboard and poured a hefty measure into a tumbler. He knocked it back, feeling the warmth. It made him feel a touch better, if only for a moment.

Memories of Caitlin from the last two days were swirling in his head as he sat down. She'd been everything he'd dreamed of and more – loving, sexy, and a total blast. Smart as a whip and a great listener, she made him feel truly alive. But the calm didn't last long; the worry of what they'd done was creeping in.

What would his family say if they found out, especially his father, that his son had fallen for a Catholic? *A Roman Catholic.* The very people his father, along with Charles Jones, had spent a lifetime mistrusting, resenting, blaming for everything. His uncle might raise an eyebrow or two, but his father? Words couldn't describe how angry he'd be. He'd never forgive him. James bristled at the thought of it.

Didn't matter though because, deep down, he knew Caitlin was the one. They came from different worlds, yes. He a Protestant and thankfully now, fairly comfortable. She a Catholic and skint. His life in Londonderry came with privilege; hers came with strain and scrutiny. They were chalk and cheese, opposites in every way. But, here he was. He was over thinking and had to smack himself to clear his head.

With a trembling hand, he poured more whiskey and muttered, 'I need to stop... please.'

He buried his face in his hands, closed his eyes, and heard his inner voice argue: You've got a beautiful woman who adores you. Intelligent, supportive and witty. Makes you laugh. Who else has ever made you laugh like that? Are you out of your mind? You've never been happier. Don't give her up now, you wally. To hell with the rest!

This time, James slammed the top of his desk, sending the empty whiskey tumbler flying to the floor, where it shattered into what looked like a zillion pieces.

A gentle knock came from his half-open office door. James kept his head down, not looking up. It was the guard, Neil, eyeing the shattered tumbler, the whiskey bottle then his boss.

'You feeling okay, Mr Henderson?' He was genuinely worried.

James felt utterly exhausted and sized Neil up for a second before trying to rise. He ended up slipping and crashing down, his hands barely missing the shards of glass.

Neil dashed over, helping him back into his chair. Both of them uncomfortable as hell. James straightened himself up and adjusted his clothes, giving the worried guard a gentle nudge.

'Sorry 'bout that, Neil. I'm all right. *Really*. I didn't eat and those few jars there hit me harder than expected. I'll sit tight for a bit.'

Neil looked at James with a frown. He liked this fella; unlike the others, the lad always took the time to say hello and ask about him and the family. He wasn't keen on leaving him like this.

'Righty-o, Mr Henderson? If you're sure. I can always whip up a strong coffee.' James eyed the broken pieces of glass and the near-empty Jameson bottle.

'I'm good. Go on now. I'll be heading out soon anyway. One thing, keep this to yourself Neil, will ye?' Neil nodded.

'Course. Goes without sayin'. As I say, I'm around if you need me.' James appreciated the gesture.

'Thanks, Neil.'

'No bother,' Neil sighed, closing the door behind him.

He'd make that coffee anyway, whether or not Henderson wanted it – seeing him like this was a real shame. They were all relying on him to keep the place open.

Meanwhile, James was in turmoil, caught in a tangle of feelings he didn't know what to do with. He cared about Caitlin, deeply, more than he'd expected to, and it shook him in ways again, he didn't want to admit. He wasn't the emotional type, had never been one for declarations or heartache, but this felt different.

He placed the whiskey bottle back in the cupboard, shut it with a bit too much force, and opened the office window for a blast of fresh air. Thick raindrops splattered against the sill and onto the carpet, and for a moment, he waited, letting the cold settle over his skin.

Shaking his head at the mess he'd made, he half-closed the window and crouched down to clear the broken glass, wrapping each jagged piece in a tissue before dropping it in the bin. The clang of the lid echoed in the quiet, but he didn't move away from the window.

The past few weeks had upended everything he thought he knew about himself. He'd come here to work, to get on with things, be a success, not to fall for some girl who'd walked into his life and somehow got under his skin without even trying. And yet, here he was, stuck somewhere between panic and elation, unsure which one was worse.

Soon enough, Neil walked in with a pot of steaming black coffee. James thanked him with a sad smile, then drank cup after cup until, satisfied, he bade James goodnight before leaving him to it.

James, needing to take his mind off things, pulled a big brown file from a drawer. The folder made him forget about Caitlin pretty fast. It was his investment proposal to save Rocola.

Hours later, he arrived home, still wired from drinking the whiskey and copious cups of strong coffee. He snatched his overnight bag from the car boot and entered Melrose.

As his foot touched the threshold, his uncle cried out urgently from the dining room, 'Is that you, James?' James groaned, placed his bag at the foot of the staircase and unsteadily entered the dimly lit room.

'Come in. Come in. Good to see you, son – by God, you look frazzled. Heavy weekend, was it?' Roger joked with a wink.

'You could say that,' James said guiltily, glancing at his uncle's guests. *Not Jones again!* He was the last person James wanted to see.

Relief swept through him when he spotted George Shalham across the room, and he moved quickly to shake his hand. Aside from James's close call in the Bogside, the chief constable admitted he'd never imagined James capable of pulling off something like this conference – getting both sides to sit under the same roof. But he had. And, by God, it was a miracle. Told him he admired James's tenacity, and that Roger was damn lucky to have him.

James thanked him with a tired smile.

Jones remained seated and stony-faced, offering James nothing more than a sullen nod. Roger noticed how rude he was, but wasn't going to let Jones ruin the evening.

'Won't you have a bite with us, James? Mrs Moore's been working on her Irish roast all day – she's about to serve. I'll grab another plate.' Sitting within sight of Jones made James squirm, but hunger prevailed, so he agreed.

Roger was pleased at his nephew's loyalty. 'Good stuff. Sit yerself down. I'll go tell Mrs Moore.'

On his way downstairs to the cellar kitchen, Roger mulled over his brother, who'd recently borrowed what little money Roger could spare and taken off to the South of France – presumably to the gambling tables of Monte Carlo. Roger told James his dad was at an army reunion in Surrey, and he didn't know when he'd be back.

Jones and Shalham were giving each other the cold shoulder all night, and Roger was so glad when James showed up. He'd noticed James sat next to George Shalham in an effort to ditch Jones.

Upstairs at the table, Shalham asked James with a curious look.

'Where've you been then James? Your uncle says, somewhere in Galway.' James shook his head.

'Not exactly... Donegal Town. I had some friends over from London. Doing a tour of the Republic.'

George smiled affably and, to embroider the lie, James remarked, 'I tried to coax them to come up here, but I'm afraid they're rather jumpy. Turns out no one wants to come up this way. Say it's dangerous. Sad, really.'

Jones took the opportunity to cut in. 'Sad, my arse!'

James stared at the man's face, thinking, 'I totally hate that guy.' Drunk, and for reasons James couldn't fathom, his uncle seemed delighted to welcome the creep. James just blew him off, and Shalham totally dismissed him. He and the chief looked at each other as Roger came back.

'All sorted. Dinner's on its way.' Roger cried. He felt the tension, and to make things less awkward, he nervously teased his nephew.

'So, aside from partying a bit hard, son, did you enjoy yerself?' He asked, in a shaky voice. James could see how unnerved Roger was by Jones.

'I did. It was lovely. I was just saying that my friends didn't want to go north.' Telling the lie was a little easier the second time around.

Poor Roger – unaware of his faux pas – answered gloomily, 'Wise of them, I suppose. Sad, really.'

Jones's face showed his annoyance. Tipsy, he snorted, stumbled backward, and rose to propose a toast.

'To the Henderson's .' Aside from a few others, the diners stayed seated, clinking glasses, and nodding politely. Jones crashed back into his chair and gave James a hard look. Then he announced angrily.

'I'm a keynote speaker at the First Derry Presbyterian Church later in the week, James. It's our second big rally here. Why don't you come? I've got everyone riled up. You'll get a good idea of what people think about those Pope-loving swine you and Roger are all about.'

Classic Jones. The room went quiet, only the clock's slow tick and the fire's angry crackle filling the gap. James and Shalham left it alone out of respect for Roger. James declined Jones's invite with polite words, though in truth he reckoned Jones could stick it where it hurt.

Everything went downhill from there. Everyone at the table except Jones wasn't hungry.

Coffee showed up, and the night was over. Jones stumbled as he got up and tried to put his chair away. A huge, muscular man ran to help. He looked like a tough guy, wearing all black, a worn leather jacket with the sleeves pushed up. James noticed a red tattoo on his arm. The 'heavy 'didn't pay attention to the guests while assisting Jones with his coat.

'Gentlemen,' Jones muttered with a sneer, looking at the diners. 'Pleasure as always.'

'Morris!' he barked, snapping his fingers at his minder.

After everyone left, Shalham, gritting his teeth, spat out, 'I hate that arrogant toad.'

'Me too,' James and Roger chimed in.

Roger figured it was time to get another drink. He had to tell Shalham and James something big, and he'd been dreading it for weeks.

'Strongly as we feel about our friend there,' he began forcefully, 'we have to remember we need him for two reasons. First, he has an overwhelming influence with the unions here – his word alone or just one snap of those fat little fingers could have them out on strike, which would hold up our containers and supplies. They run the utility companies and the local councils and have the power to stop the cogs of this province's machinery within minutes. Could cripple what's left of an extremely fragile economy.'

Shalham and James knew it was true as soon as they heard it. Roger took a deep breath as if preparing for a fistfight.

'Second, gentlemen, and here I have to be straight with you. I find myself in the unfortunate position of owing our friend a lot of money. And I mean, a lot. That is why I have no choice but to entertain Jones and insist he attend your meeting, James. You have to understand that he could call in my debt anytime. Simply put – he has me by the balls.'

The chief and James were stunned by the unwelcome news and didn't know what to say.

Roger had tried to tell them so many times, but there never seemed to be a right moment. He knew he was a coward, and his tired eyes pleaded for their support and understanding.

'You have to understand my position. I had to keep Rocola from sinking, and once the bank refused to extend my credit, I had no choice. Somehow, Jones knew all about it and offered to help. I was desperate. So unbelievably desperate.'

James gulped down his brandy. Visibly angry, he walked across to the fireplace, where he leaned his head wearily on the mantelpiece. Almost afraid of the answer, he flinched.

'How much? How much do we owe him?' he asked.

'At present, he holds a charge of forty per cent over the company. If I don't pay him back two million plus interest within three months, he can acquire another eleven per cent, giving him control. The bank wouldn't even talk to me. What else was I to do?' Roger replied, his voice breaking.

James stood dumbfounded, while Shalham looked knackered and said, 'I wish to God you'd told us, Roger. I really do. This changes everything. Don't you see? Even if we come up with a plan to keep Rocola open, the final decision could be his.'

It was James's turn to speak. 'For the love of God, anyone but him Uncle. That man couldn't care less about the workforce. Doesn't give a hoot. Hates Catholics, full stop. He'll shut the site down within days, no matter the cost. And we all know he can afford it. It's a bloody catastrophe.'

The men went quiet as Mrs Moore walked in and saw their faces. She did the minimum and retreated to the safety of her kitchen.

Shalham wandered around the dining room, thinking, while James and Roger watched him. He took a second to compose himself, then, in a resolute voice, declared.

'Okay, listen. James, Roger, this meeting of yours... You've achieved something that I and many others believed impossible. It's a huge accolade to you both – especially to you, Roger.' Roger could barely acknowledge the compliment after his difficult confession but smiled tiredly.

As Shalham continued, his voice grew more assertive.

'Between us, I've been liaising with the Secretary of State about it. And he's impressed. He even suggested he attend, however, I managed to dissuade him. It's not about politics. It's about keeping the Rocola workforce and this city alive. Gentlemen, forgive me, but I thought for a minute there, we were literally screwed. However, when I think about it, I might be onto something.'

The room itself seemed to breathe a sigh of relief.

Chapter Fifty

Tone and Timbre

'I can't get the hang of this. It's crazy! Mad!' Rob yelled at the sky in frustration.

They were into their third day of voice coaching, and it was late in the afternoon. He was tired and annoyed, Iowa was really getting into it. Her attempts at the Londonderry accent were admirable, though far from perfect. It made Rob mad as hell.

The elderly voice coach, his vowels polished in the grand old BBC style when not lapsing into the broadest Londonderry dialect, placed his hand with deliberate ceremony on Rob's shoulder.

'Now listen, my boy, listen carefully. The more you dwell upon it, the more impossible it shall become. I have already told you – close your eyes, breathe, and *attend*. Attend to the pitch, to the way the words *marry one another*. It's not unlike singing, really. Hear the timbre, the rise and fall.' Rob tried.

'Yes, yes, very good. You *can* do this, young chap.' He produced a cassette tape as if presenting a priceless artefact, wagging it before Rob with slow, dignified precision.

'Now, kindly take this to that quiet corner over there, and do exactly as I say. Concentrate on tone, on timbre, on rhythm. Take your time – proceed with deliberate slowness. And let us not, I repeat, not imagine we are in need of a Londonderry version of the Declaration of Independence. Heavens, no. We are after the *sound*. That is the essence, my boy – the art of listening.'

Rob laughed, took the tape, and, as if he were sulking, dragged his feet to the corner. He sat down, stuck the tape in the recorder, put on his headphones, and got ready to listen. At first, he struggled, but as the tape played and his earing adjusted, he began to relax and enjoy it. He recognised a few local phrases and, following the instructions, repeated them one after the other, over and over. Tone and timbre, tone and timbre...

They'd had their debriefing that Saturday morning. It had gone well. He hadn't seen much of Iowa besides his voice lessons. In class, however, she'd continued to give him the cold shoulder. He was grateful that she hadn't reported him about the girl on the bus. She'd could have thrown him in the doghouse.

For their next op, they'd been tasked with infiltrating a growing insurgent group led by an East Belfast man, Charles Jones. The dossier stated he was an ardent Loyalist who'd been speaking at Orange Order and Unionist rallies over the past few months. A fervent bigot, he was doing no good but stirring up hatred. They were sure he was involved – at a senior level – with the staunch anti-Catholic, Ulster Volunteer Force, or UVF.

He was nothing to them before, but now British Intelligence saw him as a political threat. He talked about bringing the government down, and was adamantly shouting from the rafters that there'd been a lack of control in their governance of Northern Ireland. Jones was firmly against power-sharing, and that included the government talking to the Irish in Dublin. The file also had a list of people he knew: family, friends, business partners, and the places he usually went. He had a seriously impressive portfolio, which showed how rich he was.

Charles Jones wasn't just well-connected with high-level political figures and unions in Ulster, but also troublingly engaged with several notorious right-wing factions in England. Street talk claimed he'd orchestrated the assassinations of several innocent Catholics, carried out with chilling precision in West Belfast.

Rob and Iowa's task was to observe and gather as much information as possible on him – but leave it at that. It was early days. He was planning some huge Unionist and Orange Hall rallies in the next few weeks, and they were going to shadow him.

What caught Rob's eye was an upcoming meeting at a local hotel hosted by James Henderson, the nephew of the owner of Rocola, one of the last shirt factories in the city. Rob recalled its location between Stones Corner and the Blighs Lane army compound. According to the dossier, numerous deliveries from the factory had been hijacked and set ablaze by rioters. In addition, many of the Protestant employees faced verbal and physical abuse from a few Republican rogues. Security at Rocola was a significant concern, and with the factory haemorrhaging money, if something wasn't done soon...

From 'The Toon,' Rob knew how it affected families when large employers shut their gates for the last time. Remarkably, the Henderson nephew had managed to get several of the city's prominent business people, as well as top Nationalists, Unionists, and church representatives, to meet to discuss the factory's future. He'd also included security personnel from the RUC and army hoping that, working together, they'd find a way to improve security, raise capital and keep the place open. Rob had read the report with great interest, as well as an overview of the Orange Order and the history of Unionism in Ireland. It'd been fascinating, and the more he read, the better he understood.

It also caused him a great deal of concern. He'd read the *Protestant Newsletter*, packed with pronouncements such as, 'Romanism breeds poverty, ignorance, Priest-craft and superstition,' and such comments as, 'We will terrorise the IRA terrorists, but better.'

The Unionists felt like the British government had stabbed them in the back, saying, 'No one will bargain over us!' and 'Never, never, never! No surrender. We will not be sold out!'

The cassette recorder clicked as it reached the end of the tape, and Rob switched it off. He'd had enough for one day and turned to see Iowa and the vocal coach laughing together. He'd never seen her laugh like that before, and it surprised him. Even with all that crappy stuff she wore, she was pretty. Her eyes sparkled, and she had a beautiful, radiant smile.

After removing the tape, he walked towards them, and everything changed. Iowa's eyes went dark, and she stopped smiling. He watched her thank the man and go. Rob let out a sigh and picked up his stuff. The voice coach pitied the poor chap.

'Any better?' he asked.

'Yeah, thanks. I guess I'll have to keep practising,' Rob replied.

The trainer was aware this would be difficult. The army expected so much of these undercover johnnies. Trying to pick up such a problematic accent in a matter of days was a truly daunting task. It should take at least a month.

'It is never easy at the outset with this particular accent, my boy. There is, you see, a trace of the Yankee twang in there – a curious complication, and I daresay a difficult feat for a Geordie lad such as yourself. But it all comes down to practice, practice, and yet more practice.' He allowed himself a knowing smile. 'Dear Iowa, however, is faring rather well. A clever girl indeed – most promising.'

'Hmmm,' Rob replied.

The teacher already felt something was off between them. Things were tense, which probably made it harder for his students to learn.

'I take it you two don't get along?' he asked carefully. Rob laughed. *That's an understatement!*

'No. We don't. Between us, she's a goddamn nightmare. 'Scuse my language.' Rob complained.

'No need to apologise. I agree she can be argumentative... but she'll come through.' The instructor replied. His words caught Rob off guard.

'Sorry, I didn't realise you knew each other.'

The coach regretted having said anything and hesitated. 'Well, er... yes, I've known her for some time.'

'You have?' Rob inquired. That explained why she was so comfortable with him.

'Sort of, yes. Or, no... I mean, I can't really say. Apologies Kentucky, but that's it for today.' The man picked up his belongings hurriedly, but Rob held him back.

'Tell me, please, *what* is her problem? She's been on me since day one. Her attitude, you know? I don't think she's got my back. Hates me. For sure.' The coach stared at him and grew despondent.

'Kentucky, you must surely know I cannot, under any circumstance, divulge personal details to you. I have seen, with my own eyes, this so-called partnership of yours. Believe me when I tell you, if you insist, I shall carry your concerns up the line. But let us be perfectly clear, my boy – there is the potential for danger here, for you and for her alike. This must be resolved, and the sooner the better.' Rob got it but still wanted to know something, *anything* that could explain Iowa's hang-ups.

'I understand, don't worry and don't tell our handler anything. I'll figure it out if I need to,' Rob replied.

'I shall tell you one thing,' the coach began, his voice low, each word weighed with care. 'It may, perhaps, cast a little light upon her behaviour. Iowa was once engaged to a soldier – a most capable young man, not unlike yourself. More troubling still, when one considers it, he bore a striking resemblance to you. And that, I fear, may well be the reason.' He paused, his cultivated accent softening into something almost tender.

'Alas, he was the very first soldier to be murdered in Northern Ireland.' The instructor allowed a faint, sorrowful smile, then inclined his head and bade Rob goodnight. Rob realised he'd been a real jerk. If he'd known, he wouldn't have been so uptight. Why didn't she tell him, for crying out loud?

At their Charles Jones' first Orange Order rally, they knew they had to be vigilant. Eyes peeled, ears open. It was to be held in the four-hundred-year-old First Derry Presbyterian Church, the only one of its kind within the city walls. By now, Rob's beard had thickened, and his hair was longer. It took a while, but at last, he'd shed his soldier skin.

As for Iowa, he daren't comment on her calamitous dress sense. She arrived wearing a long, loose black coat with zippers everywhere. Her clothes were covered, and Rob was cool with that - he didn't want to know. She was so embarrassing. Mad really, if anything, she drew attention to them, which was the last thing they needed.

She mumbled something that passed for a hello as they slipped out through a small, hidden gate at the side of Fort George. Without a second thought, she hooked her arm in his, trying to look like they were a pair and began walking towards the Strand Road, which led directly to the city centre. Her continued silence was killing him. He hated silence. Growing up, he'd crack jokes to lighten the mood at home since his dad would go silent for days after arguments.

Once the coach had told him about Iowa's fiancé, Rob figured he'd cut her some slack and joked, 'What's with that clobber you've turned out in today?'

'I'm talking about that coat,' he said when she froze. 'Where'd you get it?' Iowa yanked her arm free and shot him a bitter look.

'I heard you,' she snarled.

Rob chuckled. 'Well, well, it speaks!'

'Go to hell, Kentucky. I'm not trying to be your buddy for life. We're here for a job, so just do it!' Iowa shot back. She went to link arms again, but Rob pushed her away.

He didn't want to touch her and yelled, 'You can sod off an' all. Seriously, what's wrong with you? I'm done with ye!' Iowa shook her head slowly.

'Seriously, are you kidding me? Don't you get it? It's *you*!' She dug her finger into his chest.

'You're acting like a twat. You think this is all a joke, right? Who do you think you are, 007? Well, guess what? You're not!' She kept walking.

Rob sighed and rolled his eyes. He was confused for a sec, then he hurried over, grabbed her, and spun her to face him. Making sure no one was about, it was Rob's turn to point a finger.

'Listen to me, you screwed up bitch. I'll tell you why I'm here. I'm here to get those bastards who murdered Val, locked up for life, all right? They fucken tortured him, cut him, burned him, used a stick studded with nails to hit him over and over. Turned him into a fucken human ash tray. Then they battered him everywhere – and I mean *everywhere*. Even pissed on him! And finally, when the fun was over, assassinated him – one bullet through the head!' He struck his forehead in frustration. His eyes filled as the images swam before him, and for a wild moment he thought his heart might burst from his chest.

'And what bits of him left were put in black bin bags and stuck in the middle of a road, to be run over by lorry-after-fucken-lorry, tractor-after-fucken-tractor. So that's why I'm here, Iowa. I'm here to find those cowardly bastards who did all that to my marra!'

A soft drizzle fell. Rob almost welcomed it. It cooled him down and distracted him from letting her know how much he despised and resented her treatment. He paced in circles, trying to calm himself. A few people walked by, pretending not to notice the sparring couple, but still rubbernecking all the same.

Iowa was blown away by what she'd heard. His story, which she understood, filled her with sorrow. She'd heard about Val Holmes's murder but hadn't known Kentucky was so close to him. She moved to take his hand, but he shook her off.

'I didn't know. I'm sorry,' she whispered. Rob walked ahead, deflated and miserable, Iowa following a steady pace or two behind.

'How the hell would you know? We know nothing about each other. So give us a break, will ye, and get over yourself?' he said, stopping in his tracks. He waited, but she didn't answer, so he tutted and kept going.

She ran to catch him, grabbed his hand, and gave it a squeeze. She understood. Neither spoke, but their silence felt easier now – because Rob's words had changed everything, because they were bound by more than just a hand now. Revenge.

When they arrived at the church, they paid particular attention to the faces in the swelling crowd. Before they'd left the barracks, they'd studied a series of mugshots of known activists. Hundreds of people of all ages held large black-and-white placards adorned with Union Jacks and howling: 'No surrender. No surrender. No surrender!'

At the top of the church steps, they found a vantage point from which to look down on the crowd. The street was well lit, and they recognised a few faces, noting them mentally for the debriefing later.

In no time, car headlights appeared in the distance and a dark saloon manoeuvred down the narrow, cobbled street, fighting to make its way through the baying crowd who pounded on the car's sides and roof, shrieking wildly.

'No Pope here, Charlie. You tell 'em. No Pope here. No surrender!'

The vehicle came to a stop, and two burly men climbed out as quickly as their bulky frames allowed. They wore black trousers, shirts and leather jackets, each embellished with the infamous Red Hand of Ulster on the back. Rob did a double-take at one of the men. This was nuts – one of Jones's goons was Morris. Fucken Billy Morris! What the hell was he doing here?!

He watched Morris and his companion push the crowd back as the rear door of the black Rover opened, and Charles Jones stepped out. Jones waited a while before he raised his hands in the air, playing the crowd and ceremoniously closed his right hand to form a fist. Thrilled, the mob screamed their delight.

From what Rob could see, Jones wore a beautifully cut black suit, a spotless white shirt, and a bright orange tie. He walked deliberately slow up the steps into the pillared church, relishing the adoration, shaking the sea of hands thrust at him as his minders ushered him along.

Eventually, he disappeared from view, and the crowd followed like sheep, all of them desperate to get inside.

Rob grabbed Iowa, and they jumped down the steps, forcing their way through the rabble. A few spectators shook their heads, peeved at being shoved aside.

In exasperation, a teenager yelled, 'Oi! We're all tryin' to get in. Leave off!'

Iowa stared at him, and out of the blue, her entire face transformed. She broke into the most beautiful smile and beamed at the spotty youngster.

In a near-perfect Londonderry accent, she apologised, 'Sorry. Just dead excited too. No surrender. No surrender!' Raising her fist in the air, she gave him another encouraging, I'm-on-your-side smile.

The boy blushed, completely smitten. He smiled back and laughed. 'Sure, that's all right, miss. Ye see that man there, Charlie Jones. He's a hero!'

Iowa nodded enthusiastically. The smitten boy stepped aside and let them pass. A half smile lurked on Iowa's face as she glanced sidelong at Rob.

Somehow, they found a space at the back of the church, but one of the many oak pillars hindered their view. Nevertheless, they could hear everything as the speeches began.

The first speaker was boring beyond words and talked incessantly about the Protestant Reformation, his accent came thick and fast as he ranted on about his fundamentalist beliefs. Neither Rob nor Iowa had a clue what he was blabbering on about, so they continued to scan the crowd.

It appeared most of the audience didn't seem to get what the speaker was saying either. Some were yawning with boredom or fidgeting in their seats, praying the man's rhetoric would wrap up so Jones could get on stage.

Twenty minutes passed until the speaker ended their torture. A few loyal listeners clapped, and the remaining congregation half-heartedly joined in.

It was time for Jones to take the pulpit. As he strutted forward, the congregation went wild. This was their moment. They cheered, wolf-whistled, clapped like mad. Charlie was their future - the way forward for Ulster. At long last, they had someone with no hang-ups, no compromise, and the balls to say what they were thinking. Charlie Jones wasn't afraid of anyone.

Jones nodded and raised his hands to signal for calm and quiet. He fiddled with the microphone until it hit the right height, then gently tapped it.

Lowering his head, he paused, coughed, and then stared into the crowd, deliberately focusing on a few unfortunate beings at the very front. Under the weight of his stony gaze, they squirmed, distinctly nervous, and feeling like Jones was reading their every thought.

'Good evening, all of you. Thank you for being here tonight. I am privileged to be talking to you in such beautiful surroundings. Indeed, we are so fortunate to have this fantastic church to assemble in, but more importantly, within our city and within our walls.'

The crowd roared and howled their approval as Jones attempted to speak over their outburst.

'We must... we must remember the many battles we have fought to be here tonight. We must remember the siege that proves us as Ulster men and women. If we have to starve again to save this city and the Union, starve, we will. We will never give up.'

Absolute silence as he added, 'We will never give in to those Papists who breed like rabbits and multiply like vermin! This is our city, our Ulster. Our fathers and forefathers who fought at the Somme for democracy and freedom for the Protestant people, our Queen and our Empire. We must not fail them! We will never fail them!'

Thunderous applause and stomping echoed through the church, a wave of electrifying energy coursing through every man, woman, and child. Each word of Jones's message went deep, filling their hearts with pride, and leaving them in awe, as if basking in the glory of something far greater than themselves.

Rob retook Iowa's hand and tried to get closer to the front. He smiled at those who good-naturedly moved aside and allowed them through. They only got halfway up the church but found they had a much better view of the pulpit and Jones.

His speech continued, and he gesticulated to reinforce his tirade. 'I tell you this: the IRA is the military wing of the Catholic Church. Their Pope-hugging priests claim to be holy men, but no, they are not. They are the terrorists! They are men in frocks who hide guns and bombs and, even worse, hand them out! Their churches are treated as havens for those murderers who plant bombs that kill our innocent Protestant men, women and children. Get them out of our city, our LONDONderry. Am I right? Out. Out. Out!'

The frantic crowd yelled, 'Out, out, out!' Hatred tore through the church like wildfire, consuming everything in its path.

Jones continued as sweat beaded his face from his exertions and the heat of the lights.

'We must keep the thoroughfares open for our Protestant faith and our Protestant heritage. Ulster is ours!'

The crowd roared in agreement, and Jones waited for them to calm. This was what he was made for, his elated expression seemed to say. Adoration! He was telling them what they hungered to hear. He started up again, vilifying Catholics and their faith, encouraging his loyal followers to make ever greater efforts to keep the Papists in their place. By the time he'd finished, sweat was soaking his face and neck.

Rob was sick to the bone as he listened to Jones's words. 'A dog will return to its vomit. The sow will return to wallow in the mire, but by God's grace, we will not return to Popery again – no Pope here!'

Once more, the gathering erupted, and the noise of their screaming and clapping bounced off the high ceiling and intensified. Jones's face was crimson, and his thin hair plastered his forehead. It reminded Rob of the old Pathé news reels of Hitler's rallies where he'd spat out similar words of hate against the Jews. The British government was right to be concerned – this was one mad bastard.

Jones raked his damp hair back from his face, every nerve twitching with fury. He wasn't done yet.

'I'm here to tell you, as people of Ulster, to think long and hard. Listen carefully as I say this. The British government has failed us. They talk incessantly about power-sharing. Over my dead body! They are in collusion with the Catholic Irish Republican government. But will they talk to us? By God, no, they won't! *Us*, who have fought in so many wars for our Crown. *Us*, who fought and starved over three hundred years ago, to keep this city under Protestant rule.'

There was no stopping him now.

'This British government is a traitor to us. They are forcing this upon us. I say now, as God is my witness, I will not have it. We will not have it. We will not be bargained over by anybody. Ulster will fight, and Ulster will be right! There will be No Surrender!'

He stormed down from the pulpit with a fist clenched and thrust upward.

The audience erupted into a frenzy, clawing and elbowing their way through the crowd to reach Jones. The man who talked their talk. Talk they'd been dying to hear for years. They jostled and shouted, some thumping him on the back with wild admiration, others brandishing their fists and roaring with rage. The air crackled with intensity as they chanted.

'No surrender. No surrender...!'

Chapter Fifty-One

A Box of Toffees

Caitlin had been a basket case for days. For some reason, James had been distant and cold since their weekend away.

She had woken up in bed, fully dressed. It was becoming a habit, but the night before, she'd come home again so worked up she hadn't spoken to a soul, just gone straight to her room and shut the door. Apart from the green luminous hands of a cheap bedside clock, the room was pitch black. It was 4.30 AM. She yanked off her clothes and crawled back into bed in her knickers, wrapping the blankets tight around her. She longed for sleep and shut her eyes, but, as usual, no chance. The last few days had been brutal.

She turned on the bedside lamp to distract herself, then picked up a book she'd been trying to read. *The Thorn Birds*, borrowed from Maggie next door. She read a few pages without taking in a single word, eyes dragging over the text while her thoughts circled back to James, and everything that had happened.

Nervous about walking back into work after their weekend and facing him, she'd told herself she'd act like it was just another day. Let him set the tone. She'd follow his lead.

Yet, she hardly saw him. He was holed up in his office most of the time, shut away with his uncle and Alfie McScott, the accountant. When he did appear, he was in a rotten mood. No eye contact, no smile, no small talk, just asking for file after file, each demand cutting through her like a blade. She hated him for it. Hated the way Mrs Parkes's beady little eyes lit up at the tension, like she was enjoying every second of it. *Bitch.*

By the end of the day, Caitlin was starting to wonder if the weekend had happened at all. Maybe that was it - he'd got what he wanted, another notch on the bedpost. Anne and Majella had been right. And now she felt stupid, angry, and worse, ashamed. She got played and thought it was more than it was. Serves her right. Bloody fool.

Anne's brother had dropped by Blamfield Street while she was out and left a message. At last, Anne asked to see her, so Caitlin swung by her house after work. She was dying to catch up with her friend but instantly regretted it when she came face to face with her. She was a mess. The RUC had identified the bombers but weren't – or wouldn't – bring charges, saying they lacked sufficient evidence. Another one of the many injured had passed away earlier that morning, and for the thirty minutes after Caitlin arrived, Anne cried and cried and cried.

When the crying finally stopped, Caitlin suggested they have a cuppa. Without a second thought, she gave Anne the gift box of toffees she got in Donegal Town. She'd originally bought them for Majella, but after finding them untouched by the bedside, figured Anne would enjoy them more.

Anne, tear-stained and downright miserable, peeled the cellophane off the box and eyed the image of a quaint Donegal cottage on the cover.

'When were you in Donegal Town?' she asked casually. Caitlin screamed inside. *Shit!* She stammered out a lie, getting defensive.

'What you on about? I haven't been to Donegal in yonks.'

'Where'd you get those then?' Anne questioned. She tossed the box away, convinced her friend was lying through her teeth. Caitlin was caught hook, line, and sinker. There was no point in lying, so she told the truth.

'James and I went away for the weekend,' she whispered, mortified to have been discovered.

'Oh, you did, did you? Seriously, Caitlin. You promised. I warned ye about his type. Have you lost your mind?! Where did you say you were?'

'Told Mammy I was at Sinead's twenty-first in Malin.' Caitlin replied.

Anne sighed and picked up a few scattered toffees. *Might as well eat them now that they're there.* They looked really nice, though she couldn't believe Caitlin ignored her warnings.

'And your ma bought that, did she?' she asked. Caitlin shook her head.

'Mammy's a walking... no, a sleeping disaster. She was totally out of it until Granny got there.' Anne was totally stunned.

'What?! What the hell's your granny doin' there? Youse all hate her!' Caitlin got all tongue-tied. 'We... we... don't exactly *hate* her, Anne. You're going a bit overboard there. She's a cold fish all right, but she's been a real help. I swear.' Anne crossed herself twice and snickered.

'Well, would you look at that. There is a God. Top story in the *Journal*. Derry got a miracle! Call the Pope!'

She laughed as she took Caitlin's hand and gave her that old, loving look. Poor Caitlin. She looked worn out. Not like someone glowing from being in love, or drifting around in a dreamy haze after (hopefully) great sex or a fancy weekend away. Anne cared deeply for her, but couldn't help worrying. This thing with the Adonis, it had all the makings of a disaster. Men like that were users - all flash cars, swanky clothes, and charm by the bucket load. They got what they wanted, when they wanted, then tossed girls like Caitlin aside like a used tissue.

Naturally, she got why Caitlin had fallen for him. Anything different from the poverty, unemployment, and constant hassle they faced here would feel like a fairy tale – especially to someone as soft-hearted, and let's be honest, gullible, as Caitlin. A weekend away, probably to some luxurious hotel in Donegal, with a good-looking fella who reeked of money and class? Who could blame her for being swept up in it?

Part of Anne couldn't. She'd have been tempted herself. But she still hated the fucker. Hated the way he'd taken advantage. It was written all over Caitlin's face. The hurt, the confusion, the way she was clinging to the hope that it'd meant more than it did.

Anne bit back the urge to give her a bollocking, but decided no use piling it on. Caitlin didn't need a lecture, she needed a friend.

So instead, she kept her voice light, passed over the toffees, and said, 'Right. Tell me everything. And don't leave out the filthy bits. How was *it* then?'

Caitlin frowned in confusion as Anne grinned wickedly, cramming another toffee into her already bulging cheeks. Mouth full and sounding like a chipmunk, she exclaimed.

'Come on, spill it out. You and him!'

A look crossed Caitlin's face, and Anne cried, 'Jesus wept, Caitlin... *it* – the sex! The *ole va-va-voom*!'

Caitlin playfully smacked Anne's arm. She hesitated at first, shy about spilling the gory details, but Anne's relentless teasing finally wore her down. Within minutes, she'd poured out every juicy morsel of her weekend, and the pair of them erupted into giggles. At one point, Anne squealed with delight, wiping away tears as she shrieked.

'See? Told ye those dirty magazines would come in handy, didn't I?!' It felt like old times.

'You did. I "*blew*" his mind away!' Caitlin screeched.

They were nearly in stitches, and once the laughter settled, Anne gently asked how the Adonis had been in the office.

'I bet he was full of charm and smiles on Monday morning? Did he sa—' She stopped when she saw Caitlin's face fall. She knew that look.

Caitlin's throat tightened, shame and sadness rising up too fast to push down. One glance at Anne's worried face was enough to set her off.

'You've no idea, Anne. He's been awful. Rotten mood all week, barely a word out of him. I feel a right eejit. Doesn't even say hello or goodbye. Just asking for file after file after file. Day in, day out, cooped up in that office with his uncle and the accountant. I feel so stupid. A bloody fool.'

Anne had known it was inevitable - she just hadn't expected it so soon.

'I'm sorry, love. Maybe that's just how he is. You know what some of them are like. Users through and through. You've got to let it go. It could be worse. Sounds like you had a fab weekend outta it, at least. Not like Hopalong here,' she said, tapping her wounded leg, 'lying with 'alf a leg, like a broken puppet.' It wasn't funny, not really. But Anne would have said anything in that moment to make Caitlin smile again.

Caitlin sniffled and wiped her nose with the back of her hand. Anne was so brave, and, yeah, she was right, it could've been worse. God love her. She hadn't even given Caitlin a hard time, but her concerned eyes said it all: *Told you so.*

For now, what mattered was that Anne was home. Caitlin smiled, squeezed her friend's hand, and told herself she'd just have to get over it. But would she? Could she and still work there?

When she got back home, her granny and Tommy were in the kitchen, smiling and getting along fine. Majella had come down briefly that afternoon, eaten a small bowl of porridge, and gone back to bed. It cheered Caitlin up no end, and she hoped she'd get to talk to her. But when she checked in on her, her mammy was sound asleep.

After another day at work and like before, Caitlin got home, hit the sack early, saying she'd been swamped and needed an early night. Only she tossed and turned for hours.

Sometime in the early hours, she heard someone clattering about downstairs. Following the light spilling under the kitchen door, she figured it had to be Tina who was forever up for a drink of water in the middle of the night. It was time she caught up with her, anyway, so Caitlin pushed open the kitchen door and was knocked for six to find her granny sitting at the round table in a blue towelling bathrobe, puffing away like a chimney on a fag.

Caitlin nearly fell over. She'd never known the woman to smoke and was sure she'd always been dead set against it.

Mary jumped up in a panic when she saw her granddaughter, quickly snuffing out the fag and flapping her hands to disperse the smoke. Caitlin couldn't help but laugh. With a death stare at Caitlin, Mary stopped flapping her arms for a split second and let a reluctant smile creep across her face.

She patted Caitlin's hand. 'Right, right, ye got me. Whatever ye do, not a word. I'll never hear the end of it. Between us, okay?'

Seeing her so flustered, Caitlin let herself enjoy it. She pretended to mull it over, then said, 'Will do. Still, can't believe you smoke. Thought you hated it.'

Mary had despised smoking once, but after years of being more or less ignored by Majella and Tommy, she'd taken it up. Liked it. Now she saw it as an essential, a small comfort that kept her sane.

'No... I do... I did,' she stammered. 'Ah Jesus, forget it now. Sit, and I'll get us up a cuppa and a bit' a toast.' For the first time in forever, she took a proper look at her granddaughter. The spitting image of Majella at her age. But the girl looked downright miserable, so she raised an eyebrow and asked, 'Why are you up so early, anyway? It's only five o'clock. You look wrecked.'

'Can't sleep,' Caitlin sighed. 'Cheers for that.' Mary smiled gently, feeling bad, and thought she should try to be nice to the child.

With their secret shared, the two women sipped tea and munched on toast, chatting about Majella's progress. Caitlin thanked her granny for making such a difference to the household and with Majella. Thankfully, Martin's name and his latest stint behind bars didn't even come up.

The minutes passed until it was time for Caitlin to get ready. She gave her granny a peck on the cheek and thanked her with a rare burst of emotion.

'Thanks a million, Granny. It's nice having you here.'

Mary, surprisingly, was enjoying her time in Blamfield Street, and admitted it. It was nice to be needed.

'Aye, love, it is. See you after. Don't stress now. Get yourself sorted and head to work. Someone's gotta bring some money in.' She shared a knowing smile.

With a sigh, but carrying a small smile, Caitlin touched her shoulder, then, on weary legs, climbed the stairs to get dressed and, God willing, squeeze in a quick, hot bath.

On the way, she peeked in on Tina and saw her fast asleep, safe and sound. *Good.*

Later that morning at work, Caitlin sat at her desk, staring into space. James and the usual crew were, once again, holed up in his office.

She was anxious. Something wasn't right. She had a strong feeling something big was going on. This wasn't normal. From what she could tell, they'd been working flat out all night. That must've been what all the files were for. Could they be about to close this place? No way!

Her mind was racing when the office door suddenly swung open. James stepped out, looking shattered, gripping the handle like he was afraid to let go. He managed a weak smile, the first she'd seen in days. His stubble was unkempt, his hair a mess, and his skin pale, with dark circles under swollen eyes.

Her heart nearly jumped out of her chest when he called her in. 'Can you come inside for a sec, Caitlin?' *This was it!*

Caitlin figured she'd be the first to go. Dear God. They so needed the money. She nodded and walked into the office, feeling out of place and vulnerable, but still managed a brief nod at old Mr Henderson and the accountant. Each of them, looking as exhausted as James, offered their hellos with weary smiles. James fell into his seat, fixed her with a stare and motioned for her to sit down next to his uncle.

'We've gotta problem, Caitlin.' he said.

Her heart skipped a further beat, then another, as he finally told her everything, holding nothing back.

Chapter Fifty-Two

D-Day

Honey was in a total panic when the day arrived. Nothing else could describe how scared she was.

Time and time again, she kept thinking about the last time she'd seen Kieran at his auntie's place and how she'd spotted the black-clad man in the photo on Kay's sideboard. That's when an idea occurred to her. One she couldn't believe she hadn't come up with before. It wasn't just a good idea – it was a great idea. She trusted this man completely, given he'd been in her life forever. Maybe he could help, tell her how to escape this waking nightmare she'd found herself in. It had to work.

The memory of Kieran's actions that day made her shudder. She was totally gutted with fear and shame. She couldn't stop thinking about him killing her family and pinning it on her. He said if they got lifted, he'd snitch to the cops that she planned it all - to trap and kill Val. It was too much for her to take in. She wondered if she should just end it all. Unfortunately, she couldn't. It was wrong, and the truth was she didn't have the nerve. She was a total chicken. A coward whose body felt as if it had aged a thousand years overnight.

Freezing cold and sitting at the end of a wooden pew in St. Mary's Church, Honey knew she stood out like a sore thumb among a row of silent, patient, war-weary elderly men and women. A retreat was on, and the priests were hearing confessions in the early morning.

To pass the time, she watched the parishioners take their turn in the confessional and leave quietly with discreet smiles and nods. Her heart pounded. She dreaded the priest's reaction when she confessed. He'd be furious, but he had to help; he was her only lifeline.

At long last, it was her turn. She rose to enter the confessional when heavy footsteps echoed down the aisle. Turning, she was startled to see Father McGuire himself. Who was hearing confessions then? She could tell, even from a distance, he was a shadow of his former self. She froze as he mumbled something and shuffled towards the altar. He didn't see her. He seemed way less scary and kind of pathetic.

At the altar, he quickly blessed himself and hurried towards the vestry. Afraid she'd lose sight of him, she ran after him, calling out his name.

'Father. Father McGuire!'

The startled priest turned as she caught up with him, and Honey saw the raw red of his tired eyes. Even so, being near him soothed her.

'Father, I have to talk to you. It's important, I need—' she began.

The old priest raised his hand to stop her and shook his head. He couldn't face another round of minor sins or self-reproaching Catholic guilt. Not today. For years he'd kept the drink at bay, but now the devil had dragged him off the wagon. It was the first retreat opening he'd ever missed, but given the night he'd had, surely God wouldn't hold it against him.

In the small hours, he'd driven a wounded Provo over the border, hidden in the boot of his battered car. The ordeal had left him so shaken he'd hit the bottle as soon as he got back. Now he was riddled with guilt and nursing a thumping hangover. For the first time in his priesthood, he had no time, no patience, and no appetite for the day ahead. He just wanted it over. Finished.

'Ah, hello, I'm sorry, but I have to be in Magilligan Camp. There's trouble brewin', and the prisoners are in a desperate state. Sorry. I have to go. I'll catch up with you later.'

As he tried to walk away, Honey gripped his sleeve, her eyes filling up. 'But, Father, listen. I *really* need to talk to you. It's important!' she pleaded. Again, the priest tried to move on.

'No, young lady. You're not listening. I can't. I have to go. I'm late as it is,' he said.

Determined to make him listen, Honey clung to his sleeve tighter and near dragged him towards her. Through gritted teeth, she begged.

'Father, you-must-listen to me! It's Kieran Kelly... He's made me do awful things and wants me to do more. He's goin' to do something else, something dangerous, it's bad and I'm scared. Please!'

Her urgency, her boldness in touching him, left the priest speechless. Anger rising, he pulled free, then stopped and frowned at her. The girl looked dreadful – terrified, eyes red and wild - and the sight of her disturbed him. He wasn't sure he had the energy for this. All the clergy in the city were under strain, but it was breaking him in particular. His health was failing, his parish slipping, and his frustration had less to do with himself than with his crumbling faith in God and in the world.

He took a step back and glared at the hysterical, likely hormonal, girl before him. He couldn't help her. Not today. He'd no time for boyfriend troubles. Then, as if on cue, a young, dark-haired priest stepped out of the confessional and walked towards them. Father McGuire waved urgently for his novice to join him, then took the girl's arm and steered her towards him.

'Father Moore will help you now. Calm yourself. He'll hear your confession. You'll be grand with him.' But, to his dismay, Honey screamed and grabbed him again, clinging to him like a child holding onto a much-loved toy.

'But, Father, you don't get it. I trust you. It has to be you. Please, Father, you've got to listen. I'm beggin' ye'!' The confused novice sensed trouble and sped over. Desperate to leave, the old priest promptly pulled himself free from the girl's grasp and hustled her over to the young priest.

'Father Moore,' he pronounced, 'this wee girl needs to confess. Help her out, please? She's terrible upset, and I've gotta go. I'm running late as it is.'

The novice tried to take Honey's arm to guide her back to the confessional boxes, but she yanked away from his touch and glared at the pair of priests. Useless. And, with a final exasperated look at her lifelong spiritual adviser, she spat in his face.

'Forget it. And forget your fuckin' God, Father! Where is He when I need Him most, huh?'

She spun on her heel and stormed out, shouldering through the church doors and onto the steps. She sat down on the top step, oblivious to the rain, hid her face in her hands, and sobbed like she never had in her life. Every breath hurt, pins driving through her heart.

Horror flooded in at once. What had she just done?! In all her days she'd never gone on like that, and to poor Father McGuire of all people, in his own church. She prayed he would come after her. She knew she wasn't herself, couldn't believe she'd spat at him. Dear God but she needed him.

Time passed, but neither he nor the other priest showed up. Alone again. What the hell was she going to do now?

'You okay, love?' a voice asked from behind. She turned hoping it was her priest, but it was one of her daddy's old friends. *If only he knew,* she thought.

'Aye, I'm fine, Mr Gallagher. Thanks,' Honey said, trying to tidy herself up.

'Sure?' he asked again. Poor mite looked like the sky was falling in. Still, no wonder, life was shit around here these days. You were better to stay in your bed.

'I'm sure,' she repeated. 'Thanks.'

'All right, love. Mind yourself, okay. Don't forget now.'

'I won't, Mr Gallagher.' With a tip of his cap, he walked on, leaving her alone again.

Inside St Mary's, Father Moore dabbed at his mentor's face and jacket with a handkerchief. Father McGuire's trembling hand brushed him away. He'd never have imagined the girl would do such a thing. It was nothing like her. He felt a sick feeling of fear and disappointment. For her to lash out like that meant something was badly wrong. He tried to recall the name she'd hurled at him and tapped his forehead in frustration.

Kevin... no. Kieran, that was it. Ah no, not Kieran Kelly! He crossed himself.

He knew all about that waste of space from his parishioner Kay and he understood at once. 'Something dangerous...' Kelly had driven her to awful things. What awful things?

For a few minutes he stood there, turning it over, any thoughts of Magilligan Prison gone. Father Moore nudged him and reminded him he needed to get moving. They would speak when he got back from Magilligan and they'd seek her out.

Outside on the church steps, a thin, trembling voice in Honey's head told her the truth: no one was coming. She had no choice but to do what Kieran demanded. She was so scared; she thought she'd throw up. He warned her that she'd be in big trouble if she didn't follow his orders to the letter. Called it D-day. She didn't ask why.

He'd given her the keys to his flat, told her to drag out her old St Cecilia's school uniform, plait her hair, leave off the make-up. She had to act like a sweet, innocent schoolgirl and take the package he left her to the City Hotel, waiting for him there. Kieran swore again, staring her down, that he'd kill her and hurt her family if she even looked at the package or told anyone about it. Her heart felt like it was in her shoes, and she had to force herself to take a step. Barely together, she whispered a promise to herself: this was it. Threats or no threats.

She didn't want to think about tomorrow. The future was too scary to contemplate.

Chapter Fifty-Three

Morris

E arly that morning, Rob and Iowa sat parked outside Charles Jones's small hotel near Troy Park, one of the few better-off areas on the city side.

The streets were quiet, almost too quiet, and for once the silence gave Rob space to think. Since his revelation about Val's murder, Iowa had been more open, and while they both kept alert, the atmosphere between them was more relaxed than it had been. Ever.

Iowa sat beside him in a thick red jumper, blue jeans, her hair neatly tied back, looking oddly respectable, like she belonged to a different world. It was good to see. She seemed like a different person, almost gentler. It was nice.

His eyes caught sight of a teenager who moved quickly past the car, muttering under his breath. The lad was good-looking, dressed smart in black trousers, a white shirt, and a long coat that looked expensive enough to be noticed. He could have passed for a waiter, even an undertaker, but Rob's hackles rose. There was something about him not right. It wasn't the fella's walk itself, more the way he carried himself, too tuned in, too aware of everything going on around him. He kept glancing around, and it made Rob think the fella was either in trouble or about to be.

He glimpsed a name badge and for a second it made him curious, wondering what the lad did, where he was headed, what sort of life he led. Rob couldn't make out the writing from where he sat, but the fact of it, of him, stuck with him. He knew fine well he would've questioned him, no hesitation, if he'd been on the job, or off-duty, or even just feeling half himself. There was a notion in him that he ought to, but he let the moment pass and watched the teenager walk off. Maybe he was reading too much into it, maybe not. Either way, he let it pass, though the face he stored. A face like that, you didn't forget in a hurry.

Suddenly, Iowa nudged him, drawing his gaze to the hotel. Through the open glass door he saw Billy Morris standing outside, scanning the street. Billy acknowledged their battered Austin Marina and gave them a bold salute before slipping back inside.

Rob's shoulders tensed. 'Shit, what a pillock! Fucken' wanker!' he exclaimed.

Iowa, startled at such an outburst, cried. 'What is it? What's up?'

'He's seen us,' Rob noted grimly. *Bugger.*

Iowa was baffled. 'It's only one of Jones's goons showing off. What's the big deal?'

'He's not a goon. It's Billy Morris. Ex-army. Total psycho. He was at that rally the other night. I ran a check on him. Same boy's been up to his old tricks. Beat a fifteen-year-old Catholic kid half to death, nearly killed him for chucking dog shit and piss on him on patrol. I served with him.' Iowa could see Rob was well wound up.

'Bastard should be rotting in prison by now. Shows you he's got powerful mates. Charles Jones. He's a bigot, Iowa. Worst of the worst.'

Iowa was about to tell him off for not saying earlier when Morris reappeared, nudging the front door open and carrying two paper cups.

'He's coming over,' she fretted.

They were sitting targets, completely exposed, as Morris approached. He got closer, peered through the windshield, then tapped on Rob's window with his elbow. Reluctantly, Rob rolled it halfway down as Morris looked in.

'Thought you'd fancy a cuppa. You and your wee lady friend there?' Morris offered. Rob did his best to sound like a local.

'Naw, ta. We're waitin' on someone ye see.' He faked a smile at Morris whose eyes narrowed as he asked.

'I know you from somewhere, don't I?' He was sure of it.

Rob shook his head, rubbed at his bearded face, and muttered in a low, almost embarrassed tone, 'Naw, don't think so.'

Morris didn't buy it. He knew this guy. Not the girl, but the bearded fella. He offered her tea, but she wasn't having it.

With a sneer he turned back to Rob and said, 'Mr Jones and meself, well, we've had our eye on ye since you landed here this mornin'. That car of yours might as well have "Security Services" stamped across it. Stands out like a nun in a brothel!'

He let out a roar of laughter, then, for good measure, tipped both cups of scalding tea across the car roof. The liquid steamed up and ran in rivulets through the half-open window, spilling onto the driver's seat. Rob cursed as it splashed his legs and scrambled to wind the window up. Morris cracked up when he realised the truth. The penny dropped, and with bugging eyes he leaned towards the shrinking gap of the window.

'Well, I'll be fuckin' damned. Good to see ye again, Sallis. Not sure about the whiskers, mind. Ye look like a cat dragged backwards through a hedge!'

Rob and Iowa exchanged horrified looks as Morris, wearing a bitter smile and with the empty cups in hand, whistled his way back to the hotel. But, halfway across the street, he stopped abruptly, strode back to the car, and signalled for Rob to open the window again.

Rob did it, even though he didn't want to.

'By the way,' Morris grinned, his tone dripping with malice, 'I know the name of the fella that took your mate out, Robbie. So here's a wee tip for ye and that horse-faced bird beside ye. Clear off and let the real men do the work.'

Such an admission nearly sent Rob through the roof. He really wanted to know more, he was practically begging, but Morris just chuckled, turned around, and disappeared into the hotel, still smug.

In the end, Rob had no choice but to fire up the engine and tear away, the tyres screeching as his anger boiled over.

'Fuck. Fuck! I hate that knobhead. He knows who killed Val. Can you believe it? That hateful bigot knows who did it? I swear I'll get him and find out if it kills me!' His throat tightened, tears cutting hot lines down his cheeks, his heart breaking all over again. Iowa was stiff with disgust as her partner fell to pieces.

Rob cursed. Morris couldn't keep it in. Against every rule drilled into him, Iowa knew Rob's real name now.

'Kentucky, Sallis, whatever you're called, pipe down a sec. You're going to draw half the town down on us. We need to head back to the Pier right now.'

Rob hit the brakes and turned onto the side of the road, his jaw clenched. He turned to face her.

'Go back? I'm not crawling away with my tail between my legs. Did ye not hear that shitehawk? He knows who butchered Val, and he's going to tell me. I'll finish this myself if I have to.'

'No way, Kentucky,' Iowa rebutted. 'Morris knows us. Don't you get it? You can't risk going near him.'

'I don't care. I'm going back.' He went to throw the car into gear, but Iowa's nails dug into his arm, sharp enough to hurt.

'Stop and think, man. Just stop. Slow down for one bloody second. *Please.*'

Rob let out a groan, pressing his face into his hands. What a fiasco. Iowa was right about protocol. If their cover was blown, their handler had been clear: get out and report to Fort George. But he couldn't. Not now. Not with Val lying in the ground. And then he got it. Jones was due at the City Hotel. Where Jones went, Morris followed. If Iowa wanted to head back on her tod, fine. He'd find Morris there and wring the truth out of him. He lifted his head, forced a long breath, and met her eyes.

'I'm sorry our cover's blown. I am. You go back if you want, but remember - if we tell them we're exposed, we're finished. *Or* we can go to that hotel and make Morris talk. Your choice.' Iowa felt a bit queasy. She couldn't back down, not with Kentucky pushing it, and not while she could still get her revenge. She'd risk losing the op if she left him.

'Go on then,' she muttered.

Rob brought his foot down hard. The car sped away, roaring in the direction of Foyle Street and the City Hotel.

Chapter Fifty-Four

A Walking Dreamboat

The morning of the meeting Caitlin walked up the steps into the City Hotel lobby at 7.30 AM. Although it would be a long and arduous day, she felt good.

A million times better now that James had explained himself. It all fell into place – the secrecy, the files, the foul moods. She knew about Charles Jones's loan and the risk to Rocola if Roger Henderson didn't pay it back. But now, with George Shalham's brilliant plan, there was hopefully some light at the end of the tunnel.

There would be forty-five attendees – a cracking turnout. The Bishop of Derry had suggested his secretary take the minutes. Caitlin was to do the same, so they'd cross-check everything, ensuring nothing would be missed. The agenda had gone out by post, and each speaker had been briefed. She and James would meet and greet the guests as they arrived at the third-floor conference area. Today she wore her favourite black skirt, white blouse, and black jacket. Her shoes were flat and sensible. She glowed when she saw James approaching, his expressive green eyes admiring her.

Unexpectedly, Caitlin had been invited to Melrose the night before to go over some last-minute details. She was totally blown away the second she walked in. This wasn't just a house, it was a world apart from anything she'd ever known. The grand staircase swept upwards, wide enough for two people to walk side by side without touching,

polished wood gleamed beneath the glow of antique crystal chande-
liers. Every nook and crook seemed to breathe money, from the rich
rugs muffling her footsteps to the oil paintings of long-dead ancestors
staring down at her as if she'd no business being there.

For Caitlin, raised on Blamfield Street, it was overwhelming, like
standing on the set of some costume drama. She couldn't decide if
she felt awed or out of place, probably both. The drawing room had
a fire crackling in the grate, silver-framed photographs on the mantle,
and tall windows that looked out onto gardens that seemed to stretch
forever. She'd tried not to stare, but everything about the place spoke
of wealth and privilege.

And then, as if the surroundings weren't intimidating enough,
she'd been introduced to the RUC Chief Constable himself. Tall,
broad, and with that air of untouchable authority, he'd shaken her
hand as though she were someone of consequence. Caitlin had barely
managed to smile, her nerves jangling. The sheer contrast between her
world and James's was never more stark than in that moment.

At first, she found speaking to the peeler almost unbearable. Everything about him, his uniform, filled her with resentment. She hated
what he represented. Yet, to her surprise, when they were introduced,
he reached out his hand and shook hers.

His voice softened as he said, 'Caitlin... George Shalham. So sorry to
hear about your father.' She drew in a breath but met his gaze, defiant.
Bloody cheek. Caitlin didn't say anything and just let him finish.

'I was, of course, aware of the tragic incident. And after what James
here told me, I've instructed my officers to work closely with Brendan,
Brendan Doherty. I believe he's your solicitor. I'll also make a point of
keeping a close eye on things myself.'

Caitlin didn't believe a word he said, but being professional, she
forced a half-smile and thanked him.

Along with Roger Henderson, the four spent the next few hours reviewing the day's schedule and presentations with a fine-tooth comb. This was their golden opportunity to make sure not a second of the day was wasted.

As George Shalham talked about his security plan, Caitlin hated herself for warming to his enthusiasm, but the man genuinely sounded as if he wanted the meeting to be a success. He assured them that the guests in the main hotel and the wedding parties would be none the wiser about their presence, since all of James's guests would arrive by the back entrance at a designated time using the service lifts. Each attendee would be searched and escorted to the conference area, which would be closed off to the public and other guests. Only a few extra security staff, and a select number of hotel employees, would be allowed anywhere near the area.

Caitlin felt Roger eyeing her all night. It gave her the jitters. It'd been a strange and stressful evening, but a bittersweet opportunity to be close to James again.

Once they'd wrapped it up, James arranged a taxi to take her home. He apologised again for how he'd been acting as they went to the car.

'Caitlin, believe me, I'm sorry. But when my uncle told me what Jones had on him, it knocked me for six. Charles Jones is a racist thug. A dangerous man. Poor Roger only got involved with him because he was desperate.' He looked back towards the house and added.

'He's watching me like a hawk. I'm sorry. I had to pretend to be a cold-hearted bastard. Otherwise, he'd second guess how I feel about you, and right now, he doesn't need anything else to worry about. I know I've been a total arse, and seeing you so sad has been tearing me up.'

Caitlin was relieved beyond words by his apology and quipped, 'Yeah, he's been watching me too. Still, you did a good job of it. Oscar's a sure thing.'

'It's fine,' she said through their laughter. 'I have to admit, I'd thought you'd had your fill of 'you know what' and that was it.'

James shook his head. 'I know. I know and I can't blame you. I'm sorry. But once this thing is over, I promise we'll get away again. Maybe we'll go to Sligo this time, huh? I'll make it up to you, I swear.'

Instinctively, she gave him a wide, trusting smile. 'You'd better.' She knew it was a long shot, but she still secretly hoped it might happen.

Back at the hotel, a fair-haired, good-looking receptionist handed Caitlin a written message, all the while checking her out. She was hot, no question, but then he checked out the walking dreamboat coming her way, a knowing look in his eyes. He gave a quiet groan and rolled his eyes heavenward - what he'd give for an hour with that. When the hottie smiled, as if he knew what he was thinking, the receptionist turned as red as a tomato.

Flustered, he tapped at the keyboard, pretending to focus, though he couldn't resist stealing glances at them. And then he saw it - that look. *Aha!* Knew at once. A secret romance. *How deliciously exciting.*

Caitlin and James made their way to the hotel's rear entrance. As they walked, James brushed her fingers with his and whispered, 'Morning, gorgeous.'

'Morning, you,' she said. He breathed a sigh of relief. Caitlin did that to him. Everything was going like clockwork. They had it in the bag. Today was going to be a huge success and he felt bloody good.

'So, Miss McLaughlin are we ready to rock n' roll?' he whispered.

'We are indeed, Mr Henderson. Ready as I'll ever be,' Caitlin laughed nervously.

James nodded. 'Same here. We've done everything. What could possibly go wrong?' He rubbed his hands together and said with a smile, Let's get this show on the road, shall we?' Caitlin felt happy for him.

Yet. She'd one of her feelings...

Chapter Fifty-Five

Who in Their Right Mind Does That?!

B illy Morris drove his employer's Rover across Craigavon Bridge towards Foyle Street.

He couldn't get over it, remembering the look on Sallis's face when he let on he knew who killed his mate. Never liked the smarmy Geordie. A class wind-up though, given he'd no fucking idea who'd taken out that joker, Val Holmes. But seeing Sallis so desperate gave him a right thrill. Messing with the fella's head was more satisfying than anything he could do with his fists or feet.

Life was a blast now that he was out of the army, and he'd grown to idolise his new boss. If Billy were asked, he'd give his life for the wee man. Jones's preachings sat with him, and he could listen to him all day.

The British government hadn't a bloody clue – friggin' eejits – what was going on here, and what they were doing was bang out of order. When that wee Papist brat, the one who'd thrown shit at him, walked out in front of him a few days after, he'd screamed like a pig and bolted off like a dog in heat. He wasn't about to let the fucker get away this time, orders or no orders, and legged after him. Once he'd the youngster cornered, he beat the Taig bastard to a pulp and had to be pulled off.

They threw him out quick enough, service to Queen and country or not. Now, with Jones and his crew backing him, he was running his own kind of army. Like Jones, Morris had no time for Cradle Catholics, wanted them dead, and truth be told he enjoyed it, lapping up the violence the way a cat toys with a mouse.

Last night had been a high point, the wee man handing him a 'special' order that sent a thrill through him. He jumped at it, certain it would pay off, certain it would win him standing in the Orange Hall. He'd have staked his life savings on it. Life now was chaos, nothing like the army, and Jones was game for anything. His boss was going places, and William Morris from Portstewart intended to climb right up after him.

At Maggie McFadden's suggestion, Kieran had popped into the hotel a few days earlier to familiarise himself with the layout, collect his ID badge, and meet some of the staff. *Priceless*. It gave him a good chance to look around.

Now, on the job, he set about readying the conference rooms for the weddings. He charmed everyone, flirting with the staff and Maggie, and even got along with the other guys. At first, they were probably a bit suspicious and jealous of his movie-star looks, Kieran thought, but they warmed up quickly when he offered to do the hard work without complaining.

The second he walked into the staff canteen, he set his sights on a dippy looking, sparrow thin waitress, sniffling over a boyfriend who'd just dumped her. A few years older than Kieran but perfect for his needs, he fussed over her and listened while she went on and on about the ex and what a gobshite he was. Before long, she decided this fresh faced fella was a simple dote. Spotlessly dressed and gorgeous-looking, he'd listen to her moaning and cheered her up no end. Surprising for a youngster his age. She took to him and, before long, fancied him something rotten.

Kieran's efforts paid off when she mentioned that a select few, herself included, had been told to go upstairs and serve some VIPs. Bingo, he'd stick to her like glue. Maybe she could bring him along and let him have his moment. Hearing her out was worth it.

Honey arrived on time at the hotel steps, feeling a right idiot in her moth-eaten uniform. The security guard at the door spotted her and, smiling, waved her straight in. To him she was just a harmless school-girl.

Per Kieran's instructions, she quickly crossed the reception area and slipped into the hotel bar, the grill down, and tucked herself into a far corner, out of sight.

Right on the dot, Kieran turned up and found her. He was pleased as his eyes zeroed in on the school bag by her feet. As he sat down, he asked.

'Got here okay then?'

She nodded, lifted the bag up, and replied unhappily, 'Aye.'

He leaned in closer. 'It's all there?'

When she didn't answer, he grabbed her wrist and squeezed hard. It hurt so much she yanked herself away and cried, 'It's what ye left at the flat!'

'Good thinkin', putting it in a schoolbag. Should've thought of that meself. Well done.' he said, his voice icy. Although he'd praised her, he saw her eyes well up and groaned. Not today, Honey, not now. In anger, he snatched up the bag and grunted.

'Give us back me flat keys then!' She tossed the bunch of keys onto the table, then stood there, lost and unsure of what or where to go next.

Kieran picked the keys up, gave her a long, hard look, and got ready to leave.

'Get lost, Honey. Go home. I'll see you after.'

'Right,' she muttered, sounding sulky. She hated it when Kieran called her Honey now. There was a time when she'd loved it. He'd made her feel so special, important, like he loved her more than anything. Jesus wept. What a sucker she'd been, if only...

He went in for a kiss to try and fix things, but she wasn't interested. He grumbled and left the bar, hugging the bag like it was full of money.

Honey didn't want to go home. That ugly episode with Father McGuire and what she'd done, was driving her mad. The guilt. There was no point in rushing off; it was quiet here. With relief, she closed her heavy eyes and sank her head into the soft chair, feeling worn out. She'd spat at a priest! *Who in their right mind does that?* A bloody priest! The very thought of it.

Well, Kieran had what he wanted now. It was over. She wished she could just act like it never happened and everything would be okay again.

The line up of attendees was impressive: the Catholic Bishop of Derry; counterparts from the Presbyterian and Anglican churches; leaders and representatives from the Chamber of Commerce; and several senior figures from the main political parties.

George Shalham was there for the RUC, and the British Army had sent an experienced captain who knew the province like the back of his hand.

James and the rest had spent hours chopping and changing the seating plan, trying to navigate the attendees' various religious and political sensitivities. It was near impossible, but somehow, they'd done their best and were satisfied with the result.

The conference room was a pristine white-painted space adorned with ornate plasterwork ceilings and antique paintings depicting scenic Irish landscapes. However, for security, its substantial white window shutters were kept tightly closed, blocking out any natural light.

In a large square hallway outside, a few hotel staff served coffee and tea to clusters of attendees who'd been checked through the rear security point and were now gathered, ready to start.

Time to kick things off. James exhaled excitedly before announcing, 'Ladies and gentlemen, please take your seats.'

The noise level in the hallway picked up as the attendees topped up their drinks and filed into the conference room. Once everyone had settled down, James let some time pass before he nodded to his uncle to start.

On his feet, Roger Henderson felt tired and jittery as he stared uneasily at the rows of faces before him. He'd never been one for public speaking; in fact, he hated it. But then he remembered a bit of advice he'd once received many moons ago: imagine everyone naked: it wasn't working.

'Good morning, ladies and gentlemen. My name is Roger Henderson, and I'm the proud proprietor of Rocola, sadly one of the last shirt factories in our lovely city. I sincerely thank you all for being here today for the first of what, we hope, will be a series of constructive meetings.' He felt the urge to cough but held back. This was a real nail-biter.

'The purpose of this first session is to help convince you why it is vital, not only for our employees but for our city, that we keep Rocola operating smoothly and profitably for the foreseeable future.' He took a sip of water from a tumbler before continuing.

'The files we've passed out contain another copy of the agenda and important facts and figures you'll need as our speakers make their presentations this morning. For our afternoon brainstorming sessions, we've also provided some worksheets.' He looked around the smiling faces and smiled with relief. He'd done his bit.

'I'll say no more for now except to introduce James Henderson, my nephew, who will chair today's meeting. Thank you all.'

And with that, the meeting got underway.

Before returning to work, Kieran had stashed the school bag in his staff locker. As time went on, his pretence of competence and cheerfulness was wearing thin. He didn't realise the job would be so tough on his body. Full of adrenalin at first, he'd almost enjoyed it, but now he was losing the will to live. He must've lugged around about four hundred chairs for the wedding guests – the first of whom he could hear laughing and drinking at the reserved bar.

Finally, he landed down in the staff canteen for his first break. He spotted the pretty, broken-hearted waitress who, as soon as she caught sight of him, made a beeline over.

Her face was lit up with excitement, but Kieran kept eating his breakfast, noting how she fidgeted in her chair, played with her food, all the while bursting to share whatever news she had. Casually, he picked up a sausage from his plate, then put it down untouched and stared at her.

'Right. What's with all the fidgeting? You're sitting there like a cat on a hot tin roof. What's cheered you up all of a sudden?'

'Nothin'. Thinkin' how much I like ye,' she answered rather quickly. It was a lie; he knew it.

'That's nice. But I don't believe ye. Tell us. What's got into your knickers? Not me!'

She tittered and told him who she'd seen at the meeting upstairs. She'd never been so close to the bishop, not since her confirmation, and he'd been so lovely when she'd poured him his tea earlier.

After scouring the canteen, she clapped her hands and excitedly exclaimed, 'Honestly, Kieran, it's friggin' unbelievable.' They've got everyone but the friggin' Queen in that room!'

'What d'ya mean?' Kieran asked, chewing slowly as he set his cutlery down. His heart hammered. He nearly had to sit on his hands to stop himself leaping up and grabbing the silly cow by the throat.

Only then did she realise that she should've kept it shut, and wailed, 'Shit! I wasn't supposed to say anythin', was I? Don't let on, will ye? Not a word!'

Kieran pretended to lose interest, like he had when Aunty Kay opened her trap about the meeting, and slurped down his hot tea casually saying, 'Don't give a flying fuck, anyway. Nothin' to do with me. I'm only here for the day.'

She was thrown off by his sudden silence and change in mood. Touching his arm, she said, hoping to bring him back to her corner, 'You've been a real tonic, Kieran. I was dreading comin' in. You've made my day.'

'Tell us what's occurrin', then? What's everyone so wound up about?' he asked, putting her on the spot.

She paused. 'We were warned not to breathe a word, but since you've been so lovely. Well...'

Any loyalty to Mrs McFadden went straight out the window as she giggled and listed off the VIPs she'd seen. Kieran listened carefully, coaxing her on. This was it. He couldn't ask for more!

Fifteen minutes later, he retrieved the bag from his locker and slipped into a bedroom carelessly left open by a chambermaid.

Locking the door behind him, he sat on the bed and opened the school bag. Inside was a sealed plastic shopping bag, which he opened. He pulled out a handgun and tucked it down the back of his trousers. After that, he inspected a tightly wrapped package and examined a Memo Park Timer beside it, a necessity to ensure he'd enough time to get the hell out.

Finally, he slowly removed a sandwich box he'd nicked from Kay, who'd bought a load from a neighbour's Tupperware party. He pulled off its lid, and inside sat two foil-wrapped packets. The top packet, a cheese sandwich, he tossed into the bin.

Next, he carefully took out the lower one and placed it gently on the bed. Unwrapping it from the top, he smiled as he studied the sandwich filling: Frangex – a powerful and deadly explosive.

Still smiling, he rolled up his shirtsleeves and removed some fine electrical wire he'd tied around his upper arm earlier that morning. Back in the good old days with the Provos, he'd gone through some basic bomb-making training but had never used it until now. Easy-peasy.

It took a few simple steps to assemble the detonator, and... *voilà*. As he set the timer to noon, his groin fluttered. He imagined Alex lying on a sun bed next to him and moaned as he placed the components into a plastic bag. After today, he swore he'd find a way to get his queen on that plane to Miami – at any cost.

By now, Charles Jones was bored out of his skull. The meeting had been dragging on for well over an hour. He didn't give a shite about Rocola but had to make it look like he was doing his bit.

He stared across the table at Bishop Hegarty, who sat in his ridiculous purple zucchetto and over-the-top robes, looking more like a medieval character than a man of the cloth. Smug bastard. Hegarty was bright all right and carried some serious clout. Jones hated him with a passion – both for the Church he stood for and on a personal level.

Ironically, as Jones watched Henderson Jnr, he almost felt sorry for the critter. He'd bust his balls to get this bunch of misfits in one room and most likely knew by now that his uncle owed Jones a fortune. The Belfast man knew the older Henderson would miss the payment, and finally Rocola would be his.

He'd recently come up with the brilliant idea of ordering Morris and a few of his soldiers to torch some of Rocola's container lorries as they passed through the Waterside on their way to Belfast Port – putting an extra squeeze on Henderson's falling profits.

Once it was all his, in the blink of an eye, he'd make sure Rocola's machines would stop, bringing misery and poverty to thousands of Taigs. He wasn't gonna let anyone stop him, so forget any sob stories or bleeding-heart mercy missions like this, it was a lost cause. He waited too long to let anyone ruin his plans.

Before, when they went in the back of the hotel, security wanted to search his bodyguard, Morris, first. After a quick frisk, they let him pass, admiring the Red Hand of Ulster on his leather jacket. Jones was up after that.

The security guard with glasses went to frisk him, but Jones just glared and said, 'Don't you dare. Do you know who I am?' Surprised, four-eyes immediately recognised Jones and waved him in without a second thought.

Caitlin was fascinated as she watched and listened eagerly to the pre-senters. She could tell they'd done well so far from the vibe in the room, though there was one exception: Charles Jones, sitting there like a wet weekend. No surprise, really, James had pointed him out earlier. She didn't dare say what he'd called the guy.

Besides that, it was a relaxed and supportive environment while the presenter excitedly shared his ideas. You could feel his energy. James was thrilled.

Up first was Tim Hines from the Social Democratic Labour Party, or SDLP, well-known and respected in the city. Hines was trustworthy and committed to his constituents, some of whom worked for Rocola. He understood better than most the catastrophic fallout if the factory closed. James liked him and was desperate to have him and his party on their side.

He'd check on Jones from time to time. He was being an arrogant ass, checking out the room and not even listening to Hines. Jones caught James staring and smirked, as if to say, 'Give it up, pal.'

Little did Jones know, this time the Hendersons had the upper hand and were waiting for the right moment to play it.

Honey woke to find she'd drooled, a small patch damp on her chin, and she wiped it away in a hurry, embarrassed though no one was there to see. She hadn't the faintest notion how long she'd been out. Blinking herself awake, she searched about for a clock, but there wasn't one in sight. After a stretch and a quick tidy of herself, she headed down to reception to find out the time.

Chapter Fifty-Six

Lost Love

As James handed the floor over to Alfie McScott, Rocola's accountant, he only half listened.

His mind drifted back to the night Roger had revealed Rocola's deep debt to Charles Jones and how George Shalham had quickly devised a lifesaving plan: to apply for funding from the Northern Irish Secretary of State (SOS).

With perfect timing, the news had come in that morning: the SOS had agreed to a loan and had even fast-tracked it. Those in the know were ecstatic, like they'd won the football pools. Rocola had been on the brink, so close to losing all those years of hard graft and dedication from the management team and its many employees.

To his surprise, James found himself saying a brief prayer of thanks. Now, it seemed their future was secure, and the team, to whom he was forever grateful, was more committed than ever to ensuring Rocola thrived.

Even with such welcome news, James couldn't help but worry about his uncle's health. It seemed like Roger's zest for life was fading. He'd openly admitted that he felt responsible for Rocola's financial mess, and no matter how much James and Shalham tried to reassure him, he still looked like he wanted to be six feet under, leaving a heartbreaking void that his friend and nephew felt powerless to fill. They hoped that today would start his journey back to recovery.

Roger felt James's eyes on him. The loan was wonderful news, sure, but he was drowning in shame and regret. The sadness clung and wouldn't shift. Happiness felt like a distant memory, out of reach, whatever had happened or might still come. His shoulders rounded; his whole stance made him look as if he were shrinking into himself.

When Charles Jones rocked up that morning, James had noted his blatant arrogance with a wry smile. He shuddered at the thought of how he would've been if they hadn't received such positive news about the bale out. As it was, he could barely contain his delight. It meant that Jones would no longer be welcome at Melrose, no longer eat its fine cuisine, nor drink from its wine cellar. No more would they have to endure his drunken rants or blatant bigotry. To the Hendersons, Charles Jones was yesterday's fish and chips. Gone and forgotten. Even with all this, James was still frustrated that Roger had let Jones come today, despite his protests.

'Trust me, I'll handle it,' was Roger's only reply.

None of them wanted Jones catching wind of the trump card they had up their sleeve. And with no choice, James let it go. But, by Christ, he was finding it hard to keep up the business-as-usual façade around the creep.

By now, Kieran had put the explosive together. It hadn't taken long, but he was running close to time. Time to return to base, or someone might notice his absence. He grabbed his precious treasure and left the bedroom.

Back in the staff canteen, he watched the kitchen staff prepare huge stainless steel urns for tea and coffee, placing them on linen-covered trolleys, ready to be taken up to the third-floor conference room.

About to leave, the canteen's two swinging doors opened halfway and got stuck as someone tried – and failed – to push one of the heavy trolleys through. Kieran chuckled and rushed over to help pull the doors back.

On the other side stood his pretty new best friend, who groaned, 'I don't know why they asked me, of all people, to push that monstrosity. I mean, look at the size of me compared to that! Weighs a ton. And to top it all, I've got a friggin' ladder in me tights. Mrs McFadden's going to have a fit if she sees me.'

The tiny waitress turned her back, found the ladder, and tried to fiddle the ladder out of sight while deliberately giving Kieran a cheeky eyeful of what could be on offer.

Kieran was given the perfect chance to make his move. He quickly lifted the trolley's linen cloth and carefully tucked the plastic bag deep inside. *Brilliant.* With a smirk reminiscent of a schoolboy hiding a secret, he led the girl aside, seized the trolley, and navigated it through the doorway. She laughed at his cheek, fluttered her eyelashes, and smiled.

'Any chance you could give me a hand gettin' this to the lift when it's full? I'm runnin' behind. They should've had their drinks topped up by now.'

Not needing to be told twice, Kieran agreed, 'Sure, where to?' She raised her eyebrows, smiled guiltily, and giggled.

'Third floor. Ye can help me get it onto the service lift if you don't mind.'

Once the urns were refilled and ready, Kieran tilted his head and eagerly pushed the trolley towards the lift.

The waitress followed, eyeing him appreciatively. 'You're my Guardian Angel today, Kieran Kelly. Know that?' She wasn't wrong; the trolley was *well* heavy and a pain to manoeuvre.

It took longer than Kieran would've liked, but they finally reached the service lift. He pressed the call button. The waitress was getting all twitchy, pacing back and forth as the lift dragged itself down to the basement.

'Why's it takin' so feckin' long? What time is it?!'

Kieran checked his watch and said, 'Twenty-five past eleven. No sweat. It's here now, see.' She relaxed and let out a sigh.

'Thank feck.'

Alone, Morris sat outside the meeting room, waiting for the first break of the day. Suddenly, a wave of laughter and applause erupted next door. *Sounds like it's going all right in there,* he thought. *The boss'll be hating that.*

Moments later, the double doors swung open and a heavy cloud of pipe smoke rolled into the corridor, followed by a steady stream of men and women.

The smell dragged Morris back to his hateful stepfather, to the beatings. He gave a short scoff. If he'd his hands on the old man now... what he'd do to the bastard. He relished the thought. Jones was one of the first out and rushed over to him.

He brushed down his Savile Row suit and hissed, 'I can't breathe in there. That prick of a bishop is smoking a pipe like he wants to set off the fire alarms!'

Morris could sympathise. He moved closer to Jones's ear, 'Won't be long now, sir.'

The portly man grinned, his eyes narrowing as he pulled a thick envelope from his briefcase and subtly slid it over to Morris. No, *not long now.* He had the Hendersons right where he wanted, no doubt about it. They were fucked. Roger Henderson looked hollowed out with exhaustion as the deadline loomed. Jones watched Henderson's nephew mingle, grinning like an idiot and completely clueless.

The same boyo will be getting a rude awakening any time now. He'd soon find out that the Fenian women he'd been fighting so hard to keep would be out on their arses within days, worst case scenario, weeks. No jobs meant no money. No money meant no food, no nothing. And after that... well... each to their own.

Londonderry's shaky economy would likely crash and burn. Shops, restaurants, and even those Fenian-run bars that sheltered Provo murderers would have to close. *Excellent*.

And now, with Billy Morris's loyal, dogged determination as added insurance, Jones had everything sewn up. Lips tight, he glared at Derry's bishop.

Jones's anger increased as he watched the smug man swagger around, smoking his pipe as if he were in charge. Despite being vicious, evil, and ultimately expendable, Jones felt a slight twinge of remorse for Morris. It would be up to him to vanish as soon as the deed was done, while Jones, on the other hand, had his exit planned out to perfection. Amidst the inevitable confusion, he'd slip away and meet Bonner, who sat waiting in his car near the Guildhall. Then off to Belfast. Just the two of them.

Rob and Iowa arrived late after getting stuck at a busy security checkpoint and taking forever to find a parking space at the fully booked hotel.

Rob rushed up the entrance steps ahead of Iowa, but a security guard stopped him just as he was approaching the revolving doors, and with a hand on his shoulder, asked to search him. The guard was already up to his eyeballs with the day. He was the only one left minding the front while the real action was going on around the back. He motioned for Rob to raise his arms; Rob didn't move. He hadn't expected this. Both he and Iowa were *carrying*.

Iowa caught on right away and quickly stepped in to intercept. However, the gods sent yet another miracle when a large, noisy Luton van screeched to a stop right in front of the hotel steps. Everyone turned to watch as two delivery boys ran to the back of the truck, threw it open, and grabbed two massive white floral wedding displays. As if their jobs depended on it, and shitting bricks, the lads worked as fast as they could. The displays were so large that they partially hid their faces as they rushed up the steps and tried to push past the guard. A big no-no.

The guard, irritated by the intrusion, turned his back on Iowa. Taking her chance, she palmed her small handgun across to Rob, the movement quick and unseen. The delivery lads and the guard were already locked in a heated row, voices rising and hands flying. Rob gave her a quick wink, then used the commotion to slip past the guard and melt into the shadows of the foyer.

Once inside, he approached a fair-haired, adolescent-faced man at the reception desk and, with a polite expression, asked, 'Can you tell me which conference room Charles Jones might be in?'

The receptionist didn't know who Rob was talking about – he'd never heard of a 'Charles Jones'. As he checked, he found Jones's name wasn't listed.

'Sorry, we don't have anyone by that name with us today.' He turned to pick up a ringing phone with an apologetic smile, thus ending the conversation.

Rob scanned the revolving doors and saw the guard yelling to the high heavens at the two confused, sweating florists. He watched Iowa step in front of him and offer her bag to be searched. Rob couldn't hear her words, but the guard smiled, had a quick rummage and let her through.

When she got to him, Rob told her what the receptionist had said, 'Doesn't surprise me with all this security. We'll have to find him ourselves.'

He went straight to the display board, grabbed a hotel brochure, and turned it over to check a map of the conference rooms. Then he checked the foyer signboard, which listed the day's events by room: two weddings and several meetings.

'Okay. Let's think. The weddings take up the larger rooms on the second floor, and the other meetings... We know who and where they are 'cos their on that board. Morris'll probably be in one of the last ones – but which one?' He saw that only two likely venues were left, and all on the same floor – level three. He grabbed Iowa by the arm, slipped her gun back to her, and sprinted toward the lift.

Inside stood a honeymoon couple who looked like they'd finished a lazy breakfast and were itching to get back to bed. They waited impatiently for the lift door to close, but Rob blocked it with his foot to allow Iowa in. He smiled quickly at the couple, who only had eyes for each other, while pressing the third-floor button.

At the same time, Kieran Kelly pressed the button for the 3rd Floor in the service lift. He hummed a tune to the pretty waitress while pretending to adjust the linen cloth over the trolley, ensuring his package was secure and well hidden. She was still fretful about the time, but then another awful thought struck her. She was dead if anyone saw Kieran up there with her.

'You don't need to come out with me. I... I can manage. If anyone sees ye, I'm dead Kieran,' her voice caught on her every word.

He'd no intention of letting the trolley out of his sight – especially now – and couldn't care less if she was 'dead.'

'You're not that late. I'll just help you get this thing outta the lift, I swear,' he said.

She still wasn't convinced, but looking at that face she told herself he wasn't going to balls it up for her.

'Will ye just help me get it out then and go?' she pleaded.

'Cross me heart,' Kieran chuckled, stepping into the elevator as the doors slid open.

He rolled the heavy trolley onto the landing, then stepped back inside to hold the lift's wait button, knowing the girl had no chance of moving it without him.

She smiled with relief but then struggled to push the trolley along the thick, lush carpet. Shooting Kieran a desperate glance, and with a knowing nod, he stepped out to help.

Not too late, they entered the tiled hallway outside the meeting room, where Kieran parked the trolley neatly in a corner. A few attendees noticed the arrival of the refreshments and eagerly made their way over. Caitlin was one of the first, about to blow a fuse after receiving a bollocking by Charles Jones, who hadn't yet had his usual but excessive dose of caffeine.

'You're late,' she growled at the waiter by the trolley. 'You should've been here fifteen minutes ago.'

Kieran rolled his eyes. Caitlin did a double take, taking in his expression; she would speak to Maggie about him later. *Arrogant git.*

The tiny waitress, flustered, apologised profusely for the delay, then set about pouring hot drinks and offering biscuits with a warm smile.

With the trolley in place, Kieran took a slow look round the room, clocking exits and faces when out of the blue a hand yanked hard at his sleeve. He assumed it was the stuck-up bitch who'd mouthed off and spun around, ready to give her a piece of his mind. Instead, he froze. It was Alex! Alex was giving him the evil eye, and Kieran felt a moment of dread.

Alex. Here!

'What the hell are ye doin' here?' Alex hissed, dragging Kieran aside. Kieran couldn't think straight. No! Alex. Alex: the bomb, the fuckin' bomb!

'For Christ's sake, Alex. What the *fuck* are you doing here?!' Kieran yelled.

'Ssshhh... keep it down. I'm with the bishop ye eejit.' A paralysing fear gripped Kieran.

There was Father Alex Breslin, looking sharp in his all-black suit, shirt, and clean white collar, right in front of him. Kieran's pulse sped up. They had to scram. This place was ready to blow sky high!

Caitlin watched the tense exchange between the arrogant waiter and the bishop's aide. There was a problem. As she made her way over, Bishop Hegarty burst out of the meeting room, calling for his envoy.

He spun in a full circle before spotting his secretary, deep in conversation with a waiter. 'Ah, there you are, Father Breslin,' he cried, his pipe clenched between his teeth. 'Where's me tea?'

Alex instinctively turned at the sound of his superior's voice, catching the familiar whiff of pipe tobacco. He told Kieran to wait and began walking away when his world suddenly erupted. A deafening crack rang out.

In shock, he turned in time to see his bishop hit the floor hard, his old briar pipe bouncing and skidding across the tiles. Things went crazy.

Running for cover, Kieran instinctively slid the handgun from the waistband of his trousers, the cold metal steadying his grip. He kept his head down, eyes up, and swept the room in a slow, careful arc.

By the conference room door a hulking bloke stood, gun raised, shoulders set to take his next shot. A twisted grin pulled at the man's mouth. His aim had changed. He was tracking Alex now, shadowing his every step.

Kieran's breaths became more rapid. He inched his stance, brought the sights level, and settled the front post on the brute's shoulder. *Move, Alex. Move!*

Across the corridor, Morris set his feet and pushed the pistol out, arms firm, heart thudding with glee. They gave him this pair on a plate. Two Papal scumbags for the takin'. *The boss'll be pleased. Might even be a bonus,* he thought, taking up the slack and pressing the trigger as the front sight sat dead centre on Alex's chest.

Kieran saw it coming and roared, 'Alex. No!' Alex heard his lover's warning and turned around to face him.

Everything slowed as Kieran pulled the trigger, once, twice, then a third time, each round slamming into the hulk, the man's body jerking back but refusing to drop, as if sheer brute force kept him upright.

Kieran's jaw clenched and he roared, firing again, the cracks splitting the air, each impact landing with a sick, dull thud that should have ended him.

Then came another sound, not the echo of his own shot, but a blast that drove straight into his chest, stopping him cold. For a moment he thought it was nothing, just the recoil, but then a warmth spread across him, seeping fast, followed by a searing pain that clawed through his ribs and left him gasping. His body screamed to give up, to let go, but Alex was there, Alex needed protection, nothing else mattered. He planted his feet, dragged up what little strength was left, and forced himself to lift the pistol one last time, steady enough to squeeze off the round that would finish it.

At last, the gunman crashed to the floor. Kieran's eyes found Alex, there he was, whole and breathing, and relief softened his face as he gave him a small, tired smile, all the love he had left.

Kieran's hand went to his chest, curious rather than afraid, and when he looked his fingers were tacky with dark blood, his own, and the sight emptied any strength from his legs. He fell to his knees and eased down onto the floor. The room seemed to move. He blinked to keep Alex in view, not to look away, not for a heartbeat, because that face was his world. He wished he could wait, just a tiny bit longer, for another day, another laugh, another morning together, but it was slipping away, and he couldn't stop it.

'You're all right,' he breathed, or thought he did, he tried to smile for Alex. In his head he told Alex he loved him, always had, always would. He stayed with that thought as the sounds weakened and the light went soft, still keeping his eyes on Alex, refusing to let go until there was nothing left to see.

'Bye, princess,' he whispered.

Chapter Fifty-Seven

Tick Tock, Tick Tock...

With guns in hand, Rob and Iowa had just started looking on the third floor when the first cracks went off. They looked at each other, unsure, until a second burst left no doubt, gunshots!

They raced towards the noise, drawing their pistols as they drove down the corridor. A wave of screaming men and women burst towards them, pushing past them in panic.

The soldiers pushed through the crowd, and when they got to a broad square landing, they just stopped. An RUC officer in green stood with his pistol raised at a waiter crumpled on the floor, a pool of dark red blood curving in a near perfect arc from the small of his back. At the far end of the room an elderly clergyman lay motionless, one hand stretched towards a lone pipe. They watched as another officer and several security men approached a bulky, bloodied figure slumped by the meeting room door. *Billy Morris!*

The officers exchanged nods, confirming that the fallen men were no longer a threat.

Amid the confusion, Charles Jones slipped out of a stairwell at the back, half walking, half running down the steps towards the exit.

One of the RUC men spotted Rob and Iowa, armed and ready. He swung his piece toward them, shouting, 'Drop your weapons to the floor. Hands above your head!' Rob and Iowa didn't move an inch.

Iowa tried to calm the panicky officer, saying, 'Okay. Chill.' They kept their eyes on him and, together, slowly placed their guns on the ground before raising their hands as ordered. In the background, George Shalham barked out order after order.

'One of you, call downstairs and tell them to keep everyone in the foyer. You two, get down there and make sure no one leaves. I want this place sealed up tighter than Fort Knox!'

Caitlin watched as one officer nodded and ran to find a phone. Shalham hurried to check that the meeting room was clear.

She fell into a chair and shook her head. *What the hell just happened? They'd been so careful!* Her eyes scanned the room for James until she noticed something slightly familiar about the bearded man with his hands up. She needed a closer look, so she walked over to the couple, now spread-eagled against the wall.

As she studied them, the man turned to face her, and even with all his whiskers, she recognised him – the Brit from out her back garden. And then again on the bus. Up close, those glinting hazel eyes were unmistakable. She saw the spark of recognition in his eyes too.

Honey had wandered about the hotel unchallenged. Everyone was so busy, making her feel almost invisible, but she was okay with that. She'd had a quick peek at the freshly cleaned bedrooms and even the conference rooms ready for the weddings. They were out of this world.

Once upon a time, she'd dreamt of a wedding like that, fresh white flowers, beautiful porcelain table settings, shining candelabras. Aware it was so far from ever happening, especially after what she'd done, she moaned and moved toward the lift to go up to the next floor.

Upon reaching the third-floor landing, she heard what sounded like gunfire but brushed it off, thinking the staff were having a bit of craic setting off some wedding poppers. Afraid about bumping into anyone, she cautiously walked down the long corridor until the unmistakable screams of men and women reached her ears.

Out of nowhere, they started rushing toward her, and in their panic, they pushed and pulled her aside. Terrified, Tina recognised one of them from a distance – Father Breslin – crying! Not seeing her, he knocked her sideways, slamming her painfully against the wall. She pressed herself against it as the tide of people thundered past.

What the hell? And like that, she knew. Sweet Mother of God. Kieran!

She waited until the crowd had passed, then turned into a square hallway where an RUC officer was yelling. He gestured toward a waiter who'd collapsed beside a trolley. That's when Tina saw him.

His unmistakably long, black, curly hair, him lying motionless like a statue, blood pooling around him. He had a peaceful look, the same as the beginning. When he'd been funny, kind, and made her feel like the only girl in the world. She could almost feel her heart breaking, piece by piece.

A guttural groan escaped her, her heart aching with the force of it. Shock hit her like a wave as she moved toward him, but before she could get close, a pair of hands grabbed her, dragging her back.

'Ah, Kieran. What 'ave you done?' she howled. 'What 'ave you done?!'

As soon as Caitlin heard the screaming school girl's voice, her heart stopped. A silent sob caught in her throat as she ran towards the sound. She didn't want to believe it. She couldn't, but the truth was right there. Right in front of her. *Tina. Her sister!*

'Jesus Christ Tina. What the hell are you doing here?!' she yelled, glaring at her.

Caitlin tore away the hands that held her little sister and tried to take her. Instead, Tina pushed them all away, rushing to the waiter's body. She knelt beside him, trying to lift his bloodied head onto her lap. A burly peeler tried to yank her off, but Caitlin grew hysterical.

'Leave her be. She's my sister. Let me talk to her!'

She needed to understand why Tina was there – never mind why she was crying over some dead waiter. She searched her mind, recalling the nights when Tina hadn't come home until late: her silence, her aggression, her withdrawal... *No!* No way... she couldn't be involved in any of this!

The policeman, confused, turned to Shalham for guidance. His boss nodded, and with some relief, left the wailing, blood-soaked schoolgirl to her sister.

Tina couldn't believe Kieran was dead. She didn't understand how she could feel both ecstatic and completely devastated at the same time. Remembering their early days, when he'd been so loving, so kind, telling her he loved her, made it hurt even more.

She let out another ear-splitting scream, so loud Caitlin had no choice but to clout her one. It worked, and then Tina fell silent.

Rocking her gently back and forth, Caitlin whispered into her sister's red hair.

'It's me, Tina. It's Caitlin. Listen to me.' She cupped her face in her hands and made her look at her.

'What's happened, Tina? Who is he?' Tina seemed surprised at being asked such a stupid question.

'He's me boyfriend. He loves me. Loves me loads.'

Boyfriend! Tina?

At that moment, Caitlin saw her sister's eyes mist over and knew she was losing her. She took in her plaited hair, glazed look, and worn-out school uniform. What the...?

'Okay, love, it'll be okay, but why are you here, dressed like that?' Tina smiled sleepily and stayed silent. A sudden dread rose from the pit of Caitlin's soul.

'Why are you here, Tina?' she pleaded, shaking her. 'Tell me!' Tina's eyes gleamed, and without warning, she burst into a manic laugh, wild and hysterical. Between fits of laughter, Caitlin heard her mumble something about a school bag.

'What'd you say, Tina?!' Caitlin was desperate.

'What schoolbag? And who's that man, Tina? Tell me!'

Tina wanted to go home to her mammy and curl up beside her, but Caitlin wouldn't let her. Kept asking her questions and so loud, she was almost screaming. At it again, always giving off, yelling her head off.

'Tina, it's important, love. Who is he? What's he done? Tell me!' Caitlin tried again. A split second of sanity rang out in Tina's mind. She felt heartbreakingly alone. Guilt and shame tore through her. *Her daddy. Mammy. Kieran. Father McGuire. Martin. Caitlin.*

'A schoolbag, Caitlin. He's put somethin' in it. He's done cruel, horrible things. Made me do 'em as well... and hurt poor Val. Called me Flower.' Caitlin shook her head in confusion.

'What things?! Tina, please, what things? Quick! And who the hell is Val?!' But Tina's tired and fragile mind couldn't cope as she slipped into a marshmallow world where everything was soft, rosy, welcoming, and safe.

Rob and Iowa, still spread-eagled against the wall, listened intently to everything the sisters said. Rob was too far away to hear most but he heard Val's name. The schoolgirl lay there like a broken doll. It was bad enough losing Billy Morris before they could get to him, but this? Sweet fuck, don't tell me this pathetic creature was a honey trap. She's only a bairn, a child, for Christ's sake! How on earth? And the girl who let him go in the garden – the sister. You couldn't make it up if you tried.

Caitlin shook her head in despair. She held Tina close and looked up at the Brit watching them. She saw him drop his head, close his eyes, and release a deep, heartfelt groan of pain.

Farther down the corridor, James had been helping the attendees, including his uncle, escape. But as he stepped back into the hallway, the sight of blood and death rooted him to the spot. A wave of nausea hit him. He couldn't believe it when he saw Caitlin holding someone who looked like a schoolgirl and rocking her like a baby. He couldn't hear what she was whispering into the girl's hair, but the look on her face when she saw him filled him with dread.

He knelt beside her, straining to catch her words.

'It's okay, Tina. It's over love. He's gone. He can't hurt you any-more,' he heard Caitlin say.

'Who's that, Caitlin?' James asked. His throat was tight with worry. 'What's going on?'

Caitlin stared into his face and slowly released her sister, who the burly police officer quickly carried off. She began to cry so hard she didn't make a sound, struggling to tell him.

'It's…it's our Tina.' At first, James didn't understand, but then it came to him.

'Tina. Your sister, Tina?' Caitlin nodded, and through her tears, she pointed at Kieran.

'I couldn't catch everything she said, but that guy made her bring something here. Says it's in a schoolbag.'

With a horrified gasp, she leaped up and hurried to George Shalham, who was staring at her, looking both anxious and confused. Her terror was clear when their eyes met.

'What is it, Caitlin?!' he demanded, gripping her arms. Gasping, she tried again to get her words out.

'M– Mr Shalham. I... I think there's a bomb.' She pointed to the waiter's lifeless body.

'I think he's planted a bomb!'

Chapter Fifty-Eight

Darkness Looms

C aitlin's chilling words gave Chief Constable Shalham the shock of his life. Didn't he just shut this place down?!

Only a few officers remained in the hallway. One stood near the unknown couple close to Caitlin and James, while the others lingered in sombre silence by the bodies of the bishop, his unidentified assassin, and the waiter.

Pointing at British Army Captain Dolan, Shalham barked, 'Captain, get the bomb squad. Now!'

Then, turning to an officer beside the fallen bishop, he snapped, 'You, down those stairs like your arse is on fire! Get everyone out. *Move it!*' He wasn't entirely convinced there was a real threat, but he wasn't willing to take any chances.

James came over to him, raking his hands through his hair like a nervous wreck, his face as pale as a ghost. But before he could say a word, Shalham grabbed him and Caitlin, dragging them toward the nearest fire exit.

'You better get outta here. Quick!'

Shalham saw Caitlin's attempt to take James's hand but he yanked it away and turned on her, yelling, 'What the hell, Caitlin? What have you done?!'

Startled and speechless, Caitlin was caught in James's accusing gaze. Tears fell as she reached for him again, but he stepped back, as though her touch would hurt him.

Jerking his head toward her, he spat at Shalham. 'She's in on this George. Her and that sister of hers. Has to be!' His voice dripped with loathing.

Caitlin couldn't take in his words. She tried to respond, to explain, but only stammered through her tears, 'No... no, James. James, no, I—'

Shalham decided it wasn't time for a domestic, so he slammed his fist against the wall and yelled, 'Enough, get outta here I said. This minute!'

James reluctantly complied with Shalham's request, muttering curses as he made his way to the exit, leaving Caitlin standing.

'Follow him, Caitlin!' Shalham hollered, pushing the trembling girl out.

Once Caitlin was gone, the chief constable turned back, scanning the hallway to decide his next move. Aside from the bodies, the only people left were the unarmed couple and an officer.

'And who the hell are you?' he demanded, approaching the pair. The bearded man peered at his companion before replying.

'Covert, sir.' The second Shalham caught the English accent, he knew. Brits. Figured. He didn't need to know why, at least not now.

'For Christ's sake, grab your weapons and help me search this place. There's likely a bomb in here somewhere. In a schoolbag or the like!'

He paced in a tight circle, searching the room, his mind running riot. Not needing to be told twice, Rob and Iowa grabbed their handguns and began searching the floor.

'Know him?' Rob pointed at the waiter's corpse as he passed. He stared, and the realisation came quick enough. It was him. Why hadn't he stopped him? Why had he ignored his instincts? The same bloke who'd walked past the car earlier. Sod that, Rob wasn't about to say.

'Haven't a clue, but with that schoolgirl crying over him like a widow, I'd say he's the bomber,' Shalham replied.

Iowa, eyes wide, waited until they were out of earshot and muttered to Rob, 'Can't we bail outta here?' She looked ready to bolt, not really caring if the place blew. Rob shot her a sharp look, telling her to zip it.

'Go ahead if you wanna bail,' Shalham growled, his voice dripping with contempt at her cowardly suggestion.

Iowa flushed with embarrassment at being overheard, her eyes darting as they continued to scour the room.

'Come on, use your head. If there is one, it's gotta be here, somewhere.' Shalham shot a glance at his pale-faced officer, who shrugged, clueless and far from wanting to be a hero.

Rob broke left, Iowa peeled off to the right, each of them working fast, tossing chairs aside and kicking through the debris. They opened briefcases, flung handbags open, rummaged through cupboards — whatever had been left behind in the chaos.

Iowa kept hesitating, but Rob just kept on. He didn't have time for nerves. Not now. From outside, sirens wailed, and a voice over a Tannoy shouted for everyone to clear the area.

'Think that's the bomb squad?' Iowa mumbled.

Nobody answered, but Rob clung to the hope that it was. He pictured the white-haired fella from Felix, Steve something-or-other. He felt a pang remembering the pool games with him and Val after the bad day they had at the Stones Corner compound. Just the memory made him sick.

They kept on searching.

Iowa's heart was hammering as she carefully lifted the linen cover off one of the catering trollies. Her breath caught when she spotted a plastic bag. She bent down and opened it slowly. She'd found it: a sandwich box, rigged with a couple of loose wires, timer and explosives.

'Fuck,' she gasped, fear gripping her. She'd seen things like this before. Crude, but deadly. Barely above a whisper, she called Rob over, acting like any sudden noise might set it off.

'It's under there,' she said, staring at the trolley. Rob crouched down beside her, moving slowly.

'Sir,' he called out to the chief constable. 'Over here.' Shalham took a look.

'Gotta be it. Let's go. If this thing's for real, we could be mincemeat,' he warned.

In desperation, Caitlin stormed down the stairwell after the love of her life, crying his name. At the bottom, she found him as he struggled and cursed, trying to yank open the fire exit.

At last, he forced the door open, ignoring her, and stepped outside into a soaking wet goods yard. She hurried after him, panicking, then tried to grab his hand to lead him to safety.

'This way, James, *please*. I know nothing about all this. I swear. I swear, you've gotta believe me!' Instead, he shoved her hand off, glared, and his eyes were on fire as he spoke with total disgust.

'Get off and stop talking pish. We're done. You and me. Finished!' James exclaimed.

Who was this man? Caitlin shrank back at his cruel words. Anger bubbled up inside her at the unfairness of it all.

'But James!' He had to listen to her. He had to let her explain!

James wasn't having it. He stepped in close, so near she could feel the heat of his anger coming off him.

'Were you and Tina in on this from the start? Tell me!' he shouted, jabbing a finger back toward the hotel.

His dark eyes narrowed as he searched her face, then he said it again, slower, each word punched out with quiet fury.

'The two of you. Were you? In on it. Together?' His voice trembled, laden with rage.

'Were you? Were you Caitlin?!' Then, like a punch to the gut, he suddenly got it. What a complete wanker! He slammed his fist against the side of his head, furious with himself for not seeing it sooner.

'Of course. It was that Provo brother of yours. Wasn't it? Part of some grand plan, was it?!' He mocked, muttering under his breath, 'Smart, real smart. Make it a family thing, did you?'

A bitter anger crept into his voice. 'Didn't see that one coming, Caitlin. Well done.'

His temper flared the second he thought back to Blamfield Street and Creggan. The murals, the filth, the barricades. The whole place reeked of anger and desperation. Dirty-faced kids legged it between burnt-out cars and broken beds, shouting their heads off like it was normal. Jesus, the poverty of it.

And then the Bogside, those louts who tried to take his car without a flicker of fear. Bold as brass. He'd been an eejit, well and truly. His own family had warned him, told him to be careful. But he hadn't listened. Hadn't wanted to see what was staring him right in the face. It was written on the walls, in the streets, in the eyes of every person he passed. *Keep out!* What just happened confirmed everything. Caitlin McLaughlin was, and always would be, one thing: a Republican. He'd learned the hard way that she had no place in his world.

'I've been a fool, a bloody fool. I should've known,' he hissed. Watching her, he felt a deep sense of betrayal and, in that moment, he hated her and everything she stood for.

Caitlin felt completely drained, like her whole body had given up on her. Everything felt slow and leaden, her limbs numb, her mind foggy. James's accusations had sucked the breath right out of her. She kept replaying what he'd said, the way he'd looked at her, as though she was capable of something monstrous. She had no idea how Tina ended up there, bawling her eyes out over the dead waiter. None of it added up. Not one bit. And yet, somehow, she was the one left standing there, accused.

How could he, after everything, even for a moment, believe she had anything to do with it? She needed to find Tina, piece together what the hell had happened, but right now, she was broken. He'd destroyed her. She watched him open his mouth to speak but close it again, realising he'd nothing more to say. Throwing her one last scathing look, he promptly turned and ran off.

In a daze, Caitlin croaked after him. 'James, please. Wait.' A panicked RUC man hurried her away as her hands flew to her mouth, choking back cries no one could hear.

'James. Please, listen to me!'

The bomb squad arrived at the scene in what felt like minutes. Its leader was led to Shalham and the others, waiting in a public car park, well away from the hotel and safely out of danger.

'You didn't have to stay and search for it, sir,' he said politely. 'We would've found it.'

Shalham waved his hand dismissively. 'Of that, I have no doubt.' The team leader noticed the policeman's flushed complexion and offered him a drink of water.

'Thanks,' Shalham replied, taking a quick swig; his mouth was dry as a bone. He told the disposal expert where the device was.

'You can't miss it. Third floor, under a trolley in the main hallway outside conference room five. Small enough. In a lunchbox of sorts. Looks amateurish to me, but who knows?'

'Better to be safe than sorry. You've done a great job clearing the area. Thank you, sir,' the team leader replied, reaching back for his water bottle.

'I've good men. Good luck,' Shalham offered with a small smile.

He thanked the officer who stayed and told him to go home, shaking his hand. Pride swelled in his chest as he took in the empty streets. His men had done their job. The building was cleared of civilians, including, Shalham hoped, the Hendersons.

From a distance, Rob eyed Steve something-or-other, the bomb disposal expert, with his distinctive white hair. He'd managed to stay above ground then. Good to see.

Turning to Iowa, he asked, 'Where to now?'

'The Pier, I guess, now that our cover's blown,' she replied, oozing sarcasm. *Medusa's back*, Rob realised with a tinge of disappointment.

On the verge of leaving, they stopped at the sound of an urgent voice calling from behind. 'Hey, you two!'

It was the chief constable hurrying toward them. 'I need to talk to you,' he gasped.

All the pent-up tension Shalham had been holding in was finally hitting him, making him queasy and light-headed. They watched as he swayed. Rob swiftly took his arm and led him to a small wall, where he insisted he rest.

'Thank you,' Shalham murmured, pressing a hand to his heart with a worried expression.

'You gonna tell me what you were doing in there, carrying?' he breathed, nodding toward the abandoned hotel.

Rob and Iowa replied together: 'Can't say.'

'Can't say or won't say?' Shalham questioned. 'Cos no matter what, I need to know.' He wiped his brow.

Iowa knew this was the end of the road, the end of her dreams of revenge and retribution. She'd be back in uniform before she knew it. *They'd no chance.*

'Bit of both, sir,' she heard Kentucky say.

'We weren't here officially, as such. We've been monitoring a "Charles Jones" and, well... well, sir, after that, it's a bit of a long story.' He didn't mention Morris or the secret the bastard had carried to his grave – the name of Val's murderer.

'Charles Jones, eh? What's he up to now?' Shalham probed, beginning to breathe easier. Come to think of it, he hadn't seen Jones during the commotion.

'Again. Can't say, sir,' Rob replied.

The Hendersons had staked so much on today, and Shalham felt a pang of relief when he imagined what would have happened if the bomb had detonated – how many lives would have been lost, and the damage to yet another hotel in the heart of the city.

His wisdom told him that, once again, Jones was involved: had to be. He swore that after this, he'd find a way to lock the smug bastard up – for good.

'Jones has disappeared,' he declared, peering back at the hotel, 'and I think he's somehow involved. Sorry, but I need to know everything you know. Follow me.' Still shaky on his feet, he rose and wandered towards a jeep.

Rob shrugged under Iowa's intense glare – *we've no choice.* Walking reluctantly toward the armoured vehicle, she stared daggers at him.

He sneered, 'Be my guest,' at her as she followed, knowing they were in big trouble for not going back to headquarters after their cover was blown, and instead chasing Morris.

Chapter Fifty-Nine

Back to Square One

B y the time Roger and James got back to Rocola, Mrs Parkes and half of Derry knew all about it.

News of the bomb scare had swept through the factory like a shockwave. Mrs Parkes warned the remaining office staff to get on with their work, but to stay put. From the window, she saw the Jag arrive and quickly went to meet the Hendersons by the lift.

'Mr Henderson. Both of ye, I'm so glad you're back,' she rasped as Roger and James stepped out. She noticed Roger's complexion was ashen, almost ghostly, and James's not much better. After all that careful planning, the long hours, and the hopes of all the workers – including hers – life at Rocola hung in the balance again. It was dreadful, absolutely dreadful.

She ushered them into James's office, 'Come in, I'll put the kettle on.' They sank heavily into a pair of leather chairs and, with Mrs Parkes out of sight, James turned to his uncle.

'I'm so sorry.'

'You've nothing to be sorry for, son. You did your best,' Roger scolded.

'I had such dreams. We were on the brink of getting there, weren't we? And now?' Narrowing his eyes and pinching the bridge of his nose in frustration, James sighed.

'What now?' James asked, still in shock.

Roger couldn't bring out the words. His mouth had gone dry, and his thoughts were a tangle of disbelief and shame. Disappointment took his breath away. So the government pays his debt, but then what? With all the drama and risk, who would trust them now? Or even want to be in the same room. The place felt like a wake house, with both men stewing in their failures, haunted by unanswered questions.

'This wouldn't have happened if I'd never borrowed from Jones,' thought one.

'I trusted you, Caitlin, loved you even. Why? How could you?' thought the other.

Mrs Parkes rushed into the office, all excited. 'It didn't go off!' she exclaimed.

'The bomb. It didn't go off. They stopped it. Everyone's safe and sound!' She stared at the two men, expecting the news to cheer them up. It didn't.

Then she remembered. 'Apart from the poor bishop, of course.' She felt she should clarify, adding, 'Terrible as it is. Right sad that.'

Roger gave her a faint smile in acknowledgement. She didn't give a damn about the bishop, he knew, but fair play to her for her kind words. The relief of everyone's safety offered some solace, but he couldn't muster the energy to show it. Mrs Parkes sighed and went to the kitchen for the tea.

Later, setting the tray down, she studied James's inscrutable face.

'Did she come back?' he asked. The poor fella looked like death.

'Did who come back?' Mrs Parkes uttered, having no idea who 'she' was.

'Caitlin.' His jaw clenched, and his eyes blazed with anger.

'No. Why would she? I assumed she'd gone straight home.'

'She was in on it, Mrs Parkes. This whole time. Pulled us all into her web. Helped plant it.' His voice was as hard as steel. With as much energy as he could muster, Roger grabbed his nephew's arm.

'You don't know that, James! So don't go making wild accusations without proof.'

James, frightened by his uncle's urgency, glanced at Mrs Parkes. Her look totally said: Told you she was trouble.

He sneered, then leaned back, closing his eyes. It was going so well; the meeting was on track; everyone seemed genuinely interested, but then the shit hit the fan. As for Caitlin? Well...

'Have your tea now, Mr Henderson,' Mrs Parkes suggested, itching to get the dirt. Could the McLaughlin girl really be involved? She didn't think so. She wasn't that stupid.

As she poured Roger's tea, she noticed he looked worse than when he arrived. Poor man, he'd been like one of the walking dead for weeks. He appeared half-asleep with exhaustion.

'What's this about Caitlin?' Mrs Parkes asked, her voice hushed as she handed James his drink. James gestured for her to sit beside him. Seething, he told her everything.

His words fuelled her rising anger. She felt a secret pleasure, deep within herself. With Caitlin McLaughlin gone, she was free to take back her throne. Desperate to jump up and write her final pay cheque right there and then, she still doubted whether the lanky girl had anything to do with planting a bomb... A Taig, she may be, but deep down, she knew the like was a half-decent lass. After today. Who knows what's going on anymore?

Caitlin sat in their dark kitchen in Blamfield Street, feeling the outside world's madness seep in. The rioters were at it again, worse than ever – bottles smashing, petrol bombs hissing, dogs barking, and a steady stream of curses cutting through the night. Mothers were shouting, trying to keep their youngsters in line, adding to the already over-whelming noise. She'd been sitting there for hours, waiting for Tom-my, her mind a whirlwind of emotions – wavering between fear one moment, anger the next.

Tina was nowhere to be found after James stormed away. George Shalham was nowhere to be found either. Using a phone box, she got through to Tommy, who told her to head straight home and wait for him. She could barely remember how she got back, feeling utterly powerless, like a butterfly pinned to a board.

James.

She'd never forget the look in his cold, ice-green eyes when he blamed her for the shootings. For everything. His hatred was clear, like a blade in her heart. Anger rose as she remembered how he wouldn't let her speak. Not a bloody word! She wanted so badly to tell him she knew nothing about any of it, but he hadn't given her a second, not a friggin' second, to explain.

She poured herself another stiff drink, knowing that sitting here now, in this house, out of a job, meant she was right back to square one. Back to poverty - her world - while he'd slink off to the safety of his elitist bubble. She was raging. Wasn't he the one who'd played her, not the other way round? He'd said he was the fool, but no - she was the fool. And what a fool. A joke!

Majella had warned her. Anne had warned her. But she hadn't listened. She convinced herself that she could get better. She fell for a fantasy, foolishly desiring more. Got too big for her boots didn't she? And look where it got her – right in the middle of this hell. And to top it off, she was being held accountable for something she didn't do! She still had no idea why Tina was there. Her mind was scrambled. So many thoughts buzzing round like a swarm of angry bees, all trying to make sense of it.

James had been so hurt, so upset. Possibly, his anger showed he still had feelings for her. Perhaps she should call him, try to fix it. This time, he might actually listen. She understood why he was upset – course she did. Maybe he'd have calmed down by now. Don't be an eejit, an inner voice told her. Wise up, its plain as day the man hates your guts! Remember the way he looked at you? His words. His barbed accusations! Tears of rage broke out. She couldn't believe there was any left.

She jumped at the sound of the front door knocking and ran to it, praying it was James. But when she opened up, there was no one – no James, no Tommy – only an empty doorstep. The usual stench of burning tyres and petrol floating in the air.

She banged it shut and stormed back into the kitchen, slamming a half-open cupboard door that swung dangerously behind her. She wasn't about to make excuses for James Henderson. He was the one who owed *her* an apology. Hadn't he left her standing, alone and humiliated, and in front of George Shalham, of all people?!

Face it, Caitlin. James Henderson had made it clear as day, blaming her outright, not even giving her the grace of an explanation. He really did a number on her.

And Roger Henderson, dear God, the sight of him would stay with her forever, his face so pale and crushed she thought he might fall where he stood, the poor man looked devastated.

She scolded herself for sinking into self-pity and tossed back the last of the cheap vodka she'd picked up on the way home, the burn of it running through her like fire, though it did nothing to numb the ache in her heart.

'Come on Caitlin, wise up and get a grip!' she told herself.

The small kitchen felt cold and suffocating, so she stood up. Time to face it, time to take her oil, as the locals would say. Stripped of everything, she reminded herself who she was. A McLaughlin. With her family scattered, disappearing one by one, her name was the only thing she had left to believe in.

She'd try to stay strong, no matter how awful the day was. She refused to be defeated by James Henderson, even though she was hurting. Caitlin McLaughlin would show them what she was made of. She'd pull herself out of this darkness and create a good life, her own, earned and chosen.

Somewhere. Somehow...

You've only gone and done it – read Turmoil!

Out of all the books in the world, you picked mine, and I'm absolutely chuffed. This wasn't just about telling my story, it was about telling the truth. The real stuff. The grit, the grief, the cursing, the stubbornness... and the humour that got us through it. I wanted *Turmoil* to feel honest through love, laughs, politics, and pain, and I'm so glad you stuck with it. So, if you've made it to the end, you're probably wondering what happens next. Then brace yourself! *Darkness* dives even deeper. More secrets, more chaos, more reasons to yell at the pages. Use the QR below to buy *Darkness* direct from me! I get more pennies that way. Those online fellas (you know who I mean) can take up to 70%. *Ouch.*

AND... I know, I know, there's always an 'and', but if you liked *Turmoil* (even just the cover), please leave a review. It'll take two secs, and I'll love you forever. Scan below straight to my Goodreads page. Mwah!

JB x

www.ingramcontent.com/pod-product-compliance
Lightning Source LLC
Chambersburg PA
CBHW050101120726
47904CB00004B/1169